MYSTERY OF THE HAUNTED MINE AND THE SECRET OF THE SPANISH DESERT

ALSO BY GORDON D. SHIRREFFS

Range Rebel and Code of the Gun

Slaughter at Broken Bow and Southwest Drifter

Roanoke Raiders and Powder Boy of the Monitor

Barranca and Blood Justice

Last Man Alive and Now He is Legend

Too Tough to Die and Valiant Bugles

Gunswift and Voice of the Gun

Arizona Justice and The Lonely Gun

Last Train from Gun Hill and The Border Guidon

Rio Desperado and Top Gun

Rio Diablo and The Proud Gun

Renegade Lawman and The Lone Rifle

Jack of Spades and Ambush on the Mesa

Action Front! and The Grey Sea Raiders

Fort Vengeance and Shadow Valley

Judas Gun and Hangin' Pards

Ride A Lone Trail and Massacre Creek

Rio Bravo and Bugles On The Prairie

The Rebel Trumpet and The Mosquito Fleet

The Godless Breed and Quicktrigger

Son of the Thunder People and Tumbleweed Trigger

MYSTERY OF THE HAUNTED MINE AND THE SECRET OF THE SPANISH DESERT

Two Full Length Novels

GORDON D. SHIRREFFS

WOLFPACK
PUBLISHING
— EST 2013 —

Mystery of the Haunted Mine and The Secret of the Spanish Desert
Paperback Edition
Copyright © 2024 (As Revised) Gordon D. Shirreffs

Wolfpack Publishing
701 S. Howard Ave. 106-324
Tampa, Florida 33609

wolfpackpublishing.com

Paperback ISBN 978-1-63977-991-8
eBook ISBN 978-1-63977-591-0

MYSTERY OF THE HAUNTED MINE AND THE SECRET OF THE SPANISH DESERT

MYSTERY OF THE HAUNTED MINE

CHAPTER ONE

The Lure of the Lost Espectro Mine

The Espectro Mountains rose almost impetuously from the desert floor to loom high over the scattered ranches along the southern and western bases of the mountains. The Espectros dominated that lonely part of Arizona as nothing else did. They stood proudly and mysteriously against the blue, cloud-dotted sky of day and loomed dark and brooding at night.

They could be seen for many miles in all directions and had been used by travelers as the one outstanding landmark in that isolated land, for the other mountains in the hazy distance were as nothing when compared to the Espectros. They could be seen long before travelers could distinguish any particular features of the great jumbled masses of rock that formed them.

When one was near them, they seemed almost to lean over, as though to overpower insignificant humans with their ponderous might. Even when one was miles beyond the Espectros, it was difficult not to obey a compelling impulse to turn and look back at them. They had the uncanny power of making people look at them again and again and yet never tire of the view.

Still, there was a hidden seed of fear that sprouted

rapidly within those who looked at them for too long a time. Their very name, given to them by the early Spanish explorers, was an indication of the fear and respect that the brooding mountains had always seemed to instill in those who studied them.

The Espectro Mountains, the Ghost Mountains! For they *were* haunted, as surely as the fears of man could people such places with the ever-restless spirits of the dead.

———

GARY COLE UNSADDLED his claybank and placed the saddle on top of the corral rail. His eyes sought the Espectros. He well knew the aura of thrall doom, mingled with intense fear and curiosity, that hung over the Espectros like the heat haze of these late summer days. All of his life had been spent within view of the Espectros.

The night of his birth, the Thunder People had thudded their drums in the rain-streaming canyons of the mountains and had shot their lightning arrows through the dark skies to bathe the Espectros in an eerie bluish light. An old Chiricahua *vaquero* who was working on the ranch at that time had prophesied that Gary would be held in subjection to the Espectros no matter where he roamed and that he always would be compelled to come back to them.

Gary leaned on the rail and shoved back his hat. The Espectros were clothed in a smoky-looking haze which distorted and magnified them. It had been a busy summer for Gary, and in two weeks, he would be back in high school without having had the chance to explore the Espectros thoroughly.

It had been a summer of hard work with little time to play, and the money he had made was not his to keep. It was sorely needed in the Cole household, for Chiricahua

Springs Ranch was no longer a paying proposition since Gary's father had become an invalid.

He watched a puff of cloud chase its fleeting shadow down the rugged slopes of the Espectros in a race that would never end. He saw a still-winged hawk hanging almost motionless high over The Needle, like a scrap of charred paper pasted against the startling blue of the sky.

The naked pinnacle of rock known as The Needle thrust itself up from the harsh slope of a great peak like a warning finger to those who would probe into the secrets of the Espectros. But for those who *did* venture into the mountains, The Needle was always the starting point. For not only were those mysterious mountains haunted by strange and bloody tales handed down by Apaches, Spaniards, and Americans, but also by the persistent whispered rumors of vast stores of gold and silver left locked within the bosom of the mountains by the legendary Melgosa Brothers, over a hundred years ago.

Gary half closed his eyes. It was almost four o'clock. He looked directly at the sheer rock wall to the right of, and just beyond, the towering finger of The Needle, now fully lighted by the dying sun.

Just then, Gary heard the old pendulum clock in the Cole living room strike the hour. As the last stroke died away, he opened his eyes to stare at the rock wall in the canyon. For a fleeting instant, he thought he saw something like a line cut into the rock, but he couldn't be sure whether it was natural or not. Then, it was gone as quickly as it had appeared, leaving him with a bitter feeling of disappointment. Swiftly, the rock wall became shrouded in shadow until the entire canyon was dark and uninviting.

He turned quickly to walk to the house, and as he did so, he saw his father leaning on his crutches, staring toward the same canyon. Gary turned away; he didn't want to embarrass his father. He picked up his little Winchester saddle gun from its position against the corral rail. It needed a cleaning, for he had killed a rattler that day.

Gary had been guiding dudes from a local ranch, and when the rattler had struck savagely at the horse of one of the dudes, Gary had killed it with a shot through the ugly flat head. Now there was a five-dollar bill folded in his shirt pocket, a grateful gift from the sweating dude. Gary had not told him it was the only cartridge in his rifle.

"Gary!" called his mother from the kitchen.

"Yes, Mother?"

"Wash up. We're eating early tonight. Your father and I are going into The Wells tonight to stay with Aunt Marion. Do you want to come with us?"

Gary, a year before that time, would have been only too happy to go to Cottonwood Wells, but he had been a kid then. It just wasn't right for a guy *his* age to be seen riding into The Wells with his father and mother, no matter how much he loved them.

"Gary?" questioned his mother.

"Well, I was figuring on studying my maps and things, Mother."

"You know them by heart, Gary."

He filled a basin with water, washed quickly, and combed his thick, reddish hair. When he walked into the pleasant-smelling kitchen, his mother turned to look at him, brushing back a lock of her own thick, titian hair. It was a beautiful red against the blue of her eyes and the fairness of her skin.

Lucille Hart had been the belle of Cottonwood Wells before she had married Pete Cole just before Pearl Harbor when he was a sergeant in the Marines. Pete Cole had brought home a fine war record, plus a Navy Cross and a piece of steel lodged near his spine, which had partially crippled him. A strange event in a branch of Cholla Canyon had crippled him still further and had almost cost him his life.

Gary eyed his pretty mother as he set the table for her. There were dark circles beneath her lovely blue eyes, and every day, new worry lines appeared on her forehead. "I was hoping you'd go with us this time, Gary," she said a little petulantly. She didn't quite realize her only child was swiftly growing into a man.

Pete Cole came into the kitchen, slid into his chair, and leaned his crutches against the wall. "I'd rather have Gary stay here," he said. "Jim Kermit said he had seen a mountain lion prowling about the wash just east of the ranch. I think Gary had better stay here and keep an eye on the stock, Lucille."

"The *stock,* Pete?" questioned Lucille. "There's hardly enough to bother with. Now I think..." her voice broke off as she saw the taut look on his face. Pete Cole still liked to *think* he was a rancher.

Gary busied himself with his food. His father knew well enough why Gary didn't want to go to The Wells with them. It was hardly likely a cougar would be seen around there in the summer, and during daylight hours at that.

"All right, Pete," said Mrs. Cole. She had been through this before. Men always seemed to stick together, even the two she loved and cherished above everything else.

"You're off tomorrow, eh?" asked Gary's father.

"It's Sunday, Dad," said Gary.

Pete Cole fiddled with his knife. "What are you planning to do?"

There was no sense in lying, and besides, it wasn't easy to lie to his father. Gary had learned that at an early age. "I thought I'd ride up past The Needle," he said.

"Looking for more relics?"

"Yes."

"And maybe a lead to the Lost Espectro, eh, Gary?"

Gary flushed. "I didn't think there would be any harm in that."

"I've told you quite a few times this summer to forget about the Lost Espectro."

"It isn't easy, living right in the shadow of the Espectros, to forget about the treasure hidden up there." Gary leaned forward. "The Lost Espectro is supposed to be richer than the Dutchman's Lost Mine, the Lost Adams Diggings, the Lost Padre, and maybe Tayopa itself!"

"Fairy tale lies embroidered by old-timers!"

"The Dutchman brought out gold from the Superstitions, didn't he? Adams found a bonanza, and researchers agree that perhaps others found it as well and lost it again! The Lost Padre exists! You told me yourself you used to hunt for it on weekends when you went to college in El Paso. You just can't deny Tayopa, Dad. The old records in Mexico prove that Tayopa was one of the richest silver mines in the world!"

"Take it easy," said Mrs. Cole nervously. She glanced at her husband.

But Gary was warming up to his favorite subject. It was almost an obsession with him. "My great-grandfather spent a large part of his later life looking for the Lost Espectro," Gary continued, "and actually made a *derrotero* of his findings! He told your father the chart was as accurate as he could make it. He said that on his deathbed. Would he lie to his own son when he was dying? You yourself have always said that Great-grandfather Cole's *derrotero* probably held the key to the Lost Espectro if anything did!"

"Maybe it does, son," said Pete Cole quietly, "but where is it?"

This last remark was like a dash of cold water against Gary's face. The chart, or *derrotero,* had vanished years ago.

"I saw you looking for that legendary Spanish miner's symbol that is supposed to be cut into the east wall of The Needle Canyon, Gary. I know it's supposed to be visible at about four o'clock in the afternoon during the late part of the summer. Did you happen to see it today?"

Gary couldn't help himself. "Did *you,* Dad?"

It was Pete Cole's turn to flush. He glanced quickly at his wife.

Lucille Cole stood up and began to clear the table. "Yes, Pete," she said quietly, "Gary knows you still look for it. How can you expect him to forget about the Lost Espectro when you haven't forgotten about it yourself?"

"There's nothing but death up there for those who look for it," said Pete.

"Yet *you* searched for it, Pete."

"Are you siding with Gary?" he snapped.

"No, Pete. But he's as like you as you were like your grandfather. Your own father was a rancher, and he never thought about the Lost Espectro."

"I consider myself a rancher, Lucille!"

She smiled. "By birth rather than by choice, I think, Pete. I can remember when we were in high school in Cottonwood Wells, how the other girls used to talk about you. But you were always more interested in lost treasures than you ever were in girls."

"Until I got interested in you, Lucille," he said.

"But you were still looking for the Lost Espectro even after you came back from the war, Pete."

He looked down at his almost useless legs. "For a time," he said bitterly.

Gary began to help his mother. It hadn't been so many years ago that Pete Cole had been fired upon by a hidden marksman while he was searching an offshoot of Cholla Canyon for clues to the Lost Espectro. His horse had been shot to death, and in the fall, Pete had suffered damage to his spine, which had already been injured by his war wound. He had been found by Jim Kermit, a local rancher, a full day after his fall. His condition now prevented him from ever again riding into the Espectros.

Pete Cole got to his feet and reached for his crutches.

"Gary," he said sternly, "I don't want you ever to ride past The Needle. That's final!" He dragged himself from the kitchen.

Gary looked at his mother. "I'll do the dishes," he said.

"He means it, Gary."

"I won't go beyond The Needle," he promised.

He smiled ruefully. "Not much reason to, I guess. I haven't found any leads to the Lost Espectro."

She took off her apron. "Tuck called," she said.

"I'll call him right back," Gary said eagerly.

"No need to. I told him to come out and stay with you tonight."

He stared at her. "But you asked me to go to The Wells with you and Dad tonight."

She kissed him. "I don't need a lost *derrotero* to tell me the obvious," she said. "Remember, Gary! Do not go past The Needle!"

He watched her as she walked toward the door into the living room. She seemed so tired. "Mother," he called out. She turned and looked at him questioningly. He reached into his shirt pocket and took out the folded five-dollar bill. He handed it to her. "Buy a hot dog and a bottle of soda pop for yourself and Dad," he said.

She eyed the money and then her big son. "Where did you get this?"

"The Lost Espectro," he said. He swung out his arms. "The place was loaded with bales of 'em, but I wasn't greedy."

She reached out and touched his forehead. "Gold fever," she said quietly.

———

LATER, after his father and mother had left in the battered green pickup truck, Gary walked outside and looked at the dusky light over the mountains. For thirty years, persistent stories had lingered about mysterious murders and disappearances in the Espectros. Rifle shots from the clinging, dark shadows of canyons had turned back seekers of the lost treasure supposedly hidden in the mountains. Skeletons had been found in remote, sun-drenched canyons with bullet holes in the grinning skulls. Men had entered those brooding mountains and had never been seen again.

Purple shadows now filled the canyons and hollows. Only the highest peaks of the Espectros were still bathed in the intermingled rose and gold wash of the last rays of the dying sun. The mountains looked so quiet and still, so peaceful and pleasant, and yet, mysterious death waited up there, haunting the silent canyons and the lonely purple mesas, as it had haunted them for many years.

Then, the sun was gone from the upper tips of the peaks as though a master hand had flicked a switch. A cold wind began to search through the canyons and to whisper down the darkened slopes. Far across the silent desert came the drifting, melancholy crying of a coyote. Gary shivered a little.

The windmill ground into slow life, and the whirring blades sang a sad little song of their own. It was then that something seemed to catch at the corner of Gary's left eye. A pinpoint of yellow light, quickly coming and vanishing high on the rugged slopes beyond the looming pinnacle of The Needle.

Gary narrowed his eyes. No one lived up there. The local Apaches, with cold horror, shunned the thought of entering those mountains after dark. The ranchers entered the fringe canyons of the Espectros only during daylight, always armed and never alone. Those few men who were caught in there after dark never showed a light.

It had always seemed to Gary that the mountains moved in closer at night like a huge crouching beast, a beast that stared at the lonely Cole Ranch, slowly licking its thick wet lips, baring every now and then a long yellow fang, poisonous and sharp as a needle. Some dark night.

Cold green fear flowed through Gary. He glanced quickly at his rifle, which leaned against the wall of the house. "Lobo!" he called sharply. There was no answer from the huge dog. In fact, Gary had not seen him all that day.

Gary walked to the low, sprawling house that had been built near Chiricahua Springs in 1866 by his great-grandfather, a tough and hardened veteran of the Civil War. James Cole had fought Apaches and squatters to hold his land. Bullet holes and arrow nicks pocked the thick adobe walls. Beyond the ranch buildings, closer to the ever-flowing springs, was the private cemetery of the Coles'. Gary's great-grandmother lay buried there, with three Apache bullet holes in her. There were others there who had died violently, some of them by the hand of James Cole himself. It was a hard country. It was peaceable now, but it was still a hard country.

The coyote cried again. Gary shivered. The thought of entering that dark house, so full of memories, was not pleasant. A distant humming sound came across the quiet desert. Far across the black velvet shroud of the night came a flickering light, like a curious and probing finger. The light was moving with great speed along the graveled road that came from the main highway to the south. An erratic, popping, roaring noise came on the wind.

Gary grinned. It was probably Tucker C. *Tuck* Browne, riding his beloved Honda motorcycle full out, which was usually the only way he rode it. The darkness of the night seemed a little friendlier now. It was always that way when Tuck Browne came to see Gary. Tuck was a good, though temporary, distraction for the lure of the Lost Espectro.

Gary went into the house and turned on the kitchen and living room lights. Automatically, he checked the supply of food in the refrigerator. He went into the room off the back porch where the freezer was and took out additional supplies, which he brought into the house. Tuck Browne had been on a marathon eating contest as far back as Gary could remember, and that had been a good part of his life, for the two boys had been friends since preschool days.

Gary went outside and called again for Lobo, but there was no answering bark from the big dog. He looked up toward The Needle. Lobo was a prowler, but he usually did not go too far into the canyons, no matter how inviting the hunting was. Lobo had always sensed that there was something wrong with those brooding canyons. He'd go along with Gary though, no matter how much he disliked doing so, his love for Gary overcoming his fear of the unknown.

Gary saw that the motorcyclist was charging along the fence line. Any minute, he'd turn into the driveway past the windmill. Gary wisely took up a position where he could get into cover if Tuck made one of his spectacular stops anywhere near him. Tuck was gunning the motor in short, incessant bursts of power. The final act was about to begin.

CHAPTER TWO

The Mystery of the Needle

The rubber squealed as the tires of the Honda were forced into a hard, grinding turn from the road into the rutted driveway of the Cole Ranch. Tuck gunned the bike. The rear tire shrieked against the baked earth and gravel, and the Honda shot forward as though slung out of a catapult, boring through the dusk like an avenging angel.

A bent figure could be seen, hanging onto the handlebars that were even with the driver's eye level. There was a grim determination in the driver and bike as the two of them bounced across ruts and swung into the rather sharp turn just beyond the windmill. It was then that the tortured tires refused to grip the hard earth. The bike went into a spin, was wrenched out of it, then went into another sliding angle. Tuck gunned the roaring machine, and it shot forward directly toward Gary. He sprinted for cover, vaulting over the low adobe wall just in front of the house.

Tuck Browne was magnificent. He shot past the wall, skidded in a wet patch near a faucet, and then swung toward a sagging shed beyond the low barn. Gary watched in fascination as the bike bore down on the shed. Dust and smoke billowed up behind the Honda.

"Hi, Gary!" screamed Tuck a fraction of a second before the Honda battered through the thin wall of the shed. "Brakes are gone!"

"Yeh," said Gary dryly. "They sure are."

Wood shattered and cracked, dust whirled up, the bike roared once more in futile protest, then was silent. Chickens squawked and skittered as they broke madly from the ruined shed and headed for the open desert, coyotes or no coyotes. In the sudden silence that followed the roaring onslaught of Tuck Browne on the hapless shed, the roof collapsed slowly and deliberately an instant after Tuck scrambled out of the wreckage.

Gary walked slowly toward the dramatic scene. It was typical of Tuck Browne. The last time he arrived, he had ripped through a line of Mrs. Cole's washing, taking the whole mess with him like a bridal train clean through a barbed wire fence into a filled earthen water tank.

Tuck unlimbered his thin six feet of frame and removed his helmet. He tentatively touched a split lip. "Cut three minutes off my last record out here," he said slowly.

"You figuring from town to the water tank or the shed, Tuck?"

Tuck rubbed a dusty jaw. "How much difference would that make?"

"Maybe ten seconds."

Tuck nodded solemnly. "Yeh. Well, anyway, I cut two minutes and fifty seconds off. You witness to that?"

"Keno."

Tuck eyed the shed. "Was your Dad thinking of tearing that down, Gary?"

"Not that I know of."

Tuck blinked his blue eyes. "Well, maybe I can talk him into it." He grinned. "Got the whole place to ourselves, eh, *amigo?*"

Gary glanced at the shed. "What's left of it."

Tuck walked slowly toward Gary. Tuck Browne never

moved fast on foot if he could help it. He talked slowly, ate with deliberation, and never got to class or to work on time. He always seemed to be just short of standing still when he walked, that is, until he mounted the saddle of his Honda, at which time a strange metamorphosis took place, and the amiable, easygoing, lackadaisical being that was Tucker C. Browne became the personification of mad speed.

Tuck unzipped his jacket. "Got something new for you, Gary," he said. He glanced at the house. "You eat yet?"

"Yep."

Tuck's face fell. "Well, I figured on getting a bite."

"You eat at home?"

"Yes."

"Stopped at Bennie's Barbecue on the way?"

"Yes."

"Buy gas at Schick's Station?"

"A little," admitted Tuck.

"Had a Coke there and a bag of chips?"

Tuck nodded.

"And you *still* want to eat?"

Tuck looked positively mournful.

"Well, happens we have a pie left."

"What kind?" asked Tuck eagerly.

"Apple and raisin."

"You mean one apple and one raisin?"

"No, sonny, apple *and* raisin *together*."

"Well, that's good enough."

"*Gracias*," said Gary dryly.

"Wait'll I get my 'sickle' out of the shed," said Tuck. He slowly returned to the shed, and while Gary held up the shattered timbers, Tuck pulled the battered Honda from the wreckage. He eyed the bike carefully. "Not bad. Gotta get those brakes fixed one of these days. Could be dangerous."

"Yeh."

They walked together to the house. They went into the kitchen, and Gary placed half a pie before Tuck. He sat down and watched the pie vanish. "You said you had something new for me, Tuck."

Tuck nodded. His mouth was too full to talk. He jerked his head toward his jacket. "Inna pocket," he said.

Gary took out an odd-looking mass. It was a heavy lump of dirty wax, from which protruded four wicks at right angles to each other. Gary studied it, hefted it, turned it over and over, then looked quizzically at Tuck. Tuck swallowed. "Treasure-hunting candle," he said. "Got it from ol' Emilio Chavez. He said it was infallible."

"Go on."

Tuck cut another slice of pie. "Sure wish you had some whipped cream for this."

"Sorry. Go on!"

Tuck looked up. "On a dark, windy night, you take that ball of wax to a place where you *think* treasure is. You light all four wicks, then with three *amigos,* each of you holding a wick, *below* the flame of course, you watch to see which wick bums longest in the wind. That long-burning wick points the general direction to the treasure."

"Yeh...*general* direction."

Tuck swallowed. "Well, anyway, by trial and error, you finally get to where the treasure is."

"Man, you must have hit your head when you hit that shed."

"It should work, Gary!"

Gary shook his head. "I thought you might have found something that would be useful to us."

Tuck looked carefully about, as though someone might be eavesdropping. "There's something else about that candle."

"Shoot!"

Tuck's blue eyes were wide in his face. "It's partly made from dead man's fat, Gary," he whispered hoarsely.

"Oh, great!"

Tuck wet his lips. *"The fat from a man who was hung for murder!"*

A cold shiver crept up Gary's back, even though he was used to the mad ideas of Tuck Browne. He carefully placed the candle on the table and eyed it.

"Infallible," insisted Tuck.

Gary opened two Cokes. "I think I saw that light again, Tuck," he said quietly.

Tuck's jaws stopped moving. "You sure?"

Gary shrugged. "Pretty sure."

"Isn't it likely it could be any of the local ranchers up there hunting for strays maybe?"

Gary shook his head. "You know well enough no local man would shine a light up there, Tuck."

"Yeh." Tuck chewed reflectively. "Still, someone might have lighted a cigarette or something. You could see a match flare up quite a ways off. That's it! Someone lighted a cigarette up there!"

"But *who*, Tuck?"

Tuck's blue eyes studied Gary. "Who do you think it is?"

Gary walked to the window and looked out toward the huge, dark mass of The Needle. "That's the fourth time I've seen it this summer. No one lives up there. It isn't a fire. It comes and goes just like that. Always in just about the same place too."

"Yes?"

Gary turned. "Just about where that light shows is the best place around for anyone to keep an eye on a person coming up toward The Needle. From where they are situated, they can see which way a person goes into which canyon."

Tuck shoved back his plate. "Come on," he said quickly. "Tell me who you really think it is."

Gary leaned against the wall. "I'm not sure."

Tuck stood up and walked to the window. "Asesino,"

he said softly.

Again, the cold chill came over Gary. *Asesino!* The half-real, half-mythical outlaw of the Espectros. Many of the local people did not believe he was still alive or thought that he had long ago left the Espectros. There were others who were sure he had never left his hideout. A man could live in those mountains and never be seen or found if he did not choose to be seen or found.

"How old would Asesino be now?" asked Tuck.

Gary half closed his eyes. "Let's see, he was about twenty years old when he committed his first murder. That was sometime in the twenties, about 1926, I think. Thirty-five years ago. He'd be about fifty-five years old if he were still alive."

"It's possible then," said Tuck quietly.

"No one has seen him for years. There have been rumors that he *has* been seen. I've never met anyone yet who said he had seen him in the last ten or fifteen years."

"Yeh," said Tuck thoughtfully. "But there have been murders up in there the past ten or fifteen years."

"Murders or accidents?"

"A man can't shoot himself in the back of the head with a rifle, can he?"

Tuck had Gary there.

Two MEN, known to be looking for the Lost Espectro Mine, had vanished, and later, one of them had been found lying in the middle of his camp with a bullet from a large-caliber rifle in the back of his skull. The coroner had verified the fact that the rifle had been fired from some distance, at an angle indicating that the marksman had been higher than the camp. The other man had never been found. Some people said he had killed his partner. Others said he had been killed by the same person who had killed his partner. No one really knew. That had been about twelve years ago.

Asesino had been a half-breed, or perhaps more than a half-breed. His father had been a white man, a deserter from the Army, who had married an Apache woman, whose father had been a Negro, or so the story went. Asesino then had been part white, part Indian, part Negro, and all bad.

Asesino was not the man's real name. No one was sure what his real name had been. He had murdered his young wife in a drunken and jealous rage, then had fled toward the border. A posse had stopped him, and in the ensuing fight, two possemen had died, and Asesino had escaped. Trapped on three sides, he had retreated north, into the Espectros, which were an almost impenetrable fortress. He had committed several other killings, thus gaining the Spanish name he bore, a name that fitted him well, Asesino. The *Assassin*.

Asesino was one of the many legends about the Espectros, writing his legend in letters of blood. The man had the cunning and guile of a wolf, the cold ferocity of a grizzly, the stalking skill of a she-lion, the speed of an antelope, and the killing skill of a shark. The man had been an expert with rifle and pistol, bow and arrow, and knife. A man who could be set adrift in empty country without weapons and survive as his Apache ancestors had managed to survive in that wild and isolated country.

———

TUCK PEERED FROM THE WINDOW. "Whoever it is might be watching for anyone traveling toward The Needle. He could see them easily enough during the day, no matter how they went in. Dust would rise from hooves or wheels. On moonlit nights, it's almost as clear as daylight in there. On dark nights, he could see can-lights or perhaps hear wheels and hooves. That place echoes like a tomb."

"Yeh...a tomb," said Gary. "You hit it, *amigo*."

"Now, if two guys, say like you and me, were to sneak in there before moonrise, keeping quiet as the grave."

"There you go again!"

"We might just spot something," continued Tuck calmly.

"Such as?"

"That loco sign you and your pa have been trying to spot all summer long."

Gary nodded. "As long as we don't go past The Needle."

"I wasn't aiming to!" said Tuck hastily.

It was an established fact that explorers, dudes, and ranchers had never been bothered *south* of The Needle. The canyons opened beyond the landmark, to the north, fanning out to penetrate deep into the Espectros. That was where the trouble always started. First, the feeling that you were being watched. Then, the warning shots. After that, you were on your own.

"We can take the jeep," said Gary. "Drive without lights. Leave it on the playa south of the canyon where The Needle is. Walk in."

"How far?"

"Maybe a mile."

Tuck groaned. "Guess it can't be helped."

GARY PUT out the lights after he had managed to find a half dozen cartridges for his rifle. He loaded the weapon outside and stowed it in the back of the jeep. Tuck slid his six feet into the right front seat and sat with his bony knees up under his chin.

It was very dark outside. Far across the quiet desert, they could see sharp pinpoints of light. Headlights could be seen on the main highway into Cottonwood Wells. The glow from the lights of the town was visible above the rocky hills just south of it. But the Espectros were dark, a forbidding mass against the northern sky.

"Where's Lobo?" asked Gary's friend.

"*Quién sabe?* Who knows? I haven't seen him a day."

"He often take off like that?"

"Once in a while."

"Great! We sure could use him now."

Gary grinned. "You afraid, Tucker?"

Tuck nodded. "So are you, *amigo.*"

He was right. Gary started the jeep and drove out to the road, moving slowly because he had not turned on the headlights. He turned up a wide dry wash, and they bumped and clattered along it until they reached the playa, a place where sand, rock, and brush had been washed down the big canyon during flash floods.

Gary stopped the engine and clambered out. Tuck got out and stretched. Gary took his rifle from the jeep, and the two of them stood there in the velvety darkness, listening to the dry soughing of the night wind through the mesquite.

Gary shrugged. He started forward, walking quietly, although no one near The Needle could possibly have heard footsteps on the playa. Still, it was said that Asesino had supernatural powers, or at least highly sensitive hearing and sight. As long as it was dark, he could not see to shoot. But supposing he did not *stay* near The Needle?

The ground sloped upward toward the mouth of the canyon below The Needle. The two boys went higher and higher until they could see the distant lights of The Wells clearly against the darkness of the desert.

There was a faint suggestion of moonlight in the east when Gary stopped. The huge bulk of The Needle seemed to tower over them, although it was a good half mile away. The wind whispered down the canyon, rustling the brush and murmuring against the canyon walls.

"Wait," said Tuck. "Maybe we ought to wait until tomorrow, Gary."

Gary turned. "You were the one who wanted to sneak in here before moonrise, keeping quiet as the grave."

"Did you have to say *that*?" hissed Tuck.

Gary walked on, peering ahead, past the dark bulk of The Needle. There wasn't much to see. He didn't really know why they had come in there, except that this weekend would probably be his last real chance to probe the mysteries of the place.

They squatted down behind a dike of rock that hid them completely except for their heads, which protruded above the rock like the heads of two turtles encased in one shell.

Slowly, the new moon came up, first flooding the wide desert in cold, silvery light, then penetrating the canyon to light the western wall, although the eastern wall was still thick in shrouding shadows.

The two boys stared at that eastern wall. Somewhere on it was supposedly marked an ancient Spanish mining symbol. That same symbol was also supposed to be marked on the treasure chart left to Pete Cole by his father, but Pete had never been able to quite remember its exact location, or what it was.

There were quite a few symbols in the old Spanish miner's code, some of them with varying meanings, some of them important, most of them of little importance. Although the existence of the symbol on the eastern canyon wall was doubtful, it was a well-known fact that there were many symbols scattered throughout the Espectros.

Many men had seen the symbols, and Gary's great-grandfather had made a chart of them and had tracked down their meanings. Gary had been given the chart by his father, and he had memorized all of the cryptic markings. In fact, it had been that very chart that had sparked his abiding interest in lost treasures and in the Lost Espectro Mine in particular.

Time dragged past, and then suddenly, the moonlight began to creep along the eastern wall of the canyon while two almost breathless boys stared at it until their eyes ached. Forgotten was the threat of Asesino and the unsolved mysteries of the Espectros. The moonlight was now flooding the area where Gary had often thought he had seen something that was not a natural feature of the canyon.

Just as the moon completely illuminated the wall, a mournful cry came drifting down the silent canyon on the cold night wind. It seemed to emanate from the very bowels of the upper canyon, or from an opened grave.

Gary quickly levered a round of .30/30 into his rifle chamber, knowing full well that it would be of little use against the thing that had emitted that ghostly sound.

Tuck gripped his friend so hard by the arm that Gary winced. "Look!" he croaked.

The moonlight flooded the naked rock, and midway up the wall was a line, seemingly sharply etched—a long, long line that trended around a curved shoulder of rock. "Is it man-made or natural?" whispered Tuck.

Gary stared at it. "Only one way to find out," he said quietly.

"You're not going out there, are you?"

Gary did not answer. He leaned his rifle against the dike and walked around the end of the rock formation, keeping as much as possible in the shelter of scattered rocks and boulders and clumps of brush, until he could see that the line continued farther around the curve of rock. He wanted to see the end of it. Perhaps it was a gigantic arrow, pointing to the particular branch canyon where the Lost Espectro was. Perhaps it was a horizontal cross, which indicated the same thing as the arrow, or a huge depiction of a bowie knife, also indicating a specific direction. *He had to know!*

The haunting cry came faintly down the canyon. Gary's throat went dry, and his heart thudded against his ribs. He was getting awfully close to The Needle, too close perhaps. He could almost see where the line ended. He hurried forward, getting careless in his haste. He could hear Tuck panting along behind him.

The moon crept along the bald rock face. The moving light was a lodestone that Gary found impossible to resist. Forgotten were the warnings he had received.

He could see something now. He ran forward, head up-raised, staring at that thin etched line on the whitish rock. Any second now, he would know the secret.

The rifle shot crashed loudly in the stillness of the canyon. The slug whispered through the air just above Gary's head, and the harsh report of the rifle slammed back and forth between the canyon walls, raising the hollow echoes.

Gary whirled and saw that he was beyond the towering mass of The Needle. He took off down the canyon. His booted feet slammed against the hard ground like pistons, and his breath came harshly into his dry throat.

Fast as he was, and Gary had lettered in track at high school just the season before the summer, a gaunt figure passed him as though he were marking time. A strange, thin figure like an awkward crane—head outthrust, thin arms pumping up and down, big feet slapping the ground lightly, wheezing breath pumping from a gaping mouth—flew by him.

Tuck Browne easily cleared a four-foot-high rock dike, the very picture of grace and motion, in ideal high-hurdle form, striking the ground like a feather on the far side, losing not a second of rhythm in his incredible burst of speed.

They passed the mouth of the canyon and headed

toward the jeep. Gary reached it in time to see Tuck dive under it like a baseball player sliding home. He dragged the lean boy from beneath the jeep, shoved him into it, leaped in himself, turned on *the* ignition, shifted into first, and whirled the vehicle around, slamming it into second, ramming down on the accelerator to gather speed. He shifted into third as they reached the road and raced for home, raising a thick plume of dust behind them.

Not until they were inside the house with the thick door shut and barred did they look at each other with wide eyes. "It was Asesino, all right," said Tuck.

"Did you see him?"

"Sure! Rose up like a jack-in-the-box atop The Needle! Aimed right at us! Lordy! Bullet nearly parted my hair, Gary!"

Cold sweat trickled down Gary's sides. He wiped the sweat from his face and grinned weakly. "Never saw you move so fast off that Honda."

Tuck nodded. "You and your letter," he scoffed. "Man, I was accelerating! Wasn't even out of second when I reached the jeep." Tuck walked to the refrigerator and opened it. He turned, and the light from inside the box accented his sharp features. "Come to think of it, Gary, I know how he got wise to us."

"Go on."

"The moonlight was shining off the windshield of the jeep like a sheet of silver. Could be seen for miles."

Gary leaned against the wall. "Never thought of that," he said.

Tuck selected a cold chicken leg. "Close," he said. He looked at Gary. "You don't suppose he'll come down here tonight, do you, Gary?"

Gary sat down on a chair and reached for a Coke from the refrigerator. "*Quién sabe?* Left my rifle up there."

"Great, oh great," murmured Tuck. "And Lobo isn't even here." He sank his fangs into the chicken leg.

LATER, as they got into Gary's big bed, Tuck placed a hatchet under his pillow. "Might want to cut some wood later on," he said casually.

Gary nodded. He held up a butcher knife. "Or clean a rabbit," he said. His father's rifle was in town for repairs, and the double-barreled shotgun had been loaned to a friend. Pete Cole usually carried his revolver in the pickup truck. It was going to be a long and lonely night.

The moonlight flooded through the window. The wind stirred the curtains.

"Kinda cool in here, isn't it?" suggested Tuck.

Gary got up and walked to the window. He looked up toward The Needle. It was bright with moonlight. He slid down the window, and as he turned toward the bed, his eye caught a quick spark of light, high on the canyon wall beyond the huge mass of The Needle. He turned quickly. But there was no sign of light now. Nothing but the silvery wash of the cold moonlight on the silent canyon and the brooding Needle.

CHAPTER THREE

Stranger in the Dawn

The incessant barking of a dog aroused Gary from a deep sleep. He sat up suddenly, startled and confused. He recognized Lobo's deep voice. Gary thrust his legs from beneath the blanket and stood up. It was still dark outside, and he had no idea what time it was. He padded to the door of the bedroom and opened it to step into the hallway. Lobo was still barking furiously.

He walked across the dark living room and peered through a window. It was dark all right, but there was a faint suggestion of dawn in the sky. He could locate Lobo by the sound of his barking, but he could not see the big dog.

"What is it?" asked Tuck from the hallway.

"I don't know," answered Gary. He peered from one side of the front yard to the other, seeing nothing that would alarm the big dog, but he knew well enough that Lobo wasn't a habitual barker.

Gary eased the bar from the door and slowly opened it. He stepped outside and flattened himself against the front wall of the house. He could hear Tuck's quick and irregular breathing just behind him. "I got the hatchet," said Tuck.

"Shut up!" hissed Gary.

Objects in the yard were dimly outlined against the graying sky. The windmill was still. Gary crouched and walked along the porch until he was at the northern end of it. He unconsciously glanced toward the Espectros, seeing nothing but their huge and indistinct outline against the sky. A cold whisper of the dawn wind crept along the desert, rustling the leaves of the trees beside the house. The vanes of the windmill hummed a little.

Lobo suddenly stopped barking. A low growl came from him. He was near the low stock shed north of the house. Gary could just make him out. There was a pick handle leaning against the side of the house. Gary gripped it and started toward the dog. As long as Lobo was alert, no one would bother Gary.

He was within twenty feet of Lobo when the dog suddenly stopped growling. Gary had an uneasy feeling of being watched. He turned quickly, not really expecting to see anything out of the usual, but when he did, his heart seemed to skip a beat, and his throat suddenly went dry.

A hatless man stood beyond the fieldstone wall, looking directly at him. He had a rifle in his hands. Gary froze. Every instinct within him cried out to run, run, run! He glanced at Lobo. The big dog was still alert, watching the stranger, but he wasn't growling as he should have been.

Gary looked again at the silent, menacing figure, hoping that it was a mirage conjured up by his vivid imagination. It was still there. It moved. "Stay where you are!" said Gary. He raised the pick handle as though it were a rifle.

The figure raised the rifle it held. Gary's throat seemed to close up, and his stomach turned to water. "Take it easy, Gary," said the man. "Found your rifle up the canyon late last night."

Gary stared at him. "Who is it?" he asked.

"Lije Purtis, Gary. You know me."

Gary nodded. Lije was a local character. A man who prowled the local countryside at all hours of the day and night, sleeping wherever he happened to be, living off handouts, or working just enough to pay for the next few meals. Lije never bothered anyone. That was why Lobo had stopped barking as soon as he had recognized the man.

"You want the rifle, Gary?" asked Lije.

"Sure, Lije." There was no use in talking sharply to the man for coming there in the predawn darkness with a rifle in his hands. It would do no good. "You hungry, Lije?" he asked.

"Always am, Gary."

"Come on in then." Gary patted Lobo. "Where have *you* been, you bum?" he asked.

Lobo barked shortly. He was a powerfully muscled dog, like a mastiff, with a brown and white pelt and a black face, a combination of several breeds.

Lije climbed over the fence and shambled toward them. "I see him now and then in the canyons," he said.

That was another odd thing about Lije. Lije would go into the Espectros—without water, food, blankets, or arms—stay as long as he liked, then wander out again, perhaps on the remote north side or the wild east and west sides, sometimes on the more accessible south side. The local Apaches knew him well and took care of him when he wandered their way. *Mind Gone Far*, they called him, for he was protected by the gods.

Lije handed Gary the rifle. He smiled vacantly, revealing his crooked yellow teeth and the gaps between them. His washed-out eyes never left Gary's face. Gary always had an odd feeling that Lije was enjoying some vast and secret joke of his own when he looked at people. Tuck always said that he wasn't quite sure who was crazy, Lije Purtis or the rest of the world.

"Is it your rifle, Gary?" called Tuck.

"Yes."

"How did you know it was Gary's rifle?" asked Tuck of Lije.

"It is, ain't it?" said Lije.

"I know," said Tuck patiently. "But how did *you* know?"

No one seemed to know whether Lije could read and write. No one knew just how much Lije did know.

"It's Gary's," said Lije simply.

Gary looked at Tuck. Tuck shrugged. "Where did you find it, Lije?" asked Tuck. His shrewd blue eyes studied the man.

"Up the canyon."

"Where?"

"Behind a rock ledge. Lying on the ground it was."

An odd feeling came over Gary. He worked the lever. A spent cartridge case tinkled on the hard ground. Five more fresh cartridges were ejected from the rifle before it was emptied. He had loaded it the evening before with six rounds. "Did you shoot it, Lije?" he asked quietly.

Lije's eyes widened. "I don't even know *how* to shoot one, Gary," he said. "You know that!"

Gary nodded. He looked up toward The Needle, now being bathed in the cold gray light. There was no use asking Lije how he happened to be up there during the night or how he had stumbled upon the rifle if he *had* just *stumbled* upon it.

"What's wrong, Gary?" asked Tuck.

Gary turned. "One round was fired. Lije didn't fire it. You follow me?"

Tuck rubbed his lean jaw. "Yeah," he said shamefacedly. "Maybe it fell over and discharged. Maybe that was the shot that stampeded us. I had an idea all the time it was that."

"Oh sure," said Gary dryly. "Seems to me you said something like this when I asked you if you had seen

Asesino: 'Sure Rose up like a jack-in-the-box atop The Needle! Aimed right at us! Lordy! Bullet nearly parted my hair, Gary!'"

Tuck flushed. "Well, a guy gets nervous like."

"Sure does." Gary looked at Lije. "You see anyone else up there, Lije?"

"No."

"You sure?"

The veil over the faded eyes was more pronounced. "You asked me if I was hungry, Gary," he said petulantly.

Gary nodded. "Sure, Lije." There was no use in going further with the man. Gary slowly reloaded the rifle. Lije shambled toward the house and walked in as though it were his own.

Tuck studied Gary. "Well?"

Gary shrugged. "It could have been my rifle that went off by accident. I had loaded the chamber and then leaned it against the rock dike. Careless of me."

"That's not like you, Gary," admitted Tuck. "Now me, *I'd* do a thing like that."

"Lije isn't supposed to know how to shoot a rifle," said Gary thoughtfully. "But supposing he did?"

"You mean he might have shot at us?"

"I mean, maybe he shot it sometime later during the night. Maybe someone really *did* shoot at us in there. But how can we know that?"

Tuck nodded. "I've always said Lije probably knows a lot more than we give him credit for. He's smart enough not to have to work, and yet he gets by. The rest of us have to work hard for a living."

"Well, we'll never know," said Gary. He looked again at The Needle. More mystery. The place seemed to breed mysteries as it did thunderstorms in the summer and pouring flash floods in the fall and winter. "I'd like to know what Lije sees in there."

"Or *what* sees Lije," added Tuck softly.

Gary shivered. "Let's eat. We've got a long, hard day ahead of us."

———

GARY WAS KEPT busy cooking for the two guests. Voracious as Tucker C. Browne was, he was an amateur compared to the thin and gaunt Lije. Tuck finally conceded defeat after Lije started on his third plateful of flapjacks.

When they had finished eating, Lije arose. He looked at Gary. "Map," he said.

Gary knew what Lije wanted. He went into his room and brought out the large local map he had bought the summer before, upon which he had made notes, corrections, and additions for his personal quest for the Lost Espectro.

Lije knew Gary was interested in the Lost Espectro. Gary placed the map on the cleared table, and Lije leaned over it. He nodded in satisfaction. Lije might not be able to read, but he knew well enough the shape and size of the Espectros. He placed a dirty, broken fingernail on a watercourse and traced it to a huge bluff that had forced the watercourse to change its channel. "Arrastres," he said. He stabbed his finger down hard, denting the thick paper.

Gary stared at the map. The watercourse flowed out into the wild desert southeast of the range. He had been in that area the year before as a wrangler for a small party of dudes who had been looking for cliff dwellings. They had found a few crumbling structures, but Gary had not seen any arrastres in there.

Arrastres were primitive ore-crushing mills used by the early Spanish miners to crush the gold ore. Where there were arrastres, there should be, or had been, gold or silver mines. He looked up at Lije. Gold and silver meant nothing to this child of nature. There was no expression on the man's thin face, but Gary realized that Lije was paying for his meal in the only way he knew.

Lije walked to the door. He turned and eyed the two boys. "Be careful," he said. He swiftly drew his left hand across his throat in a gruesome gesture. *"Asesino!"* Then he was gone from the house.

Tuck shuddered a little. "Cheerful *hombre*," he said.

Gary eyed the map again. "Arrastres," he said thoughtfully.

"Maybe he was kidding us."

"No."

"Then we may have found a clue to the mines!"

"Arrastres weren't always near the mines, Tuck. The arrastres used in crushing the ore of the old Peralta Mines, believed to be the lode that the Dutchman found in the Superstitions, were quite a distance from the mines. The ore was brought down in *aparejos* by mule train."

"Well, it's better than nothing!"

Gary grinned. "You can say that again. You want to take a crack at it today?"

"That's why I came out here, *amigo*. After last night, I want no part of The Needle for some time."

"Yeh," said Gary dryly.

————

THEY WERE LOADING the jeep when the wind shifted. Gary quickly raised his head. "Listen!" he said.

The sound of a car engine came to them from the northwest. Gary whirled. There was only one road in there, the road he and Tuck had traveled the night before. It went in toward the western ramparts of the Espectros, then ended at Massacre Springs.

"Dust," said Tuck.

A thin wraith of dust hung over the desert, moving toward the northwest.

"Wonder who it is," said Gary.

"Which way did Lije go?"

"*Quién sabe?* He can't drive anyway."

"Sure, sure! Lije can't shoot! Lije can't read! Lije can't write! Lije can't drive!"

Gary turned. "What do you mean?"

"I've always said Lije knows a lot more than folks give him credit for, Gary. How do we know he isn't in that car right now?"

"He can't drive, I tell you!"

Tuck lowered his voice. "Sure, *he* can't drive, but he can sure ride with someone else who *can* drive."

Gary was puzzled. "I see what you mean."

"So we go chasing off after a wild goose to the *east* of the Espectros for some beat-up old arrastres while Lije goes the other way."

Gary whirled again. He snatched his father's binoculars from the jeep and ran to the windmill. He swiftly climbed the ladder to the platform at the top, took the glasses from their case, and raised them to his eyes, focusing them on the dust that seemed to be moving more swiftly. But the vehicle was below a low rise of ground, and there was no place where the road crossed an open area where Gary might catch a fleeting glimpse of it. He slowly descended the ladder. "No fish," he said to Tuck.

"Mysteriouser and mysteriouser," said the lean one.

The telephone jangled insistently. Gary ran to the house and picked up the phone. "Gary?" his father said. "Listen! Sue Browne wants to come out and spend the day with you and Tuck."

"Oh, Lord," groaned Gary.

"Your mother will drop her off at the highway in about half an hour. Pick her up there. I wasn't sure you'd be home yet. Glad I caught you."

"Yep," said Gary.

"She's a nice kid," said Pete Cole. "She'll be good company for you boys."

"Oh sure, Dad."

"O.K. Pick her up in about half an hour to forty-five minutes. Bye, son."

Gary replaced the phone on its cradle. Tuck thrust his owlish face into the room. "Who was it? Asesino? Hawww!" he brayed.

"Worse," said Gary. "That was my father. Seems like your beloved cousin, Miss Susan Browne, is to spend the day with us."

Tuck paled. "We still got time to pull out?"

"My mother will drop her off at the highway. We have to pick her up there."

Tuck seemed trapped. "Let's vamoose!" he said.

"My father told me to pick her up. I'll have to do it, Tuck."

"Why'd you have to answer that phone anyway?"

"How did I know Sue was back in town?"

"Yeh. She was away at some summer camp or something. Sure was quiet around town with her gone. By golly, I'll just bet she knew what we were going to do. I wouldn't put it past her, *amigo!*"

Gary nodded. "And just the day we get a solid lead on the Lost Espectro, too."

They walked outside to the jeep. Gary whistled for Lobo. The huge dog leaped into the back seat and settled himself with a proprietary air. Gary drove out onto the gravel road and toward the main highway. Gloom rode along with them.

"Sue Browne," groaned Tuck. "Sometimes I'm not even sure she's kin to me. No one else in the whole family is quite like Sue, odd as they all are."

"I'll buy that," said Gary gloomily.

———

THEY WAITED at the junction of the highway and the gravel road. In a short time, they saw the familiar, battered green pickup truck. Mrs. Cole drew off on the shoulder of the road. The look in her blue eyes was sufficient for her to warn Gary without opening her mouth. Mrs. Cole well knew the effect Sue Browne had on the boys.

The fifteen-year-old object of all the trouble got out of the truck, waved goodbye to Mrs. Cole, and walked quickly toward the jeep. She opened her mouth in a wide smile, and the early morning sun glinted on the braces she wore. "Brought my own lunch, Gary!" she cried happily. "Got some extra for the hungry dragon too!"

"That's *me*," said Tuck unhappily. "I'd rather go hungry, so help me, Gary."

Sue was getting taller, Gary noted. But she was still shaped something like Tuck, all odds and ends and angles. She had dark brown hair, cut short, and a battered sombrero was perched on the back of her head.

"Gary!" called Mrs. Cole.

He got out of the jeep. "Get into the back with Lobo," he said casually to Sue.

Sue had one beautiful feature, a pair of big brown eyes that seemed to dominate her face. If a fellow didn't look at her braces, tip-tilted nose, and freckles too closely, she'd almost be considered pretty because of her eyes.

Mrs. Cole leaned toward Gary. "It wasn't my idea, Gary," she said in a low voice. "But now that she is here, I want you boys to treat her nicely."

"Yes, ma'am."

She studied him. "What happened last night?"

"Nothing."

She eyed him closely. She had an uncanny knack for knowing when things went wrong with Gary. "Are you sure?"

"Yes, ma'am."

"Where are you going today?"

"Over to the southeast side of the Espectros."

She smiled in relief. "Thank heaven for that. I thought you might be foolish enough to go poking about in the canyon near The Needle."

"Not today, Mother."

She half closed her eyes. "I see. What's up at the east end?" she asked quickly.

"I thought we might find some Indian relics."

"Nothing on the Lost Espectro though?"

"Well," admitted Gary, "if we find anything, we sure won't just walk away from it."

"Your father and I will be home late this evening. Can you take Sue home?"

"Tuck can take her on his Honda."

"No! Absolutely not! *You* bring her home."

"All right, Mother."

The pickup turned and moved back toward The Wells. Gary shrugged, cleared his throat, then plodded toward the jeep. Sue was tucked in beside the bulk of the dog. She was all smiles. "Sure will be fun," she said.

"Yeh," said Tuck. He sagged lower in his seat.

Gary did not talk as he drove off to the east. Sue Browne had a hide like a rhinoceros when it came to figuring she was not wanted.

"Where to?" she asked brightly.

"East," said Gary shortly.

"I know. But where?"

"Got a lead on some Indian relics near a dry stream."

"Nothing on the Lost Espectro?"

Gary looked out of the corner of his eye at Tuck. Sue was a talker, sure enough. Tuck yawned. "Hey," he said suddenly. "You wearin' perfume, Susie?"

She seemed to swell up a little, Gary noted in the rear-vision mirror. "A little, Tuck," she coyly admitted. "Why?"

Tuck yawned again. "For a minute, I thought it was Lobo," he said. He closed his eyes as though to sleep.

She had walked right into it. Sue flushed and looked quickly away. She'd be quiet now until they reached the watercourse at least. Still, Gary couldn't help but feel a little sorry for her. She wasn't a bad kid. If she'd only learn to keep her mouth shut.

CHAPTER FOUR

Canyon of the Skull

The sun was in full spate against the eastern side of the Espectros. Gary had stopped the jeep against a perpendicular wall of rock. As he turned the engine off, the silence, with the exception of the softly murmuring wind, seemed to descend upon the empty countryside. The wide gap of the watercourse was to the north of them. Lobo, already on his way, was threading easily through the cactus and greasewood clumps.

"You sure that's the place, Gary?"

Gary nodded. He tapped the side of his head. "The map is in here."

"Lots of room for it in there," cracked Sue. She swallowed hard as she saw the looks they shot at her.

"Funny, oh *funny*," said Tuck.

"Just what are we looking for?" she asked.

There was no use in trying to deceive Sue Browne. She had the native shrewdness of the Brownes. "Arrastres," said Gary.

She nodded wisely. "Makes sense. I never could see fooling around The Needle. That so-called mining symbol in there isn't even a mining symbol, from what

I've heard. Now..." Her voice died away as she saw the intent looks on the faces of her companions.

"Just what do you mean, Sue?" asked Tuck.

"Well, when I was at summer camp, the *cocinero* there was an old man who said he had often looked in the Espectros for the lost mines. He said it was a waste of time looking about The Needle. He said he had heard about that sign in there you were supposed to see about four o'clock in the afternoon in August or September. Well, according to him, it was just a big split in the rock."

"He knows so much," said Tuck angrily.

She placed her hands on her slim hips. "Sure he does. He said it wasn't likely those old miners would make a signboard pointing *right* to the canyon the mine was *in*. That would be a little more than stupid, wouldn't it?"

Tuck looked at Gary; Gary looked right back at Tuck.

Sue slung a canteen strap over her shoulder and picked up her big lunch bag, fastening it to her belt. "So, where there are arrastres, there must be a mine. Right?"

"Right!" they chorused.

"Then what are we waiting for?" Sue took off briskly.

Tuck folded an arm across his lean stomach, rested his other elbow on it, then cupped his chin in his hand. He watched his cousin trudging through the cactus and greasewood. "Well, I'll be drowned in sheep dip," he said slowly.

Gary took the rifle, binoculars, and haversack from the jeep. "Get the rest of the stuff," he said. "Let's give her a good lead. Maybe she'll get lost."

"With *that* lunch! Sue isn't much for looks or anything else, but her mother can put up the best lunch you ever saw, *amigo!*"

They followed the slim girl through the growths. Lobo was waiting for them at the mouth of the dry watercourse. He trotted ahead of them as they fought their way through a tangle of catclaw. By the time they reached more open ground, the heat of the day was pouring into the narrow canyon ahead of them.

"How far ahead?" asked Tuck.

Gary pointed to the huge, naked bluff that seemed to block the passage of the stream about one mile ahead of them.

"Funny, I never heard of arrastres being in here," said Tuck. "Seems like someone would have spoken about them."

It didn't take them long to find out why the arrastres had been a secret for so long. Detritus had fallen from the huge overhanging walls of the canyon and had formed treacherous slopes of loose sliding rock, interlaced with catclaw and wait-a-bit-bush that tore at their clothing and ripped their skin. Only Lobo seemed immune to the sharp thorns.

At one point, it seemed as though they would have to turn back until Lobo casually trotted around behind a huge split boulder. When they followed him, they found themselves in a sort of natural passageway, affording barely enough room to squeeze through. After a zigzag passage, they came out upon a flat rock area where they could see the bluff towering above them. Here, the passage of the stream bed seemed unimpeded.

"Must have been easier to get in here years ago," said Gary thoughtfully. "No wonder these arrastres have never been seen in modern times."

"Except by Lije," said Tuck.

Sue turned. "Lije Purtis?" she asked.

Tuck nodded. "We talked to him this morning. He brought Gary's rifle back."

"From where?" she asked. "I never saw Gary leave that precious .30/30 of his anywhere."

Gary could have hit Tuck with a rock. That girl had an inquiring nose like an anteater.

"From where?" asked Sue again. She eyed them. "I'll

bet you went into the canyon near The Needle yesterday sometime."

"You know a lot," scoffed Tuck.

"What happened in there? How come Gary left his rifle in there?"

"Nothing happened in there!" snapped Tuck.

"Then you *were* in there," she said triumphantly.

She had trapped Tuck neatly, and that wasn't easy to do. She sat down on a rock and studied them.

"So help me," said Tuck. "If you didn't have that lunch, I'd leave you here."

"You *can't* leave me here! Besides, I'm not afraid of Asesino."

"Oh no?" snarled Tuck. "If he took a shot at you like he did at us last night, you'd run like a striped bird, you would..." His voice died away. A panicky look came over his thin face. "Oh, Lord," he continued. "Now I did it."

Her eyes sparkled. "I wish I had been there!"

"So help me, Sue," breathed Tuck, "if you open your mouth around my folks or Gary's folks about this, I'll never talk to you again!"

She half closed her eyes. "Well, I'll consider it," she said.

Gary picked up his rifle and walked on. He would willingly have left both of them behind. He followed Lobo through the brush and to the bank of the dry watercourse. Up and down he went, then across to the far bank and up and down that. Nothing, absolutely nothing. The words of Tuck came back to him: "So we go chasing off after a wild goose to the *east* of the Espectros for some beat-up old arrastres while Lije goes the other way."

The others joined him, and for two hours, they searched every foot of the ground with no results. The sun was at its zenith when they stopped. "Hopeless," said Tuck. "I was right all the time."

They ate their lunch in gloomy silence. Sue didn't eat

much; she never did. She left the spoils to Tuck, whose appetite was never spoiled by anything. It was almost a relief for the two boys to see her fade off into the brush. Gary sent Lobo after her.

"Blind alley again," said Tuck around a mouthful of cake.

"Yeh." Gary shook his head. "Maybe Sue is a hoodoo."

"Figures."

A wild shriek echoed through the quiet canyon. Gary moved like a flash, snatching up his rifle and then hurdling a rock. He dashed through the clinging brush heedless of the piercing thorns. He twisted his ankle on a loose rock footing, then burst into a clearing high on the slope.

He could see a dim figure beyond the clearing jumping up and down. It was Sue. Gary levered a round into the Winchester, then suddenly lowered it. Lobo had come out of the brush and was trotting toward Gary with what passed for a pleased look on his ugly black face. Nothing serious could be wrong with Sue.

Gary walked toward her. She was dancing about like an awkward marionette on a string. "Eureka!" she shrieked. Her voice echoed through the canyon like that of a banshee.

Gary winced at the piercing sound of her voice. She was pointing down at her feet. Gary leaned his rifle against a tree after emptying the chamber. He eyed a shallow circular trough worn into the hard ground. To one side was a narrow trough that angled off toward the dry bed of the watercourse. The circular trough was rimmed with low piles of material. There was little doubt in Gary's mind as to what he was looking at.

"Is it what we're looking for?" asked Sue.

He looked up at her and smiled. "It's an arrastre alright."

The circular trough was made by burros pulling a

stone to crush the ore. The other trough brought in water."

Tuck came toward them. "What is it?" he called out.

"See for yourself, Tuckie!" cried Sue.

"Tuckie!" said Tuck. He rolled his eyes upward. He looked down at the arrastre. "What is it, Gary?"

"Arrastre, Tuck."

"You sure?"

Gary nodded. He looked up at the towering walls of the isolated canyon. "What else could it be?"

"Yeh," said Tuck. He looked at Sue. "Stumbled on it, eh, Susie?"

She shook her head. "Look," she said. She led the way to a rock at one side of a scarcely definable trail. There was a faint dark mark upon it. "This mark was evidently made by a mule shoe striking it. I found the trail, then found several other marks like the first one and walked right to here."

"Just like that?"

She nodded. "Just like that." She felt in a pocket of her Levi's and brought out a curved and badly rusted piece of metal. She held it up. "Found this halfway up the trail."

Gary took it from her hand. "Piece of a burro shoe," he said quietly. "Too small for a mule or a horse."

"Now what?" asked Tuck.

It was very quiet in the canyon except for the humming of the wild bees and the soft soughing of the wind that rustled the leaves. Gary walked to the west, parting the brush. Fifty feet from the first arrastre, he stumbled into a hollow in the ground. It was another arrastre.

There wasn't much doubt about their age. No modern miners would have made them. But Gary had seen other arrastres in other parts of the Espectros, and they had led to nothing. But this was a part of the Espectros hardly visited by anyone. Gary had never heard any talk about mines in this area.

Sue and Tuck came up behind him. "Scatter," he said. "See what else we can find. Don't get too far from each other. Lobo, go with Sue."

———

AN HOUR PASSED SLOWLY, then Tuck came to Gary, holding another badly rusted burro shoe in his hand. The ends of the shoe had been flared out. He handed it to Gary. "Found it up the trail. Pretty rough in there. I poked around, but it's impossible to see where the trail goes. What do you think of this shoe?"

"It's definitely of Spanish pattern. See the flared ends? They still make the same pattern shoe in Mexico to this day though."

"Big help, eh?" said Tuck disgustedly. "Could have been left here at most any time."

Sue came through the brush. "I don't think so, Tuck. If they don't make that type of shoe around here, it isn't likely anyone would bring up a burro or mule from Mexico to go joyriding around here in the past thirty or forty years, is it?"

"There she goes again," said Tuck.

Gary hefted the shoe. "She's got something there. With this and the arrastres, we don't need much more proof that miners were in here. Spanish miners."

"But no trail," said Tuck.

Gary nodded. He looked up at the forbidding south wall of the deep canyon. "There has to be a trail!" He walked to the south, following the faint trace of the ancient trail. When he reached the place where it petered out, he could see that Tuck had been right. It just vanished completely.

He got down on his hands and knees and peered through the brush, trying to find a continuation of the trail. He tried the old trick of half-closing his eyes and then suddenly opening them, hoping to catch an elusive glimpse of the trail, but the trail was just as elusive as the mysterious light he had seen several times up the canyon beyond The Needle. There was no trail, and yet there *had* to be one. If there were arrastres, there must be a mine, or mines, even if they had been worked out.

It was a downhearted boy who walked back to the others. "I can't figure it out," he said.

Tuck had the field glasses, and with them, he was slowly scanning the canyon wall inch by inch. "I thought perhaps we'd see a trace of another canyon opening into this one," he said, "but this country is so rough and broken up it's impossible to say whether there are any other canyons beyond this one."

"There's something else over here!" called out Sue.

They walked over to see her standing in front of what looked like tumbled walls of stonework. The walls had been formed in a small rectangle, hardly more than ten or twelve feet long by six or seven feet wide. Amidst the litter in the middle of it protruded several broken poles. "Rafters," said Gary. "The roof collapsed inside the building, whatever it was."

"There's one way to find out what it was," said Sue. She placed a long leg over the wall and began to pitch out stones and beams, heedless of the two boys. They started to help her.

They uncovered several rusted pots, a broken bucket, a skillet thoroughly eaten through by rust, a pair of husk sandals, and a broken pick handle. Gary sat back on his heels and shoved back his hat. "Doesn't mean much," he said. "You can't really tell how long this stuff has been in here. Might have been in the last twenty years. Nothing to show Spanish origin."

"And nothing to sell to a museum," said Tuck. He shook his head.

"Look," said Sue in a hollow voice. She pointed just

beyond the back wall. Something white showed in the brush. There wasn't any doubt as to what it was. Gary stepped over the crumbling wall and knelt beside the skeleton. The clothing was rotten with exposure, and there was nothing to indicate how long it had been there. One part was missing the skull.

Sue was a little pale. "It's getting late," she said. "Maybe we'd better head back."

Tuck grinned. "Heck, it's not more than two o'clock, Susie. Gary and I were thinking of staying until after dark."

Gary looked up toward the canyon wall. Through the moving leaves of the scrub trees and the brush, he could see a huge boulder with a whitish excrescence atop it. Something drew him toward that boulder, and he walked about fifty yards before he stood in front of it, looking up at the whitish object. It was a bleached skull. He climbed up beside it and picked it up. A cold feeling of fear shot through him. The back of the skull had evidently been shattered by something. A bullet from a heavy-caliber rifle...

The hollow eyeholes of the gruesome relic stared up at him as though in warning. Gary suddenly had an uneasy feeling that he was being watched. He looked quickly about. There was no sign of life. He wet his dry lips and slid down to the ground, still holding the skull. He walked through the shadowy grove of trees to the tumbled ruins. Sue's breath caught in her throat as she saw what Gary held in his hands.

Tuck was squatting by the headless skeleton. "Hey," he said over his shoulder. "I found a belt buckle. Initials J. B." He turned to look at them, and his face blanched. "Where'd you get that?" he said hollowly.

"Up there on that boulder," said Gary.

It seemed unnaturally quiet just at that moment. An uneasy sort of stillness had closed in on them.

Something rustled. The two boys darted glances at

Sue. "I found a newspaper," she said in a very small voice. "A Tucson paper dated July 10, 1949."

"About twelve years ago," said Tuck. He looked at Gary, and Gary knew well enough what he was thinking. Twelve years ago, two men had been looking for The Lost Espectro. They had vanished, and one of them had been found some weeks later with what appeared to be a bullet hole from a large-caliber rifle through the back of his skull. *The other man had never been found.* Gary looked down at the skull in his hands. *Maybe he had been found at last.*

"Come to think of it," said Tuck. "It is getting late."

Sue nodded vigorously.

Gary hefted the skull. No animal had hauled that skull from the body to place it high on that boulder facing toward the camp. It just wasn't natural. Maybe it had been placed as a warning. Whoever guarded the hidden secrets of the Espectros couldn't be everywhere at once to do his self-appointed duty. Maybe he left these little relics around to hold the fort while he was busy elsewhere.

A thick, dark cloud came between the sun and the mountains, and darkness seemed to fill the canyon like the settling veil of night.

Without a word, the three explorers turned to walk back toward the arrastres. Gary picked up his rifle. None of them spoke. The wind increased, moaning eerily through the canyon.

Lobo led the way, trotting easily, but even the big mastiff seemed a little nervous. It wasn't until they were threading the narrow, natural passageway that the dog stopped suddenly and looked back beyond the three of them. His hackles rose, and he bared his strong, yellow teeth. A low, fierce growling came deep from his throat.

Tuck grabbed Sue by the arm and shoved her ahead. "Get out of the way," he said fiercely. He turned to stand beside Gary.

Gary loaded his rifle. They could hear Sue's stumbling footsteps. Lobo growled again. "Go on, Tuck," said Gary quietly. "You'd better stick with Sue."

"What about you?"

"I've got the rifle and Lobo."

Tuck swallowed hard. "I'll stay," he said hoarsely.

"Go with Sue!" snapped Gary.

Tuck moved on. Lobo moved quietly back along the passageway, ears flat and head thrust forward. Gary wet his lips. It was almost like dusk in the canyon. He glanced up at the cloud. It was then that he saw a movement high above him. "Lobo!" he yelled. The dog darted back. Gary ran like a deer.

A moment later, a huge rock crashed into the narrow passageway, scattering shards far and wide. One of them struck Gary in the middle of the back. The sound of the crashing rock echoed through the canyon.

Gary tore through the clinging brush, heedless of the clutching thorns. He saw Tuck and Sue far ahead of him, and an intense loneliness gripped him. He slipped and fell on the loose detritus, almost landing in a deep gully to one side. He scuttled back up the slope and plunged toward the open area to the east. He reached a flat area and turned to see Lobo standing on the detritus, looking back into the inner canyon. He was growling again. "Come on, Lobo!" he cried. The big dog turned and trotted toward his master.

Gary looked up at the place the rock had fallen from. There was no sign of life up there, nothing to indicate that the rock had been pushed by human hands. An icy finger seemed to trace the length of his spine. If Gary had not seen the first movement of the falling rock, he would certainly have been crushed by it.

He walked slowly down out of the wide mouth of the canyon. Far ahead of him were the figures of Tuck and Sue. It seemed as though every time he found a clue to the mystery of the Lost Espectro Mine, something interfered. Maybe it was true that there was a curse on the Lost Mine of the Espectros. The local Mexicans called it *Oro Encantado*, or Haunted Gold. Gary was beginning to believe they had just cause for their belief.

———

THE FIRST DROPS of rain struck them as they climbed into the jeep. In a few minutes, the rain was sheeting down, and by the time Gary reached the main highway, he had been forced to use low gear and four-wheel drive. The battered jeep groaned and lurched through the thickening adobe mud.

Behind them, the Espectros were sheathed in mist and rain, and thunder pealed and rolled through the hidden gorges.

Sue shivered. "I'm glad we got out of there when we did," she said.

Tuck peeled off his jacket and handed it to her. "Yeh," he said quietly. He looked at Gary. "What do you think Lobo was growling at?"

"*Quién sabe?*"

"I had a feeling all the time we were in there that we were being watched," said Tuck.

Gary nodded. He glanced toward the mountains. "There's something in there alright."

"Like what?" asked Sue.

"Gold," said Gary.

"And ghosts."

Something rattled in the bottom of the jeep. Sue gingerly picked up the bullet-shattered skull. "Alas, poor Yorick," she said. "I knew him well.'"

"There she goes again," said Tuck. "I knew it!"

It was dark by the time they reached the Cole Ranch. Rain slanted down steadily, and a cold wind drove across the soaked desert. The three of them took the relics into the little room next to Gary's bedroom. "I'll tell my father about what we found," said Gary. "He'll probably notify the sheriff about the skull."

"What do you think the sheriff will do?" asked Tuck.

Gary shrugged. "They never solved the death of the other man who was found with a hole through the back of his head. It isn't likely they'll find out any more about this one."

Tuck took his jacket from Sue. "Well, I've got to get back. You taking Sue home, Gary?"

"Yes."

Sue's braces glistened in the light as she smiled widely. Lots of girls in The Wells would have liked to ride in Gary Cole's jeep on a wet night, even if the top did leak.

"It was my mother's idea," said Gary hastily.

"Yeh, that's what I figured," said Tuck.

Gary gave Sue a jacket and one of his mother's raincoats. As they walked out to the jeep, they heard the roaring of the Honda, and Tuck Browne slithered along the road heading toward the highway, riding as though the Devil were treading on his coattails.

Halfway to the main highway, Sue kept looking back over her shoulder with a puzzled look on her face. "Is there an air warning beacon on or near The Needle, Gary?" she asked.

He shook his head, intent on his driving.

"Are you sure?"

"Positive! Why do you ask?"

She eyed him. "Because I just saw a flickering light up the canyon past The Needle."

He nearly went off the road, turned the wheel in the direction of the skid, and brought the jeep back to the center of the road. He braked it to a halt and turned to look back. The Needle thrust itself up, looming in the wet darkness. There was no sign of a light up that mysterious canyon.

"What's wrong, Gary?" she asked.

He shook his head. "Nothing." He started the jeep

and drove on. The lure of the Espectros was opposed to the mystery and death that shrouded them. It had held his great-grandfather's interest and his own father's interest, and now it had claimed his as well. He knew there would be no turning back for him now, *or ever.*

CHAPTER FIVE

Clues to the Treasure Trail

A cold, damp wind blew down Cholla Canyon early Monday morning as Gary Cole followed Jim Kermit up the wet slope toward the mouth of the great opening into the Espectros.

Jim drew rein and turned to look at Gary. "Sure, I've heard about those old arrastres on the other side of the Espectros, Gary. To my knowledge, no one has ever found a trace of a mine in there. You've got to remember this, kid: Since the old Spaniards mined these mountains, there have been a lot of changes in the canyons. Flash floods and landslides have done a lot of earth moving in there."

Gary eyed the rugged escarpment of the Espectros, sharp and clear against the rain-washed sky. "I thought we had a real lead for a change, Mr. Kermit," he said.

Jim grinned. "I've lived in these parts for a long time, and I've never yet found any float from those old mines. I'm like your grandfather, Gary. Just a rancher at heart, putting my belief into good beef. Your great-grandfather was a dreamer, lad, and I think your father is too. You forget those old lies about lost mines."

"But if there were arrastres built back in those days,

they built them to crush ore, and if they crushed ore in them, those mines had to be somewhere near the arrastres."

"Good logic, Gary. But what makes you think you can find the mines if experts have failed? Even your great-grandpa couldn't find that canyon where the mines are supposed to be, and he knew these mountains darned near as well as the Apaches did."

"The mines have to be in there," said Gary stubbornly.

Kermit shrugged. "Well, there was an aerial survey made during the war, and no lost canyons showed, kid. Those aerial cameras show everything, and they didn't show any missing canyons."

Gary looked quickly at him. "Aerial photography! That might do it!"

Jim's eyes hardened. "There you go again! Come on! We've got no time for pipe dreams! I've got strays in these canyons, and I want them out of there before dusk! *Vamos!*"

"Is there any way I could get one of those photographs?" persisted Gary.

Jim turned. "Far's I know the negatives were destroyed when a hangar at the airfield burned down. I don't know where any of the prints are. Let's go!"

Gary rode on after Jim. He had worked for Jim a number of times. It always seemed to hurt Pete Cole to have to tell Gary there wasn't enough work on the Cole place for him to do. So Gary worked for any of the local ranchers who needed help. Some of them lodged dudes at their places for extra money and had hired Gary as a guide into the fringes of the Espectros.

Strangely enough, as isolated as the area was and as mysterious and bloody as its reputation was, the dudes seemed to like it. None of them ever knew they were carefully kept away from the danger zones. More gold had been made from writings about the lost treasures of the Espectros than had been found there. These writings served to lure the dudes and put gold into the pockets of the ranchers.

Jim turned in his saddle. "Take Cholla Canyon, Gary. I'll follow Split Rock Canyon to where it runs into Cholla and meet you there about noon."

Gary rode slowly toward the looming mouth of Cholla. The Cole place would make an ideal dude ranch. It had a splendid panoramic view of the Espectros. It had a history that had served as the basis for several paper-back western novels and countless pulp westerns, none of which had paid a dime into the Cole till.

There was a bronze historical marker on the state highway south of the Cole place, which told the tale of Chiricahua Springs Ranch. There wasn't any doubt in Gary's mind that the ranch would lure the dudes. Pete Cole could handle that type of work easily enough. It would take money though, to change the ranch into a dude ranch, and as the situation was now, there wasn't enough money coming in to pay off the loans against it. Jim Kermit was anxious to buy out the Cole place, and he had the money with which to do it.

Gary guided his claybank past a towering growth of saguaros. Maybe Jim Kermit was right. If Great-grandfather Cole had been unable to find the Lost Espectro, it wasn't likely anyone else could find it. What bothered Gary was the fact that history did not lie about the three Melgosa Brothers and their fabulous discovery of gold in the heart of the Espectros in the year 1844.

Vigil Melgosa had been killed by the Apaches; Leandro Melgosa had vanished, never to be found again; Marcos Melgosa was said to have sealed off the great mine, leaving a major part of the gold within it, then had fled to Mexico, never to return again. For years after he had left, the Apaches had kept white men from probing into the Espectros. Some white men had entered the mountains despite the Apaches, lured by the promise of the Lost Espectro. None of them had ever returned.

Even today, it was said the Apaches still haunted those tangled canyons and inaccessible mesas and that they knew well enough where the lost mines were hidden. The Apaches believed the Espectros had been the home of ancient gods. Many white people thought it was the Apaches who had committed most of the unsolved murders in the lonely, echoing canyons of the Espectros. There was no proof of this of course; there never was any proof at all as to who perpetrated the murders.

The recent rains had done much damage in Cholla Canyon, sweeping earth into the water course at the bottom, piling up brush torn from its roots, moving rocks down the wet slopes. "Flash floods and landslides have done a lot of earth moving in there," Jim Kermit had said.

Gary looked up the cold canyon. A thought ran through his mind. *"Flash floods and landslides can also reveal things that have been hidden for many years..."*

He could see no strays as he worked his way up Cholla. Jim Kermit was a hard worker, and he expected hard work from his hired hands. To Jim Kermit, losing a stray was like losing a pound of his own flesh. It showed in his ranch, for he was the most prosperous rancher in that area by dint of perseverance and hard work, or so he always said. *He* took no stock in lost mines.

Cholla Canyon met Split Rock Canyon halfway up the slope of the west side of the Espectros, trending in from the left at an easy angle. Then Split Rock continued on the other, or southerly, side of Cholla Canyon, but here it was called Needle Canyon, for that looming pinnacle of rock dominated the canyon as nothing else did.

Gary rode slowly. He reached the junction and saw no sign of Jim Kermit. There was no use sitting there in the damp waiting for him. Gary rode on. It wasn't until he rode into deeper shadow that he realized he was right below the huge landmark.

Closer and closer he rode until he could clearly distinguish features of The Needle he had never seen before, great cracks and splits, crumbling ledges, and eerie-looking holes that might or might not be deep caves. Here and there, scattered growths clung to shallow pockets of soil trapped behind ledges.

He forced himself to tear his eyes away from The Needle. Weird thoughts teemed through his mind. He reached for his rifle and then thought better of it. The Cole pride would not allow him to be frightened enough to ride with his rifle in his hand. In any case, if he were shot at, he'd hardly have time to fire back, or even to see who was shooting at him. But the Cole pride would not let him turn back either. There was a job to be done.

It was a wild and forbidding place in which he found himself, a chaotic tangle of brush and rocks, bleached dead wood, and splintered boulders. He turned in his saddle to look back down the canyon and found himself looking directly at a deeply chiseled marking on a slanted rock ledge. It was an equilateral triangle with a curved line starting from the apex of the triangle and curving downward to the right of the triangle.

His breath caught in his throat. This sudden discovery, after so many months of searching, seemed to stun his senses, but not so much that he did not know what that symbol meant. "Travel around a bend from this symbol," he said aloud.

He looked to his left. A huge outcropping of rock thrust itself into the canyon like the great paw of some primeval beast. Gary slid from the saddle and snatched the reins. He led the claybank toward that outcropping. Forgotten was his father's warning about going past The Needle and also his day's work for Jim Kermit.

The sun was at its peak when he found a second

symbol, an arrow with a broad head, slanted in the direction he was going. "Trail to treasure or mine; *other signs further on...*" Gary said breathlessly.

The canyon beyond was thick with tangled brush and shattered rock, seemingly from a huge landslide of years past, leaving a narrow passageway beyond into shadowed darkness. To his right was yet another narrow canyon curving around to the south in the general direction of The Needle Canyon.

———

AN HOUR DRIFTED past while Gary hunted for another code symbol. He plowed through catclaw and skirted thick clumps of painful jumping cholla, eagerly scanning rock faces, boulders, and the high crumbling cliffs. No luck. Nothing at all.

He picketed his horse and took the rifle, walking up the side canyon, peering through the brush for symbols. There was nothing to be seen. The Needle towered to his right, and he was quite sure that if he continued on down the canyon, he would reach the great canyon below the landmark and easily see the Cole place far below on the level ground.

A cold feeling came over him as he realized he must also be close to the general area where he had seen the mysterious spurts of flickering light. He knew now that it was not a figment of his imagination, for hadn't Sue Browne seen the light just the night before?

He continued on, then turned to his left up a steep slope of loose rock. He climbed steadily until the going was a little easier. Now he could see The Needle Canyon as well as Cholla Canyon and the mouth of Split Rock where it joined Cholla. The mysterious, partially blocked canyon was beyond the crest, high above him.

He drove himself on, though his legs began to tire a little, and his breath came harshly in his dry throat. Gary stopped and leaned on his rifle for support while he looked upward. There was a dark opening in the naked rock almost at the crest. It was the mouth of a cave that had been well shielded from view below by scattered rock and a screen of brush.

Gary worked his way slowly up to the scattered rock wall and levered a round into his Winchester. He eased himself between two huge boulders and saw the cave mouth. About ten feet within it, something was hanging, something that moved a little in the vagrant wind that swept now and then up the canyon. He stared at it, suddenly realizing that it was a sheet of faded canvas dyed a dun color.

He walked forward slowly and drew back the canvas to peer into the darkened interior of a cave that went far back into the living rock. A damp odor came from the cave, mingled with the smell of old fires and other stale things. He pushed back the thin canvas so that light penetrated into the cave. As he walked into the cave, his left boot struck something that rolled beneath his foot. Gary looked down to see an empty bottle. He stooped and peered into the uninviting darkness. It was almost as though something was far back in there, watching him, waiting for him to come in. He stepped back.

The wind shifted, and a faint sound came to Gary, the sound of a man's voice calling out at intervals. Gary took his courage in his hands and walked farther into the cave. To one side was a pile of blankets. Tin cans littered the floor. He bent to look at them. Most of them were without labels, but on several of them, he saw from the labels that they had been cans of Elberta peaches. Beyond the blankets was a crude fireplace filled with ashes and charred wood. He peered into the thick darkness.

The voice was calling again. A sudden fear came over Gary. He ran back to the cave entrance and then stopped in surprise. From where he stood, he could see the entire floor of The Needle Canyon, the Cole Ranch far below, and even beyond the ranch to the distant irregular patch against the desert floor that was Cottonwood Wells. Nothing could move on that canyon floor without being seen from the cave entrance, while no one could possibly see that cave from the canyon floor.

Gary stepped beyond the rocks that shielded the cave entrance and looked farther up the slope. He could hear the voice again. He worked his way up the loose and treacherous slope to stand at last on a level area above the cave.

He stared in surprise. From where he stood, he could see into every canyon about him, while to his right, the east, was a wide tableland stretching into the heart of the Espectros, with the open areas of canyons all about it. From where he stood, a man could walk easily to the lips of any of those canyons and see who was in them. From the cave, he could see anyone probing about in Cholla Canyon or The Needle Canyon.

The voice called again. Gary turned and looked down into Cholla. A man stood down there with two horses behind him. It was Jim Kermit looking for Gary. Gary turned and slid down the slope. He reached a level place and started across it, only to slip and fall in greasy mud. He shook his head in pain, then saw beyond his muddy boots a set of sharp tracks crossing the mud area. He got to his feet and eyed the strange tracks. They were made by rather small feet and must have been made sometime that morning after the rain had stopped, for the heavy rains of the day before would have washed them out.

He walked around the muddy area and studied the boot marks. The nail pattern of the left boot heel was clearly marked a double crescent of nails. The boot heel had either slipped to one side of the boot sole or had been nailed crookedly in place. Beyond the mud, he could see tracks leading down the slope toward Cholla Canyon, only to be lost in the scrub brush halfway down the slope.

Gary slid down the slope to the canyon floor and walked quickly to where Jim Kermit stood, set-faced and with hard eyes. "You figure my strays might be up there, Gary?" the rancher asked coldly.

There was nothing for Gary to say. He was wrong.

"You don't expect me to pay you for today's work, do you, Gary?"

"No, sir."

"What *were* you doing up there?"

"Just looking around."

"Just looking around," mimicked Jim. His voice was heavy with sarcasm. "The Lost Espectro again? You're as big a fool as your great-grandfather was! You take my advice and forget about that fairy tale!" Jim mounted his horse and rode down the canyon.

He did not speak again until he was near the first symbol Gary had found, then he turned in his saddle and eyed Gary. "By Jiminy," he said. "I'll just bet you saw those phony signs in here: the triangle with the curlicue atop it and that arrow. Was *that* it, Gary? Were you looking for more of *them*?"

There was no need for Gary to answer. His red face gave him away.

Jim Kermit threw back his head. "Hawww! That's rich! I've seen those things for years, and you were following them! Hawww! Why, even my own daughter, Francie, knows how phony they are! Wait'll she gets back into high school this fall and tells the other kids about this, Gary! Hawww!" Jim Kermit shook his head in great amusement and rode on down the canyon. Now and then, he would burst into loud laughter.

Gary followed the amused rancher. He might as well go home now. He turned and looked back at the sunlit slopes high above him. If a man was staying in that cave now and then and had a fire going in there, or perhaps had lighted a cigarette or pipe when the wind flapped the canvas screen, it could be seen down on the desert. But who would stay up there? An uneasiness crept over him. He slapped the claybank on the rump. No luck with the treasure and no pay for that day. His father wouldn't be too happy about that, nor could Gary blame him.

CHAPTER SIX

The Candyman's Strange Story

It was dusk when Gary arrived home. He had not wanted to face his father. Instead of changing the fortunes of the Coles by finding definite clues to the Lost Espectro, he had just made matters worse.

An odd-looking truck was parked beside the windmill. Despite his troubles, Gary couldn't help but grin. The truck was the traveling place of business for Fred *Candyman* Piatt, as well as the only home he knew. He peddled candy, knick-knacks, notions, needles and thread, used tools and books, shotgun shells and rifle cartridges, fishing tackle, and just about every kind of thing a rancher or his family might need between periodic trips to The Wells.

The truck was something like those used by milkmen. The interior was lined with shelves and bins full of Fred's articles of merchandise. There were even shelves on the outside against the walls of the truck, which could be covered by plywood doors when required. Fred also had rigged up a bunk at the front end of the truck, and it was there he slept when on the road.

It wasn't an unusual sight to see Fred's truck parked alongside some lonely road and Fred himself seated in a comfortable folding chair, smoking his pipe and listening to his radio, miles from any other human being. It was the way he liked it. During the day, he lived for his customers; at night and on the weekends, he camped by himself, preferring his own company and finding it good.

Gary's mother turned from the stove as he entered the kitchen after washing up. "You're late, Gary," she said.

There was no use in lying to her. He told her the whole story. He could hear Fred and his father talking in the living room. As long as the *Candyman* was there, his father wouldn't make too much of a fuss.

Mrs. Cole took a big meatloaf from the oven. "I've been against this lost mine business as far back as I can remember. First with your father and then with you. Your grandfather had no interest in the story. Both of you, however, are like Great-grandpa Cole. There seems to be a curse on those who hunt for that mine. Look what happened to your father."

Gary began to set the table. But his mother wasn't through yet.

"Gary," she said, "did you ever know just how your great-grandmother died?"

"Killed by 'Paches," he said. "I know the story by heart."

She shook her head. "You know the story that is on the historical marker. The true one is not told outside of the Cole family. Your great-grandfather left her alone in this very house while he hunted the Lost Espectro. The Apaches knew he wasn't here. They sneaked up and killed three of the Mexicans who were working outside. Your great-grandmother was a brave woman, Gary. She fought from the house and kept them from killing the son who was your grandfather. She died of her wounds. It changed your grandfather's life to a certain extent. He raised his son to be a rancher, nothing more. Can you see why?"

"Yet he didn't forget about the Lost Espectro himself.

Why else would he have passed his *derrotero* on to his son?"

"I suppose he just couldn't destroy the work of years, useless as it was. Now can you see why the Lost Espectro had a curse upon it, that it brings nothing but tragedy and death to those who hunt it?"

"I guess so," said Gary.

"Will you forget about it as your grandfather did?"

He looked away from her.

"Gary?"

"No, Mother, I can't do that."

For a long moment, her soft blue eyes met those hard Cole eyes, legacy of the Cole men, and she knew she couldn't defeat her own son, or his obsession with the Lost Espectro. "Call your father and Mr. Piatt," she said quietly.

Fred *Candyman* Piatt limped into the room. He smiled at Gary. "Howdy, son! Good to see you! You're getting bigger and bigger!"

Gary smiled. Fred Piatt could cheer anyone up. "I see you're limping, Mr. Piatt. What happened?"

"Slipped pretty bad. Mebbe I'll tell you the story later. My, that meatloaf smells good, Mis' Cole."

Fred Piatt had another function in life as well as that of being a truck peddler. Fred knew all the local news. He didn't gossip but passed on anything he thought was of importance if he was sure no one would be hurt in the process. Fred was no carrier of sly tales or malicious slander; he told the news as it had been told to him, no more and no less. At dinner that evening, he passed on all the news, but he never stopped eating, for Fred was a good man with a knife and a fork, almost in a class with Tuck Browne if the truth be known.

Fred reached for the potatoes and bumped his ankle against the table leg. He winced in sudden pain. "Hurts worse than ever," he said. "Taped it up after putting liniment on it. Could hardly get in and out of the ol' truck today. Shifting gears was a hardship, I tell you."

"How did you hurt it?" asked Mrs. Cole.

"You know how hard it rained yesterday evening? Well, early this morning, I stepped out'a the truck and slipped on some 'dobe mud. Got pretty fine bones, Mis' Cole. Don't take much to hurt 'em."

"Maybe you'd better lay off a day or two," she said.

His unusually dark blue eyes seemed to flash. "I got customers to service, Mis' Cole!"

"That takes care of that," said Pete Cole dryly. "'Neither snow nor rain nor heat nor gloom of night stays these couriers from the swift completion of their appointed rounds.'"

The Candyman looked quickly at Pete. "Nice," he said. "What is it?"

Pete smiled. "Herodotus, the Greek historian, wrote that about the Persian postal system of 500 B.C. It's a quotation used to describe the present-day performance of our postmen."

Fred passed a hand over his thinning blond hair. "Well, I do my job. Folks depend on the ol' Candyman. Woman might want some baking powder, or thread, or mebbe a corn plaster. Who *else* would get it to her?"

"He's only kidding you, Candyman," said Lucille Cole.

The peddler again filled his plate. "Well, as much as I hate to think about it, I got to keep going all week. This is the week I go plumb around to the north side of the Espectros."

"Too bad Gary is working for Jim Kermit," said Pete. "He can drive as well as any man."

Gary looked quickly at his mother. She nodded.

"So happens, Mr. Piatt, that Jim Kermit let me go today," said Gary. "I'd like to drive for you this week."

"Capital!" said the peddler. "Won't be easy! Hard work! Long hours! Moving all the time! You won't get tired driving?"

"I never get tired of driving, Mr. Piatt."

"You're young. It's rough country to the north."

"Just don't let him wander off into the mountains, Candyman," said Pete Cole, half in earnest and half in fun.

Fred's eyes narrowed. "Why would he do that?" He brightened suddenly. "The Lost Espectro! I might have known! Listen, boy, that ain't nothing but a fairy tale! If there *was* such a mine, which I *doubt,* all traces of it would have vanished long ago. You won't get anywhere dreaming about those lost mines, kid. Hard work is the formula for success! Look at me! Just a grade school education, and I already got my own business! Well established! Well thought of! Welcome anywhere as a solid, respected citizen of the community!"

Fred sawed off another thick slice of meatloaf. "I pass them mountains every week," he continued. "Sure, I look at 'em and wonder if there ever was such a bonanza as the Lost Espectro, but I got enough sense to know my fortune is in my ol' truck. I *look* at them mountains, Gary, but I never go into them canyons, I tell you! Too many queer things happening in there to suit the Candyman! Lost treasures don't mean that much to me. There are plenty of other things to be interested in. Money ain't everything, boy!"

Even Lucille Cole had to hide a smile. They all knew that Fred Piatt would carry his laden truck on his back up to the top of The Needle if he thought there was a customer on that aerie. It was an obsession with Fred to serve his customers, and it was certainly not to his discredit.

Pete Cole reached for the coffee pot. "I heard that Asesino was looking for some cartridge reloading equipment for that old rifle of his," he said casually.

"Well, so happens I got a set of secondhand Lyman reloading gear," said Fred quickly. He hesitated and looked quizzically at Pete. "Did you say '*Asesino*'?"

Pete grinned. "I was only joshing you, Candyman."

"That ain't a thing to josh about, Pete! No offense to you, but some people might want to know how you found out."

"About the reloading equipment?" asked Pete in delight. He burst into laughter. "You don't believe I actually heard that, do you?"

"Pete is only teasing you, Candyman," said Lucille.

The peddler turned slowly to look at her. "I don't like being teased about *him*," he said. He glanced quickly toward the closest window as though someone might be eavesdropping.

"The man is long dead," said Pete seriously.

"No," said the peddler. "Asesino is still alive."

"You've talked to him lately?" asked Pete. "Sold him a packet of needles? Come now, Candyman!"

Fred's face was pale and taut. "There have been times I know I've been watched, the times when I camped too close to the canyon mouths. Once or twice, I saw someone moving about on the canyon rims. I'm pretty sure it was him, Pete."

There was a skeptical look on Pete Cole's face. "Come off it, Fred," he said. "Don't start wild stories about him. There are people who believe he is still alive, you know."

Fred leaned closer to Pete. "I knew him years ago," he said quietly. "I couldn't be mistaken."

"Over thirty years ago?" echoed Lucille Cole. "Do you really think you'd know him after all those years?"

Fred straightened up. "Well, I might as well tell you. I think I seen him no later than yesterday morning."

"Where?" asked Pete.

"I was camped east of the mountains. Not too far from that plugged-up canyon there. I had parked my truck close under a cliff so as to get out of the sun. That was late Saturday afternoon. Had a quiet night. Didn't do much Sunday morning except laze around and look for geodes and the like. I get a good price for them from rock hounds. I wandered quite a ways from the truck, leaving it open to air out. Well, I was getting tired, so I started back. I wasn't one hundred yards from the truck when I seen him..."

Gary felt the cold creeping of fear over his body. He remembered all too well his own feelings when he was in a canyon and thought he was being watched.

"He was standing by the rear of the truck as calm as you please, eatin' something out of a can. I was scairt, I tell you! I turned to run and kicked a rock lying there. I looked back. He was standing there looking right at me."

Somewhere out in the stillness of the desert night, a coyote howled softly. Lucille Cole shivered a little.

"His eyes was like coals of fire!" said Fred in a louder voice. "He was ragged and dirty, but he moved like a cat! His rifle was leaning against a rock! He run for it, and I run the other way! Then I fell down, and when I had the nerve to look back, he was gone. Nothing on that empty ground but my old truck! He had vanished like a ghost!"

Gary glanced at his father. Pete seemed intent on what Fred had been saying. The man wasn't known to be a liar. The fact was that no man in Gary's knowledge, and in that of his father as well, had actually claimed to have *seen* Asesino in the past ten or fifteen years, although there were plenty of rumors that he *had* been seen, but no one ever seemed to know *who* had seen him. If Fred's story was true, then here was concrete evidence that the feared outlaw was still alive.

Fred hitched his chair closer to the table and refilled his coffee cup. "When I got to the truck, I found three empty cans lying there."

"What had he been eating?" asked Lucille.

Fred looked up with an odd little smile. "Peaches! Not them little cans! The big ones! Three whole cans of Elberta peaches, Mis' Cole. That was another reason I was sure it was him."

Gary had become tense. He stared at the talkative

peddler. Elberta peaches! Some of the cans in the mysterious cave he had entered that very day had once been
filled with the luscious fruit. "Why did that convince you
it was really him, Mr. Piatt?" asked Gary quietly.

The peddler smiled knowingly. "I said I had known
him years ago. If there was one thing Asesino loved—
besides killing, that is—it was Elberta peaches! Don't ask
me why." He smiled again. "It's a cinch he ain't buying his
peaches up in the Espectros!"

"What did he really look like?" asked Mrs. Cole.

"Like a ghost! An *espectro!* Cries out like one, too."

"Cries out?" asked Gary quickly. "How?"

"Well, I can't make it sound exactly like he does it,
but it's something like this." Fred threw back his head,
cupped his hands about his mouth, and gave voice to a
wailing, eerie cry, a mournful thing, thin and haunting.

Gary paled. It was much like the sound he and Tuck
had heard that night in the canyon.

"Elberta peaches," said Pete. He shook his head.
"Anything else missing?"

"Yeah. A box of cartridges. Kinda odd caliber too:
.50/110 they was. I used to carry them for Old Man Mills
some years ago. He never came into town, so I carried
them as a sort of service for him. Well, when he died, his
son came out from Albuquerque, took one look around,
then put the place up for sale or lease and went right
back to Albuquerque. Guess he either left the old rifle in
the place or else took it with him. Well, I carried that
box around such a long time I was almost glad to get rid
of 'em. Ain't many rifles that caliber still being used."

Pete nodded. "It is an odd caliber, though not quite as
rare as you'd think it would be. Came out in the
Winchester Model 1886 repeater. Probably one of the
smoothest, level-action rifles ever manufactured. It was
usually a heavy-caliber gun in .45/70, .38/56, .40/82, and
.45/90 calibers. The .50/110 was the largest of them."

"Say," said Fred admiringly. "That's alright!"

Gary smiled proudly. "Dad is a gun crank. Anything you want to know about guns, you just ask him."

"It was a .50/110 slug that killed my horse and dumped me down to the bottom of a canyon," said Pete quietly. "I ought to know it."

"Sure could make a hole in a man," said Gary.

Fred looked quickly at Gary. "What do you mean?"

Gary looked at his father. "Can I show Fred that skull I found?"

Pete Cole smiled and then looked at his wife. "Not in here, Gary."

"I'll serve coffee and cake in the living room," said Mrs. Cole hastily.

LATER, as Fred Piatt examined the bullet-punctured skull, he nodded. "Large-caliber slug alright."

"You remember those two prospectors who went into the Espectros about twelve years ago, Fred?" asked Pete.

"Yeh. They found one of 'em with a bullet hole in the back of his head. They never did find the other one."

Pete leaned forward and tapped the skull. "This is quite possibly the skull of the one they never found. Tell him the story, Gary."

Gary told the story of finding the skeleton in the canyon of the arrastres. "There was a belt buckle with the skeleton," he continued. "Initials *J. B.*"

"I think you're right, Pete," said Fred. "The one they found dead in the camp was a man named Carl Schuster. His partner was a man named John Bellina. It all ties in."

"Gary plans to take the relics into town and have them turned over to Sheriff Gates," said Pete.

Fred hefted the skull. "I wouldn't."

"Why not?" asked Gary.

Fred looked about as though someone might again be eavesdropping. "They haven't been able to find Carl

Schuster's killer in twelve years, have they? No! And they won't either. Likely them fellas was hot on the trail of the Lost Espectro. They *knew* too much. They was killed because they knew too much, and for no other reason. Now, I think the place where Gary found this skeleton and them arrastres is mighty close to the Lost Espectro. This is a great lead, Gary. I ain't interested, naturally. All the money in Arizona wouldn't get *me* into the Espectros to look for haunted treasure, and besides, after seeing Asesino yesterday, I ain't ever going near them canyons again!"

"So?" said Pete, "But why not tell the Sheriff?" Fred smiled almost as though he were explaining something to a child. "If any man has the right to the Lost Espectro, it's you, Pete, and Gary here too. Supposing the Sheriff does get this stuff? He won't likely know any more than they did twelve years ago. But these clues won't be kept secret if the Sheriff gets hold of them. It'll be in the papers and on the radio and TV, I'll bet. In a week, them mountains will be crawling with people looking for the Lost Espectro. This time, one of them just might be lucky. No, Pete, you keep this to yourself. I won't talk. Seems like Gary has really stumbled onto something this time. Never say die, eh, boy?"

"I don't want him wandering around in there," said Pete.

Fred smiled. "He's got the Cole blood, ain't he?" He handed Pete the skull. "Anyway, I'll keep him so busy the rest of this week he won't have time to look for any lost mine. Come to think of it, I need a partner. Been thinking of expanding. Two trucks. Twice as much business. Need a young fella with energy and ideas. What do you say, Gary?"

Gary tried to make his answering smile look realistic, but he was shuddering inwardly. Some local wag would start calling him "Junior, the Candyman" or something equally horrible.

Fred got up. "I'll sleep in my truck tonight. Put that skull under your pillow, Gary. Might tell you the secret of the Lost Espectro in the dark of the moon. Hawww! Best get to bed, Gary. We leave at dawn."

"Cheerful fellow," said Pete after Fred left. He filled his pipe and lighted it. He eyed Gary over the flare of the match. "Fred might be right at that. Let's keep this skull business to ourselves, for a time at least."

"Does that mean I can keep on looking for the Lost Espectro?"

Pete puffed at his pipe. "I don't really know how I can stop you," he said. He smiled ruefully. "Almost wish I could go with you. I wonder if he really *did* see Asesino?"

"*Quién sabe?*" said Gary.

The coyote howled again. Closer to the house this time. Gary eyed the grinning skull. It was a fact that Apaches could imitate the cries of animals and birds almost to perfection. Asesino had been part Apache.

CHAPTER SEVEN

The Lone Apache

During the three days Gary drove for Fred *Candyman* Piatt, he learned things about the western and northern approaches to the Espectros he had never known before. The northern side of the mountains was almost a land apart from that which he had known around his father's ranch. Not far from it was the border of the Apache Reservation.

The last stop on Fred Piatt's lengthy and lonely northern route was the old Mills Ranch, a place that had been built some years after James Cole had established his Chiricahua Springs Ranch. It had been burned out a number of times, and once, there had been a massacre there from which there had been no survivors.

The truck ground along in low gear through the desert sands. Gary wondered how Fred could possibly make any sort of a profit by selling a packet of needles or a bag of hard candy in such a remote part of the Espectro Mountain country.

Their goal showed in a spray of dusty green against the dun of the Espectro foothills, a sure sign of water in the almost waterless land. Behind a screen of trees were the ranch buildings. A dog barked as Gary drove up and stopped the truck at the gate.

A man rounded the corner of a shed and walked easily toward the truck. He was not tall, but his chest was deep and broad, and his slim hips were the mark of the horseman. "Hiya, Candyman!" he called. "Come on in!"

"Hello, Jerry! Hot, ain't it?"

The man smiled, revealing even white teeth. Gary studied him. He had seen many Apaches in his lifetime, and he knew now he was looking at one of the pure quill. The man seemed to be staring right through Gary. "You look familiar," he said easily.

Fred nodded. "This is Gary Cole, Jerry. Gary, this is Jerry Black. Black is short for Black Eagle, ain't it, Jerry?"

"Something like that," agreed the Apache. He held out a hand to Gary. "Your dad ever tell you about me, kid?"

"Not that I know of," said Gary.

"Maybe you'd know me better by the name they called me in the Marine outfit I served in with your dad. Geronimo!"

Gary grinned. "Sure!" he said. "You were with him all through the war!"

"How's your dad?"

"Not too well, Jerry."

"War wound still bothering him?"

"Yes, but it was that fall some years ago that did the worst damage."

A fleeting change came over the dark face. "They ever find out who shot at him?"

"Some folks think it was Asesino," said Fred.

Jerry grinned and waved a hand. "Not that old fairy tale again! Asesino is dead. Long gone!"

"Are you sure about that, Jerry?" asked Fred.

"Why, it's been years since anyone has seen him!"

Fred looked at Gary. He was behind the Apache. The peddler shook his head. Gary looked up at the shimmering Espectros, vague and unreal in the shifting light. "I've heard stories he's still up there."

Jerry shoved back his hat and took out a sack of Bull Durham. He deftly rolled a cigarette and lighted it. His dark eyes studied Gary through the smoke. "I go into those mountains all the time, kid. When I got out of college, I started exploring in there. That was twelve years ago. I haven't seen Asesino or anyone like him in there. Sure, the man *did* exist. Sure, he was an outlaw and a killer. But folks have built up a legend about him like they did about Billy the Kid and Wyatt Earp, making him do things he never did."

Gary took a chance. "I thought you Apaches shunned the Espectros because of old tribal taboos and so on."

Again, the fleeting look passed over Jerry's face. "That's cornball stuff for the old rimrock 'Paches, kid. Four years in the Marines and four years in college knocked all that hokey stuff out of me, I tell you!"

"Jerry gets a little bitter sometimes, kid," Fred said. "Seems like it ain't easy for a college-educated Apache to get a good job around here."

Jerry grunted. "They still think I'd scalp anyone who disagreed with me. Well, come on in. I have some cold drinks in the refrigerator." He walked quickly to the house.

Fred limped alongside Gary, holding onto his shoulder. "Jerry leases the Mills place. Doesn't run cattle or anything though. He's writing a book or something. Spends a lot of time hunting for relics in the mountains. That's why I come out here. Don't say anything about me seeing Asesino."

————

GARY'S EYES widened as he saw the things Jerry had brought out of the mountains. They were placed on a big table in the shaded living room. Pottery, arrowheads, basketry, husk matting, and other odds and ends. Hung on the walls were rusted spurs, bits, old guns, bridles, and other relics.

Jerry brought in a tray with glasses and a sweating pitcher filled with tinkling ice and ginger ale. "What do you think of my collection?" he asked.

"Terrific! Museum pieces, some of them."

"Hardly that, Gary," said the Apache dryly. "Fred peddles some of the stuff for me."

"Now you know why I come all the way out here to this suburb of Hades," grumbled Fred.

"And this is how you make your living, Jerry?" asked Gary.

Jerry nodded. "It keeps me going while I do research on my book about the Espectro Mountain country."

"It's supposed to be against the law to loot ruins," blurted out Gary without thinking. He was guilty of the same thing himself.

Jerry's dark eyes hardened. "Maybe it is," he said in a low voice, "but the state doesn't seem much concerned about how I live. If I don't dig out those relics to make a fast buck now and then, I'd go hungry. Besides, who else would go that deep into those canyons? Remember Asesino, kid! Remember the men with the bullet holes in their skulls! Remember the mysterious marksman of death who keeps inquisitive strangers out of the inner canyons!"

"It ain't funny," said Fred sourly. "Remember, it was Gary's pa who got shot in there. By God's grace he come out alive."

Jerry rested a hand on Gary's shoulder. "I'm sorry," he said. "I get a little bitter at times. Does your father still talk about the Lost Espectro, kid? It used to be his chief topic of conversation overseas."

"I just told him the other night that he and Gary had the best right to the Lost Espectro."

Jerry's eyes flicked up. "*No* man has a right to the Lost Espectro."

Fred tinkled the ice in his glass. "Oh, I've heard tell you 'Paches know exactly where it is but you won't talk. How about that, Jerry?"

Jerry did not speak. He waved a hand toward the relics on the table. "How much of this junk do you want, Candyman?"

Fred winked at Gary. "You didn't answer my question, Jerry."

The Apache turned slowly. "Do you want this stuff or not, Fred?"

Gary wandered over to look at the items hanging on the wall. He noticed with a start that there were several mule shoes with flared ends identical to those he and his companions had found near the arrastres. Jerry looked at him. "Ever see mule shoes like those, kid?" he asked.

"No," lied Gary.

"Spanish style. They still make them that way in Mexico."

"You didn't find these in an old cliff dwelling," said Gary.

"No. Over on the southeast side of the Espectros, there is a blind canyon with some old arrastres in it. I found those shoes around there."

"Interesting," said Gary over his shoulder. "You find anything else in there?"

"Such as?"

"Lost mines?"

There was a moment's hesitation, and then Jerry spoke. "I wouldn't know," he said quietly. "I'm not interested in them as such. There are less dangerous things in there."

"Why dangerous?" prodded Gary.

"All old mines are dangerous. In the canyon where I found those mule shoes, there is always danger of falling rocks because of the rock formations in it. A man could easily get killed in there."

"Yeh," said Fred dryly. "In more ways than one. Gary,

take this stuff out into the truck and make sure it's packed right. I don't want any of it broken."

Gary carried the box to the truck and stowed it away. He walked to the windmill and scooped up some water from the trough to wash his sweaty face. As he turned away, he saw something brassy bright lying beside one of the legs of the windmill. He picked up a large brass cartridge and turned it to see the base. It was marked W.R.A. Co. .50/110 Ex. "Winchester Repeating Arms Company," he translated, "Caliber .50/110 Express Cartridge." He swiftly palmed the brass hull and slipped it into his Levi's pocket as Fred and Jerry walked toward the truck.

Fred limped to the truck. Sweat dewed his red face. "I hate to call it quits," he moaned, "but we'd better head back home, Gary. This heat and my ankle are killing me." Gary helped him into the truck. Jerry beckoned to Gary and walked toward the windmill. Gary felt a twinge of fear. Had Jerry seen him pick up that cartridge case?

Jerry smiled. "Tell your dad I'll be by the ranch to see him one of these days. How is it going?"

"Pretty tough, Jerry. He has his pension, and I work when I can, but it isn't enough to keep the ranch, I'm afraid."

"As bad as all that?"

Gary nodded.

Jerry glanced toward the shimmering mountains. "And with all that gold supposed to be hidden in there so close to your place."

"Then you really believe in the Lost Espectro?"

"Of course."

"And not Asesino?"

Jerry began to roll another cigarette. "I'll bet he's long dead, kid. You keep looking for the mine. It's in there alright. You weren't too far from it the other day."

Gary looked quickly at him. How had he known they had been looking in the canyon of the arrastres?

Jerry lighted the cigarette. He blew a smoke ring. "Dangerous in there, kid. Lot of falling rock." The dark eyes studied Gary.

If Jerry had been in there, he must have seen that skeleton and the bullet-punctured skull as well. The hole in the skull had been a big one. A .50/110 bullet might have made such a hole. It seemed to Gary that the empty hull in his pocket was burning against his flesh.

"You happen to see the skeleton and the skull with the bullet hole in it?" asked Jerry casually.

Gary nodded. His throat tasted like brass.

Jerry blew a smoke ring and stabbed a finger through it. "You going to tell the Sheriff about it?" he asked.

"Why didn't you if you knew it was in there?" asked Gary boldly.

Jerry smiled. "Remember, I'm an *Apache*, kid. Ignorant and superstitious despite my college degree. Apaches won't stay near the dead. It's taboo. Like you White-Eyes say, we 'Paches steer clear of the Espectros. There are things in there we do not like. The undead haunt these mountains. Bu, the Owl, calls at night in the voices of the restless spirits of the dead." The dark eyes studied Gary.

Jerry looked again at the mountains. "I know one thing, kid. If you ever find that old *derrotero* your great-grandfather made, you might just get a lead on the Lost Espectro."

"No one knows where it is."

"If you ever find it, keep it to yourself. There are men around these mountains who'd do anything to get their hands on it. Kill even..."

"Yeh," said Gary weakly.

"You believe that, don't you?"

Gary nodded.

"You ever see any of those old Spanish mining symbols in the canyons?"

"Yes. In Cholla Canyon. Jim Kermit said they were phonies."

"He did? Kermit said that?"

"Yes."

Jerry smiled knowingly. "Well, he might *say* so, but Jim Kermit can keep his mouth shut when it comes to making a fast buck. You ever see Jim Kermit need money? The rest of the ranchers around here are always borrowing money, but not Jim. Jim always has a buck."

"Gary!" called Fred from the truck. "You aim to let me roast in here?"

"Go ahead, kid," said Jerry. "Keep hunting for the mine. Something tells me you might be the lucky one."

Gary shrugged. All the way to the truck, he could feel those dark eyes boring into his back.

When the truck reached the road, Fred glanced at Gary. "Jerry is a bitter man. I think he knows a lot more about those mountains than he lets on. 'Course I can't see an *Indian* getting the rights *we* got, but don't tell him I said that."

"He's a citizen, isn't he? He fought in the war. He was in my father's outfit."

"Sho! What'd he do?"

"Seems to me my father told me once he was a sniper." Then, a cold feeling came over Gary. Jerry *had* been a sniper, a dead shot with a rifle in the jungles of the Pacific Islands. He had made a record for himself in that deadly game. Asesino had also been handy with a rifle. Maybe Asesino was dead, but there was nothing to stop Jerry from taking up the trade of the outlaw. Maybe it was Jerry that Fred Piatt had seen last Sunday. Maybe Jerry wanted to keep the legend of Asesino alive so that men would fear the Espectros. Killing was no novelty to Jerry Black.

Fred eased his leg. "I'm taking off tomorrow, Gary. I'll pay you anyway. Friday, Saturday, and Sunday oughta be enough rest for this game leg of mine."

"You don't have to pay me for Friday, Mr. Piatt."

"Sho! You did a good job, kid. Besides, it was nice

having company. I learned a lot listening to you, Gary. Fella gets lonesome out in these places."

Gary smiled. Fred Piatt had a name for being close with a buck, but Gary had always thought he kept up that pretense so people wouldn't know how really soft-hearted he was.

Gary glanced at the Espectros. He and Tuck would have three full days to continue their search. This time, Gary was bound and determined they would come out of there with some definite conclusion about the Lost Espectro.

CHAPTER EIGHT

Search for the Derrotero

A lone lugubrious figure was perched on the fence in front of the Cole house when Gary drove up in the truck. Tucker C. Browne looked like a dejected stork sitting there. He brightened when he saw Gary. "What are you doing here?" he asked.

Gary grinned. "Mr. Piatt isn't running his route tomorrow, so he gave me the day off with pay, Tuck."

Gary got out of the truck. He looked back at Fred Piatt. "Are you sure you can drive alright, Mr. Piatt?"

The peddler nodded. "So long as I don't have to drive too much. I got some business in The Wells and other places I can take care of without too much driving. Say hello to your mother and father, Gary."

"They ain't here," Tuck said inelegantly. "That's why I'm here. Your father's back started bothering him, and your mother had to drive him to the V.A. Hospital in Tucson. They left early this morning. They won't be back until Sunday evening if they don't keep your father there, Gary. Your mother asked me to come out and stay at the place until you got back. Between you and me, I was hoping you'd come back today or tonight. I wasn't looking forward to staying here alone tonight."

"Afraid of Asesino?" asked Fred as he grinned.

Tuck shrugged. "I never like being around the Espectros alone, Mr. Piatt. Besides, lots of people think this place is haunted, too. There were so many killings around here in the old days."

"Hokey," said Gary.

Fred eased his way into the driver's seat. "Oh, I don't know," he said quietly. "Lots of things we don't know about haunts and suchlike. Once in a while, I see things out in the desert at night I ain't sure about."

"Like Asesino?" asked Tuck in delight. "Hawww!"

"Like Asesino," agreed Fred. He glanced quickly at Gary. "You can tell him when I leave, Gary."

Gary nodded. "He won't be so cocky then."

Fred looked toward the house. "Well, now you've got plenty of time to search for the Lost Espectro, haven't you?"

"That's the idea," said Tuck brightly.

"Too bad that ol' *derrotero* vanished," said the peddler. "I always figured one of two things could have happened to it. It was either stolen when your folks wasn't around here, Gary, or it's still here some place."

"Yeh," said Gary dryly. "But where? We've looked all over the house, outbuildings, fence post holes, and even around the Springs. No luck. Not even a clue."

"Keep looking," said Fred. "Tuck, you go into the back of the truck and help yourself to a box of candy bars. You look peaked."

Tuck obeyed with a speed a little short of light. He grinned as he came to the front of the truck. "Thanks a lot, Mr. Piatt."

"Forget it. I was a growing boy myself once. Keep looking for that *derrotero*, boys. You're bound to find it."

"I got some ideas on that myself," said Tuck.

Fred started the truck and drove off. Tuck held out the candy box to Gary. "Help yourself, *amigo*. On the house."

Gary took a bar and peeled it, but his eyes were on

the hazy Espectros. "We've got three days," he said thoughtfully. "When do you have to be home?"

"Doesn't matter," said Tuck around the last half of his first bar. "My folks know I'm out here. I usually am weekends anyway. Worked all week long at Bennie's Barbecue, so I got some spending loot."

"I'll bet Bennie lost on the deal," said Gary.

Tuck peeled his second bar. "Well, I got to admit he told me to take it easy on the french fries."

"Let's get some chow," said Gary. "I have a few things I want to tell you."

———

THEY ATE in the kitchen while Gary told Tuck of his experiences and particularly of Jerry Black.

Tuck constructed his third ham sandwich. "This thing gets more confusing every time we talk it over. I always wondered why Jim Kermit never seemed to be interested in the Lost Espectro, being the man with a buck that he is. Maybe Jerry Black is right at that. Jim just might claim those markings were phonies to keep nosy people away from Cholla Canyon."

"On the other hand," said Gary, "maybe Jerry is making Jim look suspicious to keep nosy people from wondering what he's doing all the time up in the mountains."

"Yeh," said Tuck around a mouthful of bread and ham. "But somehow, I want to believe in those two symbols you found in Cholla."

"They look real enough to me."

Tuck swallowed hard. "But I've always heard that Cholla is a dead end somewhere in the Espectros."

Gary finished his sandwich and leaned back in his chair. "It looked to me like there had been a landslide in there. There's something beyond that slide, Tuck."

"Yeh, like Asesino maybe. You really think Fred saw him?"

"*Quién sabe?* He saw *somebody,* somebody that liked Elberta peaches. Like the somebody who stays in that cave now and then. Tuck, I tell you, those boot prints I saw were fresh!"

"Maybe Jim Kermit was up there ahead of you."

"I was at his place before dawn, Tuck. I was with him until we entered the canyons, and there wasn't any place he could have gotten ahead of me. No, those boot prints were made by someone else. Maybe by the person who has been staying in that cave."

"Like Jerry maybe?"

Gary shrugged. "He keeps pretty much to himself. No one seems to know much about him, even Fred Piatt, and Fred seems to know something about everybody."

Tuck nodded. "But this Jerry keeps coming back to my mind, *amigo.* I remember him all right. Looks a hole right through you. Man, he's a natural suspect for my money."

"That's just it, Tuck! He's just too much of a natural! Asesino was part Apache; Jerry is full-blooded. Asesino really knew those mountains; so does Jerry. Asesino was a dead shot; Jerry was a sniper in the Marines. Asesino was a lone wolf; Jerry likes to stay by himself. Asesino didn't seem to be much concerned about the superstitions the Apaches attach to the Espectros; Jerry doesn't seem much concerned either. Asesino was bitter against the white man; Jerry is bitter as well. Asesino quite likely carried a .50/110 caliber Winchester, and I found an empty .50/110 hull at Jerry's place."

"Sounds like a lot of circumstantial evidence," said Tuck wisely. He began to prepare a fourth sandwich, cutting into the ham with the skill of a surgeon. "It's just too pat. Besides, and don't ask me why, I happen to like Jerry Black."

"Me too," agreed Gary.

"You keep talking about Asesino in the past tense," said Tuck. "Why? Maybe Fred Piatt really saw him."

"Fred Piatt isn't a liar, Tuck. He actually knew Asesino years ago. So, Asesino swipes a box of .50/110 caliber cartridges from Fred's truck and three cans of Elbertas. Fred said Asesino loved Elbertas."

"Phooey," said Tuck. He mustarded, ketchupped, lettuced and mayonnaised his sandwich. "Big deal! I love Elbertas! You like 'em! Why, even Sue eats them like popcorn! Lije Purtis would walk ten miles to get a can of Elbertas." Tuck's voice died away, and his eyes widened. "Lije Purtis!" he added in an odd voice.

"The man who doesn't know how to use a gun," said Gary.

"At a distance, a man who looked as ragged and dirty as Lije could sure look like he'd been in the mountains a long time. Maybe Fred got mixed up. He was scared, you said, and he was quite a ways from the truck."

"I know two characters in this house who are more mixed up than he is," said Gary dryly.

"Have you thought any more about that crazy *derrotero*?"

"I think about it all the time," said Gary. "Like Fred said, it was either stolen when my folks weren't around, or it's still here. It just has to be one or the other!"

"Big help," said Tuck. "Where'd we leave those candy bars?"

Gary left Tuck and walked into the living room. It was getting dark outside. He sat down in his father's big chair, a legacy of Grandfather Cole's. Gary closed his eyes. His head ached with thinking about that lost *derrotero*. If it was hidden in the house, it surely must have been well hidden; Gary and his father had once conducted a systematic search for it, and Gary's mother had even helped them. It had been no use.

Yet something rankled at the back of his mind. He had been an infant when the *derrotero* vanished. It had been about the time his mother decided to move into town to stay with her widowed father, who hadn't been feeling too well. With Pete Cole in the hospital, the Cole Ranch was a right lonely place for a young mother and a baby boy.

Gary could hear Tuck calling to Lobo to feed him the ham bone. The big dog barked as he raced toward the back porch of the ranch house. Then Gary could hear Tuck in deep conversation with the dog. Tuck liked that. It let him do all the talking. He was telling the dog he'd have to work for the bone.

"Nineteen-forty-six," said Gary aloud. He started and sat up. Why had he said that date?

He could hear Lobo chasing Tuck around the house, and the bloodcurdling cries of the lean one were enough to send a chill down the spine of Asesino.

He stood up and paced back and forth. "I was only a baby then. That was the year my mother took me to stay at The Wells." He stared at the wall and smashed a fist into his other palm. He certainly could not remember staying with his grandfather there.

Grandfather Hart, the retired high school principal of Cottonwood Wells Union High School, had died the first year Gary had started school. Gary could remember him. He always seemed to have a pipe in one hand and a book in the other. Where Great-grandfather Cole had been a man who had probed into the mysterious Espectros to make his precious *derrotero* and to find traces of the old Spanish and Mexican miners by tracking them down, Grandfather Hart had been strictly an armchair explorer, although his interest in lost treasures and in the Espectro was every bit as keen as that of Great-grandfather Cole's.

There was a tremendous crashing noise outside and the sound of splashing water while Lobo barked in delight. Gary walked to the window. A pair of skinny legs protruded from the water trough, and then Tuck Browne's lean face showed above the edge of the trough.

He climbed out, sluicing water from every stitch of his clothing. He limped toward the house. Lobo barked again. Tuck turned. "You did that on purpose, Lobo," he said and tossed him the wet ham bone.

The Hart house, now unoccupied, still stood on a side street in The Wells. It had been left to Gary's mother, and she had kept it, always thinking that when the day came for the ranch to be sold, the family could move into the Hart house. The house had been rented several times but never for very long. There were more modern rentals in the newer part of The Wells.

"Tuck," said Gary.

The lean one was wringing out his trousers. Yeh?" he said in soppy disgust.

"We're going to take a ride!"

"To where?"

"My grandfather's old house in The Wells."

"Nothing there," said Tuck.

"I have a feeling we've been looking in the wrong place for the *derrotero,* Tuck! The *derrotero* vanished about 1946; in 1946, my father was still in the hospital, and my mother and I were staying with Grandfather Hart."

Tuck stopped wringing. "By Jiminy!" he said quietly. "Grandfather Hart was loco about such things. You think maybe the chart was taken there and forgotten?"

"I'll take a chance that it might be there."

"Keno! Let me change my clothes!"

Gary got the jeep and was waiting for Tuck. He ordered Lobo to stay behind and drove out onto the darkening road. There was an intense eagerness within him. Nothing had been changed in the old house. Every now and then, Gary would go into town and clean up the grounds of the place, cut the lawns, and sometimes, accompanied by Tuck, he'd stay the night in the gloomy old house. Not once had he ever considered that the *derrotero* might be hidden there.

IT WAS QUITE dark when they pulled up in front of the old house, dreaming on its quiet side street. Gary unlocked the double front door, and it creaked open.

"Always thought this place was haunted," said Tuck.

"You think every place is haunted," said Gary. "I'll go in alone if you're chicken."

"Who me? Fearless Browne? 'Lead on, Macduff!'"

The street lamp shone through the stained glass at the top of the big door and made an eerie reddish pattern on the faded wallpaper. Gary quickly led the way up the wide, creaking stairs. "I figure we'd better hunt in the library," he said. "That's where Grandpa Hart spent most of his time."

The library was in the front of the house, across the hall from the huge master bedroom. Gary walked into the dim room faintly lighted by the street lamp. He lighted an oil lamp and turned to look at the serried ranks of bookshelves that entirely lined the big room. "I've heard of papers being hidden in hollowed-out books," he said.

"Sounds like a story from Poe," said Tuck. "Hollowed out books! Hooooey!"

"You got any better ideas?"

"Let's look for hollowed-out books."

An hour passed while the two boys took down one book at a time and examined it. Their hands were black with dust, and dust floated about the room and swirled about the draft of hot air rising from the lamp on the table.

"Man," said Tuck in grudging admiration, "your grandpap was sure a readin' man."

Gary nodded. He had reached the end of one row of shelves, and he reached for the first book in the next row. His hand stopped partway, and he stared at the row of books.

"What is it, Gary?" asked Tuck.

"Look, Tuck," said Gary. "Every book on these shelves is marked with fingerprints."

Tuck eyed the books. "Yeh," he said. "When was the last time any of your family were in here?"

"Early last spring, and we didn't dust the books as I recall."

Tuck whistled softly. "Someone was pawing around in here then," he said. He raised the lamp. "Look, Gary. That whole wall of books back there have been handled, too. Lookit the finger marks on 'em!

A cold feeling came over Gary. Someone had been in there then. Someone who might have gotten the same idea that had occurred to Gary.

"Ghosts," said Tuck.

"Ghosts don't leave fingerprints!" snapped Gary.

"Take it easy! I was only joking, *amigo*."

Gary shook his head. He was getting discouraged. Maybe this idea was a bust too. Everything connected with the story of the Lost Espectro seemed to be a bust.

Tuck walked to the end shelf, close to the door. Here, the books still had their coating of dust. He grinned. "Just supposing that clod who was looking through these books stopped a little short of finding the *derrotero*?" he asked.

"Those holes in your thick head make your voice sound funnier than usual."

Tuck reached up and withdrew a heavy volume. He hefted it. "Seems lighter than it should be," he said. He lifted the front cover and looked down at the book. For a moment, his face was set and frozen. "Gary," he said in a hoarse voice.

"Don't tell me you've found it?" cracked Gary. He started to reach for another book.

"Gary!"

Gary turned quickly. Tuck handed him the thick volume. The inside had been neatly cut out, and the edges of the pages glued together. Within the cavity was a folded square of heavy paper. Gary slowly placed the book on the table and just as slowly removed the paper. He carefully opened it. "Gary?" said Tuck.

Gary swallowed and then nodded. "Yeh," he said. "May I never speak again if I call you loco, no matter how much I believe it!"

"You're sure that is it?"

Gary spread the chart flat on the table beneath the lamp light. He had seen enough samples of his great-grandfather's handwriting to recognize it instantly on the *derrotero*. In the lower right-hand corner was his great-grandfather's signature. "Yes," he said quietly. "This is it all right, Tuck."

"Let's get out of this creepy place then."

Gary nodded. He folded the *derrotero* and replaced it inside the book, then thrust the book under his arm. He doused the light. Tuck walked past the table, glancing out a window as he did so. "Gary!" he said.

"What is it?"

Tuck stepped back from the window. "I'm almost sure I saw someone walking toward the porch."

Gary eased open the library door and moved to the head of the stairs. Tuck came up behind him. It was very quiet, almost too quiet. The faint light of the nearest street lamp came through the painted glass at the top of the front door.

The doorknob turned slowly with a little grating noise. The door swung open, and the shadowy outline of a man could be seen standing there. He looked toward the stairwell, his face shaded beneath his hat brim. He seemed to be listening. He moved a little, and something shone dully in the darkness. A gun or a knife, Gary was sure. The man took a step forward; his hand reached for the stair rail.

Gary took a long chance. "Who is it?" he called out sharply. "Speak up, or I start shooting!"

The man spun on a heel and darted awkwardly toward the door. His boots thudded on the porch and then on the stairs.

Gary foolishly plunged down the stairs, three at a time. He burst through the doorway and saw a shadowy figure disappear into thick shrubbery at the corner. Gary dashed across the lawn and slipped on slick grass. He came down hard, and the book flew from his grasp.

Tuck grabbed the book. He looked at the place where the stranger had vanished. "No use chasing him," he said.

Gary disgustedly wiped his muddy hands on the grass. A leaky faucet had allowed a pool to form, and the water had soaked into the ground. Gary stood up. The street lamp shone on the wet spot. Boot prints showed clearly, and they were not Gary's prints. Gary bent to look at the strange prints; the left boot print had a clearly marked double crescent of nails, and the heel had been nailed crookedly in place. Cold sweat broke out on Gary's face.

"What's wrong?" asked Tuck.

"Let's get out of here!" said Gary. He walked to the house and locked the front door. He ran to the jeep and started the motor. He put the jeep into gear and flicked on the headlights. Something moved quickly in the thick shrubbery at the corner. Gary swung the jeep in as short a turning arc as he could and shifted to second. He was at the corner before he ventured a look back down the shadowy street. There was nothing to be seen. But whoever was hiding in the shrubbery had quite likely seen the book Tuck had picked up.

"Who do you think it was?" asked Tuck.

"It wasn't the Fuller Brush man, *amigo*."

"No." Tuck peered down the street as Gary turned a corner. "What scared you back there?"

Gary stopped at a stop sign, then drove on again toward the highway. "You remember the boot prints I saw up near that cave?"

"Yes?" Tuck started. He whistled softly. "The same?"

"The same," said Gary.

"Can't this bucket go any faster?"

Gary immediately demonstrated that it could. He wanted to get home and get his hand on his rifle now that they had the *derrotero*. "If you ever find it, keep it to yourself," Jerry Black had advised Gary. "There are men around these mountains who'd do anything to get their hands on it. *Kill even...*"

CHAPTER NINE

Shadows in the Moonlight

Lobo greeted the boys at the gate. Gary and Tuck knew then that no one had been prowling about the place. They went into the dark house and pulled the shades in the living room before they put on the lamp. Gary got his Winchester and leaned it against the table. Lobo would warn them if anyone came near the house, giving them time to put out the light.

"This thing gives me the jitters," said Tuck. "Maybe we ought to take someone into our confidence."

"Like who?" snapped Gary. "Jim Kermit? Jerry Black? Lije Purtis? You loco? We found it, and we keep our mouths shut about it."

"Alright! Alright! It was just a thought," Tuck shrugged. "Still, maybe we ought to hide it for a while before we try to use it. Until things quiet down a little anyways."

"You can't mean that!" said Gary fiercely. "We've been running up blind alleys too long to not use this *derrotero* now that we have it! If you don't come with me tomorrow, I'm going it alone!"

"O.K.! O.K.! I'm not one to let a buddy go in there alone! Maybe we can be buried together so's our families will only have to put up one tombstone 'stead of two."

"You're a real comedian. Too bad Jerry Lewis isn't looking for a new partner."

"I've got a partner," said Tuck seriously. "Gary, what do you really think about us going into the Espectros?"

Gary sat down and leaned toward his partner. "It isn't as though we were just going in there to take out a couple of burro-loads of gold or silver, Tuck. Even with this *derrotero,* it isn't going to be easy. Don't forget that the Lost Espectro has been lost for about a hundred years. All my great-grandfather's chart can do for us is to show us what he found, and *he didn't find the lost mine.* Sure, we can follow the clues he has on the *derrotero,* but when we reach the end of them, we'll be right where he was when he stopped looking. It's quite possible, too, that someone might have found the Lost Espectro and never opened his mouth."

"Don't say such a thing," said Tuck in horror.

"My thought is to leave here before dawn and hike into Cholla Canyon before anyone can see us from higher up, *if* we're being watched. We can take light camping gear along in case we have to stay there overnight."

"Goody, goody," said Tuck. "I can hardly wait."

"Meanwhile, let's try to learn this chart by heart. I don't want to take it in there with us."

The two of them sat at the table and studied the *derrotero* with a great deal more interest than they had ever shown in a textbook on algebra or physics. After half an hour, Tuck looked up at Gary. "I can compare everything I've seen around the Espectros against this *derrotero* except for one thing, Gary." He placed a finger on a stylized sunburst drawn in a narrow canyon.

"A sunburst like that indicates a mine or mines close by, Tuck. Any symbol of the sun indicates great mineral wealth nearby. The question mark in the center of it was probably my great-grandfather's own idea. Quite likely that sunburst is where he *thought* the mine was."

"That isn't what's bothering me," said Tuck. "Have

you ever seen a canyon in those mountains that corresponds to the one he drew and marked with that sunburst?"

Gary shook his head. "That's been bothering me too. I can identify Cholla Canyon and Split Rock Canyon, and the canyon where The Needle is, as well as the canyon where we found the arrastres, but I can't link any canyon in the mountains with that one he has marked."

"Great stuff," said Tuck in disgust. "Then just what good is this *derrotero*?"

"All I know is that he didn't make it to amuse himself. If he marked that canyon on the *derrotero*, you can bet your Honda against a dime that *it was there* when he marked it. Jim Kermit's remark that there had been a great many changes in the mountains in the past hundred years sticks in my mind. The day I was working for him, I saw up Cholla Canyon to the place where there must have been a landslide years ago. I went the other way and found nothing. I think the place to go is past that landslide."

"Behind The Needle?"

"Yes. A *long* ways behind The Needle..."

Tuck glanced at the clock. "It's getting late. If we're going to do a predawn patrol we'd better get some sleep."

They got their gear ready before they went to bed. Pete Cole's shotgun had been returned, and Tuck was to carry it; Gary had his Winchester. "You got any silver bullets, *amigo*?" asked Tuck.

"No, why?"

"Well, I heard lead bullets ain't much good against ghosts, but they might work if you rub them with garlic."

"I oughta rub your pointed little head with garlic!"

"Where do you figure on hiding the *derrotero*?" Gary grinned. "Atop the windmill platform," he said. "No one would think of looking for it there."

"No one but an eagle, that is."

IT WAS PITCH DARK OUTSIDE. Gary crossed swiftly to the windmill and quietly scaled the ladder. He secreted the *derrotero* beneath a loose board. He did not return to the ground immediately. He felt as though he was atop the mast of a sailing ship far out on the dark sea. The Espectros were dark and hulking against the night sky; the lights of The Wells could be seen in the clear air. There was a breathless feeling within Gary. Tomorrow might reveal the long-lost secret of the treasure of the Espectros.

A COLD DAWN wind swept along the lower reaches of Cholla Canyon as Gary led the way through the tangled brush to where he had found the first symbol. It was still very dark in the big canyon, and even Lobo was subdued, trailing closely at Gary's heels, with Tuck not far behind. Several times during the night, the big dog had barked, awakening the boys, but nothing had happened. They had not shown a light at the house when they had arisen, breakfasted, and left the premises in the thick darkness of the hour before dawn.

It was hard going until the first faint light of the false dawn began to show in the sky. By that time, the boys had reached the place where the branch canyon split off to the right hand. Gary looked up the dark slopes toward the unseen cave. It was as quiet as the grave. He shuddered at the simile.

Gary swiftly crossed the mouth of the branch canyon and began to fight his way through the vicious tangle that almost filled the narrow upper end of Cholla Canyon. It was quite obvious that there had been a vast slide of earth and rocks in years past. It was also obvious that the rushing waters of many flash floods had gouged the narrow passage to one side of the slide.

The dawn light was filtering down into the canyon. High above them were masses of dry brush wedged into crevices; here and there, bleached pieces of driftwood hung like bones of the long dead. They were the markers indicating the height of the floods that poured through that canyon. It wasn't a pleasant sight. The Espectros seemed to breed vicious storms in the late summer and early fall, and to be caught in a canyon at such a time was akin to a death sentence.

Beyond the slide, it was possible to see no more than a few hundred yards at a time because of the devious and tortured way of the deep canyon. Despite the coolness of the early morning, the boys were running with sweat as they forced their way through clinging catclaw and savage jumping cholla that seemed to snap at them in anger. They rounded a right-hand bend. Gary stopped and eyed a huge overhanging cliff shaped like the cup of a gigantic clamshell. "The *derrotero* shows water in here, Tuck," he said over his shoulder.

Tuck wiped the sweat from his face. "What's that up there?" He pointed to the cliff face. Clearly marked was a Spanish gourd, the unmistakable symbol for water in the vicinity.

It was Lobo who found the spring. It welled up from beneath a rock face to form a shallow pool in a *hueco* or rock hollow. The three of them drank the cold, sweet water. Tuck wiped his mouth and reached for his haversack. "Time for lunch?"

"It's hardly nine o'clock," said Gary. "I'll go ahead and see what's up there."

"Watch yourself, *amigo*."

"*I* wasn't thinking of getting careless."

GARY WAS a good five hundred yards east of the spring when he found the narrow slit that marked a branch canyon trending off to the right, deep in shadow, cold, and forbidding. He turned to look up the main canyon and saw a chiseled outline on a great slab of fallen rock. It was the outline of a tortoise. There was no way of telling to which of the two canyons it had originally pointed.

Tuck floundered through the brush and eyed the rock. "Got a little lonely back there," he said. "What's that?"

"The tortoise symbol has various meanings. Sometimes the head points toward treasure or buried possessions nearby.

"Go on."

Gary looked at his friend. "It can also mean death, defeat, or destruction..."

"But that was years ago, wasn't it?" asked Tuck in a very small voice.

"It has to be one way or the other." Gary took a coin from his pocket and flipped it high into the air. "Heads to the left. Tails to the right." He caught it deftly. "Tails," he said quietly.

Tuck eyed the narrow, uninviting passageway. "Best out of three?" he suggested weakly.

Gary shook his head. There was really no choice. If they went up the main canyon and could not find any further symbols, they would have to explore the narrower canyon anyway. He led the way. Their footsteps echoed hollowly as though they had entered a vast and empty vault carved into the very heart of the Espectros.

Neither of them spoke. Silence seemed to be the ground rule in that dark and echoing place. Silence, and a constant feeling of something watching and waiting for anyone fool enough to look for the Lost Espectro.

The heat of the midmorning sun had begun to penetrate into the canyons by the time the two explorers came to a widening of the canyon they were in. "Just where are we?" asked Tuck.

"We're heading southerly. I think we're roughly parallel to The Needle Canyon, but I haven't any idea how far we are from it."

"You think this canyon comes out on the south side of the Espectros?"

"If it doesn't, we'll either have to backtrack or stay in here tonight."

So far, they had seen no guiding symbols. That is, until Tuck fell over a rock. Gary gave him a hand to help him to his feet, and as he did so, he saw something through a screen of brush. It was another gourd symbol pointing back to the way they had come. That wasn't much help, but at least it indicated that the Mexican miners had been in there.

Tuck picked a cactus needle from his hand and looked ahead. He silently pointed at something. On an overhanging rock had been chiseled a deep Roman cross. "That's another marking with a number of meanings," said Gary. "It might mean there are church treasures buried in here, which isn't likely. It also means a Christian has passed this way. If it was lying on its side instead of being upright, then the long part of the cross would point to the treasure trail."

"As far as we're concerned then, that marking doesn't mean much."

Gary looked up at the high rims of the canyon. "It was cut in here for a reason, maybe as protection against something evil."

————

THEY MOVED ON SLOWLY, scanning the canyon walls for more markings. An hour passed before they found another symbol, and again, it was the gourd marking, still pointing in the direction from which they had come.

A sluggish wind stirred in the canyon, but it brought little relief from the gathering heat of the day. The canyon began to angle to the right with a rather sharp turn visible in the distance. The canyon floor became a mass of tumbled and riven rock intermingled and laced together by thorny brash and scrubby trees. Here and there, shattered tree trunks showed in the jumble.

"I sure could use a drink," said Tuck as he wiped his face.

Lobo moved ahead of them to vanish in the tangle. In a few minutes, he returned, and his black muzzle was wet with water. Gary forced his way through a last screen of brash and stopped in astonishment. Before him was a wide, shallow pool that had formed in the lowest part of the canyon floor. Scum floated on the surface of the water at his feet, but it seemed clearer at the base of the eastern wall of the canyon. He walked to the wall and tasted the clear water. It was fresh and sweet, and it seemed to well from the naked rock itself.

Tuck dropped on his belly and drank deeply. "Sure needed that," he said. "Let's eat." He eyed Gary. "What's the matter?"

Gary looked up and down the heat-soaked canyon. "Strange," he said quietly. "The gourd symbols point the other way."

"So?"

"If there was water here, why would they show signs to the spring so far behind us? Besides, from what I remember from the *derrotero,* there wasn't any symbol on that either indicating the presence of a spring in *here*."

Tuck was gnawing at a sandwich. He eyed the pool. "Seems to come from under that wall," he said.

Gary looked up. There was no symbol for a spring marked on that sheer face of rock.

THEY ATE and then filled their canteens. As much as Gary wanted to continue the search, he knew it was only a matter of a few hours before the canyon would be dark in shadows. A quarter of a mile beyond the water hole, they found another symbol carved into a pinnacle of rock that jutted out from the right-hand wall of the canyon. It was a neatly depicted outline of a bowie knife, pointing back in the direction from which they had come. "Trail to mine or treasure; travel on," translated Gary.

"Maybe it means travel on to the next gourd symbol," suggested Tuck.

"No. The meaning is clear enough."

Gary pushed on ahead and was rewarded fifteen minutes later by finding the next symbol, a mule shoe lying horizontally. "En route to treasure; keep traveling," said Gary. He turned and looked down the shadowed canyon. "It must be *behind* us," he said. "The symbols for water pointed the other way, away from the spring we found. Now, the symbols here do not indicate that there is water just ahead, but rather to treasure. Also behind us..."

Tuck shoved back his hat. "And the symbols in Cholla Canyon indicated that we come *this* way. I agree. The treasure, if there is any, has to be behind us, and between the last water symbol and that bowie knife symbol back there. Maybe the cross symbol indicated that the treasure was *there*."

Gary shook his head. "I don't think so."

"Maybe we ought to try the *horqueta*?" Tuck rummaged in his bulging haversack and came up with a Y-shaped bone, the bleached scapula of some long-dead animal. He inverted the bone so that the leg of the Y was upward and tapped a glass knob that had been set into the tip of the bone. There was a threaded hole drilled in the glass knob. Tuck fumbled in the haversack again. "You think the Lost Espectro was a gold or silver miner?"

"Gold," said Gary.

Tuck selected a screw from the number he had taken from the haversack. He screwed it into the hole in the glass knob. "Let's go," he said cheerfully. He gripped the two lower prongs of bone in his hands, thumbs out and palms upward.

"*What* is *that*?"

Tuck grinned. "Emilio Chavez traded me this for a double-barreled shotgun. You hold it like I'm holding it, then wait to feel the 'pull' of the minerals. That screw happens to have a speck of gold dust in it. Now if it were silver we were looking for, or copper, or whatever, we'd put in the screw with *that* mineral, you see. The screws are hollow and filled with a bit of the mineral you are hunting. Like attracts like, *amigo*. Emilio said it was infallible. Always works. Now..." His voice died away as he saw the look on Gary's face.

"If everything Emilio cons you into taking is infallible, how come Emilio Chavez is the poorest man in The Wells?"

"Well, now that you mention it," said Tuck thoughtfully.

"Tuckie," said Gary in his kindliest tone, "put one of those screws in the hollow place in your head. It's the sun, I think, or maybe your mother dropped you on your soft little head when you were a baby."

While they stood there, the sun suddenly vanished, and thicker shadows filled the canyon. A cool wind began to feel its way through the darkness.

"We'll keep moving on," said Gary. "We can make better time when the moon comes up. O.K.? Or would you rather camp in here tonight?"

Tuck smiled wanly as he stored his precious *horqueta* away.

THE DARKNESS GREW AND THICKENED. The boys did not speak to each other. There was something in the atmosphere of that forbidding place that banned conversation. Now and then, they stopped their slow progress to listen. They saw the velvety winged flight of the night-hunting owl and heard the pitiful squeaking of a mouse caught in the steely talons of that same owl. They heard the swift and almost noiseless passages of nocturnal animals through the brush. The dry wind crept through the canyon, moaning softly through crevices.

It seemed like an eternity before the first faint suggestion of moonrise appeared in the sky. Then, gradually, almost imperceptibly, they could distinguish objects and see the path beneath their tired and aching feet. The lighter it grew, the faster they traveled, and in so doing, they became careless about noise. If someone or *something* was listening to their passage...

They reached a place where the canyon widened. Lobo stopped trotting at Gary's heels. A low growl sounded deep in his throat. He laid back his stub ears, and his hackles arose. Gary moved toward the canyon wall and knelt beside the big dog. "Quiet, Lobo," he whispered. "Quiet now!"

The three of them watched and waited. The canyon floor was silvered with cold moonlight, etching sharply each shadow. Nothing moved except the wind. Minutes ticked past, and then Gary felt the hard muscles of the dog tighten against his arm. Tuck wet his lips. He pointed out toward the center of the canyon. The shadows were still motionless, and then one of them seemed to move. But there was nothing there to give body to that shadow. It seemed to move steadily and independently, drifting across rocks and brush. The shadow stopped, then moved on again. Gary saw now that it was the shadow of a hatless man. *But there was no man to form that shadow!*

Tuck touched Gary on the shoulder and jerked a

thumb upward. Gary understood now. Whoever it was, standing on the rim of the canyon, high overhead, the moonlight came from behind him, throwing his bodiless shadow onto the canyon floor. The shadow moved. It bent its head as though to listen. Something pattered dryly on the ground just to the right of the boys. It must be something living up there rather than a ghost to be able to push gravel over the edge of the rim.

Cold fear raced through Gary. His legs and stomach seemed to get weak. He swallowed hard, almost afraid to breathe for fear of making a sound. The gravel pattered closer. Tuck's breathing became louder and more irregular. Gary felt as though he were held in subjection to the thing up there. It was quite enough fear for him that night. There was a limit.

Gary jumped to his feet and grabbed his rifle. He ran swiftly out into the center of the canyon. He turned and clearly saw a hatless man standing at the edge of the rim looking down at him, but Gary could not see the shadowed face. "Who are you? What do you want?" he demanded angrily.

The man raised a rifle. Gary threw up his own gun and fired high over the unknown's head. He slammed out three more rapid-fire rounds. The man jumped out of sight. The crashing echoes bounded and rebounded between the canyon walls in roaring confusion.

"You loco?" screamed Tuck.

Gary waved Tuck on. Lobo sped toward Gary, barking deeply. Gary wasted no time. Tired as he was, his feet fairly seemed to fly over the rough ground. This time, Tuck did not pass him. They were half a mile down the canyon when Gary threw himself on the ground to regain his breath. Tuck staggered up and fell down beside him. There was now no sign of life up the moonlit canyon.

When they had their breath back, they trudged on to the south. Far ahead of them, they could see where the canyon floor slanted down toward the distant desert, silvered by the moonlight.

The haunting cry arose behind them like the dire wailing of a doomed soul, echoing eerily down the canyon until, at last, it died away. This time, the boys did not stop for breath nor look back until they reached the hidden mouth of the canyon.

CHAPTER TEN

Clues from the Sky

The moon had died, leaving behind it an intense darkness that cloaked the mountains with only the wolf-fanged peaks showing against the dark blue blanket of the sky. Two tired boys trudged toward the Cole ranch house. Gary turned to look at Tuck. "We still have two days," he said, "in which to hunt." He eyed his lean companion. Tuck had hardly spoken since they had emerged from the mouth of the canyon into the desert. Maybe Tucker C. Browne had his belly-full of treasure hunting.

Tuck yawned. He trudged on, shifting his shotgun from one shoulder to the other.

"Tuck?" said Gary uneasily. He himself wanted to keep on searching, but he'd hardly want to do it without Tuck.

Tuck yawned again. "Well, kid, it's like this," he said quietly. He paused.

"Go on, Tuck! Say it! You want to quit!"

Tuck turned slowly. "What's with you?" he said in astonishment. "I was about to say we've got as good a lead as we could wish. It's a lead pipe cinch that the treasure *has* to be back there beyond that water hole. I figure we can go right back into the canyon we just left. One of us can stand guard while the other hunts for more symbols."

"What about that man, or *thing*, we saw back there?"

Tuck spat indelicately. "Well, if it was a ghost, he won't be around during daylight hours. If it was a man, he knows we mean business. Man, you scared the Hades out of me when you opened up on him." Tuck grinned. "If that wasn't a ghost, I'll just bet whoever it was was a mite worried himself with all that lead whistling over his head. Hawww!"

Gary couldn't help but grin himself. Then he looked down at Lobo. The dog had hunched his shoulders and was standing still, looking intently toward the darkened house. "Wait," said Gary quickly to Tuck.

They stood there in the windy darkness. The windmill creaked softly. There was no other sound. "Go on, Lobo," said Gary. He loaded his rifle. The dog trotted ahead and squirmed beneath a wire fence. The two boys climbed over it and eyed the house. The dog padded on, circled the house, then came back. He looked up at Gary as though to let him know it was all right to go to the house.

Gary opened the back door and walked in. Until he lighted the room, there was a tautness of fear within him. He stared at the once immaculate kitchen. It was a shambles. Drawers hung open, tea towels were scattered on the floor, cabinet doors gaped, and even the oven door hung open. Tuck whistled softly. "Mice?" he suggested.

Lobo padded into the living room, followed by the boys. The room was a mess. Chair cushions had been removed, table drawers opened, books tumbled from the shelves, the rug peeled back, and the couch overturned, with the padding slit open by a knife.

It was Gary's room that had suffered the most damage. The mattress had been torn to pieces. The lining had been pulled loose from the closet. His books were scattered all over. The pockets of his clothing had been pulled out. Gary felt sick. He looked at Tuck. "Oh, Lord," he said, "you were supposed to be watching the place until I got back."

"Yeh," said Tuck with a weak grin. He looked about. "I don't think we have any doubt about what they were looking for in here."

Gary shook his head. "The windmill," he said quickly. "I wonder?"

"Don't go near it now!" warned Tuck.

"There'd be no one watching nearby," said Gary. "Lobo would let us know."

Tuck shrugged. "Shall we risk it?"

Gary walked to the front door. He flicked off the lights and peered through the glass window set in the door. It was as dark as the inside of a boot out there. A mysterious, clinging darkness that seemed to be a menace in itself. He eased open the door. "Take a look, Lobo," he said in a low voice.

The dog vanished in the darkness. In a few minutes, he was back, and he dropped to his belly on the porch. Gary walked to the windmill and looked up the ladder. It was possible that a person at a distance might be able to skyline him up there. It wasn't a pleasant thought, and a .50/110 slug could bore a big hole in a man. He climbed slowly and as quietly as possible, reached the top, felt beneath the loose board, and almost panicked. The *derrotero* was not there!

He clung to the ladder and peered out into the darkness, wondering who or what was out there. Perhaps the person who had removed the *derrotero* was still somewhere nearby. There was a green sickness within him. To find the *derrotero* after years of search and then to lose it again!

He eased his hand beneath the board and felt along it. Something rustled dryly and fell from the platform. He almost panicked again. Swiftly, he descended the ladder and dropped to hands and knees, pawing the damp ground. When at last his hands closed on the folded chart, he breathed a silent prayer, then hurried back to the house.

He did not feel at ease until the door had been locked and barred behind him. He wordlessly handed the *derrotero* to Tuck, who took it as though it were red hot. He juggled it a little. "What do *I* do with it?" he asked.

Gary leaned against the wall. "We'd better take it with us tomorrow. Right now, I'm going to get some sleep. I want to be out of here before dawn, as we were this morning."

Tuck nodded. "I'll take the first watch," he said. "Tired as I am, I can't sleep right now."

Gary walked into his room and lifted the ripped mattress onto his bed. It was no time to be choosy. He pulled off his hat and boots and dropped onto the mattress. It seemed as though he were asleep the instant he hit it.

————

WHEN HE OPENED his eyes again, it was still dark. He had no idea as to what time it was. The house was deathly quiet. He sat up and dropped his legs over the side of the bed. Something seemed to warn him as he sat there; he reached for his rifle and then stood up. He stood there for a few minutes, listening with a cocked head for a sound.

Gary walked softly to the bedroom door and through the dark hallway to the living room. Gentle and steady breathing sounded from the couch. Gary tiptoed across the littered room and looked down at Tuck, sound asleep, faithful as ever to his trust. He couldn't help but grin. He was a little startled when the pendulum clock struck one. It seemed much later than that. He reached out to arouse Tuck, and his hand stopped midway. A grating noise came from the back of the house.

Gary turned quickly. Lobo was either sound asleep or had wandered off, as he often did at odd hours. The kitchen door squeaked as it was opened, and Gary remembered then that he had not locked it. He reached down and clamped a hand on Tuck's mouth. He looked down into Tuck's wide eyes and shook his head, then released his grasp. Tuck stood up and reached for his shotgun, but Gary again shook his head. The scattergun was too dangerous in close quarters.

Something moved just beyond the doorway to the kitchen. Gary pointed down, tapped his chest, pointed up, and touched Tuck's chest. His sign language was clear. They'd take the intruder by force, Gary in low and Tuck on high.

Somebody loomed in the doorway, and Gary drove in hard, arms outspread to grip the legs while Tuck closed in. The stranger thrust out a balled fist, and Tuck smacked into it and grunted in pain as he fell sideways to land on top of Gary.

The intruder broke loose. Tuck came up and caught a boot heel against his chin. Down he went again.

Gary darted after the intruder as he ran for the back door and dived for him, catching him about the waist and driving him hard against the wall. Fingernails clawed Gary's face. "Let me go, you big ape!" screamed a thoroughly feminine voice.

"It's Sue!" yelled Tuck. "We might have known she'd be nosing around."

Gary could feel the blood running down his face. She had put up one whale of a defense. "Don't put on a light," he warned Tuck. He pulled the blinds on the windows and locked the door.

"Man," said Tuck. "I ran right into that fist of yours, Susie. Were you holding a flatiron in it?"

She laughed shakily. "I was so scared I didn't know what I was doing."

"I'd hate to see you in action when you *did* know what you were doing," said Gary ruefully.

"I didn't want to disturb anyone," she said. "Besides, I wasn't sure you were here. Lobo wasn't around."

"He usually isn't when we need him," said Tuck.

"Would you mind telling us how you happened to come here at this hour?" asked Gary.

"Well, I was going to stay with Francie Kermit this weekend," she said.

"Just by coincidence," said Tuck dryly. "I never thought you and Francie were buddy-buddy. The only reason you were going to stay there was to keep an eye on us."

"What difference does it make?" she said. "Don't answer that! Well, anyway, Mr. Kermit is gone for the weekend."

Gary looked quickly at Tuck. "I wonder?" he said, thinking of the shadowy figure that had been watching them.

"Wonder what?" asked Sue.

"Nothing," said Tuck. "Go on with your lying, Cousin Sue."

"Well, Mr. Kermit had left something for Gary at the house. I wanted to bring it right over, but Francie said it could wait until tomorrow, *today*, I mean. I couldn't sleep. So I sneaked out of the house and came over here."

"You could have got killed," said Tuck fiercely.

They could see her inspecting her nails. "Oh, I don't know," she said archly.

"Listen to her!" snapped Tuck.

"Forget it," said Gary. "What was it he left for me?"

She took out a roll of heavy paper from within her shirt and handed it to Gary. He got a bull's-eye lantern from a cabinet and lighted it, holding it close to the floor so that no glow would show through the blinds. It cast a bright circle of light on the floor. Gary unrolled the paper and saw that it was an aerial photograph an aerial photograph of mountains cut with deep twisting canyons. His breath caught in his throat. "The Espectros!" he said excitedly. He looked up at her. "Tell me about this!"

"He wasn't there when I got there. Francie said that he told her he found out that one copy of the aerial photograph made during the war was still in the files of *The Cottonwood Wells Courier,* so he picked it up for you."

Gary eyed the photograph. "The negatives were destroyed in a fire at the airfield, and Jim told me he didn't know who had any prints of them."

"That was darned nice of him," said Tuck.

"I wonder?" said Gary quietly.

"What do you mean?" asked Tuck.

Gary stood up and turned off the lantern. "Maybe Jim Kermit has been looking for the Lost Espectro all these years without any luck. Perhaps Jim figured that we might find it with the help of this photograph coupled with what we already know. He'd let us go poking into those canyons, trailing us maybe, until we did find the mine, then close in for the kill."

"How you talk!" said Sue. "After he was nice enough to get that photograph for you!" Her voice changed. "Is he a prime suspect, Gary?"

"Forget that TV talk," said Tuck. He paced back and forth. "He's not at home this weekend. Who knows where he really is? Might be outside right now. Maybe he was at your grandfather's house in The Wells when we found the *derrotero* there..." His voice trailed off. His eyes widened. He clamped a hand over his mouth.

Sue seemed to expand a little in the darkness. "So," she said slowly, "you *did* find the *derrotero?*"

"You and your big flapping mouth!" moaned Gary to Tuck. "Well, she knows now!" He picked up the photograph and the lantern and took them to the little windowless room next to his, where he kept his relics and other odds and ends. He put the photograph on the table, then placed the faded and wrinkled *derrotero* beside it. He did not look up as the other two quietly entered the room behind him.

Gary traced a finger up Cholla Canyon on the photograph and located the water hole, hardly more than a dot on the narrow floor of the long canyon. To the east of the canyon and slightly north, the terrain seemed a lighter hue, hardly distinguishable from the rest of the land, but still obviously lighter. He studied the *derrotero*. The sunburst with the question mark in it was marked to the east of the water hole canyon in yet another canyon, nothing more than a narrow slot in the rough terrain, but plainly marked on the *derrotero*. *There was no such canyon apparent on the photograph.*

Tuck traced the line of another twisting, narrow canyon. "That's where we found the arrastres," he said. He moved his finger to the right and placed it on the area where the canyon showed on the *derrotero* but not on the photograph. "It figures," he added. "There was a canyon there in the old days, in the time of your great-grandfather, Gary, that could be reached both from Cholla Canyon and the canyon of the arrastres. It isn't there now, that's for sure."

"Buried forever in a landslide," said Gary gloomily. He reached for a magnifying glass he used on his rock specimens and began to study the photograph inch by inch. The lighter area held his attention. There wasn't any doubt in his mind that the lighter area indicated the massive slide. He noted, too, that on the *derrotero,* water was indicated as flowing down the canyon of the arrastres, but no water showed on the photograph.

He looked for the time of the year when the photograph had been made. It had been taken in the wintertime, and there surely should have been drainage water in the canyon at that time. Yet no water showed there. But water did show in the photograph of the narrow canyon they had explored and *did not show on the derrotero*. Surely, his great-grandfather would have marked such an important thing as a water hole in that dry land.

Then, too, the very carved symbols in the canyon did not indicate water there, but rather farther on, at the spring they had found in the upper reaches of Cholla Canyon. So there had been no water in there during the time of the Mexican miners either. "No wonder the Lost Espectro has never been found," he said. "The land changes have been too great." He quickly related his thoughts to his two friends.

Tuck placed a finger on the water hole they had found. "The key is right here somewhere," he said. "You think it's possible that the landslide may have diverted the original water source in the canyon of the arrastres back into the canyon where we found the water hole?"

"I'm almost sure of it," said Gary. He passed a hand over the lighter area of the terrain. "I wonder how many thousands and thousands of tons of rock may be atop the Lost Espectro?"

"It won't hurt to look," said Sue courageously.

"Who said anything about *you* going?" demanded Tuck.

Again, the fingernails were inspected. "When I tell the story about how two rough, tough juniors from Cottonwood Wells Union High School tangled with a little slip of a girl and darned near got whipped this summer, I wonder how your standing will be?"

"You wouldn't!" said Tuck.

"Just you try me, Mister Tucker C. Browne!"

"She would too," said Tuck to Gary.

A cold anger grew within Gary. "All right," he said harshly. "I'm sick of her poking her nose into everything we do. If she wants to risk it, I don't care! We're going back into that canyon today."

"When?" asked Tuck.

"I'm not sleepy. How can you sleep at a time like this?"

"Who said anything about sleeping? I was hoping you'd want to go right now."

Gary rolled the *derrotero* and the photograph together and wrapped them in plastic sheeting. "I don't want to stay around here any longer than I have to."

Sue grinned, and the lantern light glistened on her braces.

"No wonder, the way you characters have been keeping house. What a mess!"

Tuck raised his eyes toward the ceiling. "Lord," he breathed, "make me strong. We didn't mess up the house, Sue! It was that way when we got back. Somebody must have been searching for the *derrotero.*"

"Oh," she said in a small, weak voice.

"Now do you want to stay behind?" asked Tuck.

"No," she said firmly.

"Well," he said in resignation, "I have only one deep consolation. Being a female, you'll probably get married someday to some unfortunate male, which means you have to change your name from Browne to whatever *his* name is, which makes me, as your beloved first cousin, happy indeed!"

"Enough of that," said Gary. "This is no class picnic we're going on. It might be dangerous in there. It's bad enough that Tuck and I are taking this chance, Sue, without involving you too. You've been a big help, and we appreciate it, but you're going to have to take orders from us. Is that clear?"

"I like taking orders from you, Gary," she said.

Tuck grunted and rolled his eyes up. "We have to have *one* leader. I nominate Gary Cole. Any seconds?"

"I second the nomination," said Sue.

"Motion made and seconded. Any objections? None? Those in favor say aye. Aye!"

"Aye!" said Sue.

"Motion made and carried. All hail, Leader!"

"That means you have to take orders from me too," said Gary with a grin.

Tuck frowned. "I never thought of it that way."

"Let's get moving. We'll need our gear, digging tools, rope, food, guns, and one blanket apiece."

"Why?" asked Sue.

"We might have to stay in there overnight."

She smiled weakly. "Oh," she said.

"We'll take the jeep toward the highway, then cut east on the old gravel road," said Gary. "We can leave the jeep about a mile from the canyon mouth and walk in. It will still be dark. We can make the water hole about dawn. You still sure you want to come along, Sue?"

"Absolutely."

"On your head be it," said Tuck.

They wasted no time thereafter. While they were loading the jeep, Lobo, as though conjured up by magic, appeared in the dimness and jumped casually into the back seat. Gary started the jeep and drove out to the road, turned left, and headed for the highway. Before he reached the main highway, he shut off the headlights, then turned left onto the old gravel road.

They wouldn't be fooling anyone who might have watched them leave the house, but the desert was wide and dark, so the chance was worth taking that they might get away with it. Gary really didn't care as much as he thought he would. He was sure they were on the right trail this time. The next day or two would decide if the mine was buried forever, or if the Lost Espectro really could be found.

CHAPTER ELEVEN

Into the Heart of the Espectros

The water hole was a sheet of smooth pewter-colored liquid in the faint cold light of dawn.

Something splashed in the water, and then came the scurrying of small feet on the hard ground and a rustling in the brush as some small animal fled from the pool. The concentric ripples spread smoothly and began to lap softly on the shore. The faint musical sound died away, and the canyon was as quiet as before.

Tuck took up position as guard in the thick tangle where he could see both rims of the canyon. Gary placed Sue near the water hole and told Lobo to stay with her. Gary pushed on, scanning the wall of the eastern side. There was nothing to be seen.

Two hundred yards beyond the water hole, he came to a huge, tiptilted slab of rock, which forced him to step down into a deep hollow. He was about to pass on when he saw the carving beneath the slab. He crouched to see it clearly. It was the familiar equilateral triangle with the curved line sprouting from the tip, pointing onward, indicating the treasure trail was around a bend or curve.

Gary stepped up out of the hole. The huge slab had obviously been moved by great brute force from its original position to lie so. He walked up the canyon in the pale, watery light. Beyond him, there was no indication of a curve or bend to the right, as the symbol indicated, nor was there even a bend or curve to the left. The canyon here was as straight as a mine drift. It was then that he noticed the formation of the canyon wall.

It was made up of tumbled and shattered rock, bleached wood, and tangled brush. He compared it to the rock of the west wall, which was darker and smooth, almost as though it had been polished. It was quite evident then that the bend or curve indicated by the symbol no longer existed; it had been filled in by huge masses of fallen rock and earth.

He scanned the walls, both old and new, and saw no symbols. He turned and trudged back toward the water hole. He squatted at the edge of it and looked at the slightly disturbed surface of the water right where the rock wall met it. "Go get Tuck," he said to Sue. "You take guard. Don't do anything if you see anything suspicious. Let us know."

She hurried off. Tuck scrambled through the brush and squatted beside Gary. "Speak, O Leader," he said.

Gary told him of his deduction. Tuck nodded wisely. Gary dabbled a hand in the cool water. "You said it might have been possible for the land changes to have forced the water that used to run down the canyon of the arrastres into this canyon, Tuck," he said quietly. "Supposing we could trace the source of this water? Maybe it might lead us to the Lost Espectros."

"That's loco," said Tuck. He looked up at the towering canyon wall above them. "We can't get over that."

"Maybe we can go *under* it," said Gary. He stood up and peeled off his shirt. "I'm going for a swim."

Tuck watched him with wide eyes as he stripped to his shorts and waded into the pool. Gary walked to the wall and began to feel along it under the surface of the water. His hands probed into nothingness. He took several deep breaths, held the last one, and submerged, leaving a series of ripples that lapped at Tuck's feet. Tuck Browne closed his eyes and prayed for the first time in a long while.

Gary rose a little, and his head struck solid rock. He dived down again, felt his knees scrape the rough gravel bottom, and then came cautiously upward again. When his head broke the water, he found himself in a domed cavern illuminated from some dim source ahead of him. He swam slowly to the side of the cavern and crawled out onto a narrow ledge, shivering from mingled cold and fear. He realized now that his swim had been a very short one. He could hardly be more than twenty feet from where he had started. It had seemed such a long one, but all out of proportion as when one's tongue explores a tooth cavity and magnifies it tremendously.

Gary stood up and began to explore the ledge. There was shattered driftwood scattered along it. A cheerful thought, for the water had brought it into the cavern from outside. But how *far* outside? He walked forward slowly and saw that the ledge petered out. He took a staff of driftwood and probed the dark water; it was about two feet deep. He waded in and followed a bend in the cavern, testing the depth all the way.

Then suddenly, everything seemed clear to the eye, and he waded out into a narrow slot of a canyon, if one could correctly call it that, hardly more than twenty feet wide. High, high above him, was the sky, now lighted with the rising of the sun. To his right was a narrow strand, uttered with dead brush and driftwood. He waded to it and walked along it. He could see fairly far ahead. Gary shivered. The deep, narrow trough seemed to penetrate into the very bowels of the Espectros.

He returned to the cavern and eyed the dark and

uninviting surface of the water, dreading the thought of having to enter it again. Something scuttled over his bare feet, and he almost screamed in sudden panic. He saw that it was a gecko lizard scuttling toward the dark wall at the forward end of the cavern. Lizards were usually creatures of the sunlight. He walked to the place where he had seen the lizard vanish and got down on his hands and knees. He was relieved to see a faint line of light. He got down on his belly and squirmed beneath the rock. There was soft earth beneath him. He shoved some of it aside and crawled out into broad daylight to look up into the grinning face of Tucker C. Browne. "Dr. Livingstone, I presume."

Gary dressed quickly. Tuck got Sue. The two of them listened to Gary's story. "So," concluded Gary, "the only clue left to the lost mine, at least in my opinion, is the canyon beyond the cavern."

There was a long and deathly silence from the two Brownes.

"I'm going back in," said Gary quietly.

"I'll side you," said Tuck.

"Me too," said Sue.

"No," said Tuck.

"You can't leave me here," said Sue stubbornly.

She was right.

———

WHILE GARY WIDENED the entrance to the cavern, Tuck and Sue got the gear. Gary carried it into the cavern. The two Brownes came in, followed by Lobo. The dog trotted ahead along the narrow ledge. "Aladdin's Cave," said Sue. "Who's got the magic lantern?"

Lobo turned suddenly. He trotted back past the three of them and began to growl. Gary stared at him. Suddenly, there was darkness beneath the wall as rock and dirt fell heavily. Gary ran forward and got down on his knees. The hole had been blocked. He pushed against the rocks and could not move them. A cold feeling of dread came over him.

"Rockfall?" said Tuck from behind Gary.

"Maybe," said Gary. He stood up and looked at his two companions.

"We can always swim under the wall," said Sue.

"You might as well face the truth," said Gary. "If that wasn't a rock fall, someone blocked that hole, and that same someone could be waiting for us to pop up out of the water."

"Like who?" asked Tuck.

"Whom!" corrected Sue.

Gary shrugged. "Someone might have been watching us all the time," he said.

"Well, if we can't get out, he can't get in," said Sue.

"Yeh," said Tuck. He shivered.

Another cold thought came to Gary. They were unable to return through the hole, but that did not mean whoever had blocked the hole could not clear it and follow them if he so desired.

Gary took his gear and waded into the water. He led the way out into the tunnel-like canyon. There was no way to scale those sheer walls. He walked on, keeping his face turned away from the others so that they might not see the fear etched upon it.

They splashed steadily onward, sometimes wading, sometimes clambering over loose detritus that had fallen from high above. The echoes of their slow passage made strange and eerie sounds as though someone, or *something*, was laughing at them.

Now and again, they had to squeeze between the damp walls which had closed in together. If a flash flood should strike suddenly, as they often did, it would fill the narrow trough with roaring waters that would drown anything living caught in the canyon.

AFTER AN HOUR'S SLOW PROGRESS, they stopped to rest. Gary unwrapped the *derrotero* and the photograph to study them. He took out his compass and checked the direction in which they were traveling. It was almost due east. Yet the canyon they were in did not show on the *derrotero* or on the aerial photograph. The three of them discussed it quietly. "It's possible that the photograph might not have picked up this canyon. Sometimes, at certain angles, things can be hidden," said Tuck.

Gary took out his magnifying glass and studied the photograph of the general area in which they now were. Suddenly, he started. His lens had caught a very faint line, barely discernible, running along the mesa top in an easterly direction from the canyon of the water hole. He eyed it closely, but he could not distinguish any features. "This might be the canyon we are in," he said, tracing the line with his finger. "Maybe you're right, Tuck. The light or angle or something might not have caught the canyon quite right."

"But it's not marked on the *derrotero*," said Sue.

"Which means it either did not exist at the time the *derrotero* was made or my great-grandfather left it out because it had no bearing on the treasure trail," said Gary. He tapped the sunburst marking with the question mark inside of the circle. "But from what I can figure, this *has* to be ahead of us. With luck, this canyon might just run into the canyon where the sunburst has been marked on the *derrotero*."

"And if it doesn't?" asked Sue.

Gary did not answer. He rolled photograph and *derrotero* together and replaced them in the plastic wrapping.

"Maybe this canyon doesn't lead anywhere," said Sue. "Maybe it is a dead end. What do we do then, partners?"

"Go back," said Gary shortly.

Her eyes were wide, and her face was taut. "But what if... Say he is..."

Gary walked on, followed by Tuck. Both of them were just as concerned as Sue was, but the lure of the Lost Espectro took precedence over their concern and fright.

THE MORNING WAS at mid-passage when they reached a place where the canyon widened. The right-hand side of the canyon was still that sheer wall, so steep and high it seemed to be leaning over the canyon, but the left-hand side was now lower and composed of shattered rock and great boulders stippled with long-dead trees and brush, a treacherous-looking and impassable mass. Here, the canyon trended to the left and narrowed again, and on the left-hand side appeared a dark opening from which the stream emerged, much as it had back in the canyon of the water hole.

Tuck eyed the dark orifice and shivered a little. "We have to go in there now?" he said.

Gary grounded his rifle and looked farther up the narrowing canyon. "Not until we see what is up there. This is evidently the place where the stream broke through when it was blocked from the canyon of the arrastres. *Adelante*!" He led the way to the east.

The sun was at its zenith when they reached a place where their narrow passageway joined yet another canyon, and despite the light of the sun, this was a gloomy place, for the walls leaned inward, forming a rough bottle shape, with the mouth of the great bottle high overhead. There was a strange brooding quality about this place that repelled Gary. Lobo growled low in his throat and pressed his muscular body hard against Gary's leg.

"I'd almost rather go into that water cave back there," said Tuck. "This place is downright creepy."

Once again, Gary checked the *derrotero* and aerial photograph against each other. This time, he was quite sure that the sunburst with the question mark inscribed inside of it must be quite close, but there was no indication on the aerial photograph that such a canyon as the one that loomed before them existed at all.

If the sunburst *was* in that canyon, it was an indication that his great-grandfather had, in all likelihood, penetrated in there, but the question mark within the circle of the sunburst clearly indicated that either he had not believed that the symbol was true, or that he had not been able to find further clues to the lost mine. *"I know one thing, kid,"* Jerry Black had said cryptically. *"If you ever find that old derrotero your great-grandfather made, you just might get a lead on the Lost Espectro."*

Gary rolled the *derrotero* within the photograph and replaced them in his pack. He started down the slope to the floor of the gloomy canyon. Lobo stood still, then turned slowly and looked back along the way they had just traveled. He growled low and flattened his ears. The three explorers looked back. There was nothing to be seen. Lobo growled again.

Gary motioned to his two friends to take cover. He sank down behind a boulder and peered down the quiet canyon.

"What do you think it is?" hissed Tuck.

Gary wet his lips and felt for the field glasses. He focused them on the canyon and slowly swept every foot of it with the glasses. Nothing was to be seen, at least nothing that would threaten them.

"If that wasn't a rockfall that blocked us from getting back through that hole, and someone did block it, then mightn't they have waited until we left the cavern, then removed the blockage and followed us?" said Sue quietly.

Gary shrugged. He looked at Tuck. "You stay here with Sue and watch," he said. He handed Tuck his rifle and took the shotgun. "Don't do any wild shooting!"

Gary trudged down the slope, followed by Lobo. The dog kept looking back. Gary forced his way through a tangle of brush and then walked alongside the dry watercourse of the canyon. To either side, below the overhanging walls, were slopes of talus formed from the loose hanging rock that seemed ready to drop if one were to raise his voice in that echoing place. Thick and thorny brush had laced itself through the jumble. A snake would have had a hard time finding a way through the entanglements.

He rounded a curve and was a good half mile beyond the place where he had left his friends when the canyon widened. Here, it was a mass of rock and brush through which the dry watercourse crept, almost turning completely back on itself at times. Sweat broke out on him as he forced his way through, grunting in pain as thorns pierced his clothing and flesh.

He was finally forced to stop. He sat down on a flat rock and reached for his canteen. It was then that he saw the faint symbol carved into the opposite wall. He was on his feet in an instant, forcing his way across the tangle despite his weariness. He stopped on the treacherous slope below the symbol and stared at it. It was not familiar to him, although he lashed his flagging memory until his head ached. He then saw that the upper left and center part of the place where the symbol had been cut had flaked off through weathering.

He half closed his eyes, and then the realization came to him. The left-hand part of the symbol, as he faced it, should have been a reversed numeral 3, although in the case of this particular symbol, they were not numerals but rather brackets on each side of a word, which was now incomplete. The complete symbol meant to stop and change direction.

Gary plunged down the slope, heedless of the thorny brush. He followed the rough bed of the old watercourse back along the canyon, studying each foot of the walls as he went along. He was almost back at the canyon junction before he knew it, and he had seen no further symbols.

Sue came down to him. "We haven't seen anything," she said.

"Forget about that!" said Gary. "Get Tuck!"

"Here," said the lean one as he came toward them. He eyed Gary. "You look excited, *amigo*. You see Asesino?"

Gary told them of his find. "We'll have to work to the other end of this canyon for more clues."

"What about *him*?" asked Tuck, jerking a thumb over his shoulder toward the canyon through which they had just traveled.

Gary whistled sharply for Lobo. He pointed to the narrow canyon. "Go, boy," he said. The dog trotted up the slope and vanished in the brush.

"No one will get past him," added Gary. "At least he'll let us know if anyone is around."

Gary led the way. They had walked a quarter of a mile when they turned a bend to find themselves looking at a thoroughly blocked canyon filled with masses of rock and earth. There was no way under, around, through, or over that blockage.

"Crazy," said Tuck. "From what I figure, the canyon of the arrastres must be somewhere beyond that blockage. No wonder we couldn't find a way from there into here."

Sue was poking about with a stick. "Hey," she said. She picked up a rusted mule shoe, one of the type with the flared ends. "I wish this thing could talk."

"We'll have to work back," said Gary.

Slowly and carefully, they scanned the walls until they reached the place where the narrow canyon joined the one they were in. Lobo dozed on a rock. "Well," said Gary, "that shows he didn't find anyone."

"Or whoever was in there went back," said Tuck.

They all looked at each other. The threat from the unknown was being far overshadowed by the thoughts that the mine must be somewhere close to them. "*Adelante!*" said Gary.

———

MORE THAN AN HOUR PASSED. It was Tuck who made the next discovery, a rather curious symbol on a flat rock, almost completely covered by brush and a litter of gravel. The symbol was a stylized snake with the head pointing across to the western side of the canyon. There wasn't any doubt that the rock upon which it had been carved had been in that particular position a long time. They crossed the dry watercourse, for the symbol was plain enough. "Treasure on opposite side," it seemed to hiss.

The western side was a terrible jumble of rock with labyrinthine passages, some of them thoroughly choked with brush, weaving through the mass. The three of them examined every open rock face, then began to poke through the brush to examine others. Time drifted past, and there were no new discoveries. Nothing but naked rock and cruel brush.

Tuck climbed a sloping rock ledge, then jumped down on the far side. There was a crashing sound and the hoarse voice of Tuck mouthing imprecations.

Gary grinned. He walked up the slope and looked down. All he could see was Tuck's head. The rest of his body was concealed by the ever-present brush.

"Anything down there?" asked Gary.

Tuck was still muttering. "Nothing but black dirt," he growled.

"Black dirt? In there?"

Tuck held up his hands. They were mottled black. "Well, anyway, it's charcoal or something," he said.

Gary dropped on his belly. "Kick around a bit," he said.

Tuck's head vanished. In a few minutes, it appeared like the head of a busy gopher. "Charcoal, all right," he said. "Seems like someone had a big fire in here."

"Gary!" called Sue from the other side of the ledge. "There's another hole here, and the bottom is black too. Charcoal, I think."

"Eureka!" said Gary. His eyes widened.

"You loco or something?" asked Tuck.

"Charcoal, you dope! Charcoal pits were used by the old Spanish and Mexican miners to heat their drills so they could temper them! Man, we're close! We're *so* close!"

"There's another charcoal pit over here," said Sue. She paused. "Something else, too! Another one of those snakes! Pointing right up this slope, Gary!" She popped out of the hole and pointed up the almost impassable slope toward the masses of rock clogging the western side of the canyon.

"We're almost right on top of it," said Gary in a hushed voice. "Up the slope! *Adelante!*"

They wasted no time, tired as they were, for the fever was now upon them, the treasure-hunting fever that begins slowly and then steadily and ever increasingly takes over the mind and the body until it reaches the raging heat that sometimes consumes those who harbor the insidious disease.

"There's one of those crazy mule shoes," said Sue, pointing to a symbol carved on a squat boulder.

Gary looked at it. It did look like a mule shoe except for the three dots within the shoe. "It's not a mule shoe," he said slowly and quietly. That symbol means a flight of steps, indicating that the treasure is down in a shaft or a cave."

"But *where?*" said Sue. She looked at the wild and

forbidding area about them and then dropped her hands helplessly by her sides.

"Fifty *varas* away," said Gary in a faraway voice. He walked to the upper end of the squat boulder and pointed to an odd-looking symbol carved there.

"*Varas*?" questioned Sue.

"A *vara* is thirty-three and one-third inches," said Gary.

"Which way?" asked Sue.

"Will that help?" asked Tuck. He pointed beyond the boulder to yet another symbol, a horizontal cross. The long part of the upright pointed directly up the slope.

"About forty-six paces," said Sue, "figuring on a three-foot pace, or thereabouts. There should be something else in that area to show us the rest of the way."

"How confident she is," said Tuck.

Gary began his pacing, but it was almost impossible to keep to a standard pace because of the terrain. When he reached the end of his pacing, he stood in an area where openings of all sizes and shapes, some of them in the ground, others against the side of the canyon, showed like the unseeing eyes of the blind. There must have been at least two dozen of them.

In and out of the holes they popped like busy ground squirrels, but found nothing to indicate that the holes were anything but works of nature. Gary looked along the slope. "There are other holes along there," he said wearily.

"Too far from the symbol," said Sue.

Gary nodded. He shoved back his hat. He leaned back against a flat slab of rock upon which Tuck Browne stood like a gaunt statue, eying the jumbled slope. The flat slab was almost against the canyon wall. Tuck moved his feet. Gary's mouth dropped open. He leaned forward and shoved Tuck's left foot over. "Say!" said the lean one. His jaw dropped too as he saw Gary pointing to a carved sign where Tuck had been standing. "Treasure in a tunnel, *directly beneath this sign*," said Gary.

An intense, brooding quiet seemed to shroud the canyon. Then, the faint, far-off muttering of thunder sounded over it.

somewhere Tuck had been reading. "Because of a rattler, you must have come down." said Sue.

And, as he walked along, they seemed to swoosh
suddenly. Then the same far-off chattering of the fast sound reached after him.

CHAPTER TWELVE

The Lost Espectro

G ary got down on his knees and examined the thick slab of rock supposedly resting atop a tunnel that held the treasure that had been lost for so long. It would take powerful modern equipment to move the slab, yet it had either been placed there above the tunnel about a hundred years ago, or the tunnel had been dug *beneath* it.

Gary reached for his pack and took out his light, folding entrenching tool. He pulled loose rock aside and then began to probe into the hardened earth beneath the slab.

"Chow time," said Sue laconically. She placed the food on the slab.

Gary nodded absent-mindedly. Tuck came up the slope and dumped a load of driftwood near the slab. "I picked out the strongest of the stuff for shoring, Gary," he said. He shook his head. "I still don't like the idea of digging down under that slab."

"How else do you expect to get into the tunnel?" snapped Gary. His nerves were getting edgy.

"We could go back outside and get help," said Tuck.

Gary stubbornly shook his head. "We've got to find

out what is under here first, Tuck, before we go and make fools out of ourselves."

"He's right, Tuck," said Sue.

They ate quickly and with little talk. Now and then, they could hear the far-off rumbling of thunder high over the darkening Espectros. The canyon was a gloomy, forbidding place at any time, but now, with the darkening sky, it was positively frightening. A cold wind swept through it now and then, thrashing through the brush and moaning around the bends.

Gary finished his meal and set to work again, driving a shallow hole beneath the edge of the slab. Tuck and Sue looked at each other over Gary's head. Now that they had reached their goal, they were feeling somewhat let down; both of them had expected to walk into a neatly shored drift and find piles of gold ingots covered with dust, ready for the taking. Now, they did not know how long it would take to find out just how true those symbols atop the rock slab might be.

The noise of the thunder, and the wind, and the utter loneliness and isolation of the place had begun to prey on their nerves. Yet neither of them had the courage to tell Gary what they thought. Gary was stubborn, and he was determined to get beneath that slab. Meanwhile, the sands of time were running steadily and a little too swiftly to suit the Brownes. Darkness would trap them in the canyon if Gary did not agree to leave soon.

He was on his belly now, driving the tool deep beneath the slab. Despite the coolness of the air, he was dripping sweat, and his hands had begun to redden with forming blisters from the hard work.

Tuck shrugged at Sue. "Let me take over, Gary," he said.

"I'm doing all right," said Gary.

"Two of us taking turns can dig faster than one alone."

Gary looked up. He wiped the sweat from his dirty

face. "The quicker we find out, the quicker we can leave, eh?" he said a little sarcastically.

Tuck picked up the tool. "Take it easy," he said quietly. "No use getting gold fever."

"Sure," agreed Sue. "Like in the books where one man goes loco and kills off the others once they find the gold. You know, in that picture we saw one time. I..." Her voice trailed off as she saw the look on Gary's dirty face. "Heh, heh," she said. "Well, I better do the dishes, fellas, being as how I am *cocinera*. Heh..." She began to gather the food supplies and to repack them in Tuck's haversack.

"See if you can find a water hole," said Gary shortly. "Don't go too far!"

"I'll be all right," she said. "Besides, Lobo is down the slope. He won't let anyone bother me."

Tuck was digging steadily. He looked back at Gary. "You think this slab might cave in?"

"Most of it seems to be resting solidly."

"Yeh, well, I don't want it resting solidly on *me*."

Gary walked around the slab and examined the ground between it and the cliff face. He took the other entrenching tool and began to dig. Here, the earth seemed softer, and in no time at all, he was down several feet. He threw off his hat and shirt and began to dig steadily.

Tuck stood up and wiped the sweat from his face. "Well, that was a waste of time," he said. "Struck solid rock down there."

"Give me a hand!"

The two of them made the earth fly until they were waist-deep in the hole. Gary crawled out to get his canteen, for it was hot, dry work. He drank and then started toward the hole to give Tuck the canteen. He stopped as though he had run into a stone wall when the terrified scream came from the canyon below him.

He dropped the canteen and snatched up his rifle. He

ran down to the place where he had last seen Sue, for it was her voice that was awakening the echoes. Then she appeared, legging it up the slope as hard as she could go. Gary ran down to meet her with a ready rifle. She staggered a little. "Don't go down there!" she gasped. She reached Gary and gripped his arm. "I saw somebody down there!"

Gary crouched behind a rock ledge and motioned her to do the same. He eyed the lower canyon. There was no sign of life down there. "Did you see who it was?" he asked.

She swallowed hard. "All I really saw was a head. I had found water in a hole and was just bending down to see if it was good enough to use when I had the oddest feeling I was being watched. I looked up, and there he was about fifty yards from me, on the other side of the dry watercourse, staring right at me, Gary. I got scared, I tell you! I opened my mouth to yell, and nothing came out."

"That was a switch," said Gary dryly.

"Funnee, oh funnee! Well, I got my voice back, and when I screamed, he vanished. Poof! Just like that!"

Gary eyed the far side of the canyon. It was almost impossible to distinguish things because of the gloom. "You sure you didn't see who it was?" There was no answer from the girl. "Sue?" he added. He turned.

"It was his eyes," she said shakily. "Gary, I'll swear it must have been Asesino!"

His blood ran cold. Despite himself, he shivered a little. "Cut it out!" he said.

"No," she insisted. "He wasn't wearing a hat, Gary, just a band of cloth about his thick dark hair like you see in the pictures of the old-time Apaches."

"He's just a legend now," he said firmly.

"No one knows for sure if he is dead," Sue said quietly.

Lobo came quietly up the slope. Gary eyed the big

dog. It was strange that he had not made some commotion. "Lobo didn't seem to see or hear anything," he said.

"Can a dog *see* or *hear* a *ghost*," she said in a low voice.

"That's loco!" he said. "Let's get back to Tuck."

She walked up the slope ahead of him. Gary looked down at Lobo. "Didn't *you* see anything?" he asked.

Lobo looked back at his master. There was no trace of excitement about the dog. Gary shook his head and walked up the slope. Now and then, he looked back down toward the floor of the dark canyon. There was nothing to be seen, yet he, too, felt as though he were being watched.

"Tuck!" called Gary.

There was no answer from the lean one and no sound of metal striking earth.

"Tuck!" called Gary again.

There was no sound from Tuck. Sue looked quickly at Gary. A veil seemed to pass over the canyon as a cloud drifted high overhead; the canyon now had a twilight gloom about it.

"Tuck?" called Sue.

Gary looked down the slope again. It was as deserted as a lunar landscape. He walked around the rock slab; there was no sign of Tuck. A cold feeling came over Gary. Supposing, somehow, Asesino had gotten up *behind Gary* and Sue and had spirited away Tuck? It was really impossible for a being of flesh and blood to do it, but then Lobo had not seen or heard anything. His heart skipped a beat. "Tuck?" he called.

Nothing, not a sight or a sound of the lean one. The hole was empty. The slope showed no signs of Tuck. Gary peered about; he was downright frightened now. He almost wished he had listened to the others and had left while they had had a chance to leave. "Lobo," said Gary. The dog sniffed up and stopped beside him. "Go find Tuck, Lobo."

Lobo padded off through the brush. He stopped at a

clump of thick and tangled brash that was matted against the rock wall. He looked back at Gary.

"Go on, Lobo!" said Gary. "Find Tuck!"

Lobo stood stock-still. He whined a little.

Gary walked to the dog and stared at the brash. He looked down at Lobo. "Find Tuck," he repeated angrily.

Lobo whined and poked his nose into the brush. Gary pulled some of it aside, and a cool draft played about him. Suddenly, his hair seemed to stand on end, for a ghostly, faint voice was calling his name. "Gary! Oh, Gary! Gary!"

Gary shivered. The voice seemed to come from the brush itself. He pulled more of it to one side, and the cold draft grew more pronounced. Then, he plainly heard the voice beyond him and much lower than he was. "Gary! Oh, Gary!"

He started forward. Lobo barked sharply. Gary's left foot began to sink, and he jumped back, slipping and falling heavily. Gravel rushed from where he had been standing and pattered hollowly down below somewhere.

"Thanks, *amigo*!" came the strangled, hollow-sounding voice. "Whyn't you dump down that rock slab while you're at it?"

Gary got down on his hands and knees and worked his way back into the brush. His right hand struck a rounded edge of earth and then probed into nothingness. He bellied forward and found an irregular hole close beside the rock face. The cold air played about him as it rose from the black depths. "Tuck?" he called. His voice echoed below.

"Yeh, it's me," answered Tuck. "Black as ink down here. I got tired of digging. Saw a rabbit run into that brush. Thought it might taste good if we needed more food. All of a sudden, I found myself falling, and I landed down here."

Gary closed his eyes. Green sickness welled up within him, and his throat tasted sour. Many a man had been lost forever by fooling around just such old mine shafts and caves.

Sue came up behind Gary. "Where is he?" she asked.

"Don't come any closer," warned Gary. "He's all right."

"I got lonesome out there," she said.

———

GARY GOT THE PACKS, tools, rifle, and shotgun and brought them to the place where Tuck had dropped from the face of the earth. There were two coils of light nylon rope in the packs. He took one of them and fastened a bull's-eye lantern to it. "Line and lamp coming down, Tuck," he said. He lowered away.

He could see the lantern light alternately illuminating each side of the deep hole as it swung about. Then he saw Tuck's dirty, frightened face in the yellow pool of light, only to lose it again. He lowered the light a little more, and it swung about to light something else, something white and bony, a human skeleton complete with a grinning, hollow-eyed skull. Then it, too, was lost from sight as the lantern spun about once more.

Tuck's shriek blasted against Gary's ears. Gary had the presence of mind to whip the end of the nylon rope quickly around a shattered tree stump that was near the edge of the brush. The rope tightened, and feet scrabbled against the sides of the shaft. Tuck's harsh and erratic breathing echoed hollowly. In record time, his head popped up out of the opening. Gary grabbed him and dragged him out on the ground. Tuck lay there shivering with fright, taking in air with great gulps.

Gary gathered his courage and looked down in the hole once more. The lamp twisted and again lighted the human relics. Shreds of rotted clothing hung on the pitiful framework, and one bony hand rested on what seemed to be a book. It was then that Gary noticed the thick tree trunk to one side of the hole; it had deep notches cut into it. His heart leaped. It was a sure enough Spanish miner's chicken ladder!

Tuck gasped. "It wasn't that skeleton that bothered me, *amigo*, it was the bad air down there."

"Sure, sure," said Gary soothingly. He looked back at Tuck. "I think you literally stumbled into the Lost Espectro, Tuck."

"You sure?"

"No, but I soon will be."

"You going down there?"

Gary nodded. "It isn't the skeleton I'm afraid of, Tuck, it's what Sue saw down in the canyon." He told Tuck of Sue's experience.

"Who do you think it was?" asked Tuck after a long pause.

"*Quién sabe*? The dog didn't see or hear anything."

"You think she might be kidding us?"

"I am not!" said Sue angrily from the background.

Gary looked up at the dark sky. "It's getting late," he said. "We can't possibly get out of here tonight. I say we stay here. Hole up in one of those caves. Two of us stay on guard all night. Lobo won't let anyone get near us without a warning."

"Sure," said Sue sarcastically. "He sure gave us a warning about that somebody down there, whoever it was."

"Maybe he knew who it was," said Tuck thoughtfully. "Someone *he* wouldn't be concerned about. How would he know about our suspicions about certain people?"

"You might have something there," said Gary.

"Whoever it was sure looked like an Apache," said Sue. "How many Apaches does Lobo know?"

"Jerry Black?" said Tuck.

Gary shook his head. "I don't know if he ever saw Jerry," he said. He looked at the two of them. "Maybe someone is *playing* Apache."

"Fine time to be playing cowboys and Indians," growled Tuck.

"That's not exactly what I meant," said Gary. He picked up his rifle and checked it. "A white man can have dark hair and bind it with a cloth like Apaches used to do. *Someone whom Lobo knows*..."

"I'm scared," said Sue. There was a catch in her voice.

"Look, Sue," said Gary, not unkindly, "we're stuck in here. If anyone is looking for trouble, we're better off staying right where we are and letting them come to us than trying to get out of here in the dark. We don't know any way out of here other than the way we came in, and it would be pitch black in there before we ever reached the cavern. We can't take a chance of trying to find another way out of here, if there *is* such a thing."

"Besides, Susie," said Tuck bravely, "we've found the Lost Espectro. We can't just go off and leave it here, can we now?"

"How do we know it's the Lost Espectro?" she demanded.

"There's one way to find out," said Tuck with a brave and careless smile. He seemed to grow a little in height. "Go on down there and make sure."

"Bravo," said Sue.

Tuck turned. "Don't you worry about a thing, Gary," he said. "I'll keep good watch up *here* while you're down *there* making certain it is the Lost Espectro."

"I might have known," said Gary dryly. "O.K. I didn't come all the way into this hole in the mountains to turn away from the Lost Espectro at the last minute." He handed Tuck the rifle, put on his shirt, and picked up his hat. Gary formed a sling for the shotgun from a length of rope and slung it over his back. Then he took the second coil of nylon rope and slung it over his arm. He lowered his legs into the shaft and felt for the first rungs of the chicken ladder, holding onto the rope that he had dropped for Tuck. Gary tested the ladder all the way down and found it solid, preserved from rot by the dry air of the shaft.

He detached the lantern from the rope and flashed it about. Behind the sprawled skeleton was the dark, irregular opening of a drift. He flashed the light on the skeleton. It had been there a good many years. He knelt and examined the clothing. It was so old that some of it crumbled in his grasp, releasing a little cloud of musty dust that swirled about in the lamplight and then rose up into the shaft.

An eerie feeling, as well as the ancient dust, seemed to float about Gary. He gently removed the leather-bound book from beneath the bony fingers and opened it. It was a Spanish Bible. A nameplate showed in the yellow light, and written upon it in a spidery script was a name. "Leandro Melgosa," read Gary quietly. He looked at the skeleton. According to history, Leandro Melgosa had been the youngest of the three Melgosa Brothers. Vigil Melgosa, the second brother, had been killed by Apaches, while Marcos, the eldest, supposedly after hiding the mine, had fled to Mexico and had never returned. Nothing had been known of the fate of Leandro. He had vanished in the Espectros like the snows of yesteryear.

Gary stood up. He stepped over the skeleton, and as he did so, a queer, sickening feeling of cold horror came over him. He could see the back of the skull, *and in it was a large and ragged hole*. Someone had evidently killed Leandro, if indeed it *was* Leandro, from behind, unless of course, he had fallen and fatally struck himself. Gary reached out a trembling hand to touch the hole. As he did so, the skull fell to one side. Something rattled on the floor of the shaft. Gary knelt and picked up a mutilated lead slug. He had been killed by human hands then.

Thoughts of the other killings in the Espectros flooded through his mind. *Killings in which men had been shot through the back of the skull!* He was confused. No one murderer could have spanned the long years from the time of the killing of Leandro Melgosa up until twelve years or so ago when the two prospectors, John Bellina and Carl Schuster, had been shot to death through the back of the head. There was an eerie puzzle here.

He stepped over the skeleton and raised his lamp. The rays picked out a sketchy carving on the drift wall. "*Dios Mio, ayudame,*" read Gary. He wrinkled his brow. "My God, help me," he translated. Farther down, a deep cross had been cut into the rock, and beneath that was more writing. "There is nothing but death in this canyon," he translated. There was a signature beneath the last word. "Marcos Melgosa, August 17, 1844," he added slowly.

There was mystery and hidden tragedy in those words. Gary flashed the light up the drift. Here and there on the floor were pieces of wood that had fallen from the sagging pit props supporting the narrow runnel. Amidst the litter were woven baskets. Gary recognized them as *mecapals,* used by the Spanish and Mexican miners to carry ore from mines. There was also a pile of sotol stalks, once used by the old-timers as torches.

He raised the lamp and shot the light down the drift. It had not been cut straight as American miners would have done—driving in a drift, then crosscutting to get at the vein—but in the old Mexican method of following the vein itself and not removing any more earth and rock than was absolutely necessary.

Something held Gary back. The prospect of walking alone up that twisted, dark, and echoing drift was not too inviting. He stepped back, hesitated, then walked forward again along the drift. What puzzled him was the steady current of fresh air flowing about him. It indicated only one thing, there was another opening to the mine somewhere in the bowels of the rock ahead of him.

He saw a worn-out husk sandal on the floor and a rawhide *zurron* bag that had once been fastened to the head of the man who had carried ore in the *zurron* from the mine. On and on he went, his boots crunching in the debris fallen from the roof and walls of the drift, watching carefully for holes or weak spots in the packed earth of the drift bottom. The draft still blew about him, but there was no sign of a gold vein in the walls or any caches of the precious metal that had been left behind so long ago.

The place was too much for his nerves at last. There was a brooding, haunting air about the drift. He turned to go back, and instantly, it seemed to him as though something had moved up close behind him out of the fearsome darkness to reach out bony claws for him. He almost panicked. Then, he began to count each step to himself. He had taken thirty paces into the drift. He held off gibbering panic and at last reached the shaft. Gary forced himself to stand there, disciplining himself. "Tuck!" he called.

Sue thrust her head into the hole. "What is it, Gary?"

"I haven't found much of anything," said Gary. His voice cracked a little.

"You want Tuck to go back with you?"

She knew all right. She knew Gary was fighting for self-control down in that drafty, dark hole in the ground. Sue smiled. "Maybe Tuck ought to stay on guard," she said. "I'll go with you, Gary."

He swallowed hard. "It's all right," he said. He knew she was as scared as he was. The kid had guts alright. Scared as she was, she didn't want him to go in there alone again. She came lightly down the ladder. She eyed the skeleton. "Who was he?" she asked.

Gary shrugged. "Leandro Melgosa, as far as I know. The brother that vanished."

She gingerly walked past the skeleton. "Seems to me his brothers should have buried him."

"Vigil was killed by Apaches. Marcos returned to

Mexico." Gary looked down at the remains of Leandro. "I think he was murdered right here, Sue."

She smiled wanly. "Why?"

"Someone shot him through the back of the head." Gary's eyes narrowed. He flashed the light on the writing. "I wonder," he said quietly.

Sue was an A student in Spanish. She quickly translated the inscription. "My God, help me! There is nothing but death in this canyon. Marcos Melgosa, August 17, 1844." She looked at Gary. "He was just frightened, that's all, Gary. His other brother had been killed by the Apaches; then Leandro was killed, and Marcos knew he had to get out of here or die as well. He didn't have time to bury Leandro."

"But he had time to cut that inscription into the rock," said Gary quietly. He looked down at the skeleton. "He didn't even take the time to lay out his brother properly. Just let him drop there in death right across the drift entrance."

There was a puzzled look on Sue's face. " So?"

"Maybe Marcos left Leandro as the *patron*."

"So what? A *patron* is an owner, an employer, Gary. Maybe Marcos..." Her voice trailed off. "How could a dead man be an owner or an employer?"

Gary felt a creeping horror within him. "There is another meaning to the word *patron,* Sue. The old Spanish miners would sometimes take as much gold or silver from a mine as they needed or could carry at the time, then to guard the mine, they would kill one of the peons or Indian slaves so that he would be a *patron*, a ghostly warden or guard of the mine to keep out intruders."

"But Leandro was his brother!"

"Yes. But Marcos had gold fever. He knew he had to leave the mine, and there was no *patron* to place on guard. *No one but his own brother*."

Sue shuddered. "Now we know why he never came

back here again. Imagine coming down here to see Leandro still on guard!"

"I saw him," said Gary dryly. "So did Tuck. I don't think we'll be bothered by the ghost of Leandro Melgosa. I have a feeling his ghost was waiting for one man alone. Maybe the ghost, if there is such a thing as a ghost, left here and went to look for Brother Marcos. *That* would have been a meeting!"

Now that Sue was with him, Gary felt his courage return. If a girl had the nerve to come down into that dark mine, he could hardly back out now from further exploration.

"Maybe there is nothing in the mine," said Sue.

"Then why would Leandro have been left behind as *patron?*"

"That's true," she said. "Won't hurt to look. It doesn't seem to be much darker or any more dangerous down here than it is up there."

Gary smiled at her, then turned to lead the way back along the dark and echoing drift. A stone struck the bottom of the shaft. A moment later, Tuck whistled softly. "Gary," he croaked in a low voice. "There's someone coming up here!"

Gary shook his head at Sue, then swiftly ascended the ladder, crawling on his belly through the brush to lie beside his partner. He raised his head and caught a swift and furtive movement amidst the tangle of rocks and brush. The canyon was very dark now, and the wind was getting colder. Gary flipped off the safety on the shotgun. Tuck raised the Winchester and fully cocked it.

Minutes ticked past. There was no further sign of life. Gary's eyes ached from peering into the gloom. He raised his head a little higher, then some strange intuition made him quickly turn his head to the left. A man was standing behind a shattered boulder with only his head and shoulders showing; his thick hair was bound with a cloth, exactly as Sue had described the stranger.

Gary threw up his shotgun, and Tuck turned, raising the rifle. Gary sighed, and then his breath caught in his throat. The man stood up in plain view and smiled widely. He waved a hand. "It's Lije Purtis, fellas," he said. There was no sign of a weapon on him.

"Come out in the open," said Gary coldly. "What do you want?"

Lije shambled out into the open and smiled again. "I wanted to tell you someone has been following you. You got anything to eat?"

"Yes," said Tuck. "Who is following us, Lije?"

Lije shook his head as though to clear it. "I followed him through that cave way back there, at the water hole. I was goin' to ask him for some—" The rifle cracked flatly from a hundred yards down the slope. Lije fell heavily. The echo of the shot slammed back and forth in the canyon as the boys dropped flat. Gary crawled to the edge of the rocks in front of him, and just as he did so, lightning flashed high in the heavens. The eerie light played full on the gaunt face of Lije Purtis. His mouth gaped open, revealing his yellow teeth. His eyes stared at the dark sky, but they did not see. They would never see anything on earth again.

CHAPTER THIRTEEN

Trapped

The canyon was quiet again, except for the moaning of the wind. The acrid odor of burnt powder drifted away. Nothing had been seen of the hidden marksman except the quick, stabbing spurt of flame from his rifle muzzle. His accuracy had been remarkable at that distance, firing uphill and in the uncertain light. If he had done nothing else, he had at least cleared poor Lije Purtis of any suspicion, not that it would help Lije now.

Gary passed the shotgun to Tuck and took the rifle. Tuck was a good shot, but not in a class with Gary. There was no use in fooling themselves. The chips were down, and it might soon be a question of kill or be killed. Strangely enough, to Gary, there was almost a feeling of relief within him as he peered through the shifting light. He had become tired of the unknown and the unseen. He knew now it was no ghost that haunted the Espectros. It was a man of flesh and blood, armed with a heavy-caliber rifle, who thought nothing of killing. Lije Purtis had known who he was; therefore, Lije had died. It was as simple as that.

This time, Gary would shoot to kill rather than fire warning shots as he had done at the shadowy figure who had been watching for them that moonlit night in the canyon of the water hole.

Lobo rounded a huge slab of rock and dropped to the ground beside Gary. Gary looked curiously at the dog. If it had been Lije Purtis whom Sue had seen, it was logical enough that Lobo wouldn't have barked at *him*. Lobo knew Lije and knew he was harmless. What puzzled Gary was the fact that Lobo was so calm now. Had he seen the man who had killed Lije? *Did he know that man as well as he had known Lije?* Was that why he was so unconcerned?

Tuck was evidently puzzled as well. He looked down at Lobo and then up at Gary, shrugging his shoulders. Gary worked his way over to Tuck. "What do you think?" he asked.

"*Quién sabe?* Lobo must know who it is. Someone *he* thinks is all right."

"That's what I'm thinking. On the other hand, if it was Asesino, he wouldn't stay any longer in one spot than it takes to fire a shot. He's too slick for that, Tuck."

Thunder rumbled in the sky. A few cold drops of rain pattered quickly on the rocks. Gary eyed the position they were in. The mine was just below them, probing beneath the sheer cliff behind them. To the right and the left, the cliff walls curved down toward the floor of the canyon. Before them was the tangled slope covered with shattered rock from which the killer had fired. If he were still on that slope, he could easily see anyone trying to make the floor of the canyon.

When full darkness came, he could move in, taking his chances on the fact that Lobo knew him. He could wait through the darkness of the night, watching and listening for any movement, and when the light of dawn flooded the canyon, he could pick his position so that he could see a fly crawling across those rocks near the mine.

Gary took stock. They had enough water for another day or so and enough food for about the same amount of time with short rations, of course. Gary had a full magazine in his rifle and about a dozen extra cartridges, totaling twenty rounds. Tuck, with the short-range shotgun, had only half a dozen cartridges. At close range, the shotgun was a deadly weapon, but if the unseen marksman stayed away from it, he would be safe enough.

The wind shifted and carried another sound with it. A thin, mocking laugh that came from up high. Gary raised his rifle, but he decided there would be no sense in shooting at the elusive voice. Maybe that was what the killer wanted; the quick spurting of fire from the Winchester would enable him to pinpoint Gary. The way he could shoot, he'd hardly need more than that.

Tuck paled. He crouched lower, and his knuckles whitened as he gripped the shotgun. He looked toward the sound of the voice, and even as he did so, the swift red-orange spurt of flame etched itself high on the canyon wall to the right. The slug splattered itself on the rock a yard above the two boys as the echo of the shot tumbled in raucous confusion down the canyon.

"Get down," said Gary. He jumped up and then dropped. The rifle flashed again. This time, Gary saw the darkness of a man behind the flash of the rifle, and he fired twice. He knew instantly that he had fallen victim to the instinctive bad habit of firing too low when shooting upward.

The mocking laughter came again from a different place. There was an eerie, haunting quality about it, as though it came from the lips of a madman.

Gary lay low. The quick sight he had had of the man had been long enough for him to see that the man did not wear a hat. He remembered the old saying of years ago in Arizona in reference to fighting Apaches. "Shoot 'em if they don't wear a hat!" It was a fair rule of thumb.

"Asesino?" queried Tuck hoarsely.

"I don't know."

"Who else could it be?"

They were interrupted by a shaky little voice emanating from the shaft behind them. "I'm scared down here," said Sue.

"I'm scared up here," said Tuck.

Darkness was swiftly filling the canyon. The thought of lying there in the open in the coming darkness with a madman stalking them was a frightening one.

————

TEN MINUTES PASSED. Something struck the rocks ten feet in front of them and shattered, scattering shards of broken rock through the air like grenade fragments.

A moment later, another rock plummeted down and crashed five feet to one side of Tuck. He grunted in pain as a bit of the rock slashed across the back of his right hand. The laughter floated across the canyon and echoed back so that no one could say where it came from. So confusing were the echoes. The laughter was followed by the crashing impact of more rocks.

"Get into the shaft," said Gary quickly.

"We'll be trapped," said Tuck.

"You want your skull smashed! We haven't any choice!"

Tuck scuttled down the ladder. Gary backed up against the rock wall. He pulled up the nylon rope and tied it about Lobo, then lowered the heavy dog into the shaft. It was too dark to see anything now. Swiftly, he lowered their gear down into the hole. He looked up at the dark rim of the canyon and saw someone flit past, then vanish. "Who are you?" he yelled. "What do you want?" The echoes fled down the canyon. *"Who are you? Who are you? Who are you? What do you want? What do you want? What do you want?"* They died away to be replaced by the moaning of the dusk wind.

There was no answer. Gary glanced once more toward the still form of poor Lije Purtis. His last words came back to Gary. "I followed him through that cave way back there, at the water hole. I was goin' to ask him for some—" What had he wanted from the unknown person?

The voice came clearly from the darkness, now to the left. "Asesino...Asesino...Asesino..." It was followed by that eerie, mocking laughter slowly dying away.

Gary wasted no time. He clambered down the chicken ladder with the strong premonition that it wasn't quite the thing to do; they might be trapped in there forever. But there was no choice. He was confused, and he could not think clearly. "Get back into the drift," he said.

The three of them stood there in the pool of light from the bull's-eye lamp. The draft played about them. Gary looked along the dark drift. "The draft means there must be an opening somewhere along there," he said.

"Somewhere," echoed Tuck. He swallowed hard.

"It's a chance we have to take," said Gary.

Tuck looked upward. "Maybe he knows where the opening is. Maybe he'll be waiting there for us."

"Cut it!" snapped Gary. "We've got guns! We can shoot, too! We're not licked yet!"

"Hear! Hear!" said Sue.

Something pattered on the floor of the shaft.

Gary flashed the lamp that way. Silvery drops of rain showed in the yellow light. Faintly and insistently, the muttering of thunder came to them.

"Well, anyway, we're out of the rain," cracked Tuck. He subsided immediately when he saw the looks shot at him.

"Keep guard here, Tuck," said Gary. "I'm going to explore this drift." He walked to the pile of sotol stalks he had seen and gathered some of them, returning to Tuck to give him the lamp. He lighted one of the sotol stalks and started down the tunnel, followed by Lobo. "Go back," he said.

He went on alone, following the winding passage, holding the flaring stalk high. His footsteps echoed on the hard, dusty floor of the drift. Now and then, he had to squeeze under dangerous places where the props had sagged; at other times, he had to clamber over piles of rock and earth that had fallen from the sides and top of the drift. It was reassuring to feel the constant draft blowing about him. The air was a little musty, but it was fresh enough to indicate that it came from the outside, no matter how far it was up the drift.

Here and there were the dark and narrow entrances to crosscuttings. Some of them had been filled by earth and rock when the props collapsed. Some of them were not very deep. The old miners had followed the winding of the vein, scooping out the rich ore wherever it was.

So far, he had seen nothing of the ore itself, for they had been thorough enough in their digging. He wasn't much interested at this point in the legendary tales of the wealth of the Lost Espectro, if this was indeed the Lost Espectro. He knew now that life was more precious than finding the treasure reputed to be buried in the old mine. Lead fever had replaced gold fever, the lead from Asesino's rifle.

The flickering light revealed a roughly squared-off room cut into the drift. Suddenly, Gary realized he had just enough of the sotol stalks to light his way back to the shaft. He peered into the room, saw that there was a further continuation of the drift on the opposite side, then turned back. He did not want to have to traverse any of the distance back in the darkness.

The last stalk flickered out as he turned the last bend in the drift before reaching the shaft. The light went out, and he was in complete darkness. He should have been able to see the light from the lamp by now. He hesitated as he stared into the blackness, feeling sweat from his perspiring hands beginning to grease the stock of his rifle.

Supposing something had happened to his two friends? Supposing he was now alone in that drift? *Supposing somebody was waiting for him in the blackness after disposing of Sue and Tuck?*

He tried to call out, but his mouth was as dry as ashes. Then he whistled softly. Something pattered on the floor of the tunnel, and he heard Lobo's welcoming bark. "Tuck?" called Gary softly.

"Quiet!" said the lean one from the blackness.

Gary felt his way along until he touched Tuck. "What is it?"

"We thought we heard someone up there."

Gary cocked his head to listen. The rain was still pattering down, and some of the drops fell into the shaft. He was about to chide Tuck for a false alarm when he heard the scuffling of feet at the top of the shaft. He stepped back into the drift and raised the shotgun. Gravel dropped into the shaft. A moment later, the eerie, mocking laughter came to them. There was a haunting madness to it.

This time, Lobo sensed something. He barked savagely and then growled deep in his throat. Gary held him back as more gravel rumbled into the shaft. If that unknown made a move to reach the chicken ladder, he would meet the full blast of both shotgun barrels. And even Asesino couldn't evade that.

There was a scuffling noise, and something heavy dropped at the top of the shaft. Gary reached for Tuck and took the lamp from his hands. The scuffling noise came again. This time, Gary chanced a light, flicking it up the shaft in time to see a heavy tree trunk fall across the opening and the quick withdrawal of a wet hand. He saw, with a sickening conclusion, that there were several other timbers already in place across the narrow opening. He flicked out the light as gravel tumbled down toward him.

Cold sweat trickled down Gary's sides. The madman

was blocking them in as he had blocked the dry entrance to the cavern far back in the canyon of the water hole. "What do you want?" yelled Gary. "Tell us! *What do you want*?" His voice seemed to boom in the shaft.

"Gold," said a faraway-sounding voice. "The gold..."

"We haven't found any!"

Gravel trickled down again. The scuffling continued. Gary chanced another lighting of the lamp. This time, he clearly saw the wet face peering down between two of the logs. The dark hair, bound by a dirty wet cloth, and painted across the nose, were two bands of white paint, while the dark eyes seemed to burn with madness and hate. Then the face vanished, and the eerie laughter drifted down to them again.

Gary stepped back. His hands were shaking. Tuck gripped him around the shoulders. "Who was it?"

Gary shivered. "It was him all right. Asesino. I saw him, Tuck. *I saw him*!" Gary's voice rose sharply.

Tuck's hand cracked against Gary's head. "Snap out of it, *amigo*!" he said. "Don't *you* go loco on us! We need you, Gary! You can't let us down now!"

Gary's nerves calmed down. "Thanks," he said quietly. "Never thought I'd be thanking a fella for bopping me."

Gary walked back into the drift. They could hear their attacker hard at work up there, blocking the way. It would have been better to have hunted for him as he had hunted for them. But with a man like that, an outlaw hunted for so many years, his senses would have been honed to the edge native only to animals.

"He said he only wanted the gold," said Sue.

"He said he wanted gold, and there wasn't any *only* in what he said," corrected Tuck. "In the first place, we haven't got any gold. In the second place, if we did have it, and we let him have it, do you think he'd let us get out of here alive?"

Lobo was now almost in a paroxysm of rage. He barked and growled, and the sound of it was a terrible thing. Gary finally managed to quiet him. There was no sound coming from above. Gary aimed the light up the shaft again. All he could see were the logs, with packed dirt and rock showing between them. They had been neatly sealed into the shaft, and there wasn't any doubt in Gary's mind about who was waiting up there for them if they tried to dig their way to freedom.

Gary lighted the lamp again when he was in the drift. "Come on," he said. "There's air coming in here from somewhere. We've got food and water. We're not licked yet!"

Tuck grinned. "I never thought I'd have to belt you, Gary, but now that I did, I'm not sorry. *Adelante!*"

————

GARY LED the way back to the large squared-off room and into the drift beyond it. Ten minutes later, the three of them stopped in dismay. The drift had narrowed, and a heavy fall of rock had almost completely sealed the passageway. Air drifted through the narrow space between the top of the drift and the piled-up debris.

Gary crawled up the pile and flashed the lamp over it. The air blew damply against his face, but he could see little with the lamp. They'd have to dig through.

The three of them set to work, with Sue relieving the boys in turn while Lobo stood guard behind them. Now that the entrance to the shaft had been sealed behind them, the draft died away, and the stifling dust hung heavily in the drift, but the air was fresh enough.

Gary was ten feet into the pile when Sue crawled up beside him. "Maybe we ought to rest," she suggested wearily.

Gary shook his head. "No," he said. "We keep on!"

"It's after eleven o'clock, Gary!" she protested.

Gary jerked a thumb back over his shoulder. "He isn't sleeping," he said quietly. She knew whom he meant.

Hours passed, and then Tuck weakly drove his entrenching tool against a big rock. The handle snapped, and then the rock slid heavily down a steep slope, followed by Tuck riding the slide to the bottom of the drift. Gary crawled after him and flashed the weakening lamp up the drift. The way seemed clear enough now. The two of them crawled through their little tunnel to get Sue. She was sound asleep with her back against a pit prop and with Lobo's head nestled on her lap.

Gary walked partway back into the drift to listen. It was as quiet as the grave. He winced mentally at the simile. That squared-off room had been puzzling him all night. He walked slowly back to it and flicked out his lamp to replace the batteries. He lighted the lamp again and instantly saw a niche cut into the far wall with something resting upon it.

"Come on, Gary!" called Tuck. "The bus is leaving!"

"Wait a bit!"

The two Brownes came into the room. Gary walked toward the niche and flashed the lamp upon the shelf. His breath caught in his throat. There were half a dozen objects resting upon it, somewhat brick-shaped but about half the size of a common brick, and the edges were roughly rounded. Dust was thick upon them. He reached out a hand and then quickly withdrew it, stepping back to flash the light on the roughly hewn wall.

"What is it, Gary?" asked Tuck.

Gary turned slowly. "I think we have found what we've been looking for," he said quietly.

"A way out?"

"No. Gold, *amigo*!"

"Those bricks?"

Gary nodded.

"Let's get 'em and get out then!" Tuck started forward.

"Wait!" snapped Gary.

Tuck turned slowly. "Why? You loco?"

Gary shook his head. "We've got to watch for traps." He picked up his entrenching tool and firmly lashed it to the barrels of the shotgun. He raised the gun, then jerked his head at the two Brownes. "Get back into the drift," he cautioned. He reached forward, slid the edge of the tool beneath an end brick, and lifted it up. He turned and passed it back to Tuck. Again, he reached out and scooped up another brick, passing it back to Tuck. Sweat appeared on his brow as he lifted the third one. Nothing happened. He was almost ready to grab the rest of them by hand, but something held him back. He scooped up the fourth brick, and as it cleared the shelf, something creaked dryly.

"These are *pure gold!*" said Tuck wildly.

"Gold!" shrieked Sue. "Gold!" She danced madly about. "Get the rest of 'em! *GOLD!*"

Gary began to lift the fifth brick, and as he did so, the creaking noise came again, but this time it was louder. He dropped the brick and jumped back. As he did so, Tuck flashed the light on the wall. The wall was moving, falling forward with a creaking, grating noise. Then it fell heavily and solidly, some of the material striking Gary's feet.

The wall was completely collapsed, and the rays of the lamp reflected dully off piles of the roughly shaped bricks set into the hewn-out area behind the wall. Then the roof dropped to conceal the amassed wealth of the Lost Espectro. Gary slammed full tilt into Tuck and Sue, driving them along the drift as rock and earth thudded behind them, raising a thick, choking cloud of dust. "Run!" yelled Gary. He turned to look back. Tuck flashed the lamp, and through the thickening dust, they could see a bizarre sight. A lean, wet face streaked with white paint peered through the swirling haze, then the mouth opened to shriek madly.

Gary raised the shotgun and wildly fired both barrels, not even bothering about the lashed entrenching tool that thrust itself out from the barrels like a spade bayonet of ancient times. The noise from the gun was deafening. The face vanished behind the dust and more falling rock and earth.

Gary did not stop to see the result of his firing. He was running for dear life along the drift, with rock and dirt pattering down behind him. He saw Tuck's legs wriggling out of sight atop the tunnel block, and he dived in after them. Tuck broke into the open and slid wildly down the slope, with Gary helter-skelter, head over heels, atop his partner and Lobo atop Gary.

Gary handed the shotgun to Tuck and took the rifle. The three of them had their gear slung about them. It was no time to be choosy. There was one way to go. They slogged on along the echoing drift, spurred on by their fear.

Twice more, they had to clear their way through blockages, but they were nothing compared to the big one far behind them. The drift sloped upward, and the draft became stronger; a wet, freshening smell replaced the dusty odor of the drift.

Gary rounded a sharp turn in the tunnel and saw a steep slope. He scrambled up it. They had been climbing steadily almost since the time they had left the gold cache. Water was trickling along the side of the drift now, and he could have sworn he heard the faint rumbling of thunder. He rounded yet another turn and found himself in another large room. At the far side was a tattered sheet of cloth waving in the strong breeze that blew into the room. He started toward it, then stopped short. An odd, eerie feeling came over him. Tuck and Sue came into the room, puffing and blowing.

Gary turned slowly and swung the lamp. To one side was a crude bunk, and in the bunk was a hunched figure covered with a filthy blanket. One arm hung over the side of the bunk, and the hand that rested on the floor was nothing but drawn, parchment-like skin that clearly showed the bones.

"What is it?" said Sue weakly. "Not *again,* Gary!"

"He's long dead," said Tuck. "The *dead ones* don't bother me anymore."

Gary's feet grated on rusted tin cans as he walked toward the bunk. He slowly and steadily pulled back the blanket to look into a mummified face framed by thick, coarse black hair. The mummy had been there a long, long time, preserved by cool, dry air. A dingy headband bound the hair to the head.

Gary stepped back. His feet struck tin cans again. He flashed the light down on them. Some of the labels were still legible. "Elberta peaches," he said quietly. He raised the lamp. A Winchester rifle leaned against the wall, covered with a patina of rust and dust. Gary walked to it and picked it up. He knew enough about guns to recognize a Model 1886. He worked the stiff action and ejected a heavy brass cartridge. He picked it up and looked at the base of it. "A .50/110 caliber," he said. Gary looked at his two friends. "I think we've found Asesino. He's been dead many years."

Sue shivered in the draft. The wind whipped the tattered cloth at the room entrance and moaned down the drift.

"If that's Asesino, and I don't know who else it could be," said Tuck quietly, "*who was that back there?*"

Gary leaned the heavy rifle against the wall, flicked out the lamp, and walked to the curtain. He pulled it to one side and stepped out onto a rock shelf with a rough and almost natural-looking breastwork of rocks along the outer edge. For a moment, he expected to be looking down the canyon of The Needle. Instead, he saw the thick grayness of the false dawn and, far below, a canyon.

For a moment, he was confused, until he realized it was the very canyon in which the entrance to the Lost Espectro was. From where he stood, he could easily see anyone who moved on the slopes or in the canyon. Even now, he saw a stealthy movement. Someone was skulking along the edge of the canyon. Someone with a heavy rifle in his hands and a dirty cloth bound about his dark, wet hair. He was looking down toward where the entrance to the mine should be.

Gary stepped back into the room. He lighted the lamp, knowing well enough the man outside could not see the light. "Our little friend is out there," he said, eying his two partners closely, "looking down toward the mine entrance. Maybe he figures we just might dig ourselves out that way. He knows now we found the gold. What do we do? Sit it out here? Try to make a break to get away? Or clean his clock for him?"

Tuck grinned. "You think I'm leaving here without taking a crack at him? After the way he scared me? No, sir!"

Sue spat inelegantly into her left palm and smacked it with her small right fist. "Let me at him," she growled fiercely. Lobo began to growl, too, as he started for the entrance.

Gary flicked off the lamp. "Quiet, Lobo," he said. "Stay! Our boy probably won't look back this way. That's a break for us. If we get close enough, we can get the drop on him."

"Supposing he doesn't surrender?" said Sue anxiously.

There was a long moment of quietness.

Sue spoke again. "Now that was a stupid question, wasn't it?"

The rain pattered down steadily, and the wind whined through the canyon as the three of them made their plan.

CHAPTER FOURTEEN

End of a Killer

The rain was drumming on the Espectros, streaming from a real buster of a cloud that hung over the mountains. The cloud was a huge and threatening mass with a distended belly of gray and black, which held a mighty tonnage of water.

The Espectros had long been notorious as the breeding place of storms, and when the Thunder People rumbled their great drums in the deep canyons and lanced the streaming skies with their shafts of lightning tipped with flashing death, it was no place for a frail man to stand up against nature.

The wind bellowed through the gorges and lashed the scrub trees. Water had begun to course through the dry stream beds at the bottoms of the canyons, rising with frightful speed and sweeping everything before its fluid power.

Gary Cole knew it had been pouring rain for most of the night while he and his companions were burrowing in the belly of the Lost Espectro. There had been other rainstorms of more than average intensity over the Espectros that summer, but he could not recall any as fierce as this one. It was almost like dusk in the canyon country as he peered from behind the breastwork to spot the killer who haunted the canyon rim. Then, he saw a movement in a clump of brush at the very edge of the chasm. "Ready?" he asked over his shoulder.

"Hold it a minute," hissed Tuck from within the cavern. "I'm not finished with my makeup!"

Gary turned to look at Sue, and his heart went out to her. Her great brown eyes looked like those of a frightened doe as she hunched back against the rock face out of the driving rain, holding onto Lobo's collar. "Remember, Sue," he said quietly, "I want you to release him only if things turn against us."

She nodded. "I'll remember," she said.

Gary looked at the shotgun beside her. "It's loaded. I showed you how to throw off the safety catch. Don't fire both barrels at the same time! If anything happens to Tuck and me, lay low. He might not find you. If he gets too close, let the dog go at him, then use the gun."

She closed her eyes, swallowed hard, then nodded again.

Gary crawled around the edge of the tumbledown breastwork and bellied down the slope behind a screen of wet rock. In no time at all, he was wet to the skin, but it didn't matter. The hunt he was on and the tension of it was enough to keep his mind from his discomfort. He was halfway down the slope when he looked back. Tuck's head popped up. The lean one waved, then vanished again. Gary gave him time to get into position, then crawled on.

The killer was well hidden in the tangled brush that covered one side of a huge tilted slab of rock at the very brink of the canyon. Gary could just make out the outline of his prone figure. Gary inched along, cradling his Winchester in the crook of his arms, until he reached a place to one side of the slab of rock where the ground was a little higher. He was no more than thirty yards from his quarry.

He waited again, feeling the cold rain beating steadily

against his back. Minutes ticked past, and then he saw a furtive movement to his right, beyond the slab of rock. Tuck was in position now with Asesino's old rifle.

Gary bellied down the harsh, wet slope. Then he stopped short, for there had been a movement in the tangle of brush. He saw two boots protruding from beneath it. They were small boots, and the heel on the left one had been set crookedly in place. The sight laid nerve-chill upon rain chill. It was too far away to distinguish the double crescent of nails set into the crooked heel, but as sure as his name was Gary Cole, he knew that the crescent was there.

The rain slackened a bit. Gary picked up a fist-sized rock and threw it over the brink. He hardly heard the sound of it striking far below, but the killer heard it. He must have hearing like a dog. As he moved, Gary saw the wet, dark hair bound with the dingy cloth, but the man's painted face was turned away from Gary as he peered intently down into the canyon.

Gary moved closer. He eased the hammer of his Winchester back to full cock. It would be an easy shot. He could hit the killer, and he'd never know what had hit him. But it wasn't in Gary to kill that way. An intense curiosity came over him. Gary wanted the man to turn his face so that he could see it plainly, for his other views of it had been too short to know who he was. Maybe he would not know the man at all.

Gary shifted to raise his rifle, and the metal shod stock struck a rock. The effect of the noise was instantaneous on the killer. He turned and was on his feet, crouching flat against the rock. As he raised his rifle, he was looking directly at Gary. It was no one Gary recognized.

Higher on the slope, a heavy rifle crashed. The killer's eyes widened. He looked past Gary, and his mouth squared like that of a Greek tragedy mask. He was trying to yell or cry out. Gary turned to see a tall, gaunt figure striding down the slope, a figure wearing ragged clothing, with long black hair bound by a dingy cloth and bands of white paint drawn across his nose and upper cheeks. A heavy Winchester was in his hands, and as he came down the slope, he gave forth with a piercing, wailing cry that seemed to congeal Gary's blood.

"Asesino!" screamed the killer at last.

"Throw down that gun!" yelled Gary.

The man turned to stare at Gary. Gary ran forward. The rifle came up, and the stock struck Gary on the shoulder. He dropped his own rifle and then ducked under another blow of the rifle, staring into the wild, dark-blue eyes of the killer. "Tuck!" screamed Gary. He jumped to one side and saw the disguised Tuck fall head-long over a rock, his rifle clattering down the slope.

It was no time for niceties. Gary kicked the killer in the belly, and as he came down with his head in a reflex action, Gary rammed his right knee up to meet the down-coming chin. The man grunted in pain. He staggered to one side and fired his rifle.

The blast of flame and smoke half-blinded Gary. He threw his hands over his face and fell backward against the rock slab as the killer levered another round into the smoking rifle. A lean figure hurtled down the slope. The rifle roared, and Tuck hit the ground an instant ahead of the bullet, but the stock struck his head and kept him down there.

The killer jumped back to reload his rifle. Gary could hardly see him. At this moment, a dark shape came roaring into battle. It was Lobo. The dog rose cleanly from the ground and struck savagely at the killer. The man fell backward. His feet clawed for a hold on the crumbling brink of the canyon, and then, with a wild, piercing scream, he went down. There was a thudding noise just below the rim of the canyon, then the distant clattering of the rifle as it struck far below.

Thunder roared in the canyons, and lighting etched

itself across the dark sky to lance into a distant peak. Gary rubbed his eyes and then crawled to the edge of the canyon to look down. Twenty feet below him was a narrow ledge, and lying flat on the ledge was the killer with his wide, dark eyes staring right back at Gary, but they could see nothing. Gary rubbed his eyes again. The man's hair was no longer thick and black but rather thin and blond. Just above his head lay a rain-soaked black wig.

Tuck bellied alongside Gary. He stared too. "The *Candyman*," he said in an awed voice.

Gary nodded. He began to feel his intense weariness, the pain in his shoulder, and the bitter coldness of the lashing rain. "You played a great part, Tuck," he said. He gripped his partner's shoulder.

"It was your idea, Gary."

Gary stood up. "It was too close to suit me."

From somewhere up the canyon came a subdued roaring that gained intensity as they listened. Then, it seemed as though the canyon was filled with a towering wall of gray and white. It was water, a great mass of drainage water trapped in the narrow canyon and raging along through it to seek an exit. It leaped from side to side like some insensate and blinded primeval beast as it battered at the walls, carrying within its swirling liquid belly tons of rock, brush, shattered trees, and anything else it could gobble down, using the rough mass to scour the bottom of the canyon like some gigantic sanding machine.

It was a mad orgy of sound, a world of insane water and crackling lightning underscored by the rumbling of the thunder. From high on the canyon rim came silvery streams of rainwater to add to the flash flood. The water swirled with incredible speed up the slope below the cliff upon which the boys were standing in wide-eyed awe. It swept against the cliff base, rising higher and higher until it seemed as though it might even lap around the feet of the two watchers, then slowly, ever so slowly, it began to subside. The swirling surface was stippled with drowned animals, tangled mats of thorny brush, and splintered trees.

Despite the danger and the cold rain, they could not leave until the flood began to recede. Farther along the canyon, the crest still roared and raged.

Gary dropped to his belly and stared down at the base of the cliff as the water trickled off. Where the great rock that marked the site of the Lost Espectro had been was now a smooth area of gravel and sand overlaying the original rocky slope. Even as he watched, great masses of rock fell from the cliff face and shattered on the slope. There was no way he could locate the shaft now. Perhaps it was lost forever. No one could ever trace it without the cryptic symbols left by the Mexicans over a hundred years ago.

They did what they had to do. They got the nylon ropes, and Gary let himself down the crumbling ledge where the Candyman lay. They hoisted the body and placed it beneath the rock slab, covering it with rock to keep the coyotes from it. They did not look back as they returned to Sue. Despite the pouring rain, none of them wanted to take shelter in Asesino's cave.

They packed their gear. Now they had only three gold bricks since one had been left behind somewhere along the winding drift. But nothing in the world could have made them go back after it. Even the gold they had saved didn't mean much to them. They wanted, above all, to get away from the dripping mountains of violent death.

They were south, a good mile away from Asesino's cave, on the rugged mesa top, when the lightning struck with fearful intensity against the bald rock face high above the concealed cave entrance, the back door to the Lost Espectro. Slowly at first and then with gathering power, a great side of rock and rain-loosened earth cascaded smoothly down the slopes until the once rough facing was a smooth mass of rock and mud at rest, with

Asesino entombed, perhaps forever, beneath the great new covering.

They did not look back again as they picked their way down a crumbled cliff into a wide canyon, which Gary recognized as the lower part of the canyon where the water hole that had been formed by the great landslide of years past was located. Three horsemen urged their mounts toward them, and the worn-out trio recognized Sheriff Larry Gray, Jim Kermit, and the dark, smiling face of Jerry Black.

Jim Kermit shook his head as he unscrewed the top of his big Thermos and began to pour coffee for them. "You kids had everyone worried sick," he said. "My Francie found out Sue had left the house, and she called me at Millerton to tell me about it. I found the jeep you left behind and got in touch with the Sheriff here. Luckily, Jerry Black was in, making his monthly report to the Sheriff, so he came along. Believe you me, kids, you had everyone scared to death. Mrs. Kermit called Tucson and got in touch with your mother, Gary. She's on her way home. Your pa is all right. I also called *your* pa and ma, Tuck."

"Thanks, oh thanks," murmured the lean one.

Sheriff Gray looked at Sue. "I have a rough idea who is going to get the worst of this thing," he said with a sly grin.

"Yeh," said Sue. "Jolly, isn't it? Heh! Heh!"

Gary looked at Jerry Black. "Monthly report?" he said questioningly.

Jerry nodded. "The state assigned me as a special investigating agent to see if I could get any ideas as to who was killing people in the Espectros. That's why I pretended to be writing a book while I stayed at the old Mills place. It gave me an excuse to look about in those mountains. Frankly, I didn't believe much in those killings, but I liked the freedom the job gave me, except when I was keeping an eye on you two characters.

"What do you mean?" asked Tuck.

Jerry grinned. "Oh, I was watching you. It wasn't easy because of that dog. He seemed to know a real Apache was prowling about. The only time I really got worried was the night you boys were coming out of this canyon and Gary took a couple of potshots at me."

"So that was you!" said Gary. "You nearly scared us to death!"

"How do you think I felt when you shot at me?" said Jerry. "Kid, you shot as fast and as accurately as any combat Marine I ever knew."

"I wasn't trying to hit you," said Gary. "Just scare you off."

"You did that!"

"Did you ever really suspect anyone?" asked Sue.

Jerry shook his head. "I had no leads at all. Of course, I knew there were all kinds of oddball characters poking about those mountains. I had nothing on any of them."

"Did you ever suspect Fred Piatt?" asked Gary.

"Him?" Jerry threw back his head and laughed. "The Candyman is scared to death of those mountains. He is the last person I'd ever suspect."

"That's rich," said Jim Kermit with a grin. "The Candyman! Hawww!"

The sheriff shook his head. "You kids," he said with a smile.

"Tell 'em, Tuck," said Gary.

The lean one emptied his coffee cup. He *told 'em,* complete with histrionic gestures and intonations that would have put a Barrymore to utter shame. At the conclusion of his harrowing tale, Sue took out the three gold ingots and handed them to the sheriff. He hefted them and whistled softly. "You say there are a lot more of 'em in that mine?"

"Enough to make all of us richer than Croesus," said Sue offhandedly. She casually inspected her dirty and broken fingernails. "Maybe buried forever, of course," she added.

"Incredible," said the lawman.

––––––

THEY TOOK the three worn-out kids up behind them and rode to the jeep. Gary got the motor started on the third try.

Jerry leaned on his saddle horn and eyed Gary. "Did you know there were a number of rewards posted for the murderer?" he asked.

"No," said Gary. He was sick of talking about the Candyman.

"Amounts to somewhere between three and four thousand dollars as far as I can recollect. *Dead or alive,* Gary."

"We can guide you back to the body, Jerry," said Gary. "But I'd rather not talk about it now."

"I understand."

Gary drove to the graveled road and then along it toward the main highway. Tuck spoke when they were on the pavement. "Well, we found out the truth about Asesino *and* the Lost Espectro. I wonder what Fred Piatt thought when he saw me coming down that slope. Must have been quite a jolt."

"It was," said Gary. "Enough of a jolt to kill him off. The Candyman. When I think of those four days I rode in the same truck with him, shooting off my mouth about my theories on the Lost Espectro and all the clues I had, it makes me pretty weak inside, I tell you."

"He must have spent a lot of time in those mountains," said Sue, "without even a good lead on the Lost Espectro until *we* showed him the way."

"Poor Lije," said Tuck. "All he probably wanted was a can of Elberta peaches from the Candyman. It was his death sentence. They'll never find Lije's body now."

"Maybe that's the way he wanted it," said Gary quietly.

"There will be more ghosts in the Espectros tonight," said Sue. Suddenly, she shivered.

"As far as I'm concerned," said Gary, "they can have the Espectros. I've had my fill of them."

"Me too," said Sue fervently.

A gentle and melodious snoring came from the lean one, seemingly echoed by the low growling of thunder over the rain-misted Espectros.

CHAPTER FIFTEEN

A Person Without Dream is Dead

G ary Cole came out of the shop with his mother's Christmas gift tucked under his arm. The cold December wind swept down from the Espectros and moaned through the lamplighted streets of Cottonwood Wells. Gary looked up and down the street for Tuck and his Honda. The lean one was standing at the nearest corner beside his motorcycle, talking to a girl. Gary walked toward them.

It would be a good Christmas for the Coles. What with the reward money and the money from the gold they had taken from the Lost Espectro, the Coles were making plans for the dude ranch Pete had always wanted.

Gary eyed the girl as he came up behind Tuck. She was a doll, tall, dark-haired, and well-dressed. "Hey, *amigo*," he said. "Introduce me!"

Tuck turned slowly. "You loco, man? Remember our partner when we hunted the Lost Espectro? The one who got shipped off to boarding school in Phoenix to keep her from fooling around the Espectros?"

Gary stared at her. Gone were the ugly braces and the generous sprinkling of freckles. Gone was the short-cropped and untidy hairdo. Gone were the Levi's and the faded checkered shirt, the battered old hat, and the dusty boots. Susan Alice Browne was no longer the hoyden who had helped solve the mystery of the Espectros. She was now a young lady.

"Close your mouth, Gary," she said gently. "You look much better that way." She smiled. "I was allowed home for Christmas."

"You make it sound like a reform school," said Tuck.

Gary swallowed. "How is it, Sue?" he asked.

She raised her head a little. "I must say the atmosphere is more congenial and *much, much* more *polished* than that of Cottonwood Wells Union High."

"Yeh," said Tuck. "Lookit her, Gary!"

Gary actually felt embarrassed. The metamorphosis of Susan Browne from lowly caterpillar into lovely butterfly was almost impossible to believe.

Tuck grinned. "Gary doesn't have a date yet for the Christmas dance, Sue."

She smiled gently. "A *kid* dance? Rock and roll, no less!"

Gary eyed her, and the devil took over. "Well, Sue, I'd be happy to take you, but I'm not sure I want to go myself. Jerry Black thinks he has a good lead on a couple of burro-loads of silver that were buried near Massacre Spring about seventy years ago, and since we have Christmas vacation now, Tuck and I figured we'd take a crack at looking for it. So we have to get our plans made and our gear ready. Sorry about the dance. Good night, Sue." He started to walk toward his jeep.

"Gary Cole!" she snapped. "So happens I *do* want to go to that dance with you! So happens I have a Christmas vacation *too*! And if you think for one minute that you and my cousin Tucker C. Browne are going to look for that silver without *me*, you have another thing coming!"

Tuck rolled up his eyes. "Now you've done it, Gary," he said. "Can't trust you one minute."

THE THREE EXPERIENCED treasure hunters started out through the cold night air toward the Cole ranch, Sue Browne riding beside Gary in the jeep and Tucker C. Browne leading the way on his roaring Honda, trying to cut down his time between The Wells and the ranch. To the northeast bulked the dark and brooding Espectros, still holding many of their old secrets and perhaps some new ones as well. They held a spell over those who had been born in their shadows, a spell that could never be broken in a lifetime. For if the Espectros had not given the trio of treasure hunters great riches, at least they had given them a place to hunt for them, and a person without a dream is dead.

THE SECRET OF THE SPANISH DESERT

To Gary Mark and Dale Allen

CHAPTER ONE

Prowler in the Dark

The rain was moving swiftly across the cloud-darkened desert far south of the legendary Espectro Mountains that notched the dim northern horizon. Beyond the huge silvery column of slanted raindrops, the sun was shining brightly, forming a magnificent double rainbow that arched through the swirling pillar of rain to touch one shimmering leg above the soaked hills beyond Lechuguilla Wash.

The rain swept on, almost like a searchlight beam from the heavens, and where it touched, the parched land was thoroughly soaked and darkened, while, beyond the wetness, the yellow sands and the dark rocks were as bone dry as they had been for many months.

It was a lonely country, seldom traveled by man, and only alive at night with the coming of the hunters and the hunted. The silent bobcat hunted down the dainty kit fox while the kit fox was pursuing the timid pocket mouse, and overhead, the velvety winged owl drifted its swift shadow between the earth and the ice-chip stars, searching with its uncanny vision for game.

With the coming of the dawn, they would all disappear, and for a time, the birds would make music heard only by their own kind until they too vanished before the enervating and deadly heat of the desert day.

The day's heat had passed with the coming of the flash Storm that was beating its slow and majestic way across the land toward the distant mountains to the west. Within a matter of several hours, the twilight would follow the path of the rain.

It was the kind of country where a traveler seemed almost suspended in a sort of limbo, for the mountains never seemed closer no matter how long he moved toward them, and, despite the almost utter loneliness, there was always the feeling that one was under surreptitious surveillance from someone, or *something*, always just out of eyeshot no matter how swiftly and suddenly one turned his head to look.

Gary Cole turned in his saddle, almost expecting to see someone watching him, but the desert was as devoid of human life as it had been before, exclusive of himself, of course, and the bayo coyote horse he was riding.

The east wind had swirled up a dust devil, and it was racing parallel with the course of the rain, gathering up dust, rootless brush, and other odds and ends from the desert floor as neatly as a housemaid sweeps a floor, only to perversely scatter the debris somewhere else and then rush on to other areas to repeat the same senseless process over and over again.

The Espectros were now nothing but dim humped shapes against the sky. Gary's father's ranch nestled close to the base of those mountains, but nothing of it could be distinguished. Gary was reaching the end of his second day's ride across the eastern approaches to the legendary Spanish Desert. It was but one of a number of names by which that vast area of wasteland was known.

Indeed, most of the modern maps did not call the desert by its old name, but to Gary Cole, incurable romantic and hunter of lost treasures as well as of the fascinating legends that surrounded them and at times obscured them entirely, it would always be the Spanish Desert.

The Spanish Desert was the lure that had called to Gary many a sleepless night as he lay in his bed at Chiricahua Springs Ranch looking from the open window toward the moon-bathed hills far to the south of the ranch.

No one bothered much about the Spanish Desert in these times. It was so *highly* prized that the Air Force had used it as a gunnery and bombing range during World War II and the Korean conflict—and then even that use had run its course, and the old desert had been allowed to return to its native state, still pocked here and there by rocket, bomb, and machine-gun holes.

In time, the yawning desert would slowly and carefully fill in the holes, cover the bits of rusted metal, sweep away the debris, and then settle slowly back into its ages-long rest. Yet, all the time, it seemed to Gary Cole as though the Spanish Desert was hiding things... things of great interest to that person who would brave that deserted and yet enchanted land to search for them.

Gary reached the first of the low, sand-buried hills and rode up to its crest to look to the south. There were more hills dotting the more or less level desert floor, and beyond them, like a great backdrop, rose the humped shapes of mountains, lead-colored and hairless of growth like the wrinkled hide of an old elephant.

The rain was north-west now, rushing on toward far-distant California, but it probably would never get there. The sun was slanting low as well. The rays picked out bright flecks of mica and quartz on the desert floor. Something caught Gary's eye. A lone stone, rather smoothly shaped, thrust itself up through the encroaching sands, and nature, by some touch of worship, had carved deeply into the stone the shape of a cross.

Gary rode down the wet slope of the hill. He was

riding now just about where the end of the rainbow had been. He grinned to himself.

"Oughta be a pot of gold around here, Mickey," he said to the horse. He grinned again. "I haven't been away from those dudes at the ranch for two days, and already I'm talking to my horse like the hero in a western!"

He was riding past the stone when he suddenly drew rein. He kneed the bay closer to the stone and looked down upon the eroded cross. He narrowed his eyes. No quirk of nature, by wind, rain, and frost, had so neatly incised *that* stone.

Gary whistled softly and then dismounted. He knelt on the damp sand and traced the shape of the cross with a forefinger. There wasn't any doubt in his mind but that that cross had been cut by the hand of man, and a long time past—perhaps as much as a century or more. He examined the stone for other markings, but nothing else had been carved upon it.

Gary squatted on his heels and looked about the area. He was in a large, bowl-shaped area encompassed by the low hills. There were no signs of past habitation. No low, eroded adobe walls or rusted stretches of barbed wire met the eye. It wasn't cattle country. Little life could exist there except the furtive and rarely seen creatures native to it.

There were tiny placitas much farther south, but more to the east, for the country due south extended deep into Mexican Sonora, and the features of it hardly changed. No one had lived there in centuries past, and no one lived there now. Even legend would admit little about man living in that harsh and pitiless desert.

Gary stood up and shoved back his hat. Perhaps some poor fellow had died in the Spanish Desert and had been buried here. A Spanish conquistador, perhaps a wandering padre, or a leather-jacketed lancer from Mexican times. It wasn't like the Americans who had flooded that country after the Civil War and then passed on after realizing that it held no profit other than a harsh beauty singularly its own to leave such markers as this. They might place a cross atop the grave of an unfortunate companion, but Americans were jackknife artists, whittlers in wood, rather than carvers in stone. They would have placed a crude cross of time-silvered wood atop the grave.

It was almost an eerie feeling that crept through him as he stood there. Who had placed this marker here, and why? Some of the canyons of the Espectros held carved symbols. He knew them well enough, for the summer before, he and his pal, Tucker C. "Tuck" Browne, along with Tuck's cousin Susan Browne, had solved the long-standing mystery of the Lost Espectros Mine, after some hair-raising adventures in the mysterious canyon depths of those lonely and seldom penetrated mountains.

Gary Cole had been an avid student of lost treasures ever since he could remember; a far better student of such matters than of his school work, he had to admit. He would have been much higher in the final standings of his June graduating class at Cottonwood Wells Union High School if he had applied himself more to his school work. As it was, he had just managed to keep up a good enough average to be admitted to State in the coming fall.

"I'm supposed to be looking for riding trails for the dudes back at the ranch," Gary said aloud, as though to steady himself on his course of duty. He grinned. "I wonder if Dad really believed that whopper," he added.

————

IT HAD BEEN A LONG, hard, early summer for Gary. Chiricahua Springs Ranch had started business in the spring with a small group of dudes wintering in Arizona, not really expecting any of them to remain for the late spring and early summer. But such had not been the case.

The ranch was situated in a breezy area, shadowed for part of the day by the nearby mountains and thus avoiding the terrible heat of the desert summer, and so some of the dudes had lingered on and on, keeping the three Coles, Pete Cole, Gary's father, managing the ranch, Lucille Cole, Gary's mother, handling the domestic duties, and Gary acting as jack-of-all-trades.

There had been help, of course. Tuck Browne worked part-time, but some of the situations for which Tuck had a natural bent had almost ruined business once or twice. But he was a willing worker—too willing, thought Gary wryly.

Business would pick up in the fall, from all indications, and State wasn't so far away that Gary could not make it home weekends with Tuck to help at the ranch.

Meanwhile, business had quieted down enough for Pete Cole to let Gary take off a few days to explore for new riding trails. Fact is, Gary had never been able to fight off the lure of the Spanish Desert country.

He had had to come alone. Tuck had gone to Phoenix to see about a new motorcycle to replace his beloved and battered Honda that had reached a tragic end one dark night on a rutted road by running into the business end of a Hereford bull. As well built as the Honda had been, the bull had won the challenge match and had gone on off into the night, bellowing in triumph.

THE SUN WAS TIPPING the far western range. Already, a cool and questing breeze was tentatively feeling its way across the Spanish Desert, bringing its warning of the coming night. Gary looked down at the marker again, then withdrew his map case from a saddlebag and carefully marked it on the empty spaces of the sketch map he was making. Later, he would fill in the features on the large, carefully plotted map he had at home. He made compass bearings and entered them on the map, then placed it back in the saddlebag.

He had reached the far hills at the southern end of the bowl-shaped depression when the sun seemed suddenly to drop from sight. He led the bay up a slope and found an area of jumbled rocks that would give shelter from the cold night wind.

It was only a matter of minutes to make his simple camp, throwing down his sleeping bag, beating the ground to drive away possible snakes, placing his food and cooking gear on a flat rock, and kindling a fire from dry greasewood that had been blown into crevices among the rocks.

While the fire was burning down into coals, he watered the bay, filling his own dusty hat with water for the bay to drink from. He picketed the horse where there was a scanty patch of grazing, supplementing the food with oats from a sack he had slung across the cantle of his saddle.

He dined well on crisp bacon, canned beans, preserved peaches, and a slab of his mother's prime apple and raisin pie, slightly dry and stale, but not enough so a hungry man would notice it. He boiled his coffee and then sat down on a rock to pull off his boots to let the night air cool his feet. He had done a mess of walking that hot day to rest the bay.

The fact that he was alone in a lonely country didn't matter to Gary. He had been raised on the ranch—lived there almost all his life, in fact—working now and then for local ranchers, searching the canyons and the range for strays for days on end, so being alone hardly mattered to Gary Cole.

Still, he missed Tuck and his almost ceaseless chatter. Come to think of it, he missed Sue Browne as well. She was a good companion and brave as all get out. She'd be returning to boarding school in the fall, as well as Tuck and Gary. She had changed quite a bit in the past year, but the tomboy still in her had a way of taking over now and then, to the deep distress of her mother.

He climbed up on a tip-tilted slab of rock, still warm from the day's heat, and looked north toward the unseen Espectros. There was a faint, winking yellow eye of light over there, but he knew well enough that it wasn't from Chiricahua Springs. Even as he watched it, it vanished. Probably a car speeding across the empty country in a hurry to reach someplace where there were lights and people.

He looked south. The wind had shifted, whispering to him of what lay to the south. Mexico was down there beyond the vast wastes of the Spanish Desert. A man could hardly tell when he left Arizona and crossed into Mexican Sonora in that look-alike country. Faintly seen in the darkness were those brooding mountains. Not a light showed on them or near them.

Gary slid down the rock and fed his fire. The comforting glow of the flames lighted his tanned face, revealing the thick reddish hair and the steady gray eyes that always seemed to others to be looking through them, on into distant vistas of lost treasures and fascinating legends.

He thought again of the marker. It puzzled him. There were a few dim roads in that area, used decades ago and later by patrol vehicles when the area was a bombing and gunnery range, but none of those roads would have been marked by a cross-inscribed rock. No, if it was not a grave, it had been placed there to mark something of importance to the person or persons who had put it there.

Gary half closed his eyes and riffled through his mental files, trying to recreate some of the dim history of that lost land. The exploring conquistadores and brave padres had traveled either farther east or farther west, avoiding this country because of the harshness and the deadliness of it too.

There was reputed to be no water in the country except for the little that was left in natural rock tanks, or *tinajas,* in the granite mountains. A man, if he was lucky beyond all good fortune, might just be able to dig in the bed of a dry wash not long after one of the infrequent flash storms and find water. Even the barrel cactus, which held some moisture in its fat little belly a good part of the year in other parts of the Arizona deserts, was seemingly always shrunken and withdrawn in the Spanish Desert.

Gary unconsciously glanced at his canteens. He had three of them—two large ones and a smaller one—just enough to get him and the horse perhaps fifty miles or so into that lonely country and out again. If something should happen to that water... He cast the haunting thought from his mind.

He lay back against his saddle, moving his scabbarded Winchester to one side. He'd have to head back in the morning, perhaps after going a few miles farther south. There was always the long chance that he might find something interesting beyond the next hill. It was a sort of a curse, he supposed, having that foot itch to go on and on, always trying to see what was beyond the next hill, and the next, and the next...

There are some people who can live alone in remote and isolated country and like it, while others must have people about them. Most people are naturally gregarious, but Gary Cole was one of the fortunates: he was equally at home with others and with himself when alone.

A man can hardly be "alone" while watching the fleeting clouds race their drifting shadows across the desert and up and then down the mountainsides in a race that can never be won or lost, or in watching a fast-striding roadrunner run down a lizard or race ahead of a car down the center of a rutted road.

Then, too, there are voices in the vagrant wind, and in the dry rustling of the mesquite. There is the lonely hawk, so high in the clear air that he looks motionless, as though pasted against the sky like a scrap of charred paper. Best of all are the deep thoughts of past history and forgotten peoples, of lost mines and hidden canyons, of soldiers, priests, traders, Indians, and pioneers.

Gary thought again of that strange marker. He stood up and walked to the edge of the depression where he had made his camp. The bowl-shaped area was thick in velvet shadows now. It seemed as empty and primitive as it had been since the beginning of time. He shook his head. There was no answer yet, but, in his own slow and stubborn way, he'd mull over the puzzle, constantly seeking a solution until he found it. He'd have to find the answer, or he'd never rest.

———

LATER, he crawled into his sleeping bag and lay for a long time looking up at the winking ice-chip stars. Somewhere, far across the emptiness, a coyote howled into the night. Lonely as the sound was, it still sounded good to Gary. At least he wasn't completely alone in that long uninhabited desert.

He rolled over in his sleep and half opened his eyes. Something seemed to probe into his mind... A subtle warning of something wrong. He raised his head and peered about the dark depression in which he lay. A faint trickling sound came to him. A moment later, the bay whinnied sharply.

Gary was out of the clinging sleeping bag in an instant, gripping the cold metal and wood of his rifle, peering into the darkness, swinging the rifle to cover the area. The trickling sound annoyed him. He peered toward it, then suddenly realized what it was. He darted to the rock ledge where he had left his canteens. The bay whinnied again. Gary's Winchester butt struck metallically against the rock.

Even in the darkness, he could see that the canteens lay on their sides, the caps removed and hanging by their metal chains, and a dark, spreading mark of wetness on the dry rock. He snatched each canteen in turn and stoppered them, then spun on a heel to run toward where the bay had been picketed. Something sounded low on the southern slope. He jumped up on the rocks, forgetting that he shouldn't silhouette himself, and stared down into the concealing shadows.

Cold sweat worked its way down his sides, chilling him as the night wind whispered across the empty miles and swept about him. There was nothing to see or hear. He pulled on his cold-stiffened boots and walked slowly and quietly to the bay. The bay shied and blew, then nuzzled up against him. Gary picked up the picket line and followed it to the pin. The pin lay on the ground. He had set it well into the ground between two rocks. It was hardly possible that the bay could have pulled it loose.

He looked off into the darkness again. There was nothing to see...not a sound except the dry whispering of the wind through the scanty growths that stippled the harsh earth.

A colder feeling came over Gary, this time engendered by the unseen face of fear, gibbering at him, slack-mouthed, from the darkness. He gripped the rifle tightly. A flesh-and-blood creature would feel the weight of a .32/20 slug, but the supernatural would not be harmed.

He fought for control, then walked back to his camp, leading the bay behind him. He tethered it to a rock, then lifted his saddle and placed it on the horse. The dawn wasn't far off. Already, there were faint pewter traces in the eastern sky, and the wind was shifting.

He reached for his saddlebags to fill them with the odds and ends that lay scattered about. They were surprisingly light. He thrust a hand into them. His food was gone.

Gary looked about the camp as the faint dawn light

began to filter through the gloom. There was no trace of the food containers. He walked over to his canteens. He was too experienced a traveler in desert country to leave his canteens unstopped. He shook each canteen. There was hardly enough water in the three of them together to fill a quart bottle. One of the stoppers might have come loose, but certainly not all *three* of them.

Someone had been about the camp, prowling on silent feet within a yard or so of Gary as he slept peacefully, and helplessly, if the truth be known. Maybe a desert rat looking for loot. He had likely taken the food and might have been trying to steal the horse as well about the time that Gary had awakened. It was the matter of the missing water that really bothered him. If the man had wanted water, he'd hardly have let all three canteens fall over to lose their precious contents. Why had he taken the food and not the water?

"Who?" said Gary aloud.

The bay whinnied as though in perplexity.

————

HE WORKED his way down the south slope as the light grew. Halfway down the slope, he found that for which he was looking. He squatted to study the ground. Several small rocks had been disturbed, for the heavier, darker sides were upward. Rocks tend to lie with the heavy sides down, and of course, being beneath the soil, they would be darker than the constantly exposed tops.

Beyond the disturbed rocks were faint marks, hardly distinguishable to anyone but a person who was well trained in such matters, and Gary had had the best of instruction. One of his instructors had been Jerry Black Eagle, a pure quill Chiricahua, who had served with Gary's father in the Marines in World War II, and was now a special law officer for the state.

The sun was tipping the eastern ranges when he

walked back to his camp. There was no chance now of continuing farther south. He was almost out of water; indeed, he had just about enough to make it back to Mesquite Wells. He'd *have* to go back.

He looked down into the bowl-shaped depression and then narrowed his eyes. Faintly seen on the harsh surface of the dry ground were parallel lines. He had not seen them the day before, but now the rising sun was casting the minutest of shadows across them. Even as he watched, they vanished as the sun rose higher. Unless nature was playing another trick on him, he had seen ruts from an ancient road. Maybe the marker he had seen had something to do with the road. Road? What road would lead anywhere in the Spanish Desert? It just didn't make sense.

Gary hefted his coffee pot. There were about two cupfuls of the strong fluid left from his evening meal. He might as well drink it, for in the hours to come, it would grow a little on the bitter side. He kicked some brushwood together, then walked toward a deep crevice to pick up a chunk of wood that lay there. As he lifted it, he noticed curiously that it was shaped. He stared at it. It was familiar enough. An ox yoke! "Curiouser and curiouser," he murmured. It had been generations since oxen had been used in Arizona.

Later, he sipped his coffee, eyeing the ancient yoke. A strange cross-inscribed marker, the faint traces of an ancient road, a long-weather-beaten ox yoke. It all added up to something—but what?

———

HE RODE the bay down the slope, looking for the faint ruts, but could not distinguish them. A person had to see them at just the right time. The ox yoke bumped behind him where he had lashed it to the saddle cantle. He reined in the bay to look at the cross-inscribed marker.

There was something else on his mind, however, as he felt the first strong blast of the summer sun on his shoulders and the side of his face. Whoever had taken his food had deliberately emptied out his water, knowing well enough that whoever was without water in that area had at least fifty thirsty miles' travel to the north to get more water. It was almost like premeditated murder.

"But why?" he said aloud.

"*Why indeed...why indeed...why indeed?*" intoned the dry, hot wind as it swept across the lonely Spanish Desert.

CHAPTER TWO

Legend of the Lost Mission

Tuck Browne and Gary Cole walked slowly down the wide steps in front of the Cottonwood Wells Library. Tuck leaned his head back and stared in wide-eyed astonishment at the motorcycle parked at the curb. "Man!" he said. "You don't suppose some good little boy, with a gold-plated heart and the purest of motives, a lad who helps old ladies across the street and puts out the trash when his Momma tells him to, got *that* for his good deeds?"

Gary grinned. "Yeah," he said drily. "About six feet of good little boy by the name of Tucker C. Browne."

Tuck's lean face split into an expansive smile. "Of course! It was *me*, alla time!"

Gary stopped at the curb and eyed the resplendent machine. "Personally, I'll take a horse."

"Why?"

"It'll take you places that thing won't go."

"Wanna bet?" snarled Tuck. "We've been through this before, friend." He tilted his head to one side. "Anyways, it don't take water like a horse, and it gets you there and back a lot faster."

There was something in Tuck's tone that caused Gary to study his friend. "Meaning?" he asked quietly.

Tuck shrugged. "Meaning you darned near didn't get back from that solo performance of yours in the Spanish Desert last week, that's all!"

"Listen, Tucker," said Gary patiently. "In the first place, I wasn't quite in the Spanish Desert. In the second place, it wasn't any fault of mine, or of my horse, that I lost the water."

"Even so. Personally, I think you've flipped your wig."

"Meaning?"

Tuck straddled the seat of his bike. "All this talk about finding that cross marker, a road that shouldn't be in the desert, an ox yoke, so forth and so forth. Can't mean a thing, *amigo*. You heard what Mrs. Wittman, the librarian, said about a road being out there."

Gary waved a hand. "Sure, she didn't have any record of it. Maybe a record was never made of it in English."

"You're talking kookie."

"Look," said Gary. "That is an *old* road. A *very* old road. That road existed before the time of the Americans' arrival out here. Maybe when the Spaniards were fooling around out there."

"I can't believe it. You see a couple of lines on the sand, and you claim right away it's a road. Big deal! Who'd put a road out there? You said yourself there wasn't any reason for a road being out there."

"There's no reason *now*," said Gary quietly. "Maybe there hasn't been a reason in a hundred or more years, but there *was* a reason at one time."

"Such as?"

"Something the Spaniards built out there."

"Like what?" jeered Tuck.

Gary looked up and down the empty sidewalk as though not wanting to speak so that someone might hear him. "You ever hear of the Lost Mission?" he asked softly.

Tuck stared at him. "*That* phony story? Man, I take your word on lots of these phony-baloney lost treasure stories, but I don't bite on that one. Gary, they've *found* all the old missions in Arizona and the Southwest. You oughta know that."

Gary shook his head. "There are lost missions in Sonora," he said,

"You said Sonora. That proves you don't believe there's a lost mission south of here."

"Man, you ain't too bright. Tucker. Sonora and Arizona were all one country in those days. Those old Spaniards and Mexicans didn't have to get an O.K. from the customs to come over here. They built missions at Tumacacori and Tucson and around where Yuma is now, didn't they? There was another one somewhere northwest of Nogales, I think. Why couldn't there be one around here?"

"You're hopeless."

"A little one?" said Gary.

Tuck fiddled with the throttle of the bike, then looked sideways at Gary. "When do we leave?" he asked.

"I'll pop in for a burger and fries at Bennie's Barbecue and outline my plan."

Tuck hesitated. "That include a double-thick malt?"

Gary took out his wallet and studied the contents, wrinkling his brow. "I can just make it," he said.

"Hop on, gourd-head!"

They shot down the street as though the devil was riding on their coattails. Gary closed his eyes. It was better that way. He didn't want to see the way Tuck was driving.

"Haven't broken her in yet!" said Tuck over his shoulder. "You just wait, pal!"

"Yeah," said Gary faintly. "What *else* I got to do?"

———

LATER, as they sat at an outside table, shielded from the burning sun by a large and gaudy umbrella, Gary told

Tuck of his ideas. "Somewhere south of where I camped are those lonely old mountains. The road must go that way, for it was a north-south road. When I was making my way back to Mesquite Wells, I kept looking for other markers, or ruts, with no luck, which doesn't mean a thing, for the road could have been wiped out of existence by drifting sand and flash storms or it could have turned east or west without my seeing the turn. I figure that if we go to where I camped, then keep on south toward those old mountains, we might pick up more clues."

"Yeah," said Tuck. He noisily drained the last of his malt through the big straws. "But what about that monkey-business at your camp? That stealing of your food, the dumped water, and so on?"

Gary shrugged. "A desert rat, maybe. Two-legged variety."

"Yen," said Tuck softly. "Seems to me, though, when I last heard about the Lost Mission, there was a story about something else."

"Like what?" asked Gary.

"Every story I ever heard about the place mentioned that it was haunted. Haunted, maybe, by the old padres, guarding something there."

"Oh, you always hear about those places being haunted and full of treasure, which no one ever finds. I don't think those old missions were that rich that they'd leave buried treasure lying around. They'd take it with them when they went."

"So?" said Tuck. "Then why are we going there?"

Gary looked out across the empty, heat-shimmering country to the southeast of Cottonwood Wells. "Because it's there," he said quietly.

"We hope," said Tuck. "Maybe we ought to wait until the weather cools off. It's like hades out there now."

"Not at night," said Gary. "The new moon is due. We can travel at night and hole up during the day."

"You're always thinking with your head," said Tuck. "But *I'm* still thinking about whoever it was, or whatever it was, that kiped your food and dumped your water. Another thing, pal, it doesn't seem possible that a big building, like most of those missions were, could just be *lost*. If it ever existed, there couldn't be much of it left to see. A lot of planes have flown over that country in the past twenty years or so. Isn't it a sure bet that *one* of those pilots would have seen something?"

"Sure," said Gary, "but they weren't looking for *lost* missions, Tuck. They were on bombing and gunnery missions, and both times the area was used for such missions, it was during war—World War II and the Korean conflict. All those Air Force boys were interested in was completing their gunnery course and getting back to other duty."

"What about commercial planes?"

"There are no commercial routes over the Spanish Desert."

"Private planes?"

"They don't like to fly over it. They follow the highways or the railroads, makes navigation simpler. Besides, ever since that one private plane force landed out there some years ago, most other private planes stay away from the desert."

"Yeah," said Tuck thoughtfully. "Come to think of it, they found the plane intact, ready to fly, except that it was out of gas. They never did find the people who had been in it. I wonder why?"

Gary picked up the check and stood up. "Likely they needed water and went to look for it. It wouldn't take long for heat and thirst to overcome them. It was the middle of the summer. You don't last long out there without shelter and water. Likely their bodies are out there somewhere. Maybe they'll find them some day, and maybe they won't."

"You make everything sound so cheerful," said Tuck. "When do we leave?"

"Give me a lift back to the ranch. Dad wants me to do an errand. After that, I'll have some free time."

"Not too busy these days, hey?"

Gary shook his head. "The Gatewoods are leaving today. The Penders left two days ago. I think someone else is due out today or tomorrow. Some people from the Los Angeles area."

"Any work for good ol' Tucker C. Browne? I have to keep that bike up in the style to which it is accustomed."

Gary grinned. "You can ask Dad. After the way you loused up that windmill-fixing job, you think you ought to ask him?"

"Well, it is an old windmill. All I was trying to do was give it a little more pep. How'd I know one of the vanes would fly off in that wind storm, thus unbalancing the wheel, which in turn cast off a few more vanes until you could get it stopped? How is it now?"

Gary took care of the check and walked toward the shining new motorcycle. "You'll see the ruins of it when we get out there."

———

THEY RODE east on the highway, with the distant loom of the Espectros to the northeast rising up magnificently from the desert floor. Gary had lived in their shadow almost all his life and had penetrated many of the mysterious canyons and gorges, but there were still a great many things he did not know about the Espectros, named well by the old Spanish explorers—the Ghost Mountains.

Tuck, Sue, and Gary had solved a mystery of many years' standing when they had found, and lost, the famous Lost Espectro Mine, but even in losing, they had gained, for their experiences and the solving of some baffling murders had given them much.

Tuck turned off on the road that led to Chiricahua Springs Ranch, raising a streamer of dust that could be seen for miles as he gunned the bike, driving with all the skill he possessed.

A chaparral cock burst from the brush and raced ahead of the roaring bike, full out, then darted off to one side when he realized that he'd never outrace Tucker C. Browne. A stray steer bolted clumsily out of the road and bellowed angrily as the bike roared past his tail.

The bike slammed across a wooden bridge, squirting dust up between the planks, the noise of its crossing causing low thunder that echoed back from the foothills of the Espectros. Tuck shot off the road just before a curve, threading his way through the thick and dusty brush.

A giant jackrabbit bounded out of the way. Desert quail broke from cover like the explosion of a shotgun shell. Lizards scuttled frantically out of the way. Tuck hit the road on the far side of the curve just as an oncoming station wagon came up out of a dry wash. There was nothing for Tuck to do but take to the fence line. The bike shot past the car, and Gary, glancing sideways, saw his father's stern face peering from the window.

The bike slammed through the fence, bounced down into the wash and up the other side like a surfboard taking a big wave, literally leaped into the air, and came down in a floundering crash in a hole that had been used for a dumping ground for many years. Rusted tin cans, broken bottles, sheets of metal, and broken dishes all arose in a shower about the bike.

It was then that Gary Cole abandoned ship, leaping like a frog from the rear of the seat, to land in a patch of cholla cactus, and as the needles tore into his shrinking flesh, his screams carried above the noise of the engine as Tuck throttled it down, righted the bike seemingly by sheer will power, and roared off through the brush in a mad swirling of dust.

Gary painfully crawled from the cholla patch and saw his father walking toward him with the faintest suggestion of a limp, a relic of his almost fatal war wounds. Pete Cole stopped at the broken fence, eyed the pall of dust in the quiet air, then looked at his only child. "You're either the most courageous lad in Arizona or the maddest," he said drily. "Riding with that madman."

Gary picked a cactus needle from his left hand. "He's always pretty sensible until he gets on that bike," he said. "I'm sorry, Dad. I'll fix the fence."

Pete nodded. "Forget the apologies," he said. "I think you've suffered enough. Did you find anything out about the Lost Mission?" There was the faintest suggestion of a twinkle in his eyes.

Gary limped out of the trash hole. "Nope," he said with a mournful sigh.

"I didn't think you would, but thinking about such things keeps you out of trouble. Well, I've got a job for you. Pardy Willis has some old relics he wants to get rid of. Said I could have them. I'd like to gussy up the ranch a bit with them. You know, for the dudes. You know where Pardy lives, don't you?"

"Uh-huh." Gary inspected a hole in the knee of his levis. "Down south, near Lookout Rock."

"You were there some years ago, as you may recall. Pardy will probably remember you. Pardy is getting crotchety, but underneath it, he's a fine old man."

The roaring of the bike had died away. The dust drifted off beyond the ranch buildings. Tuck had gotten that far, at least. Gary idly wondered what had stopped him. Likely a building or at least something other than a fence.

"I've left the pick-up for you. I've got to pick up some new dudes in the station wagon."

"That's good news, anyway."

Pete Cole nodded. "I think we'll have a good year, kid. Not enough people staying here, so we have to knock ourselves out taking care of them and plenty of time to get ready for the winter season."

"I won't be around to help much after college starts. Dad."

Pete Cole smiled. He placed a hand on Gary's shoulder.

"Listen, kid. If it hadn't been for you, we might have lost the ranch altogether. That gold and the reward money you brought in from the Lost Espectro thing saved our hash. But, beyond that, it's something else."

"So?"

Pete nodded. He looked up at the looming mountains, now thickening with late afternoon shadows. "Publicity," he said quietly. "People around here have always known of the history of Chiricahua Springs Ranch and the legends of the Espectros, but it took all those newspaper stories and that magazine article to bring in the dudes. God bless 'em! I don't think they've been disappointed."

Gary grinned. "Personally, I think it's Mom's cooking that does the trick."

Pete Cole nodded. "It's kept the two of us happy."

"And Tucker C. Browne as well."

Pete's face sobered. "Yeah. Well, take him along, but don't let him con you into taking the bike with him. Another thing: *you* do the driving! Got it?"

"Yes, sir."

Gary watched his father walk back to the station wagon. Pete Cole had changed a lot in the past months. Before that time, his war wounds and the fact that he might lose the ranch, passed on in the family for almost a hundred years since tough James Cole had built the place in Apache-infested country a year after the end of the Civil War, had deeply shadowed Pete Cole's life. James Cole had fought Apaches, squatters, desperadoes, and anyone else who had disputed his right to that land. His son, Gary's grandfather, had also held out through drought and the depredations of rustlers to hold the ranch. It would have gone hard with *his* son to lose it in times of peace and prosperity.

Gary walked slowly back to the fence and along the fence line toward the ranch buildings, relishing the late afternoon quiet after the noisy approach to the ranch.

Local wags said that someday Tucker C Browne would roar on into the twilight and never return but that his lean ghost, bent low over the handlebars, masked face staring intently ahead, would haunt the roads of that country for generations to come, something like the Flying Dutchman, forever doomed to travel on and on through eternity.

It was better to travel at night, thought Gary, as he reached the main gate of the ranch. If they got to Pardy's too late, they could always bunk in the back of the truck, rigged out as it had been by Pete Cole, a handy man with tools, in the form of his own ideas of a camperback. There was a thirty-gallon water tank with an outside spigot placed on the truck body, as well as an extra gas tank. The truck wasn't new, but it was in good shape, with four-wheel drive and a winch on the front of it. A man could go most any place in comparative safety in the truck.

Gary's mother was waiting for him on the front porch of the house. "Gary," said Lucille Cole quietly, "I'll have to forbid you to ride with Tucker on that bike of his. If there was no way for you to get back from town, I would have come for you."

Gary smiled. "Wasn't Tucker's fault," he said. "He didn't see Dad coming up out of the wash."

"He would have seen him if he wasn't driving like a madman as usual."

"Well, it was a little dusty," said Gary.

"With no wind? All the dust we saw here at the ranch

was caused by Tuck's bike. Some of the guests thought it was a whirlwind coming."

"It was," said Gary drily.

"I'll have to talk to his mother about his driving," said Lucille Cole.

Tuck poked his dusty face out of the nearby window, mouth full as usual. "Won't do any good, Mrs. Cole," he said soberly. "She drives that ol' bike faster than I do. You should see *her* go!"

Lucille shook her head. "I give up. When are you leaving, Gary?"

"Tonight, if it's all right."

"It's all right with me. Do you want to eat now?"

"You're too busy. We had a burger and fries at Bennie's."

"I'll round up something for you. There's half of a fresh apple and raisin pie left over."

"*Was,*" said a mysterious masculine voice from beyond the window...

It was Sue Browne, Tuck's dark-haired cousin, who made up the food for the boys under the close supervision of Tuck. "Some people have all the luck," she said crossly.

"Meaning you can't go along, eh?" said Tuck. "Put in a couple more cans of sardines, Sue."

"There are two cans in there now," Sue said.

"Sardines go good on ham sandwiches."

"Oh, Lord," breathed Sue.

Gary knew what was bugging her. She wanted to go along in the worst way. "Nothing but dusty old desert down there, Sue," he said.

"Don't butter me up," she said as she finished packing the food. "You two characters aren't just going down there to get some rusty old relics from Pardy Willis' junk-yard of a place. You've got something else on your feeble *little-boy* minds."

"Like what. Sue?" asked Tuck.

"I've heard something about you two getting interested in the Lost Mission. If it *does* exist."

Tuck opened his mouth to argue with his cousin. As skeptical as he acted toward the Lost Mission when around Gary, he'd defend Gary's belief in it to the death if need be. Gary quickly shook his head. Tuck closed his mouth. He really didn't look too bad when his mouth was closed, thought Gary. Rather an unusual way for Tucker to be, though. Gary often wondered if he kept it closed when he was asleep.

"Lost Mission!" snapped Sue. "Pah!"

"Pah to you, too," said Tuck impolitely as he picked up the food hamper. "Kinda light," he complained. He headed quickly for the door before Sue could grab the hamper from his greedy little hands.

"All we're doing is going down to Pardy Willis' place," said Gary in a kindly tone. "Maybe we can take you some place when we get back, when you're not helping my mother."

"That's more than you're doing," said Sue.

Gary shrugged. Sue was in one of her tiger moods. Not that he could blame her. The flame of adventure, the seeking of the lost and the mysterious, burned as brightly in Sue as it did in Tuck and Gary.

"Well, I hope you don't learn anything at all down there," said Sue. She banged her way out onto the back porch.

"Pardy Willis! Humph!"

Gary walked outside. The sun was gone, and the sky was dark. A faint feeling of wind was in the cooling air. "We'll be back late tomorrow night, most likely. Mom," he said. "You know Pardy. Great talker when he gets started on one of his favorite subjects."

"I know you and Tuck too," she said drily.

Gary got into the truck. Lobo, his big dog, came swiftly out of the darkness and eyed the tailgate, readying himself for a leap. Those bunks in the back were right comfortable for a dog who had spent a good part of his day chasing around in the heat. "Not this trip, Lobo," said Gary. "You stay here and guard Mom, Sue, and the guests."

"Maybe somebody oughta guard against Sue," said Tuck. He climbed into the pick-up and settled the hamper between his bony knees, as though it was a rare treasure not to be let out of sight. Gary drove out onto the road, glancing back to see some of the guests riding toward the corrals. His mother would soon be serving them. There was a different air about the old ranch now, a feeling of life and gaiety, and it seemed to suit his mother, but then she too had once been depressed about losing the ranch.

"Times have changed," said Tuck.

Gary glanced at him. "Yeah. Sue was sure angry about us going without her."

"Can't take her everywhere," said Tuck. "She seems to think we've got ulterior motives or something, instead of going down there for a lot of rusty junk."

"Yeah," said Gary. "Funny thing about Sue, though, pal, she's usually got a nose for the unusual."

They were rolling swiftly along the highway, heading east toward the turn that would head them south, when they suddenly looked at each other. "By golly," said Tuck. "I think she *knows* something!"

"It just registered on me too," said Gary. "I just remembered that Pardy Willis is a walking encyclopedia when it comes to stories of lost treasures, legends, mines, trails, and anything else that went on in and around the Spanish Desert."

"Lookout Rock overlooks the beginning of the Spanish Desert," said Tuck. "Come to think of it, that's how it got its name."

A mile farther on, Gary turned onto the road that led to Pardy's place many miles to the south. "Another thing," he said quietly. "Dad didn't need that stuff from

Pardy in such an all-fired hurry. It could have waited. You don't suppose he thought up this trip just to help find the Lost Mission, do you?"

"He's a Cole, ain't he?" said Tuck. "Devious and sly, underhanded and subtle, crafty, wily, artful, shrewd, acute, and intriguing."

"Knock it off," said Gary. "I get the point, lunkhead."

The faint light of the moon showed against the eastern sky. In time, it would flood silvery rays down the western side of the mountains and reach out to expose the sleeping and brooding Spanish Desert west of the old paved road upon which Gary and Tuck were traveling. They'd not likely see any other travelers on that road. The county kept it in some sort of repair only to service the few people who lived near it. There weren't many living east of it and none at all west of it, for that was the mysterious and deadly expanse of the Spanish Desert.

Now and then, as Gary drove on, while Tuck nodded, half asleep beside him, he'd glance out across the lightening desert. It was calling to him again. Someone had once lived there. Someone who had made a road generations past and had left a marker beside that road. A marker with a cross cut into it. Somewhere at the end of that road might be the Lost Mission.

CHAPTER THREE

The Hermit of Lookout Rock

No one lived near Pardy Willis, which was all right with them and even more so with Pardy Willis. It was easy enough to find his place if one wanted to go there. Thrusting itself up from the rolling desert floor, a mile from the seldom-traveled branch road, was the naked pinnacle of rock known as Lookout Rock. It seemed to be a warning linger of stone to keep the curious from penetrating into the dangerous wastes of the Spanish Desert to the south and west.

One could not see Pardy's place from the road, for he had established himself on the far side of the rock many years ago. Some said to take advantage of the dubious shade of the rock in the hellish heat of the summer and to shelter from the bitter sweeping winds of the winter. Others said that old Pardy, out of sheer dislike for the human race individually and in general, hid himself from the sight of anyone who traveled the lonely road.

Pete Cole had said more than once that the Spanish Desert held a curious spell over Pardy Willis. At one and the same time, he loved it and hated it. He loved it for the drawing fascination such places have for some men, despite the innate cruelty and treachery of the place; he hated it because of what it was said to have done to him. Whatever the reason, Pardy Willis lived alone at Lookout Rock, gazing out over the heat-shimmering wastes by day and the gleaming, moon-lighted sands by night, or perhaps into the velvety darkness of the desert night, that seemed to be a living, breathing thing, waiting for the unwary to stumble into its meshes of heat, thirst, and eventual madness.

The moonlight picked out each mark and crevice on Lookout Rock, bathing the pinnacle in cold light and etching a shadow as sharp as a die upon the sand of the desert westerly beyond the rock. There were no other such formations with-in sight, although far to the southwest, just now being lighted by the moon, were the naked, hairless humps of the mountains, which were part and parcel of the deadliness and the brooding mystery of the Spanish Desert.

Tuck Browne shivered a little as he eyed the rock. Gary down-shifted gears to get the feel of the loose, sandy ruts of the winding trail that led toward the rock. Pardy's mailbox shone in the moonlight, nailed loosely to the top of a weather-silvered post, hanging at a drunken angle toward the sand, with a tumbleweed wedged up beneath the box. "Wonder how long since a Scars catalog was stuffed in there?" said Tuck.

"Last time the Pony Express went through here," said Gary drily. "I'm wondering when was the last time a car or a truck drove on this road, if you can call it that."

Tuck grinned. "Probably to deliver Pardy's draft notice for the Spanish-American War."

"Didn't have cars then," said Gary.

"Sure! That's why ol' Pardy never got his draft notice! Haw! Haw! Haw!" Tuck nudged Gary. "Get it? Pretty good, eh?"

"Oh, Lord, deliver me," said Gary, casting his eyes upward.

They drew closer to the rock. As yet, there was no

sight of Pardy's place except for the drifted ruts. The grinding of the truck wheels through the sand and the sound of the engine was about all that could be heard, and it seemed inordinately loud in the night. If there was anyone around the rock, he'd have heard the truck by now, but there was no sight of anything living.

"Like landing on the moon," said Tuck.

Suddenly, as they rounded a spur of the rock, they saw something glittering sharply in the moonlight. Gary slowed the truck. Both boys stared at the sight. It was a brass bedstead of ancient vintage, knobbed and furbelowed, posted and rodded, standing starkly on the bare sand, as though on display in the window of a furniture store before the turn of the century.

"You don't suppose?" said Tuck. He shook his head.

"Nawww!"

"I don't ever remember seeing that standing there when I was here before," said Gary.

"Might be some kind of spaceship," said Tuck.

"You've flipped."

"How do *we* know what one looks like?" retorted Tuck. "I saw a space movie one time when the Martians landed out here in the desert in something that looked like an Erector set gone completely crazy! Man, when them Martians came out of it, they *flowed* out. Big and green they were, with tentacles waving all over the place, and you could see their brains inside this green stuff like fruit in a gelatin salad like my Mom makes."

"Maybe you're right," said Gary. "Look, Tuck! *It's rising.*"

"*Urk!*" said Tuck. He ducked his head and bumped it against the dash of the truck. It seemed to ring like a bell.

Gary grinned. "You must have some silver in that head of yours," he said. "Like when the old Spaniards wanted to make a bell have a sweet tone, they'd mix a little silver in with the copper, or brass, or whatever they used. Sure made a difference."

They passed the brass bedstead and came closer to the towering pinnacle, grinding in low-low through the clogging sand. Between growths, they saw piles of rusted tin cans, an anvil nailed to a thick piece of log standing on end, a pile of ancient rubber tires gone gray from being so long exposed, a number of long-dried-out wagon wheels both of wood and of metal, rusted sheets of corrugated iron, a sagging sawhorse, and many other curious odds and ends, none of which the boys could identify.

Tuck looked about a little nervously. "You sure he still lives here?"

"Dad said he did. Dad was down this way some months ago, looking for relics for the ranch. Pardy always liked Dad. He knew my grandfather real well. Prospected with him and used to stay out at the ranch years ago, before my time."

"What's Pardy like?"

Gary shrugged. "All right, from what I can remember. I was just a kid then. Dad had heard Pardy wasn't feeling well, and he and Mom decided to come down and see if they could do anything for him. He liked Mom as well as he did Dad. That was on account of Mom's father. Pardy always admired a man with an education."

"Like me, eh?"

"You know how Grandfather Hart was about lost treasures and suchlike," continued Gary, ignoring Tuck.

"Weren't many that knew as much about such things as he did," said Tuck. "Beats me how such a fine man could end up being a high school principal," he added darkly. "Especially of Cottonwood Wells Union High School."

"They did the best they could with you," said Gary.

They rounded another spur and saw the shimmering expanse of the desert lying spread before them, sloping down from the base of Lookout Rock. By half closing the eyes, one gained the effect of a vast area of water, sparkling under the light of the moon. It almost looked frosty cold, but that was an illusion, for despite the coolness of the desert night, the sands still held much of the heat of the day.

A scattered group of shacks stood close to the westward base of the pinnacle. The moonlight glittered from the window glass of some of them, but no lights showed from within. There was no sign of life. No dog barked. Nothing moved.

Gary stopped the truck and turned off the ignition. The silence seemed to flow in upon them, broken only by the ticking sounds of the cooling engine. Gary opened the door and stepped outside to look about. The moonlight was sharp and distinct, clearly revealing everything it touched, and the accentuation seemed to make the shadows even more intense.

Gary walked toward the largest building. It was built of rocks from the talus slope below Lookout Rock, roofed with corrugated iron and tar-paper—indeed, anything that would serve as a cover. The door gaped open. The windows looked at him like the eyes of the sightless.

Gary shivered a little in the coolness, not at all sure that something else was not helping him with his shivering. Vague memories of the place began to sharpen in the files of his past experiences, like a photograph beginning to reveal itself in developing fluid.

The place had changed scarcely at all. Gary looked back at the truck. Tuck was standing close beside it, ready to take off at a moment's notice, but meanwhile, to sustain his weakening spirit, he was munching on a thick sandwich. Tucker C. Browne might conceivably go to a sudden grave without confessing his sins and asking for absolution, but it was *a* lead-pipe cinch he'd never go there with an empty stomach.

Here and there on the ground between the buildings were scattered more of Pardy Willis' strange collection. Boxes of bottles and other glassware tinted by the rays of the sun. Piles of mineral specimens, including some good-looking geodes Gary would like to have. Various pieces of wagon gear and equipment, such as brake shoes, iron tires, hooks and tugs, tar buckets, whip sockets, parts of running gear, hub caps, and wheel spokes. A rusted double-barreled shotgun leaned against an old army forge.

Gary walked to the doorway of the largest building, "Mister Willis," he called into the uninviting darkness beyond the door.

"Mister Willis..." echoed the interior.

Gary waited and then walked inside, almost wishing he had taken his rifle from the truck. Pardy Willis wouldn't bother him, if he recognized him, but if he didn't... Pardy Willis had long been notorious for his hair-trigger temper. There were those who said that knowing the untold story of Pardy Willis might disclose the fact that the old man was a living legend from the bloodshot past of the Southwest.

"Pardy?" he said dubiously into the clinging darkness.

Gary snapped a match on his thumbnail and looked about by the dim, flickering light of the match. The place was as cluttered as the outside. Shelves and racks held piles of indistinguishable objects, thick with dust. The floor was littered with other objects. There were two doors at the rear of the place, and close as it was to the base of Lookout Rock, it was quite possible that old Pardy might have burrowed deeply into the living rock to store more of his possessions.

Gary shrugged. Pardy, if he still lived there, must bunk in one of the other buildings. A mouse scuttled for cover as the match flickered out. Gary walked back to the doorway and looked out into the frosty moonlight.

Tuck was burrowing into the hamper with his back toward the buildings.

Gary started walking toward one of the other buildings. He glanced uneasily up at the towering pinnacle of Lookout Rock. It reminded him too much of The Needle in the Espectros, a similar pinnacle, much larger of course, that had always been the starting point for those who wished to probe into the mountains behind it to hunt the Lost Espectro mine. He took three more paces, then stopped short to turn slowly and take another look at the rock formation.

"What's wrong, Gary?" called out Tuck.

"Look up there," said Gary.

High on the side of the formation was what seemed to be a carving made by wind, scouring sand, rain, and cracking frost. It looked like a white-bearded old man sitting in a natural armchair hewn into the living rock by the hand of nature. His thin arms hung across bony knees. His graven face stared steadily out across the moon-lighted wastes of the Spanish Desert.

Tuck walked up beside Gary. He narrowed his eyes. "Looks natural enough to be real," he said in a low voice.

Gary wet his dry lips. The figure did not move. "It is real," he said at last.

"Pardy Willis?"

"I think so."

"Is he dead?" whispered Tuck.

Then, the moonlight glittered from the staring eyes as the head moved a little. The faint wind creeping about the pillar of rock moved the thick beard.

"Pardy Willis!" called out Gary.

"*Pardy Willis...Pardy Willis...Pardy Willis...*" echoed the rock.

The figure did not move.

"Let's get outa here," hissed Tuck. "I don't like this at all."

"Go on, if you like," said Gary. "I came here to see Pardy Willis, and I aim to see him."

"You are seeing him, ain't you?" snapped Tuck. "Or what *looks* like him?"

"Meaning?"

Tuck swallowed hard. "How do we know the ol' boy didn't cash in his chips? This place don't exactly look like Times Square, pal. Looks like nobody's lived here in months."

Gary felt in his heart that maybe Tuck was right, but it wouldn't do to admit it. "Pardy Willis!" called out Gary.

"*Pardy Willis...Pardy Willis...Pardy Willis...*" echoed Lookout Rock.

The head moved. The eves looked down at the two boys so far below.

"Lordy," said Tuck. "Now you did it! He sees us!"

"So? If it is Pardy Willis, he won't bother us. If it is his ghost, that can't bother us either."

"Listen to him!" hissed Tuck. "Who are you? Edgar Allan Poe? I say we ought to pull foot out of this place. Now! *Pronto!*"

The figure moved again. It stood up right at the very lip of a hundred-foot drop, the beard lifting in the wind.

"You and your big mouth," said Tuck. "Whatever it is, it's seen us now!"

"Go hang some garlic around your neck," said Gary cruelly.

"That's for vampires, you dope!"

Gary grinned. "I knew you'd know all the answers. Here he comes, kid."

Tuck wanted to run, but he'd never leave Gary, and if the truth be known, if Tuck *had* run, he'd hardly have beaten Gary to the truck.

Slowly and carefully, the old man clambered down from his lofty perch on a narrow pathway that could hardly be seen from ground level—a mere scratch against the sheer wall of rock. As he came farther down the trail, they could hear his harsh breathing, which gave the boys assurance that Pardy Willis was still a creature of flesh and bone.

The old man reached the bottom of the trail, perhaps twenty feet above the roof of the biggest of the buildings, and then, before their very eyes, he vanished into thin air.

"Ulp!" said Tuck. "I told you so!"

Both of them wanted to run, but neither would start ahead of the other, so they both stood there with cold sweat trickling down their sides, staring at the empty trail.

"What is it you want? Who are you?" said a harsh voice from the dark doorway of the biggest building.

"It's Gary Cole, Mister Willis," said Gary,

"How'd he get down there?" whispered Tuck hoarsely.

There was a moment of silence. "Who's the skinny critter with you?" asked Pardy Willis.

"Listen to him," said Tuck angrily.

"Tucker C. Browne," said Gary. "He's a friend of mine, Mister Willis. Dad said you had some things for him. Told us to come down and see you. Maybe you weren't expecting anyone."

The silence hung heavily in the quiet air. "Well, I was, and I wasn't. Leastways not from your direction."

Tuck looked about. "Does he mean out there?" he said in a barely audible tone, pointing back toward the emptiness of the desert. "*Who'd he be expecting from out there?*"

Pardy appeared in the doorway as though manipulated like a marionette by the unseen hands of a master puppeteer. He narrowed his eyes. "You've growed a bit, Gary," he said.

"It's been a long time since I was here."

"Look something like your Pa. Touch of your mother, too, about you. Ain't as handsome as your Pa or as pretty as your Ma."

"Thanks," said Gary drily.

"Didn't you see or hear us, Mister Willis?" asked Tuck.

Pardy walked slowly toward them. "I was looking and listening for something else," he said.

"There he goes again," whispered Tuck.

Pardy stopped ten feet from the boys. He tilted his head to one side. "You boys eat?" he asked.

Tuck expanded. "Well, Mister Willis, we did, and we didn't!"

Gary shot a hard glance at Tuck. "We figured you'd like to eat with us, Mister Willis. My mother sent down some things."

"Fine woman. Pretty as a calico dress," said Pardy. "I'll go light the lamp, boys." He walked to the building he had just left and disappeared inside.

Tuck shook his head. "Man, he won't like it when he sees how much we left in that hamper."

"You mean how much *you* left."

"Either way, he won't like it."

Gary walked to the truck, glancing back toward the biggest building as he did so. The place was nothing but a storeroom for Pardy's assorted junk and other possessions. Gary shrugged. Maybe he had a lamp in there he needed to light one of the other buildings. Gary opened the back door of the camperback and reached under a bunk to withdraw a box heavy with staples and other foods, including some of his mother's canned delicacies.

Tuck stared at the box. "How'd that get in there?" he said suspiciously.

"The Brownies put it in there," said Gary. He carried it toward the buildings.

"Of all the dirty tricks," said Tuck.

———

THERE WAS no sign of Pardy in the building. Gary stood there hesitantly. One of the two doors at the rear of the big room was opened. Pardy Willis appeared. "Come on in, boy," he said.

Gary carried the box to the doorway and followed Pardy as he led the way into what looked like a hallway, but it was more of a tunnel cut into solid rock. The tunnel made a sharp turn left and then right, angling somewhat sharply upward, and at the far end was the welcoming glow of a lamp.

Gary followed Pardy into a low-ceiled room hewn from the solid rock. It was well furnished with a big brass bedstead, a large ranch stove, a plain wooden table, chairs, and other furniture. A huge fireplace filled most of one wall, and the rock was blackened by the smoke of many fires. Gary placed the box on the table and whistled softly.

Pardy peered at the box. "Dug out the place myself, boy," he said. "Warm in the winter, cool in the summer. Nobody can get in here unless I let 'em." He glanced at a double-barreled shotgun hanging on the wall.

"You used to live in one of the other buildings, as I recall," said Gary.

"Got too drafty in the winters."

While the old man poked about in the box, Gary walked to a squared opening in the rock. He reached forward and opened a heavy wooden shutter. Moonlight flooded into the room. Gary whistled softly. From his viewpoint, he could see the entire area below them: the littered junk, the sagging fence, the decaying buildings, and the pick-up truck, while Tuck stood in the open looking about. A man could hold off a company of troops from the place. Beyond the immediate area was the flat expanse of the approaches to the Spanish Desert, stippled here and there with mesquite, cactus, and tumbleweed.

Pardy was starting a fire in the big range. "You boys staying a while?" he asked.

"Yes, if we can."

"Got another room or two beyond this place."

"We can bunk in the truck," said Gary.

"Suit yourself."

"You've got a nice view here, Mister Willis."

"Call me Pardy, darn it! I ain't used to formality, boy."

"You must like looking out over the desert. You were up there on the rock when we came, and you can sure see a lot from here. Quite a view, Pardy."

There was a moment of silence. "I hate it," said Pardy in a low, hard voice.

Gary turned slowly. He was startled at the expression on the old man's face—a mingling of fear and hatred, changing the visage into something he hardly recognized. Gary almost recoiled at the sight.

"Close that winder! Go get that skinny fella!" snapped Pardy. He turned back to the stove.

Gary walked back down the sloping tunnel, followed the turns, and came out into the building. He walked outside. Gary whistled at Tuck. Tuck was standing near the sagging, rusted fence, looking to the southwest. Gary whistled again. Tuck turned and walked slowly back toward Gary with an odd look on his face.

"What's bothering you, man?" asked Gary curiously.

Tuck jerked a thumb over his shoulder. "That," he said.

"The desert?"

"The *Spanish* Desert. I see what you mean now, Gary."

"Like what, for instance?"

Tuck shrugged. "I really don't know," he said seriously. "It sorta grows on you. I didn't think too much about that story of yours, losing the food and water when you were out there alone, but just standing here, thinking about it, it makes more sense."

"Such as?"

Tuck turned to look at his friend. "They say the Spanish Desert is haunted."

Gary laughed. "Now you're flipping your wig. Besides, it's supposed to be the Lost Mission that's haunted, not the whole desert."

"That's exactly what I mean!"

"You've been out in the moonlight too long. 'Lunar madness,' they call it. Pretty soon, you'll be howling at the moon."

Tuck lowered his voice, although there was no one around to hear it other than Gary. "Maybe you were closer to the Lost Mission than you thought you were."

"And the ghosts of the old padres came out to kipe my chow and dump my water."

"Well, if they didn't, who did?"

"That's a mighty good question. Tucker. I don't know, but I find it hard to believe in ghosts wandering around out there."

"You weren't so sure a little earlier this evening," jeered Tuck.

Gary turned and walked toward the biggest building. "Come on," he said quickly. "Pardy is going to fix up some chow."

"Whyn't you tell me! Standing around here talking alla time!"

Gary stepped aside to let Tuck enter the building. He looked out across the quiet desert. A curious feeling came over him—a feeling he had experienced the last time he had been on the approach to the Spanish Desert. Despite the utter loneliness, there was the constant feeling that one was under surreptitious surveillance from someone, or something, that was always just out of eyeshot, no matter how swiftly and suddenly one turned his head to look. He hurried into the building after Tuck to show him the way to Pardy's hideout.

———

THE MOON SHONE into the open window cut through the rock into Pardy's big room. The window framed the bearded face of Pardy Willis, and there was a strange look upon that face. When he saw Gary vanish into the building, he quickly stepped back and closed the heavy wooden shutter, then hurried to the stove as he heard the boys' voices in the tunnel.

CHAPTER FOUR

The Ghost Dog

Pardy Willis was an unrecognized genius in the art of simple cookery. There was little conversation while the three of them ate, for the two boys were hungry, and Pardy seemed to have thoughts of his own behind his strange and piercing eyes. The fire crackled on the great hearth, filling the room with pleasant heat and the astringent odor of desert wood. Pardy had placed a dutch oven in the coals to raise biscuits made from the dough he kept in a covered pot. With a thick layer of Mrs. Cole's strawberry preserves on such biscuits, the combination was downright delicious.

Pardy slowly filled his corncob pipe from the big tobacco tin Pete Cole had sent him. He lighted the pipe with a spill from the fire and blew out a ring of smoke. "Prime," he said quietly. "Run outa real tobacco weeks ago."

Tuck deftly scooped up a biscuit, ladled preserves on it with the skill of a past master, and then popped the biscuit into his mouth, closing his eyes in deep satisfaction. "Prime," he mumbled. He looked at Pardy. "How do you get around, Pardy?"

Pardy took his pipe and pointed down at his two feet. "Them," he said.

"No car or truck? No horse or burro?"

"None," said Pardy.

Gary shoved back his plate. Pardy Willis was a *walkin' man* if there ever was one. Pardy had been a foot-prospector in the old days. He had been the old-fashioned type of infantryman, vintage of World War I, and before that, a foot-slogging, beetle-crushing doughfoot. It was said that Pardy Willis had walked into and out of places that few other white men, if any, had ever visited.

They said that Pardy had once walked across Death Valley in the very core of the summer's heat at night when the furnace winds blew and no living creature had much of a chance of surviving. Pardy had done it. It was also rumored that he had walked down into the Grand Canyon and up the other side.

"I ain't been out of my place here for quite a spell," said Pardy. "Sometimes I run out of things, but someone remembers old Pardy and comes through. Sometimes it costs me something, sometimes it don't." He chuckled. "I can't say they get much of a bargain with what I sell them."

"Relics?" said Tuck. He reached for another biscuit.

"That junk out there? Hell, that's for dudes. I'm too lazy to get rid of it until somebody like you comes along to clean it up."

"Thanks," said Tuck drily. "What do you sell them, Pardy?"

"Information," said the old man.

"Such as?" asked Tuck patiently.

"Old mines. Lost treasures. Trails. Ruins. Suchlike."

"Ruins?" said Tuck.

"Yup. Cliff dwellings. Old frontier forts. Trading posts. Old Indian villages. Anything they want to know, old Pardy tells 'em."

Tuck looked at Gary. Gary shook his head slightly. Pardy had a perverse streak in his nature. Say the wrong thing, and he'd clam up.

"You know the Spanish Desert real well, then?" asked Tuck.

"Better'n any living man." Pardy grinned crookedly. "Better'n most dead men, too. Ain't nothing goes on in that hellhole I don't know about."

The firewood snapped and crackled. Pardy looked into the wreathing flames and smoke with a faraway look in his eyes. It was almost as though he had forgotten that the boys were there.

"What about that plane that was found out there?" asked Gary. "The one that was out of gas. They never did find the people that were in it. Do you know anything about that, Pardy?"

There was a long silence, and then Pardy nodded. "I know all about it. You see, it was me that found the plane."

"But no sign of the people?"

Pardy shook his head. "They walked away from it to look for water. Heat and thirst got at 'em. Likely then they crawled into any shade they could find. Maybe under a sand bank. They died there. The wind blew, and the sand drifted. The plane was found. The bodies weren't. The old Spanish Desert likes its privacy. Maybe it allows a lone man to travel across it, *if he's careful* and don't let the desert trick him into thinking he's real safe. Maybe it even lets men build things out there, while biding its time, lulling them into a false sense of security. Then it strikes, one way or another, and either kills them off or drives them out. Then, the old desert settles down to get rid of the buildings, like trying to get rid of an abscess or a scabbed wound.

"Takes time. Bit by bit, the sand drifts. Bit by bit, the wind works. Together, the two of them work, and in time, they take back what is really theirs. The naked desert, like God made it during the Creation. You can't ever lick the Spanish Desert. It don't make any difference if you wore moccasins and came to it before Columbus discovered America, wore a Spanish pot helmet and rode a horse, or walked afoot in a black robe carrying a cross. Maybe you wore a slouch hat and chewed tobacco, talking with a Yankee twang or with a soft Southern drawl, velvet in your voice and steel in your eyes, but the desert licked you just the same. Horses, mules, cars, and then planes. The desert licks them all!"

In the silence that followed, the two boys eyed the old man.

"You make it sound as though it is alive," said Gary at last.

The strange, piercing eyes probed into Gary's eyes and gave him the uncomfortable feeling that they were probing into his very mind. "*It is alive,* boy," said Pardy Willis in a low voice. He glanced over his shoulder at the shuttered window.

Gary remembered all too well the sight of Pardy seated in his natural armchair high on the sheer face of Lookout Rock, staring out across the Spanish Desert, newly lighted by the moon, seemingly oblivious of all that was going on far below him. What was it Pardy had said when Gary had said that maybe Pardy wasn't expecting visitors? "*Well, I was, and I wasn't. Leastways not from your direction.*" Later, the old man had vehemently said that he hated the Spanish Desert.

What had changed Pardy Willis from the man who knew the desert country like the palms of his gnarled old hands? A man who had always preferred his own company? A man to whom the deserts and the mountains were home? Certainly, the Spanish Desert had a strange, haunting quality about it, a leave-me-alone-or-suffer-for-it quality. The spell of the place had worked on Pardy Willis years before Gary had been born, and it had worked on Gary as well. Even Tuck had noticed the strange, brooding quality of the place.

"Any roads out there, Pardy?" asked Tuck at last.

"Some. On the edges."

"None going through the middle, maybe?"

"Nope."

"A trail, maybe?"

Pardy laughed harshly. "I said the desert gets rid of man-made things."

"Certainly the old Spaniards were out there," said Tuck.

Pardy nodded. "Two things they wanted, both of them powerful enough to make a man fool around out there. Two things: to carry the Cross to the heathens who were hardly fool enough to live out there, and the other thing they wanted was gold! They found some gold."

"Did they find the heathens?" asked Tuck.

"I said they were hardly fool enough to live out there," said Pardy.

"Then why would the Spanish padres build a mission out there?" said Gary quietly.

Pardy slowly took the pipe from his mouth. He just as slowly turned his head to look at Gary. Once again, Gary felt as though Pardy was trying to plumb the depths of his mind. "Mission?" said Pardy in a low voice. *"What* mission, boy?"

"There's a story about a lost mission out there."

"There ain't any out there!"

"They say it's haunted, Pardy," said Tuck.

Pardy stood up and knocked out the dottle in his pipe.

"Time for bed," he said. "Thanks for the vittles, boys." He walked to the shuttered window and dropped a wooden bar across the hooks.

Gary and Tuck stood up and walked to the door. Gary turned.

"Maybe it's only a legend, Pardy," he said.

"Likely."

"But you've heard about it?"

"Likely."

"Can you tell us about it? Isn't there a road out there that might lead to it? A road marked by cross-inscribed rocks?"

"Did you come out here to pick up some relics for your father or to plague me with loco stories?" snarled Pardy.

Tuck jerked his head toward the door. He should have known Gary Cole much better than that. Gary was usually pretty quiet, but he was the bulldog breed. Let him get his teeth into something, and nothing could shake him loose.

"You know more about the Spanish Desert than any living man, Pardy," said Gary quietly. "You said so yourself, and it's likely true. Do you deny there is a road out there?"

"Yes."

"No cross-inscribed marker rocks?"

"None! Not a blessed one! Another thing: don't go fooling around out there. It ain't no place for boys like you or men either! Now get outa here before I lose my temper!"

They walked down the dark tunnel, lighting their way by matches through it and the dark building. The moon was low in the west. They walked toward their truck with the sand grating beneath their boots.

"You got a lock on the back of that truck?" called out Pardy from his window.

Gary turned. "Yes," he said.

"Then lock it once you get into the truck." The shutter slammed shut, and the bar dropped.

"What's buggin' him?" asked Tuck. "Man, he was riled about that mission business. He's right, I guess. He oughta know."

"No," said Gary. "He's lying to us, Tuck. I don't know why, *but he's lying.*"

Tuck shrugged. He walked over to a shack and looked at the door. Two heavy locks hung from the hasp. The windows had been boarded shut. It was the same with the other shacks. "Sure guards his junk well," said Tuck.

Gary nodded absent-mindedly. He looked up at the moonlighted face of the rock pinnacle and the tightly shuttered window. Something *was* bugging Pardy Willis. He walked toward the truck. A low mound of rocks was beside the sagging fence. Dark-looking rocks, rather alien to that particular area. They were mounded above something that looked like a grave. Gary saw a board thrust into the ground at the head of the mound. He knelt to read it.

"Barkus," he said aloud.

"Friend of his?" asked Tuck curiously.

"His dog," said Gary. "He had a dog named Barkus when I was out here years ago. Barkus was his friend, all right."

"Sounds like that character out of Dickens," said Tuck. "'Barkis is willin',' or something like that."

Gary nodded. "I think it was my mother who gave Pardy the idea to call his dog that. The dog was a pup then."

Gary stood up. He looked down at the dark rocks. The moonlight slanted down on them. He narrowed his eyes. One of the rocks was incised with the shape of a cross, almost exactly like the other rock he had seen out in the desert. He knelt beside it and traced the course of the cross with a finger. "Look," he said quietly.

"Is that like the one you saw?"

"Almost exactly."

"And he said he had never seen any such rocks."

"Might be coincidence."

"Yeah," said Tuck softly. "Look there!" He pointed at another of the rocks lying on its side. He turned it over with his foot. The surface was carved with a cross.

In a matter of minutes, the two boys had checked all of the upper rocks. *Each and every one of them was cut with the cross inscription.*

Tuck glanced toward the pinnacle of rock. "What's his game!" he said.

Gary wiped the dirt from his hands. *"Quién sabe?"* he said. "Who knows?" He rubbed his jaw. "He must have walked miles to pick up each of these rocks and carry them here for grave markers."

"Maybe he found a bunch of them together?"

"What difference would that make? He'd still have to lug them here. They must weigh at least fifty pounds apiece. Some job for a man his age."

"Yeah," said Tuck, "and if you're right about that road, each and every one of these markers was beside that road. Maybe the road had vanished, but the markers were still there. My guess is that those markers led straight to the Lost Mission."

"Elementary, my dear fellow," murmured Gary.

"But why wouldn't he tell us about it?"

"Because he's deathly afraid of something, Tuck."

Tuck shivered a little in the cold wind that was creeping across the darkening desert. The moon was seemingly resting on the fanged mountains miles and miles to the west. In a short time, it would disappear on the far side. "Let's hit the sack," said Tuck. "All of a sudden, I'm tired. How about you?"

Gary nodded. He followed Tuck toward the truck. Tuck climbed into the rear and flicked on the dome light. Gary locked the front doors of the cab and followed Tuck inside the camperback. They sat on opposite bunks, pulling off their boots, each occupied with his own thoughts. By the time they had undressed and turned out the light, the moonlight was gone, and the darkness became colder.

Gary peered from the window to look out toward the desert. It seemed to creep in toward the truck. He looked toward the dark and brooding bulk of Lookout Rock. He lay back on his bunk and dropped a hand to the floor to feel for his Winchester.

"It's right in the middle of the floor," said Tuck from beneath his covers. "If anything happens tonight, may the best man reach it first."

"I hate to go straight home tomorrow," said Gary.

"Meaning?"

"It's shorter if we cut through the edge of the Spanish Desert."

"No roads."

"Pardy said there were some on the edges."

"Yeah. What happens if we get off one of them?"

"We've got four-wheel drive and low-low."

"Goody! Goody!"

Gary grinned. "Of course, if you're afraid..."

"You know blasted a-well I'll go!"

Gary grinned again. "You feel the fever the same as I do."

"You figure we'll have any luck?"

Gary raised himself on an elbow. "Maybe," he said. "There *is* a road out there despite what Pardy says. The markers prove that it existed. If we could get Pardy to show us where he got those markers, we'd have a terrific lead to the place."

"You won't get him to show you."

"No, but I can find the one I ran into. The road runs north and south. It's a cinch the Lost Mission isn't north, for the desert peters out on the way to Mesquite Wells. It *has* to be south."

"Near them mountains, maybe?"

"*Those* mountains, you dope! I think it must be in or around them, for if it was still standing on the open desert, it would have been found long ago."

"Maybe Pardy is right when he says the sand and wind take care of covering up things like that."

"That's hardly likely. Those old Spanish padres knew how to build such places, and they built them big and strong, to last for generations. Besides, they'd build them nearer the mountains so they could get building materials such as stone and timber."

"Yeah. I buy that, pal."

"We don't have to take any unnecessary risks. Pardy will know where we went. We can stay on the road for quite a way, and around where I found the marker, the ground is hard and flat for the most part. We don't have to go deep into the desert."

"Oh, no, not us," said Tuck sarcastically. "Once you see another one of them markers, you'll be off like Alice in Wonderland chasing that crazy rabbit with an Ingersoll in his pants pocket."

Gary pulled up his covering. "Sweet dreams," he said.

A gentle snoring answered him. Tucker C. Browne could go to sleep in the middle of a sentence—sometimes a phrase—and once, as Gary recollected, he had stopped in the second syllable of a three-syllabic word.

Gary stared up at the dark ceiling, thinking of those markers gathered with infinite patience and terrible hardship by Pardy Willis to cover the grave of his beloved dog, perhaps the closest friend the strange old man had ever had. Gary could vaguely remember the dog, for it had been hardly more than a pup when he had seen it years ago—a gangling, clumsy thing with a patient insistence on following Pardy wherever he walked.

In those days, Pardy called the dog Hey You. It was Gary's mother who had started to call him Barkus, based on the character "Barkis" in one of Dickens' novels: first, because the pup always was "willing," as Barkis had been in the novel, and secondly because of his peculiar barking. Gary thumbed through his mental files. Surely one of his friends might have a pup Gary could bring out to the old man to replace Barkus, if that was ever possible.

The mission had to be in or about those mountains, and if that was so, surely Pardy Willis must have seen it, *if* it existed. The legend hadn't just started out of thin air. Legends must have a source of some kind. There must have been an original Beowulf and an original Robin Hood, no matter how fantastic and impossible some of their feats would be considered in modern-day light. It had been so, too, about the ancient Greeks and the legendary Trojan War, considered as myth and fantasy because of the curious mixture of men and gods in the cast of characters, until it was proved in recent times that Troy *had* existed, and that there *had* been a Trojan War—without the help of the gods, of course.

Gary slowly drifted off into sleep, with the cool desert wind creeping through the window vents and rustling about the truck, now completely shrouded in thick, velvety darkness...

———

THE SOFT GRATING sound awakened Gary, although his mind was still drugged with sleep, and his body seemed reluctant to respond to its commands for movement. He opened his eyes and then closed them. The grating sound came again, closer to the rear of the truck this time. Gary opened his eyes again. He shook his head to clear it from sleep. Then he raised it suddenly. The door handle had been moved a trifle. Gary slowly reached down for the rifle. The touch of the weapon gave him courage.

The lock jiggled again. Gary tried to remember whether he had locked it or not. It was the last thing Pardy Willis had said to him that night. He quietly cased his legs over the side of the bed. The grating sound came again, alongside the truck, and he could have sworn that he saw something dark and indistinct pass by the side window of the truck on Tuck's side.

Gary sat up. The truck moved a little as something heavy rested on the left running board. Again, a door handle was jiggled. There was an opening between the camperback and the rear window of the truck, the glass having been removed, and a flexible connection fitted between the window and the front window of the camperback. Gary eased toward it, trying to see who was up there, but it was no use. A moment later, the right-hand door handle was moved a little.

Gary crouched low as the grating sound came along his side of the truck. Then, it was quiet for a few minutes. Suddenly, metal touched metal, and the rear door handle jerked. It was being forced. Gary raised the rifle butt and knocked it sharply against the inside of the door. The grating sound came again, this time much faster, and then it died away toward the darkness of the desert.

"What's the matter?" said Tuck sleepily.

"Nothing."

"I heard a knocking sound."

"I bumped my head."

Gary wet his dry lips. His heart was thumping erratically. Cold sweat from his hands greased the stock of the rifle. He swallowed hard. Supposing he had left the rear door unlocked?

"What woke you up?"

Far out in the desert, a faint howling sound arose.

"That," said Gary. "That coyote."

"Never seemed to bother you before, pal."

"I just happened to wake up."

The howling sound arose again, carried by the night wind.

"Listen to him," said Tuck. "Craziest-sounding coyote I ever heard."

Gary raised his head. The howling broke off into a sharp barking sound that rose and fell, rose and fell, then died away into the silence of the desert night.

Tuck was snoring again. Gary placed the rifle on the floor of the truck. He lay back and stared at the ceiling. No use in alarming Tuck about the night prowler. It wasn't that which was now bothering Gary. That had been something alive. A man, naturally, and certainly not a ghost. It was the howling and barking that was smearing a green film of intense fear across his imagination.

That had been no coyote out there. It had been years since Gary had heard the howling and barking of Pardy Willis' dog Barkus, but he could never forget it. Whatever it was that was howling out there sounded exactly like Barkus. There was no mistaking the sound. But if that was Barkus out there, *what was buried beneath the pile of cross-inscribed stones?* Maybe it *was* the body of the old dog under there. If so, the Spanish Desert was haunted, indeed—not by a man, but by a dog.

An icy shiver of fear crept through Gary Cole. There was something intensely horrible in the thought of a dog's ghost prowling the lonely wastes of the Spanish Desert in the darkness after the wane of the moon. No wonder Pardy Willis was afraid of that desert; no wonder he stared out at it with eyes haunted by fear

CHAPTER FIVE

Stay Out of the Spanish Desert at Night!

Pardy Willis was up at the crack of dawn, hauling all manner of things out of nooks and crannies, which Tuck and Gary loaded into the rear of the truck. Gary's eyes widened now and then, for as a collector, he knew the value of some of the items despite Tuck's continual mumbling about "junk." Some of the items would have brought a nice price from other collectors or museums.

There was an old Spanish morion helmet, Spanish brass shoe stirrups, several excellent metates used by the Indians and the Mexicans to grind their corn, a number of percussion rifles and carbines, a brass-trimmed "Jennifer" saddle of the Civil War period, a number of horse bits, a box full of various spurs, some of which Gary recognized as being of Mexican, Californian, Texan, and other styles.

There were several metal bootjacks, metal hat ornaments, quirts, a lovely Navajo bridle, a bundle of branding irons from famous Arizona ranches, leather *tapaderos,* and a big box full of buttons and ornaments. There were a number of lamps that would bring a sparkle to the eyes of Lucille Cole: a Betty lamp, a Phoebe lamp, an exquisite Argand lamp with a marble column, and another Argand lamp of the wick type, a camphene lamp, a Rochester hand lamp, and a magnificent Rochester brass hanging lamp of the harp type.

Pardy was gone quite a while on the last trip into one of his hideaways after they had finished a huge breakfast, and when he returned, he had a flat wooden box under his arm. He looked up at the sun. "Gettin' late," he said. "You boys will soon be on your way."

Gary nodded. "We want to cut across the north end of the Spanish Desert," he said.

"That's loco!"

"Maybe so," said Gary quietly. "It won't be so bad if you tell us about the roads."

Pardy hesitated. "All right," he said gruffly. "If you insist." He got down on one bony knee, and with a piece of stick, he traced lines on the sandy ground. "You drive south of here on the main road out there in front of the Rock."

"Some main road," said Tuck.

"Four or five miles south of here, you'll go down into a deep wash. Turn right up the wash. It's a washboard bed there, but better than the sand. Watch your mileage. Four miles west, the country slopes down quite a bit. Look for another wash that comes in from the north. Follow it a quarter of a mile or so, and you'll see a road." He stopped and looked down at the tracing he had made.

"Yes?" said Tuck.

"The road trends west, sometimes turns south, then north. You got to watch close for it. They's an abandoned well out there. No water at all. Usedta be, years ago. Just run dry. No one ever lived there. You got to watch sharp beyond it, for the road turns sharp right, trending north. After a time, it peters out, but the ground is hard there, and you can go straight north and come out near Mesquite Wells."

Tuck looked at Gary over the white head of the old man. Pardy was' describing the country where Gary had camped, then had returned north, past the marker he had found, for Gary had said that the ground was hard and flat for the most part—no problem for the truck. Pardy evidently knew it well.

"No road markers or anything out there?" asked Gary.

Pardy slowly got to his feet. "You'd better get on the way," he said quietly. "Look here, boys, you can reach the area where you can head for Mesquite Wells across country 'bout four or five o'clock this afternoon. You'll have enough daylight to reach within a few miles of the Wells, then the moon will help out. I can't stop you from fooling around out in that hellhole by daylight, but *don't you turn south,* and *don't you stay out there overnight.* If you get caught in there by the dark, you just keep heading for the Wells!"

Gary had a dozen questions on the tip of his tongue, but he knew that the old man was through talking. Hot irons would never get another word out of him.

Pardy handed the flat box to Gary. "This is for you, boy. Thanks for the vittles and the company. You got to forgive an old desert rat for being cranky."

"It didn't bother me," said Gary. He took the heavy box.

"Open it, boy," said Pardy.

Gary placed it on the tailgate of the truck and opened it. He whistled in surprise. A pair of matched and engraved Frontier Colt six-shooters were neatly fitted into the green velvet lining of the box. The butt plates were of carved ivory. The sun glinted from the exquisite weapons. Gary looked at Pardy. "I can't take this. Mister Willis," he said.

"Why not, boy?"

"It's worth a great deal of money."

Pardy spat. "Money ain't worth nothing," he said. "A good friend is worth all the money in the world. Your folks was always good to me, boy, and you are too. Whenever you look at them guns, you think a kind thought or two about old Pardy Willis."

"I sure will, sir," said Gary.

Pardy turned and looked at Tuck. "You're the champeenest eater I ever seen," he said. "Best man with a knife and fork in this state, but then you skinny critters are all mouth and appetite, anyways."

"Gee, *thanks*, Mister Willis," said Tuck.

Pardy shoved a hand into his pocket and withdrew a small leather-covered box. He shoved it toward Tuck. "This is for you, boy. Does me good to see a man who appreciates good vittles like you do. Open it up, boy! Open it up!"

Tuck opened the lid. It was his turn to whistle softly. Tucked into the silken lining of the box was an exquisite double-barreled derringer, silver-chased, with smooth ivory grips.

"The little gun with the big bite," said Pardy. "Carried that derringer with me for years. No use for it now. Kinda like you, boy."

Tuck smiled uncertainly. "Yeah," he said.

Gary looked at Pardy. "You know you've got a standing invitation to come and stay at the ranch, Pardy."

Pardy smiled. "Like one of the relics," he said.

"You know my father and mother don't mean it that way."

"Sure, boy." Pardy shook his head. "Thanks, but this is my home. Maybe not for long, but it's home. Old Barkus is lying there, and maybe, when my time comes, you and your folks will see to it that I lie here too."

Gary closed up the rear of the truck. He held out his hand to Pardy and was surprised at the still-powerful grip of the old man. "Goodbye," he said.

THEY MOVED SLOWLY through the clinging sand past the buildings, with Pardy standing there in the bright sunlight, the hot wind moving his full beard, and then he was out of sight. The truck ground slowly through the sand to the road and turned south on it, picking up speed.

Tuck looked up at Lookout Rock. "Strange old man," he said.

"He's got you pegged, kid."

"Yeah, wonder what he meant when he said the derringer was like me."

"*Quién sabe?* Something about a little gun with a big bite."

"Lordy, but those guns are expensive, aren't they?"

Gary nodded. "I'll keep them for him. If he needs money, my father can sell them and send the money to Pardy."

"I was thinking the same thing myself, but I'll bet he won't like it."

They reached the place where the wash crossed the road, or the road crossed the wash, depending on the way you figured it, for, in time of a flash flood, the road would be half a dozen feet deep in rushing water. The truck bumped along the washboard bed of the dry watercourse while Gary kept an eye on the mileage. The country sloped down as Pardy had said it would.

"There's the other wash," said Tuck. "Man, it's hot out here. We got plenty of water?"

Gary nodded. "The truck tank is full, and so is the desert bag, and I filled three canteens while you were eating your third serving of pancakes."

Gary turned into the second wash, and they bumped along that until they saw the place where the old road crossed the wash. The truck ground slowly up to the ground level, and Gary stopped it on the old road.

It wasn't much of a road. Great patches of it were full

of holes, and as far as the eye could see, there were areas where the road was completely covered with drifted sand.

The sun was beating down with full force now. A leaden-colored haze hung over the distant mountains like a fog hanging on a sea coast. Now and then, a thin wraith of dust spiraled slowly upward, as though exhausted by the heat, whirled across the shimmering wastes, and then disappeared as mysteriously as it had appeared.

"Any minute I expect to see Rudolph Valentino gallop up on a white horse, or a file of French Foreign Legionnaires come plodding along looking for Fort Zinderneuf," said Tuck.

Gary nodded. He drove slowly along the execrable road. Pardy Willis had been right when he had said that one must watch carefully for the road, for there were times when it vanished altogether, and there was nothing to do but downshift and keep going until a patch of the old surfacing appeared again, orienting Gary so that he knew which way to drive.

The sand was pretty bad in this part of the desert—deep and clinging, moved by the hot winds, restless and shifting. The truck might have a difficult time if it got away from the road. Maybe it hadn't been such a bright idea, after all, to take this route home to Chiricahua Springs Ranch, but there was a hard-headed streak in Gary that would not let him turn back. "Well," said Tuck. "A *well* out here? When did they ever have water out here?"

"Pardy had a well back there," said Gary. "Said it never ran dry."

"Yeah, back there. What about out here? Any water at all?"

Gary shrugged. "*Charcos, pozitos,* and *tinajas* is about all."

Charcos were holes scooped in clay basins, *pozitos* were dug in the sand washes, and *tinajas* were natural tanks eroded in rock and filled, if one was fortunate, with water from the infrequent rains. None of them could be relied upon.

———

AN HOUR PASSED, and the heat grew by the minute. The flat and burning surface of the desert reflected the cruel heat into the cab of the truck.

"We ain't too bright," grumbled Tuck.

"Look ahead," said Gary.

A tilted structure showed against the dun yellow of the sands. A wooden-framed windmill tripod, with the fan wheel hanging drunkenly to one side, half the blades missing.

"It's been a long time since that ol' mill ran," said Tuck.

Gary stopped the truck beside the old structure. He looked up at the barely decipherable name on the battered metal sail that used to keep the fan turned into the dry wind. The mill had been one-of-a-type famous in its day, the Eclipse.

Gary got out of the truck and took the cased binoculars from under the seat. He climbed the ancient structure, half expecting to feel the rungs snap beneath his boots. He sat on the top of the tower and uncased the glasses, focusing them, and then began to study the terrain. There wasn't much to see west, east, or north, but to the south were those same intriguing mountains. The sun was at high noon now, beating down with its full and implacable fury.

The haze that shimmered and danced across the desert and hung over the mountains actually hurt the eyes.

There was no sign of life in all the vastness of the desert. Not a tree, building, fence, or any other sign that man might have dwelt there long enough to leave traces of his passing. Nothing but the dun and yellow of the desert and the lead-colored mountains. Gary lowered the glasses and wiped the sweat from his face to keep it from misting the eyepieces.

He raised them again, and as he looked toward the mountains, he saw a quick flash appear in a notch in the mountains, as though the sunlight had reflected from some highly polished surface like metal or glass. He shook his head and studied the notch again. For a moment, he thought he saw something white in the notch, and then it was gone, although he wasn't quite sure he had actually seen anything.

"What are you looking at, man?" said Tuck. "Maybe some bathing beauties in bikinis, hey?"

Gary lowered the glasses and eyed those mysterious mountains. They weren't too far away, although distances were always deceptive in such country. Not too far away for the truck to reach them and have plenty of gas to get back to Mesquite Wells. It wasn't the gas that worried Gary, for he had a spare tank full, and it wasn't the water, for they had plenty of that too. It was the prospect of getting the truck bogged down, or having a mechanical failure out there in the middle of nowhere that plagued him.

He came slowly down the ladder and walked to the truck. He looked toward those mountains again, and as he did so, he saw that quick and mysterious flash, like a spot of quicksilver against duller metal. He got into the truck and drove west, and in a short distance, he saw that the road did, indeed, turn sharp to the north, almost at a right angle. It puzzled him, for there was all the room in the world to make a sweeping curve instead of such a sharp angle.

He stopped the truck and got out of it. Here and there, as the ground sloped gently upward to the north, he could see traces of the road. He turned and looked south. There was no trace of the road there. He eyed the drifted sand, and then half closed his eyes to study it.

Faintly, he perceived something on the desert floor. Parallel lines, about the width that ruts would be separated on a road, could be just distinguished, and they were a continuation of the road that continued north.

Tuck was rooting around in the food hamper, grumbling to himself as Gary walked around to the other side of the truck and up the road that led north. Fifty yards up the road, he squatted, half closed his eyes, and then sighted along the line of the road he was on. Sure enough, the faint line of ruts were in almost perfectly straight alignment with the road upon which he was squatting. Even as he eyed the faint line of ruts, they seemed to vanish, so hard were they to distinguish.

The road that came from the highway farther east— the one that ran past Pardy's place—had not been designed as it now appeared to have a sharp right-angled turn onto the road north. Perhaps at one time, it had ended as it met a road that ran both north *and* south. Somewhere during the passage of years, a new surface had been placed upon the road past the well, and then the surfacing had been continued north on the old road, *but not south*.

Gary stood up and sighted along the line of the road. There was nothing out there but heat-misted desert and, as a brooding backdrop, the mountains far to the south. Something seemed to reach out from those haze-shrouded heights to beckon on Gary Cole with a bony, spectral finger, and the almost unheard siren voice crept into his mind and settled itself there as though it was at home like a kitten on a cushion before the fire.

Gary walked slowly back to the truck. Tuck was chewing, as usual. "What's a delay?" said Tuck around a mouthful of ham, cheese, and rye bread.

Gary told him of what he had seen. "Funny thing Pardy wouldn't tell us about any road going south," he said, shaking his head from side to side.

"Maybe he didn't know about it. No, he'd know about it, wouldn't he?"

Gary nodded. "It's pretty early yet," he said.

Tuck stopped chewing and eyed Gary. "Go on," he said, "as if I didn't know."

"Maybe there's another of those markers out there," said Gary quietly.

Tuck finished his sandwich and eyed another one. "No," he said. "Be tough. Tucker, be brave and disciplined, for the food you don't eat now, you may need before you get out of the wilderness with ol' Dan Tucker here!" Gary got into the truck. He eyed the mileage gauge. "How far?" he said.

Tuck shook his head casually. "Strike an arbitrary figure, my boy. Say a thousand miles. I always wanted to see Acapulco in the summer."

"About ten miles?"

"Fair enough."

———

GARY DROVE out onto the hard surface of the desert. The sand had evidently been blown into the lower areas by the strong winds that swept the area, leaving a good hard surface upon which the ancient wheel tracks had made an almost permanent impression. Who had driven wheeled vehicles on that road? How long ago? Where did the road go?

The questions teemed through Gary's mind as the truck rolled to the south, and in a little while, through passing lower and lower toward the vastness of the true desert to the south, the old windmill vanished from sight, and no signs of man could be seen. At times, even the ancient road was gone, and Gary drove in as straight a line as possible. There was a good compass mounted on the dash, but it was of little help, for a deviation of a few yards either way would lose the trace of road altogether.

There was nothing to do but drive straight and hope that the ruts would appear again.

They did appear again, just enough now and then to lure the boys onward and assure them with a dry chuckle that they were, indeed, following the old road. The full heat of the day now struck as though a thick, enveloping blanket had been lowered upon the Spanish Desert. The sun seemed to be pouring through an immense magnifying glass, the focal point being the Spanish Desert, for it was almost the core of the summer's heat in that area. The boys were silent as the heat beat down upon the truck and the baked earth of the desert.

By three o'clock, it was almost more than a human could bear, but there was nothing to do but keep on going or return to the newer road to the north. The heat would be the same, of course, but at least the truck would be heading for Mesquite Wells.

Tuck raised his suffering head. "Suggestion," he said.

"Shoot."

"How far have we come?"

Gary eyed the mileage gauge. "Fifteen miles," he said.

"What happened to the ten miles we were supposed to stop at?"

"Forgot."

"Me, too."

"What's the suggestion?"

"The sun will be going down in a couple of hours. Maybe we ought to drive back in the darkness. I can't stand much more of this, pal."

Gary nodded. "It was a mistake," he said. "I'll turn around now."

He guided the truck down a hard-surfaced slope and looked ahead to see if he could see the ruts. Something caught his eye. A dark rock standing alone in all that emptiness... A peculiar feeling welled up within Gary, for he knew, without seeing the rock close up, that it had to be another of the markers.

He stopped the truck beside the rock and got out, feeling the full blasting of the sun. He knelt beside the rock, wincing as the baking ground burned through his levis and seared his knees. The cross was very faint, almost imperceptible, but it was there, sure enough!

"Well," said Tuck.

Gary stood up and looked south. The ruts showed for a stretch, then vanished again. He was quite surprised to see how close the first rough hills of the mountains appeared.

"We've got a couple of hours of daylight left," said Tuck. "There will be a moon again tonight."

"You game to go on?"

"Why not?" said Tuck drily. "Out here, the petty ambitions of man are as nothing. The dross of one's soul is burned away by the heat of the sun, his sins vanish like snow beneath the rays. What can one lose but his worthless life from heat or thirst? I have spoken."

"The Omar Khayyam of Arizona," said Gary.

It was slow going for a time, for here, the wind had drifted the sand between low ridges, and the truck had to plow through it with the temperature gauge rising steadily. The sun was low in the west when they found another of the marker rocks, but here, there was absolutely no sign of the road. The hard patches of ground were now few and far between, and just about the time the sun dropped out of sight and the mountain fringe was very close, the truck became firmly stuck in a low area between two ridges. Nothing that Gary could do would move the vehicle out of its trap.

"Great," said Tuck. "What was it Pardy said? *Don't you turn south, and don't you stay out there overnight. If you get caught in there by the dark, you just keep heading for the Wells.*"

"We'll have to unload the truck," said Gary.

"I knew it!"

They hauled out all the things Pardy had given Gary and most of the other gear in the back of the truck.

Sweat dripped from their faces, for it was still very hot despite the fact that the sun was gone.

Before they attempted to get the truck up onto firmer ground, suggested Tuck, they had better eat to gain additional strength, which struck Gary as rather superfluous, for no matter how much Tuck ate, he always seemed to get a little more tired.

They sat on the tailgate, munching the dry food, listening to the dusk wind creeping across the desert. They had just finished eating when the cry came across the desert from the direction of the nearby mountains. Gary recognized it at once, and a shiver crept through his body.

"There's that crazy-sounding coyote again," said Tuck. "He's out early tonight. Didn't even wait for the moon to rise."

"Yeah," said Gary softly.

There was no doubt at all that the howling and the barking, distant though the sound was, was the unmistakable voice of old Barkus, supposedly buried deep beneath the sands, covered with heavy rocks, miles and miles away at Lookout Rock.

CHAPTER SIX

The Fleshless Hand

"It's no use," said Tuck as he peered into the cab of the truck, wiping the sweat from his lean face. "We can't get any traction this way. We'll need something under the wheels. Once we get her moving, we can reach that harder ground up ahead and turn her around."

Gary shut off the ignition. It was still hot in the desert, although the sun had long gone. It would be some time yet before the moon rose. "We'll need some timbers or something," he said.

"Out here? You loco? There ain't even enough brush to cut to put under the wheels."

Gary stepped out of the truck. "I'll walk to those hills," he said. "I saw a wash or two before it got dark. There might be brush or driftwood lying about there. All we'll need is enough for the wheels to back up on, Tuck."

"Yeah." Tuck looked toward the hills, dim and indistinct in the clinging darkness. "Scary sort of a place. Sure you don't want company?"

"You scared to stay alone?"

"Who? *Me*?"

"Yes, you!" said Gary with a grin.

"Yeah," said Tuck. "Maybe we oughta stick together, though, man."

Gary shook his head. "I don't want to take any chances. You know how I lost my water supply the last time I was fooling around in this desert. I don't want that to happen again. You keep the rifle handy."

"What about you?"

Gary reached into the cab and opened the box that carried the matched pair of Colts. He took one of them out and felt about in the case until he found a box of cartridges. The weapon was a .44/40, and the cartridges seemed fairly fresh. He opened the loading gate and filled the cylinder with cartridges, slipping the extra cartridges into a pocket. He thrust the gun through his belt. "It'll be moonrise by the time I get there," he said. He looked at Tuck.

"You get in any trouble, you just start shooting, and Old Dad will be right along, pal."

"Same to you, Tuck."

Gary hooked a canteen to his belt and picked up a length of rope. He strode off into the darkness.

Tuck picked up the rifle and loaded the chamber. He walked about the truck, whistling softly until, at last, the sound of Gary's passage was gone. Then Tuck sat down on the tailgate, staring off into the darkness, and his thoughts were not good.

———

GARY PLODDED across the warm sands, eyeing the dim hills ahead of him. The howling and barking he had heard had done his peace of mind no good, but if he and Tuck were to get out of the desert that night, they'd have to have timbers or something to put beneath the wheels of the truck. They had already chewed up two of the blankets from the truck and various other odds and ends under the spinning wheels.

There was a faint suggestion of moonlight in the east when he reached the first spur of the hills. He walked toward a deep-cut wash, scanning the ground for pieces of wood. He found a piece about four feet long and another two-foot piece, hardly enough for what they needed. He worked his way up the wash. It was deep enough to remain in shadow while the moonlight crept toward the hills and bathed their tops in soft, silvery light.

He was halfway up the wash when he suddenly remembered the notch he had seen and the reflection of sunlight from something, and he realized that he must be within walking distance of whatever had reflected the sunlight. Might be an old mine structure, or a deposit of mica, or perhaps some shining rocks, he thought.

He found a piece of wood, rather wide but thin, and a piece of timber balk about five feet long. He placed them together and worked his way up the steepening wash. Sweat dripped from beneath his hatband and ran down his face. He winced as he felt the stinging bite of a catclaw and raised his head in pain.

He narrowed his eyes. Ahead of him, perhaps a quarter of a mile or more, the light of the new moon was reflected softly and luminescently from something white and rounded, like a huge, white-washed boulder. He stared at it. There was nothing else like it anywhere in sight, nor did he recollect having seen anything else like it on their approach to the hills.

A cool wind crept down the deep notch and touched his heated face with gentle, invisible fingers. He turned and looked down the wash. He could just make out the pick-up truck, like a toy sitting out there in the middle of all that emptiness. Gary turned and looked up the wash again, and as he did so, he could have sworn he saw a shadow move quickly as though to avoid being seen.

His throat grew dry, and his stomach moiled a little. Maybe it had been a shadow of a moving brush, but then he realized that the wind was not strong enough to move the brush that much. His hand crept down to the butt of the Colt. He waited, eyeing each boulder and each clump of brush, half expecting to see a bushy-headed Apache warrior leap from cover and speed down on him with an upraised knife.

Gary saw another piece of wood. He picked it up, and as he turned to carry it down to the mouth of the wash, his foot struck something. The moon was peering into the hills now, lighting the western wall of the wash. Gary looked down to see an almost perfect metate at his feet. He dropped the piece of wood and knelt to examine the metate. It was heavy—hardly the thing an Indian would haul with him on a waterless journey through the inhospitable desert and hills.

He knew of no Indian villages, new or old, within miles of this area. He squatted on his heels, studying the metate, and as he did so, he saw something else. Beyond the metate, embedded in the stony side of the wash, were pieces of pottery. There was no mistaking them. He walked to them and pulled several of the shards free from the imprisoning earth.

Gary looked up and down the wash. There was no level spot for a village anywhere within several hundred yards. The shards had been swept down by rains, or perhaps had been thrown there when the pots had been broken. The metate was another matter, but it was quite possible for a flash storm to arise over the hills and deluge them with blinding rain, sweeping everything before it.

Gary had experienced such floods before, and he knew the awful, insensate power of them. He had often listened to the grinding sounds of big rocks and sometimes boulders being swept along the bottom of a canyon or an arroyo by the racing waters.

Gary shoved back his hat. There must have been a village somewhere within the shelter of the hills. Perhaps at a time when there was water there. Perhaps the water supply had failed, or the predatory Apaches and Yanquis had driven out the more peaceful Indians—perhaps Pimas or Sand Papagos. He began to forget his mission to get timber. Once again, he looked at the whitish surface, wondering what it was, and then he remembered that he must get back to Tuck. They could come this way again, or perhaps explore a bit after they freed the truck.

He stepped back and felt the quick driving pain of a cactus needle that pierced the side of his left boot and sank into the flesh. He winced and sat down, feeling for the broken-off needle with his fingertips. The needle had firmly pinned the boot, sock, and flesh together. He took out his knife and pried at the needle until it loosened a little, then he eased off the boot, feeling blood trickling on his flesh. He worked the needle out of the tough leather. The needle could almost have been used as a nail, so stout and tough was it. He flipped it away and raised his head.

His blood seemed lo congeal into icy red crystals. He was looking directly at a hooded figure standing on a rock at the top of the wash, and it was looking directly at him, although he could not see the face. For a long moment, they looked at each other, and then the robed figure raised an arm and pointed down the wash toward the desert, and Gary Cole could have sworn that the hand at the end of the dusty, draping sleeve was *fleshless!*

He mechanically pulled on his boot, never taking his eyes from the spectral figure, and then he stood up. His heart thudded against his ribs. His throat turned brassy dry. He opened his mouth to yell in fear and panic, but nothing came from his dried-up throat.

He stepped back, and his foot struck the metate. He looked quickly down, and when he looked up again, the figure was gone. If there was ever a time when fear almost loosed Gary's sanity, it was at that instant. He closed his eyes to get a grip on himself. Maybe he had imagined seeing the robed figure. Gary had seen and heard many strange things in the deserts and mountains, but there had always been some explanation for them, or at least he had thought so.

Gary opened his eyes. The figure was gone, sure enough, and the moonlight revealed a dreamy, almost unearthly, landscape. The wind had died away. He slowly moved down the wash, picking up his pieces of wood, looking back over his shoulder every now and then, half expecting to see the spectral figure closing in on him, but he *would not run*. Once fear was the spur, panic would follow, and then all control would be lost.

The wash seemed ten times rougher and longer than his memory recollected, but at last, he reached the desert floor with his wood tied together and slung over his shoulders. He did not look back. Maybe he had conjured that ghostly-looking figure out of moonbeams, shadows, and pure, unadulterated imagination, and if he had, he had done a prime job of it.

———

TUCK'S lean face was always a welcome sight to Gary Cole, but this night, Gary could have kissed it. He dropped the wood. "Let's get going," he said breathlessly.

"You pooped?"

"No, why?"

Tuck shrugged. "You look as though you'd seen a ghost."

"Ha, ha, ha," wheezed Gary.

"You sound a little loco, pal."

Gary did not answer. He glanced back at those brooding hills, now fully bathed in ghostly moonlight. They were as still as the grave. He turned to the truck and busied himself. He wanted, above all, to get that truck out on firmer ground, turn it back to the north, and keep it going until Mesquite Wells was in sight.

He worked his way down under the rear of the truck, forcing pieces of wood here and there to give the rear wheels traction. He was crawling out when the howling sound drifted from the hills and broke down into a ragged barking noise. He closed his eyes and felt the icy sweat work down his sides. This was getting to be too much.

"There's that crazy coyote again," said Tuck.

"Yeah." Gary crawled out and walked to the cab, wiping the sweat from his face, hardly daring to look ahead. He started the engine, shrinking within himself as the sound carried loudly toward those lunar-looking hills.

He eased the truck into low-low and felt the wheels grip. They whirred on and on, and the smell of burning rubber hung about the truck, but slowly and steadily, the truck moved forward with a loud crackling and snapping of the dry wood beneath the wheels until, at last, the truck was on firm ground. "March order!" snapped Gary to Tuck.

Tuck looked curiously as Gary heaved the relics into the back of the truck with calm disdain for their value. "You inna hurry or somethin', pal?" he asked.

"I'd like to get out of here, is all," said Gary curtly.

"You want to throw in the wood too?"

"Might as well. Might need it again."

The wood clattered into the truck. Tuck raised the rifle to place it inside the camperback.

"Keep it with you," said Gary.

Tuck lowered the rifle and eyed Gary again. "What's wrong, Gary?" he asked quietly.

"Nothing."

"Don't kid me, Gary. I've known you too long not to know when something is bugging you. What is it?"

"I saw a ghost, is all."

"Oh, *that*? I thought it was something important!" Tuck grinned as he walked toward the front of the truck.

He stopped suddenly and turned slowly. "You're kidding, of course?"

Gary slammed the rear door shut and locked it. He walked to the front of the truck. "No," he said.

Tuck tilted his head to one side. "Man, oh man," he said. "You've been out here too long. You're getting like Pardy Willis."

Gary shrugged. He reached for the door handle and froze in the motion. For a moment, he was sure he was seeing things, but there was no mistaking the same robed and hooded figure, standing this time atop the low sand ridge south of the truck and between it and the hills. Once again, the arm raised slowly, and the fleshless hand pointed north. "Get on your way," the thing seemed to be saying in sign language.

"Look," gasped Gary.

Tuck looked up toward the robed figure. His eyes narrowed. "What is it?" he said.

"I *said* I had seen a ghost."

"Lordy! What is it, man?"

The figure was motionless, as though carved from dusty brown rock, and the outstretched arm did not waver. The moonlight shone on the fleshless hand, glistening from the thin white bones.

As one man, the two boys were inside the cab. Gary shifted gears and drove in a wide sweeping path around the soft sand and set the truck at the northern ridge. It wasn't until the truck topped the ridge that he dared to look back as he steered a slantways course to descend the ridge. The other ridge was as empty as it had been before the apparition had been seen.

"Faster," murmured Tuck through set teeth. His face was wet with cold sweat.

Gary drove with all his skill. It was almost as light as daylight, and by following the marks of their passage to where they had gotten stuck in the sand, he was able to avoid the softer areas. If they got stuck again, with that *thing* hanging around...

They passed the cross-marked rock and drove on, and it seemed as though somehow they had wandered into a sort of limbo, unmarked by man, roadless and pathless, with now and then the faint marks of their earlier passage to guide them.

The moon was at its zenith when, at last, they reached the road that led north and could make better time. Neither of them looked back. Tuck went so far as to move the outer rear-view mirror on his side so that he couldn't see behind the truck. Neither one of them spoke. They had each had a bad fright. Reason would return in time, but now fear held the reins, with a spade bit in their mouths, and he wasn't about to let control get out of his hands—not until he had seared their souls a bit.

The road wasn't too bad, but even so, the truck bumped and slewed, slammed and swayed in its too-swift passage to the north. Gary Cole didn't want any part of the Spanish Desert in darkness *that* night.

"Ol' Pardy was right, at that," said Tuck. "'Don't you turn south, and don't you stay out there overnight,' he said. That ol' man knew what he was talking about."

Gary nodded. Reason was returning ever so slowly. He began to reconstruct incidents in his mind. It could have been a man in that dusty old robe, but if so, he was well concealed, and there had been no mistaking the fleshless hand. Gary's own flesh crawled at the thought of it.

"Funny thing," said Tuck slowly. "He was wearing a robe like them old padres wore."

"Brown," said Gary. "Dusty old brown. Franciscans wear brown robes."

"No, it's the Jesuits that wear brown. The Franciscans wear black."

"It's the other way around," said Gary.

"Have it your way. Whatever he was, if it was a he, I

don't like him in black *or* brown." Tuck began to poke about in the food hamper, a sure sign that he was feeling normal. "Maybe he was a Mexican monk or something just poking around."

"Miles from any road? In waterless country on foot? Besides, *how about that hand of his?*"

Tuck stopped fooling in the food hamper. "Yeah," he said slowly. "That sure gave ol' Tucker a jolt. You said you saw him in the hills?"

"Yeah. Right at the top of the wash I was in."

"What'd he do?"

"Just stood there as though he was watching me. He pointed down the wash as though warning me away, then vanished."

"Just like that?"

"Well, I stepped on a metate and looked down, then when I looked up again, he was gone."

"A metate? In *those* hills?" asked Tuck incredulously.

"There were some potsherds there, too."

"I'll be darned! I never heard of any Indians living in them hills. Never heard of anyone living there, as a matter of fact. No one is that loco."

"Maybe not, but someone must have been living there."

"Like maybe a Franciscan padre?" said Tuck quietly.

Gary looked at him. "Yes. There were Jesuits in the Southwest in the seventeenth century. They founded Tumacacori in the Valley of the Santa Cruz. The Jesuits were expelled from the New World empire of the Spaniards about the middle of the eighteenth century. The Franciscans came then and took over the missions. That was about two hundred years ago. It was the Franciscans who actually built the mission, as we know it, at Tumacacori. More than a hundred years ago, the Franciscans were also expelled, this time by the Mexican government. So it would be more likely that Franciscans were in this area, to build missions at least."

"I find it hard to believe."

"There was *something* in those hills. Tuck."

"You bet!" said Tuck fervently. "You just bet there was, and I don't want to see *him* again!"

"I wasn't thinking about that. There must have been a village or a settlement in those hills, perhaps a hundred years ago or more. If there was a settlement, there could have been a mission."

"Meaning?"

Gary looked at him again. "The legendary 'Lost Mission,' pal. Everything points to it, Tuck. The faint traces of a road, the cross-inscribed marker rocks, the old ox yoke, the metate and the potsherds. Everything points to it, I tell you!"

"Yeah," said Tuck drily, "and that ol' padre with the bony ol' hand points *away* from it."

There was no answer from Gary. There was no possible explanation for the eerie visitation of the brown-robed figure. Gary didn't believe in ghosts or psychic phenomena; at least he *thought* he didn't. He knew, too, that ancient superstitions are not easily expelled from the primitive depths of the human mind despite great advances in science and education. He also knew that there were well-documented accounts of strange and inexplicable happenings sworn to by people whose intelligence, honesty, and sanity were above reproach.

There was one more thing Gary Cole knew as sure as he was sitting in the truck, bouncing his way in haste toward distant Mesquite Wells under the clear light of the desert moon. He had to go back some day. There would be no denying the call of those strange and brooding hills.

CHAPTER SEVEN

Clues to the Lost Mission

The day's work was done at Chiricahua Springs Ranch. The last of the summer's guests had departed in the afternoon, being driven to town by Pete Cole, and he had taken along Lucille, his wife, for dinner and a show in town after the guests had been seen off. There would be peace and quiet at the old ranch for some weeks to come, before Gary and Tuck went off to State and Sue Browne returned to her boarding school.

There had been no chance for the boys to return to the Spanish Desert for some weeks. There was just too much to do, and as Pete paid them by the hour—for an hour's work, according to his figures—but two hours' work for the price of one, according to Tuck—the opportunity to make a few dollars before starting college in September was too tempting for the boys to pass by.

Tuck Browne slowly clambered down from the windmill platform and wiped the grease from his hands. "Well," he said slowly, "I took care of all the damage I did when I tried to speed up that ol' relic. How come your father wants to keep it, anyway, Gary? He's got that terrific new pump for the well."

Gary grinned as he threw a stick for Lobo to chase. The big dog lumbered clumsily after it. "Gives authenticity to the place. Color, you know. The dudes like to see it. Personally, the crazy thing keeps me awake on windy nights."

Tuck looked up at the wheel. "I could sneak up there and make a few adjustments," he said darkly. "Get a night of big wind, and them vanes would take off like crazy across the desert. Whoeee! Just like that!"

"Yeah," said Gary drily, "and we'd be right after them. Whoeee! Just like that!"

"We can't win for losing."

"Come on in," said Gary. "Sue is making supper. She's got one of those mysterious smiles of hers on her face, like a cat that just ate the pet parakeet."

"Oh, Lord, deliver me," said Tuck. He rolled up his eyes. His nose wrinkled. "Man, what's that I smell!"

"Tamale pie," said Gary.

Tuck rubbed his hands together. "How many of them?"

"How many do you think?"

"Just one?"

"It's big enough for a squad of Marines," said Gary.

"That ain't hardly enough, but it'll have to do." He eyed Gary. "You think she's got something up her sleeve?"

Gary nodded. "With that smile and tamale pie on the table? Besides, my mother gave her the secret of apple and raisin pie, and Sue made three of them."

"One apiece!"

Gary nodded again. He was barely listening to Tuck. Day after day, he had been thinking about the Spanish Desert and the Lost Mission, but somehow or other, his thoughts would get on a merry-go-round, and he couldn't get any leads worked out. There was only one thing to do, and that was to return to those hills and check them out thoroughly. Time was running out, however, and once he and Tuck started college, they'd hardly have much free time in their first year to search for the Lost Mission.

"Looks like we'll *never* get back there," said Tuck. He

jerked his head toward the south. "Our ol' pal down there will be missing us."

"You think we really saw him?"

"I don't know about *you,* pal, but ol' Tucker C. Browne saw him."

"Beats me," said Gary. "I've tried to believe it was imagination or maybe something that looked like an old padre in his brown robe, but somehow or other, I know that's wrong. We saw *something,* whatever *it* was."

"I was in town a couple of days ago on an errand for your father. I talked with Mrs. Wittman again about roads out there and about the Lost Mission. She said she had been asking questions about it and corresponding here and there with people who might know something. She didn't get a single lead. Beats me, pal."

"Well," said Gary gloomily as they walked toward the ranch house, "it's only a matter of time before we're off to State. It isn't going to be easy to pay much attention in classes thinking about that old mission out there, if there is one."

"There is," said Tuck soberly.

"You think so, too?"

"I *know* it," said the lean one. "Man, smell that pie!"

Both boys surreptitiously eyed Sue as she primly served them, exquisitely neat in her housedress and apron. Now and then, they glanced at each other when she wasn't watching them. She was up to something.

The blow fell about the time Tuck was working on his second helping of tamale pie, meanwhile eyeing the three apple and raisin pies cooling on a side table. He was eating so fast that his teeth seemed to be stumbling in their haste to switch from tamale pie to apple and raisin.

"Got a letter today," said Sue.

"Fan mail?" mumbled Tuck.

"Pen-pal," said Sue.

"A chimpanzee in the San Diego Zoo writing to you?" said Tuck.

"Well, yes," said Sue sweetly, "but I couldn't translate chimp language, so I thought I better have *you* do it."

"*Touché*!" said Gary.

"Dirty pool," said Tuck.

Sue smiled at Gary. "So happens," she said, "that I have a pen-pal in Durango, Mexico. We practice on each other with English and Spanish."

"Some practice," said Tuck. "Man, when that kid comes up here thinking she can speak English after what you done to her! Hawww!"

"I had straight A's in English," said Sue smilingly, "and intend to major in it—for one purpose, to spread the English language to heathens such *as you*, Tucker C. Browne! By the way, how were your last English grades? A step above D, perhaps?"

"Just about," admitted Tuck. "Sorry, Susan Alice Browne."

"Apology accepted," she said.

Gary grinned. Sue could take Tuck on any time in a verbal duel and whip him easily, which was more than Gary could do or most any of their friends and friendly enemies at Cottonwood Wells Union High.

"Serafina's father is Professor Roderigo Abeyta, and he's an authority on Mexican history."

"Serafina?" said Tuck. He rolled his eyes. "Sounds like some kind of a cereal."

"Serafina knew we were interested in finding the Lost Mission," continued Sue. "She asked her father about it."

"We?" asked Tuck. "*We*? Since when did *you* get in on the deal?"

Sue tilted her head to one side and eyed her fractious cousin. "Look, *bomber*," she said in a cold fiat voice, "I'm dealing myself in. *Comprende*?"

"Not exactly," said Tuck.

"You two clods have been fooling around trying to get a lead on the Lost Mission and haven't got much of a lead at all. Have you?"

"Well, no," said Tuck, "now that you mention it."

"Listen to *me*, then. *Escocbar*! There never were any records in English written about that missing mission. Missing mission? Clever, eh?"

"Ha, ha, ha," said Tuck. He closed his eyes and shook his head. "That's awful."

"In fact, no one seemed able to find records of the Lost Mission written in Spanish, either," said Gary.

"Sure," said Sue wisely. "That was because those records were lost themselves."

"Very clever," said Tuck.

"When the Jesuits were expelled by the Spanish Crown in 1767, the Franciscans took over," said Sue. "When the Franciscans arrived, everything was changed from the Jesuit regime to that of the Franciscans. All the places of worship, either missions or *visitas,* were rebuilt or made over to conform with Franciscan ideas."

"Listen to her," groaned Tuck.

Gary shot him a hard glance. "I am," he said. "You ought to try it."

"Many of the old Jesuit Church records were lost or stolen. No one seems to know much about what happened to them, but in some rather vague references, Professor Abeyta pieced out some information about a mission somewhere between the Colorado River and the Valley of the Santa Cruz."

"That's an awful lot of country," said Gary.

"Wait until I finish," pleaded Sue. "There was a small village of Papagos—I *think* they were Papagos—that was isolated from the rest of the area by deserts and mountains, a difficult country to cross because of the lack of water, roads, and the great heat. Beyond those hardships, there were the Apaches who periodically raided around there. The word of God was taken to these Indians by the Jesuits way back some time in the early part of the eighteenth century, and for some reason or other, they pledged themselves to build a mission, or a chapel, near their village. This village was situated in a valley, well protected and with a fine supply of water. Perhaps the only water for many miles. The mission *was* built. The Jesuits abandoned it later, probably when they were expelled, and the records were lost."

"Big deal," said Tuck.

"Go on," said Gary to Sue.

"Many years ago, a small party of Franciscans pledged themselves to find the old mission and the Indians and restore the place. They journeyed into that desert and *were never seen or heard of again...*"

Tuck looked at Gary. Both of them had vivid memories of the brown-robed figure that had warned them away from the hills.

"So, that's why there are no records on the place," said the girl. "The Jesuit records were lost. The Franciscans evidently couldn't find the place. They wrote off the party of padres that tried to find it and went about their other business."

"What about the Indians?" said Tuck slowly. "You can't lose a whole village of Indians just like that."

"There was evidently a gap of some years between the time the Jesuits abandoned the place and the Franciscans went to look for it," said Sue. "A lot of things could happen in that time in such a country. Maybe the water ran out, or they had a plague, or they moved somewhere else, or they were massacred by Apaches or Yanquis."

"Makes a lot of sense," said Gary. He stood up and paced back and forth. "We might as well tell you all we know," he added. He filled Sue in with the details of the cross-inscribed markers and other facts—the finding of the metate and the potsherds—but he did not dare tell this sharp, intelligent girl about seeing that ghostly figure.

"Then the Lost Mission must be in those hills," said Sue firmly.

"It's still a lot of country," said Gary. "As I told Tuck,

there was no border in those days. This was all part of Mexico. That Lost Mission could be in Arizona or, more likely, south in Sonora. Between the Colorado and the Valley of the Santa Cruz? There are hundreds, if not thousands, of square miles in that area. Was the mission or chapel named?"

"Professor Abeyta thinks it *might* have been named Mission de la Purisima Concepcion."

Tuck looked at Gary. "Didn't you once tell me about some mission on the Colorado named Concepcion?"

"Yes. Built by the Franciscans. Wait a minute." Gary walked into his room and brought back a notebook he had filled in with such information. "Here it is," he said quietly. "Padre Francisco Garces instigated the building of it about 1779. He was of the Franciscan Order. In 1781, the Yuma Indians arose against it and massacred many of its people. It was named Mission de la Purisima Concepcion." He shook his head. "It can't be the same place. A wrong lead again?"

Sue began to cut one of the apple and raisin pies under the fascinated eyes of her cousin Tucker.

"Isn't it possible," she said over her shoulder, "that there might have been *two* missions by that name? The Jesuits founded the first one, abandoned it, and the Franciscans never found it again or weren't much interested later in finding it. Years later, they built a mission on the Colorado and used the same name all over again?"

Tuck looked at Gary. "Sometimes she does make sense," he said.

Gary nodded. There had been a gap of twelve years between the expulsion of the Jesuits and the building of Mission Concepcion on the Colorado, but Sue had said that the Jesuits had abandoned the mission they had built somewhere between the Colorado and the Santa Cruz Valley, and they might well have abandoned it *before* their expulsion in 1767.

Sue served the pie and sat down. "Serafina mentioned that her father said it was quite possible the so-called Lost Mission was somewhere southwest of Cabeza Negra and possibly in the Sierra Lechuguilla."

"Cabeza Negra," said Gary. "Black Head. I never heard of such a place."

"What about the Sierra Lechuguilla?" said Tuck around a wad of pie.

"Lechuguilla means ruche or ruching," said Sue.

"You don't say!" said Tuck. "What does *that* mean?"

"Like frills, or folds, or something," she said.

"There's a Lechuguilla Wash south of here, before you hit the true Spanish Desert," said Gary. "There's a Lechuguilla Desert, too, between the Gila Mountains and the Tinajas Atlas Mountains to the west and the Copper Mountains and Cabeza Prieta Mountains on the east. Not too far from the Colorado, as the crow flies."

"Hope he carries his own water," said Tuck.

"You don't know of any Lechuguilla Mountains, then?" asked Sue.

Gary shook his head. "Names have changed over the years. Some of these mountains and deserts have two or three different names. Both of those names have me licked. Black Head and Ruching Mountains. Great!"

"We're back where we started," said Tuck as he deftly slid a second slab of pie onto his plate. "You got any ice cream for this pie, Susan?"

"Only licorice," she said sweetly.

"Well, that's better than nothing," he said resignedly. His eyes widened. "*Licorice!*"

"Just whipped up a batch," she said.

"Will you two stop feuding!" snapped Gary. "Feed that creature anything you have in the line of ice cream, Sue, and let's study this thing out."

"What do they call those mountains we were heading for when the truck got stuck?" asked the lean one.

"The San Vigils," said Gary. "They are also known as the Papago Mountains, I think."

"Any other names?" said Sue.

"There are some hills down around there called the Ruffled Hills, but it isn't commonly used in referring to them."

"Sounds cute," said Tuck.

Sue ladled ice cream atop Tuck's pie. "Ruffled Hills," she said musingly. "Lechuguilla Mountains. Lechuguilla means ruche, or ruching. Ruching could also be called ruffling, couldn't it?"

Gary stared at her. "Of course!"

"We're looking for mountains, not hills," said Tuck.

Gary waved a hand. "Maybe they called the foothills of those mountains the Ruffled Hills. They might also have called the mountains the Ruffled Mountains. The similarity is too close just to overlook it, pals."

"So now we've found the Sierra Lechuguilla...maybe," said Tuck. "All we have to do now is to find Cabeza Negra."

Gary nodded. "I'll have to dig through all my old maps, charts, and accounts. There should be a reference to such a place."

Tuck finished his pie and stood up. "I've got a chore to do," he said. "Got to clean out the ol' pick-up. I'll give you a hand when you're ready to start hunting through those records, pal."

Sue started clearing the table. "Me too," she said, "as soon as I clear up this mess."

———

GARY LEFT the house to take care of his chores. There wasn't much to do, and every now and then, he found himself looking off to the south, toward the unseen mountains where he had made those fascinating discoveries and had seen that mysterious robed figure.

He could hear Tuck grumbling and complaining as he worked on the truck. Wood clattered to the ground. The rear door of the truck was closed. Wood clattered again as Tuck picked it up. Then, all became very quiet. Minutes passed. "Hey, Gary!" yelled Tuck. "Come on the double, man!"

Gary ran around the side of the house. "What's wrong, Tuck?" he cried.

"Take a look at this piece of wood!"

Gary took it from Tuck, recognizing it as one of the pieces he had found in the dry wash in the hills to the south. He looked at it and then at Tuck. "You flipped?" he asked.

"Turn it over, gourd-head!"

Gary turned it over. The wood seemed to be engraved with lettering of some kind. He traced the letters with a fingertip. "Miss," he said aloud. "De...Puri...Cone..." He looked at Tuck. "I don't dare to believe what I'm thinking."

Tuck handed him another piece of wood, about the same size. "This has letters on it too."

Gary eyed the faint letters, "n...ma...ion..."

Tuck nodded. "This piece split under the wheels. Maybe we left the middle piece of it out there."

"No!" yelled Gary. "I nailed it across a hole in the back of one of the sheds! Come on!"

———

SUE BROWNE STOOD on the back porch of the house watching the two boys racing to the rear of the shed and then listened to the sounds of the two of them arguing to take it easy, etc., while nails grated in wood. "Men," she said in a tone of disgust.

A moment later, the two of them sped past, whooping at the tops of their voices, with Tuck dragging a piece of wood behind him. Sue walked through the house and out onto the front porch to see the two of them on their knees, fitting three pieces of wood together. Tuck's ungodly shriek, a combination of a train whistle, coyote's howl, tires protesting against pavement, and the rising incantations of a Druid priest, arose into the quiet.

Lobo came rushing around the side of the house, teeth bared. The cat lit out for the tall timber. The chickens cackled in their house, a steer bellowed out in the darkness, and birds flew out of the trees in panic.

"Mission de la Purisima Concepcion!" screamed Tuck.

Sue ran to the boys and looked down at the three warped and sun-silvered pieces of wood fitted together on the ground, and she saw the faintly carved letters. "Where did you get it?" she cried.

Tuck smashed Gary between the shoulders with his two fists. "The gourd-head picked them up in the wash!" he shrieked. "We used them to help get the truck outa the sand! Thank the Lord I thought of keeping them when we got out, and I kept 'em stored in the back of the truck!"

"Listen to him," said Gary drily. "He thought of storing them in the truck. Dad has been trying to get him to clean out the truck for a week or more."

"I'm psychic," said Tuck. "I had a feeling alla time these pieces of wood were valuable!"

"That's why you let me nail one of the pieces to the shed, then?"

"Well, any dummy could have seen the wood was carved."

"I'll have to buy that," said Gary. He stood up. "We've got a sure lead now. Those potsherds and the metate indicate that there *was* an Indian village in those hills, and these pieces of wood indicate that the mission must be up in there, too. The wood was likely washed down during a flash flood, maybe buried for years."

"Or maybe dropped there by someone who picked it up somewhere else," said Sue.

"Listen to her!" shrieked Tuck. "Spoil-sport!"

"She might be right," said Gary. "Besides, those are pretty wild and rugged hills and mountains. A flood could sweep things for miles and miles." He looked about. "Where's the rest of the wood?"

Tuck kicked at the pile with his feet.

Gary knelt and turned over the widest of the pieces.

"Look," he said. The thick wood had been carved into a panel design similar to that found on doors common in Spanish and Mexican Colonial architecture. "No Indian would carve a door like that," he said, "and if by chance he did, he was most likely taught by a padre. Like those *santos* you see in New Mexico. Indians carved them, and they therefore look like Indians. The padres supervised the work of building their churches and missions and likely did the most difficult work, but they did it with Indian labor."

"It's a perfect lead," said Tuck. "Now all we have to do is get back there."

Gary picked up the pieces of wood. "I doubt if we can make it back there this year," he said quietly. "Maybe during the Christmas holidays. I hate to wait, though."

"We agreed to help your father until college starts," said Tuck.

"Cheer up," said Sue. "Who else knows about it? It'll be safe enough until we go look for it."

Gary shrugged. "I suppose you're right," he said, "but I always have the feeling someone will beat us to it."

"Yeah, I know what you mean," said Tuck. "Like when you know there is a slab of pie or cake left over, just waiting for you, and you get your sharp little fangs all set for it, and when you go to get it, savoring it until the last possible second, you find out that someone beat you to it."

Sue smiled. "Leave it to ol' Tucker to work out a simile like that."

"Let's go hunt through my records for Cabeza Negra," said Gary.

They all walked into the house, carrying the old wood, and as they did so, the new moon began to rise, shedding its soft, silvery glow over the wide country, lighting the mysterious wastes of the Spanish Desert and the brooding hills to the south.

CHAPTER EIGHT

Where Is Pardy Willis?

Chiricahua Springs Ranch was sleeping in the bright moonlight when Pete Cole drove the station wagon into the wide front yard. He shut off the ignition, got out of the car, then walked around it to open the door for his wife. She looked up at him. "Are you going to tell the boys now?" she asked.

He looked at his wristwatch. "It's only twelve o'clock," he said. "I'd like them to get an early start." He looked about.

"Quiet, isn't it?"

She nodded. "I'll miss the guests," she said.

"We'll have more of them in a few weeks. I'm glad this thing about Pardy Willis came up. I haven't enough work to keep the boys busy. Besides, they've been wanting to go south again."

"What about Sue?"

"Can you spare her?"

"Of course!"

They walked into the house. Pete Cole walked to Gary's door and tapped lightly on it. "Gary?" he said.

"Yes, Dad?" answered Gary. "We weren't asleep."

Pete opened the door and walked in as Gary lighted

the bedside lamp. Tuck raised his head. "What's up. Mister Cole?" he asked.

Pete sat down on the side of the bed. "I met Sid Fleischer in town tonight," he said. "Sid works for the state. He had to go down Pardy Willis' way a few days ago. He stopped to see the old man and said Pardy is in pretty bad shape."

"Sick?" asked Gary.

"Well, maybe not physically. Sid said he was acting strangely. Looking out into the desert all the time, mumbling to himself. Sid thinks he's been out there too long by himself. I'd like to have you boys go down and see how he is and bring him back here for a while, if he'll come."

Gary felt Tuck's leg bump against his.

Pete stood up. "There isn't enough work to keep you two workhorses busy." He never cracked a smile. "Your mother said Sue can go along if it's all right with you two fellas."

"Well, now," said Tuck.

"You'll take her along, then?" said Pete. "*Bueno!* Your mother saw her mother in town tonight after we talked to Sid. Mrs. Browne said it was all right to take Sue along."

"She would," said Tuck in a strangled voice.

"You can pull out any time," said Pete. "You can take the station wagon if you like."

"I'd rather take the truck, Dad," said Gary.

"Suit yourself. You might have to stay down there overnight, so take along plenty of chow. Remember you have Tucker C. Browne, the lean and hungry one, along."

"Gee, thanks," said Tuck.

"We'll pull about before dawn," said Gary, "to miss some of the heat." He reached out for the alarm clock.

Pete noticed the sly look on Tuck's face. "Oh, before I forget, Gary. Your mother is telling Sue about the trip right now." He grinned as he closed the door behind him.

"Sometimes he acts just like you," growled Tuck.

"I think this big act of yours is as phony as a three-dollar bill. Besides, who knows, along with your back and my brains, we might need a little feminine intuition in case we run into something. Just in case, mind you!"

––––––

IF TUCK BROWNE had had any ideas about leaving Sue behind in the darkness before the coming of the dawn, he was sadly mistaken. A slim figure moved about the back of the truck, stowing away supplies and softly whistling when the two boys struggled sleepily out to the truck. Sue smiled cheerfully at them. "Top of the morning!" she cried.

"I ain't well," groaned Tuck.

"Get in the back. Tucker," said Sue brightly, "and I'll tuck you in, Tucker! Pretty good, hey?"

"Oh, my head," said Tuck. He crawled into the back of the truck and reached for a food hamper. Sue deftly closed the door. "Ready, chief?" she said to Gary.

He handed her the keys. "Stay out of the ditches," he said.

She drove the truck expertly from the yard out onto the gravel road and turned south, heading for the east-west highway. Gary sagged in the seat beside her. "You know where to turn off?" he asked.

"Sure do!"

"Listen to her at this time of the morning," a muffled voice said from the back of the truck.

There was no answer from Gary. He was already asleep.

––––––

THE SUN CAME up beyond the eastern range and began to flood the cold desert with its warming light. The rays lanced through the window on the driver's side of the truck. Sue Browne reached over and shut off the blower fan of the heater. She had turned onto the little-used road that led in time to Pardy Willis' place at lookout Rock. It was going to be a hot day.

Gary opened his eyes as the sun touched his face. "How is the lean one?" he asked.

"He fell asleep with half an apple in his mouth," said Sue.

"I hope he keeps it there all day," said Gary. "Maybe he'll give us some rest from that constant chatter of his."

"Well, it doesn't make any difference," she said. "You shut up one Browne, and you have another to deal with. Like me, man."

Gary grinned at her. He could never get over the change that had taken place in Susan Alice Browne between the time of their adventures in the Espectro Mountains the summer before and her appearance that Christmas upon her return from boarding school. There was one thing that had not changed about her, though; she still had the same inquisitive quality, coupled with a sharp mind and more than her share of courage.

"I wonder what's bothering Pardy Willis," she said.

"You know him, then?"

She nodded. "A long time ago, he was in town. He knew my Uncle Mark pretty well. You know, the one that's something like you. Always poking around out in the desert looking for things. Pardy liked my Uncle Mark. Pardy stayed in town for a few days and left as quietly as he came. It bothered me then, for he didn't have a car or a truck—not even a horse."

"He walks," said Gary. "That's the walkingest man you ever saw. Or used to be," he added quietly.

"Why do you say that?"

Gary told her about the old man and his seeming fears. "There's something out in that desert that's bothering him," he said. "Besides, he lost his old dog Barkus."

"Lost him?"

"Well, he died, and Pardy buried him. Remember we told you about those cross-marked rocks on the dog's grave?"

"You knew he was dead," she said, "and yet you said Barkus was *lost*. Why lost instead of dead?"

"Well, I thought I heard the old dog out in the desert a couple of times. He has a peculiar howling, barking sort of a way of making noise."

"You couldn't have been mistaken?"

Gary did not answer. The memories of that crying out in the desert still brought an eerie feeling to his mind. "Pardy sits up on the side of Lookout Rock and looks out on that desert as though expecting to see something he didn't exactly want to see."

"Such as?"

"*Quién sabe?*"

"Maybe a ghost or something?"

"Why do you say that?"

She looked sideways at him. "I have a feeling you and Tuck are holding something out on me."

"Why should we do that?"

She smiled. "Because I know you and Tuck. Something happened out there, and you two have clammed up on me about it."

A tousled head was thrust between them from the rear of the truck. "There she goes again," said Tuck. "Making like J. Edgar Hoover or Sam Spade."

She eyed Gary. "What made you two characters come out of that desert so fast?"

There was no answer as the truck pounded along the uneven highway.

"Well?" said Sue.

"How about some coffee, Gary, ol' pal?" said Tuck.

"Suits me, Tucker."

"I'll find out one way or another," she threatened. "I'll never dig it out of you, Gary, but my loquacious, garrulous, talkative cousin will slip, one way or another."

"That'll be the day!" boasted Tuck. "Hey, Gary! Supposing ol' Pardy don't want to come with us?"

"I've been thinking about that," said Gary. "He's a stubborn old man."

"Man, I wouldn't stay out in *that* place. How about them mysterious footsteps you heard the night we were there, Gary? You know, when somebody tried to get into the truck. Then there was..." Tuck's voice died away. "Uh-oh," he said in a very small voice indeed. His head vanished from the window.

"See?" said Sue with a knowing smile.

Gary shot a murderous glance at Tuck. He hadn't told Tuck about that until they had reached Mesquite Wells for fear of worrying his partner, but he hadn't wanted to frighten Sue with the story.

"Who do you think it was?" asked Sue.

"Probably Pardy. Checking the locks. He told me to make sure the truck was locked."

"He did? Why?"

Gary flushed.

"Ol' loquacious, garrulous, talkative Gary," said a muffled voice from within the depths of the camperback.

"Oh," said Gary lightly, "Pardy is just nervous. Been out there too long. Something was bothering him, that's all."

"I'll bet something was bothering him. Why didn't you two scaredy-cats get out and see who it was?"

"Scaredy-cats!" shrieked Tuck. "Listen to her! Man, if *she'd* seen what *we'd* seen out there in the moonlight near them foothills! Ha, ha, ha! She'd be the *scaredest-cat you* ever saw! Pointing with a hand with no meat on it." His voice broke in a paroxysm of anger.

It became very quiet in the truck except for the humming of the motor and the singing of the tires. Gary looked out of the window across the approaches to the Spanish Desert. He began to whistle softly.

"Ha, ha, ha," mimicked Sue. "A hand with no meat on it? Ha. Ha, ha."

Tuck had vanished completely, as though he had stepped into a hole. Not a sound came from the back of the truck. Not even the rustling of wax paper being stealthily removed from thick sandwiches, the crunching of sharp fangs into a juicy apple, the snap, crackle, and pop of king-sized, crinkled potato chips being crushed, the hissing sound of a bottle cap being removed... Nothing at all.

Even Sue dared not look at Gary. She was adept at trapping her cousin, but Gary was another matter. This time, Tuck had floundered into a neat trap of his own making. Gary and Sue had a healthy respect for each other's keenness of mind, like two master swordsmen touching foils, testing each other's skill before they fought it out.

"You can let me out here, Gary, ol' buddy," said a sepulchral voice from the depths of the camperback.

"There's Lookout Rock," said Gary.

The rock thrust itself up into the sharp, clear morning sunlight. There was nothing quite like it for miles and miles. It was almost as though the good Lord had built Himself a desert out there with the extra sand he had left over from the Sahara and then, as an afterthought, had dropped the great pinnacle of dark rock into the sand as a marker, in case he ever wanted to find the Spanish Desert again, which wasn't at all likely.

"How can he live out here all alone like that?" mused Sue.

"To get away from talkative women," said Tuck darkly.

Gary turned. "Speaking of talkative people," he said.

Tuck vanished again.

"Solitude doesn't seem to bother Pardy much," said

Gary. "At least it never did. Something was bothering him when we were out there, though."

"Do you think it was really him checking the truck?"

"Who else could it have been?"

Sue steered past a dead jackrabbit lying in the middle of the road. "Maybe the hand with no meat on it?" she said bravely.

Gary turned off the heater. Already, the sun had driven the cold from the truck. "Well," he said quietly, "we might as well tell you. There'll be no rest until we do." He told the girl about seeing the brown-robed figure near the wash and then near the truck.

"Whameee!" crowed Sue. "This is really something! A real ghost! One of those old Franciscans guarding the treasures of the Lost Mission, warning trespassers away! Man, oh man! This is the best yet. Can we get a chance to see him, Gary?"

"Listen to her," said Tuck. "Once she gets a load of that ol' boy, dressed in that ol' dusty robe and them ol' bony fingers pointing out the way. Man, oh man!"

"You sure you saw him?" asked Sue.

"No doubt about it," said Gary.

"It wasn't imagination?"

"Not on your life," said Tuck eagerly. "He was there! You want, we should drive you back to the ranch now, Sue?"

"You just try," she said. "I'll give you such a *knock* on the head!"

"She means it, too," said Tuck gloomily.

———

THE ROCK WAS NEARER NOW, towering above the level land, while far beyond it, to the southwest, were the dim hills and mountains, just now being lighted by the rising sun. There wasn't a sign of life anywhere. Not a house, fence, car, bird, or animal. Nothing but the brush-stippled desert and the straight road, dotted here and there with holes and great cracks. Pardy Willis had chosen his place of self-imposed exile with great skill.

Sue stopped the truck at Pardy's mailbox. "You'd better take it in, Gary," she said, "I might get stuck."

Gary got into the driver's seat and drove onto the sandy road. It was just as it had been the last time he and Tuck had been there. The naked pinnacle of dark rock. The desert beyond it already starting to feel the growing heat of the sun. The humped mountains to the southwest, still clear and sharp before the coming of the dull heat haze that would change them into something unreal-looking later on in the day.

The brass bedstead was still there. Gary and Tuck grinned at the look on Sue's face as she saw it. None of the scattered junk had been moved or taken away. The road was still thick with clogging sand. Yes, everything was quite the same, and yet, to Gary's quick imagination, it was *not* quite the same.

"The Spanish Desert," said Tuck as they rounded the pinnacle of rock. He nodded his head toward the great panorama ahead of them.

Sue nodded. "Maybe those are the Lechuguillas," she said, pointing to the distant mountains.

"Could be," said Gary. He glanced toward the shacks as the truck rounded the talus slope north of the rock. There was no one in sight, just as it had been when he and Tuck had arrived there in the moonlight. He stopped the truck in almost the same place he had parked it the first trip they had made there, weeks past. He shut off the engine. The three of them sat there. For some peculiar reason, none of them was in a hurry to get out.

"Quiet, ain't it?" said Tuck. He cleared his throat. There wasn't a sign of life about any of the buildings. Gary got out and held the door open for Sue. She got out and stood beside him. Tuck rounded the front of the truck. Both he and Tuck automatically looked up toward the still shadowed western face of Lookout Rock, half expecting to see old Pardy seated in his rock chair, staring out into the limitless expanse of the Spanish Desert. The seat was empty.

"Where is he?" whispered Sue. "This is like a ghost town."

"Might be in his hideout," said Tuck.

Gary nodded. He walked toward the largest of the buildings. "Pardy Willis," he called out as he had done the first trip there.

"Pardy...Willis...Pardy Willis..." echoed Lookout Rock.

Gary walked to the biggest of the buildings. He eased open the creaking door and felt the cool air of the interior flow about his face. He walked inside. Something scurried for cover in the darkness. A mouse, most likely, or perhaps a gecko lizard.

"He ain't anywhere out here," said Tuck from the doorway.

Gary walked back to the rear door that led into the tunnel so laboriously carved by the old man into the living rock. He opened it. "Pardy Willis?" he called into the cool darkness of the tunnel.

"Pardy Willis? Pardy Willis? Pardy Willis?" questioned the tunnel echo.

Blast him, thought Gary. Where *is* he?

Gary didn't exactly want to walk into that tunnel. He knew old Pardy wouldn't bother him. It wasn't the thought of Pardy that took the keen edge from his courage. It was something else. The unseen is always more fearful than that which one can face. There was a haunted, brooding quality about the place that hung like a veil over everything, like the thick dust in the rooms of a long-abandoned house.

Gary forced himself to walk up the sloping tunnel into the room where the old man made his living quarters. The place was empty. He opened the shutters and let daylight pour into the room. He looked down upon the area in front of the great rock. Sue was peering into one of the shacks. Tuck was prowling about behind another of them. Beyond was the implacable face of the desert, and not a sign of life upon it. Nothing but a lone hawk hanging as though pinned like a specimen against the clear blue of the sky.

The room was as neat as could be. Gary felt the fireplace. The ashes and stones were cold. The bedding was rumpled, but it didn't look as though it had recently been slept in. The old shotgun hung on its pegs. Gary even looked under the bed. There was nothing there but a pair of ancient carpet slippers.

Gary walked down through the tunnel, through the big room of the shack, and out into the bright sunlight. There was almost a feeling of relief within him in getting out of the rock. He took his binoculars from the truck and found a way to reach the narrow trail that led up to Pardy's lookout. It was about a shoulder of rock in the tunnel just as one entered it from the shack. The way up to the trail was cut neatly through the rock itself, and one emerged about twenty feet up from ground level.

Gary worked his way slowly up the trail, not looking down until he reached the natural armchair carved by nature into the rock. Then he sat down and took the glasses from their case, adjusting them so that he could scan the desert. The excellent lenses picked out features in sharp detail in the clear morning light. He could even see what he took to be the top of the abandoned windmill to the southeast, just short of where the road made its sharp right-hand turn. To the south of that were the faint traces of the older road that led to the low foothills still farther south, where Tuck and Gary had seen the ghost—if that's what it really was.

Twenty minutes ticked past while Gary patiently studied the Spanish Desert through the glasses. There was nothing to reveal human life out there. Not a thread of dust, not a sparkle of reflected sunlight, not a movement of any kind. It was almost as though the Spanish Desert was a place of death for all forms of animal life. Nothing moved. It was too early for the heat of the day to raise its shimmering haze and for the hot wind to whip up dust-devils.

"Beats me," said Gary. He shook his head. The sun was rising higher, and already, a faint suggestion of the day's heat hovered about Lookout Rock.

He could see the white faces of Tuck and Sue as they looked up at him. "See anything?" called Tuck.

"*See anything? See anything? See anything?*" echoed Lookout Rock.

"No," called down Gary.

He had cased the glasses and slung the case about his neck, preparatory to returning to ground level, when something caught the corner of his eye. It was an instantaneous flash from the low foothills against the dull-looking mountains, as though the rising sun had reflected from some glistening surface. He stared at the hills. He had had the same experience the day he and Tuck had driven south to those mysterious hills, so he took out the glasses again and swept those hills from one end to the other without seeing anything that would reflect the sunlight.

Again, he cased the glasses, and as he picked his way down the narrow trail, he remembered something else: while he had been prospecting for timber in the wash that led into the hills, he had seen something upon which the moon had shone softly; something like a huge white-washed boulder. Maybe it was a deposit of caliche or mica, or perhaps a place where minerals had leached out to the surface to form a natural reflecting area.

What had puzzled Gary then, as it did now, was the fact that those hills were of rather dark rock and earth, as were the mountains behind them—hardly the place for something so light in color to appear. It was not natural.

He stopped suddenly. "It might be something that *man* put there!" he exclaimed aloud.

The lure to go to those hills was on him again, despite the presence of the fearful unknown, as exemplified by that haunting robed figure.

Gary passed through the shack to the open ground. "It's no use," he said. "The old man isn't around here, that's for danged sure."

Tuck nodded. He squatted on the hard ground and slanted his hat across his eyes to peer out toward the desert. "Maybe he's off on one of his walking tours?" he said.

"Worries me," said Gary. "Sid Fleischer said he wasn't well. My Dad was positive that he wanted us to bring him back."

"We'd better not leave until we find him, or at least find out where he went," said Sue.

"Maybe he'll show up yet," said Tuck. He glanced up at the rock pinnacle. "Maybe the old boy is hiding out watching us right now. I wouldn't put it past him."

Sue shivered. "Gives me the creeps," she said quickly.

———

THEY SEARCHED the area until the sun reached its zenith and the great heat of the day became too much to bear under their exertions. It was Sue who suggested that they prepare the noonday meal in Pardy's quarters. They carried a hamper up into the room and kindled a fire in the great fireplace, while Sue took over the duties of chef.

Tuck occupied his time peering from the opened window with the binoculars. Gary examined the room, hoping for a clue as to the whereabouts of the old man, but it was no use. Pardy Willis had vanished from his place as though spirited off to another world.

The three of them were pretty quiet during the fine

meal Sue had prepared. Even Tuck, at his best in spirits while eating, seemed depressed. Now and again, he would look back over his shoulder. "Beats me," he said at last. "The old man is gone, sure enough, but I always get the feeling he's standing in a corner watching me, but when I look quick-like, he isn't there."

Gary nodded. Sunlight was starting to stream through the window. It was then that he noticed something on the rock wall at the head of the old brass bedstead. He got up and walked to it, pulling the bed to one side so that he could examine the wall more closely.

Pegs had been driven into holes drilled into the rock, and from the pegs hung various articles of equipment and clothing, concealing much of the wall. Gary passed a fingertip along what appeared to be a deep crack close to the corner. He stepped back and eyed it. He kicked at the adjoining wall with a boot toe and winced as it met solid rock. He kicked at the wall behind the head of the bed. Not only did it sound different, but also it didn't feel quite the same. Gary rubbed his jaw as he studied the wall. On a long chance, he gripped one of the pegs and pulled at it. Nothing happened.

"He's flipped completely," whispered Tuck hoarsely to Sue.

The third peg did the trick. Gary pulled down on it. There was a soft grating sound, and the wall, or at least a narrow part of it, swung inward as though on concealed hinges, and a cold draft of rather musty air flowed about Gary.

Gary noted that whoever had built the doorway into the rock wall had done a terrifically fine job. The fitting had been almost perfect, and the hanging of the articles on other pegs had been a stroke of genius, concealing most of the cracks where the door fitted into the wall. "Light that lamp. Tuck," he said.

"You goin' in there?" asked Tuck.

"Why not? We came to find Pardy, didn't we?"

"In *there,* pal?"

"He isn't anywhere else around here that I can see," said Gary.

Even so, it took quite a bit of nerve for Gary to take the lighted lamp from Tuck's hand and step inside the unknown area beyond the doorway.

The flickering light of the lamp showed a neat flight of steps carved into the rock, leading down into the utter blackness of the depths below Lookout Rock. A faint whispering of wind seemed to emanate from those depths, like the muted crying of a lost soul.

CHAPTER NINE

The Secret Below Lookout Rock

A hollow echoing raced ahead of Gary down the stairwell—if one could call it that—as he placed one foot before the other in his slow descent. The flickering lamplight revealed the walls, roughly hewn as compared to the walk of the rock room above him. Gary wondered how long it had taken Pardy to dig his way into the dark depths below Lookout Rock. The old man had lived there for many years, with much time on his hands, and he was a skilled hard rock miner, one of the many careers he had pursued and mastered in his long and adventurous life.

He glanced back and saw the white faces of Sue and Tuck at the top of the stairway. For the first time in the hours they had been on the way to Lookout Rock, and on their arrival there, the two of them were silent.

The stairwell turned right rather sharply to disclose a narrow, roughly hewn tunnel probing into the darkness. Gary raised the lamp. "Pardy?" he called out. The echoes raced along the tunnel and died away. "Pardy Willis?" There was no answer.

Gary walked along the tunnel and suddenly found himself in a low-ceiled room. The air was cold and damp. The faint trickling sound of water came to him. He raised the lamp. The far wall was wet with trickling water, sheeting the solid rock wall and then filling a shallow basin hewed into the rock floor. Half immersed in the water were a number of crocks. Shelves had been built along the walls, and they were lined with bottles and jars of preserves and other foods. Gary scanned the room closely. It was nothing more than a sort of cooling vault for Pardy's store of perishable foods. There were no other doorways or cracks in the damp walls indicating that there might be an opening in the walls.

Gary placed the lamp on a barrel top and shrugged. Wherever Pardy Willis was, he wasn't around Lookout Rock, or in it, or *under* it, for that matter.

"You all right?" called down Tuck.

"Yeah," said Gary. "Found some treasure."

"*Treasure?*" shrieked Sue. Her booted feet beat a tattoo on the stairs and she burst into the room. A moment later, there was a thudding sound, a muffled exclamation, and then Tuck rolled into the room, head over heels, to land with a crash against a wall. A jar of preserves fell from the shelf over Tuck's head, bounced from his skull, and smashed on the rock floor between his knees. Tuck shook his head, thrust a finger into the mess on the floor, and tasted it. "Sweet pickles," he said. "Not bad, either."

"Where's the treasure?" demanded Sue.

Gary pointed to the shelves. "I think this is Pardy's spring cellar," he said quietly. "Nothing more."

"No Pardy, eh?" said Tuck.

"No Pardy," said Gary. He shook his head. "Beats the devil out of me."

"Where do you suppose he got all this stuff?" said Sue.

Gary shrugged. "Traded off things for it, I suppose. The old boy is dead broke, except for some of the relics he owns."

Tuck was scanning the shelves, muttering to himself

like a miser counting his hoard. "Watermelon pickles!" he said. "Just my dish!" He reached up for the jar.

"Big deal," said Sue. "Here I thought we were really getting into something."

Gary nodded. "Come on, Tuck," he said. "The old man won't like it if he finds us down here."

Tuck was struggling with the top of the jar. "Lemme taste just one, man!"

"Wouldn't you know it," said Sue. "Look at him."

Tuck had unscrewed the lid. He placed it on the shelf and sniffed at the contents of the jar. A puzzled look came over his lean face. He poked a finger into the jar.

"Come on," said Gary impatiently. He picked up the lamp.

"Wait," said Tuck. "There aren't any watermelon pickles in this jar. Just a wad of paper." He withdrew his finger and turned the jar upside down atop the barrel, emptying out a thick roll of paper. As it was released from the confines of the jar, the paper unrolled and lay almost flat. Tuck whistled softly. "Look at that! Watermelon pickles, hey?"

"Money," said Sue quietly. "Hundreds of dollars in fresh new bills."

Gary placed the lamp beside the money. He picked some of it up. It was all in twenties. A quick calculation of the number of bills gave him a figure of about two thousand dollars.

"Look here," said Tuck. He took a bottle of preserves from the rear of the shelf and opened it, dumping the contents beside the bills. "Peaches, hey? There's more money in this jar than in that one!"

It was Sue who opened one of the crocks in the water basin. She thrust a slim hand into the mouth of the crock and brought out another wad of bills.

"Man!" said Tuck. "Let's open all of them!"

"No," said Gary. "It isn't our money."

"That old shyster," said Tuck. He shook his head.

"Playing like he was stony broke and alla time he was loaded with this green bread. What a phony!"

Gary rubbed his jaw as he eyed the money. "There must be at least six or seven thousand dollars there," he said, "and Lord knows how much more in the rest of these jars and bottles."

"We can look," said Tuck.

"No!" snapped Gary. "It isn't ours. We've got no business fooling around with his money. It's his own business how he wants to keep it."

"Burns me up, though," said Tuck. "Him and that pauper act of his."

"It's his business," insisted Gary. The puzzle bothered him as well as it did Tuck. The old man was secretive and mysterious, but neither Gary, nor anyone else he knew, had any idea that Pardy Willis was a rich man.

Gary wondered just how much more money, in fresh, crisp bills, was stored away in those dusty-looking containers lining the shelves. If most of them were full, Pardy Willis was the Croesus of Arizona. "Put the money back where you found it," he added.

They replaced the money and left the room to ascend to the upper level, where the bright light of day came through the open window, bringing with it waves of heat. As bright and hot as the day was, there was a chilling air of mystery about Lookout Rock.

"Better scatter and search this area inch by inch," said Gary. "There's bound to be some sign of the old man."

———

AN HOUR PASSED before Tuck's keen eyes found something in a wash several hundred yards from the shacks. The clear, sharp tracks of low-heeled boots crossing a patch of soft sand and earth, trending toward the southwest, in the general direction of the old windmill—and, of course, the distant mountains hovering behind the shimmering heat haze.

"They're pretty fresh," said Gary thoughtfully.

"How fresh?" asked Sue.

"Several days, I'd say."

"Doesn't mean much, does it?" she said.

"Everything or nothing," said Gary. "Those are big footprints, and Pardy wears a size twelve at least. Few people ever prowl about here, so I'd be willing to bet it was Pardy who made those tracks."

"Yeah," said Tuck. "Besides, who but Pardy would *walk* out there?"

"It's pretty flimsy evidence," said Sue.

"What else we got to go on?" said Tuck inelegantly.

"You've got a point there," she said. She turned to walk back toward Lookout Rock and then stopped short. "*Look!*"

Both boys looked in the direction she was pointing. Tuck glanced at her. "You flipped your wig? That's Lookout Rock, Susie."

"Look how dark it looks," she said. "Notice how the top is shaped like something?"

"A man's head," said Gary. "Never noticed that before."

"Never looked at it from this angle," said Tuck. "At least this close, anyway."

Sue eyed them. "Are you thinking what I'm thinking?" she asked.

"Whoever knows what *you're* thinking?" said Tuck.

"Keep talking, Sue," said Gary.

She smiled, slightly superior, and looked at the rock. "The rock looks almost black up near the top. It's shaped like a man's head. Black head, if you'll pardon me saying it that way."

Tuck narrowed his eyes and looked at Gary. Tuck shrugged. "She's far gone," he said.

"Black head," said Sue patiently. "Black is *negra* in

Spanish. Head is *cabeza*. Cabeza Negra. Simple, isn't it?"

Gary stared at her and then at the rock. "She's hit it!" he said.

"I'll be darned," said Tuck. He looked at the rock and then toward the distant mountains. "The Lost Mission. Southwest of Cabeza Negra and possibly in the Sierra Lechuguilla. It all adds up. The old road, the markers, the pieces of wood, and the metate and potsherds. That Lost Mission has to be somewhere in those hills near where we got stuck."

"And it looks as though Pardy Willis was heading that way, too," said Gary.

"So maybe we have to go look for him?" suggested Tuck.

They walked slowly back toward the towering rock. Gary wasn't thinking about the Lost Mission now. He was thinking about old Pardy Willis wandering out there in the killing heat, in an almost waterless land, and no one to look for him or care whether he lived or died.

Sid Fleischer had said that Pardy wasn't acting right.

"That poor old man," said Sue quietly. Her voice broke a little.

Tuck nodded. "He was pretty nice to us when we were here last. Fed us like we were kings. Gave us those swell guns."

Whatever had been bothering Pardy Willis had at last drawn him back into the deadly Spanish Desert, a place he had once loved but now feared and hated. It must have been some powerful lure, or perhaps his mind had snapped and he hadn't known what he was doing.

"We can't waste time in letting the authorities know," said Sue. "It might be a matter of life and death for Pardy."

Gary nodded. "I'll have to go," he said.

"What about us?" said Sue.

"I'll go," said Tuck. "You can stay here and play house, Susie."

"Not on your life. Buster!" she snapped. "You won't get me to stay around this place by myself. It's bad enough when you two characters are around."

"Well, I tried," said Tuck resignedly.

"Check the water tank, the canteens, and the waterbag, Tuck," said Gary. "There are a couple of G.I. cans under one of the bunks. You'd better rinse them out and fill them too. There are some old burlap sacks in one of those sheds. Throw them into the rear of the truck, for they'll make good matting in case we get stuck again. Sue, you check the food. If we need anything else, take it from Pardy's place."

"Stick in some of them bottles of watermelon pickles," said Tuck with a grin.

"Hop to it!" said Gary.

"Say," said Tuck slowly. "While I am doing the water and burlap sack bit and Susie is making with the chow, what will *you* be doing, chief?"

Gary took a spade from the rear of the truck and walked toward the mound of rocks atop the grave of old Barkus, the dog. "I'm going to do a little digging," he said quietly. "Just to satisfy myself."

"He's gone completely," said Tuck. "Now he thinks he's a Resurrection man, although I ain't sure just what that is."

"You'd make a good team," said Sue. "Cole and Browne, like Burke and Hare."

"Burke and Hare?"

"Yup," she said. "Burke and Hare lived in Edinburgh, Scotland, many years ago. Doctor Knox at the university would buy bodies for dissection. It got to a point where men who dug up bodies to sell to Knox were called Resurrection men because they resurrected the dead, see? Burke and Hare figured a quicker way. Burke would kill people, and Hare would take the bodies to Knox to sell them. Saved bothering to dig them up."

"Got rid of the middle man," cracked Tuck.

Sue shivered a little despite the heat of the day. "How did we get started on that?" she asked.

Tuck watched Gary as he pitched the rocks from the top of the grave. "Sometimes I wonder about him," he said.

"Sometimes I wonder about both of you," she said.

———

GARY QUICKLY DUG out the loose earth atop the buried dog. A few feet down, the spade struck wood. Gary unearthed a neat, dog-sized coffin. A brass plate had been nailed atop it, and the name BARKUS had been inscribed on it. He took out his sheath knife and began to pry off the lid. He knew Sue and Tuck were watching him from near the truck, but it didn't bother him.

As much as he hated to do what he had to do, he could not stop now. The lid fell off to one side, and within the cloth-lined box was the stiffened body of a dog. The odor sickened Gary and he stepped quickly back and turned his head away. There was no doubt in his mind that he had seen the decomposing body of old Barkus.

Gary quickly placed the lid on the box, holding his breath, and hammered home the nails with a rock. He slid the box into the grave and quickly covered it up, then replaced the rocks. Sweat dripped from his face and body as he walked toward the truck.

"Well?" said Tuck.

"It's Barkus, all right," said Tuck.

There were a few moments of silence, then Tuck spoke up again. "If that's the body of Barkus in that grave, Gary, what was that we heard out in the desert?"

Gary threw the spade into the rear of the truck. 'That's what I'd like to know," he said quietly.

"Maybe a coyote," said Sue.

"No," said Gary.

"You could be mistaken," she insisted.

"No!" he snapped. "It was Barkus, all right! Or his ghost!"

Sue looked curiously at Tuck. The lean one shrugged. It was obvious that he, too, tended to think along the same lines. The sharp memory of that haunting robed figure was still in Tuck's mind. It was also obvious that Sue thought her two companions were playing up the ghost angle a little too much, but, on the other hand, *she* hadn't seen that robed figure and the bony hand pointing the way north, away from whatever was hidden in the Lechuguillas.

———

THE TRUCK WAS ready to roll, water tanks full, food stowed away, burlap sacking and pieces of planking in place on the rear floor of the truck. The truck was pretty much of a self-contained unit as it was. It had an extra-large gas tank, as well as a spare fuel can. There was a well-equipped first-aid kit, complete with snake-bite packet. Gary's Winchester rifle, a pump action 16-gauge shotgun, and a .22 caliber pistol formed the armament, with plenty of extra cartridges.

Gary went back into Pardy's hideout and carefully rehung the clothing and the equipment that concealed the doorway leading down into Pardy's spring cellar. There was nothing else to do around the place. Pardy sometimes left his home for days at a time whenever the wandering fever came over him. Evidently, it had come over him again—or at least Gary hoped so, for in his right mind, the old man could well take care of himself. But if something had gone wrong, it would be quite a different matter.

He carefully closed the shuttered window and barred it, idly wondering as he did so what had been bothering Pardy the last time the boys had been there. He walked down the sloping tunnel and closed the tunnel door behind him, then closed the rear door of the shack and piled some boxes and other items against it so that intruders might not see it.

The sun was slanting to the west, pouring down all its concentrated strength on the Spanish Desert and the great mountains that ringed it in the hazy distance. Gary's two companions stood beside the truck, looking out across the shimmering expanse of the desert. They sincerely wanted to find old Pardy Willis, but there was more to their interest than just finding the old man.

The lure of the Lost Mission had entered into their blood stream like an insidious virus that would never be eliminated until the haunting mystery of the place was solved. Perhaps, if they had not worked out the approach to the puzzle by carefully sifting out information and aligning the clues they had stumbled upon, they might have returned home to find, in time, the Lost Mission fading away from their minds in favor of other and more important matters.

Perhaps it would be so with Sue and Tuck, but not with Gary Cole. He had been through these bouts of fever before, and there wouldn't be any cure until the mystery was solved.

Gary glanced at the mound of rocks over the grave of old Barkus. Once again, the haunting feeling about the old dog came over him, making him shiver a little, even in the burning light of the sun. There was something ghastly and horribly alien about the thought of a ghost dog running loose in the Spanish Desert—far more horrible and chilling than the thought of the ghostly Franciscan and his fleshless hand. It was hard for Gary to believe that the Franciscan, if he was a ghost, would harm mortals, for he was of a gentle and submissive order. On the other hand, perhaps the thing was guarding in death that which it had attempted to guard in life...the Mission de la Purisima Concepcion

CHAPTER TEN

The Hell of the Spanish Desert

T he sun was moving slowly down toward the western mountains as Gary turned the pick-up truck south on the faint trace of road west of the long-abandoned windmill. Here, the surface of the desert was hard, and the twin ruts, almost imperceptible to the eye, stretched south toward the softer areas, where, at times, the ruts vanished completely. Sue squirmed a little as she saw those ruts, and her brown eyes seemed to light up.

The truck moved slowly down into wide hollows and up and across wind-blown ridges where the winds had driven the sand from the basic rock to form treacherous overhanging lips through which the truck could plunge to destruction if one was not careful to avoid them. It wasn't easy driving, and the memory of how hard he and Tuck had worked to free the truck from the sand near the hills was too vivid in Gary's mind for him to make the same mistake again. Even so, now and then, he was forced to shift into low-low to creep through the softer patches.

The heat seemed to be a living thing. It was hard to breathe with the mouth closed, for the lungs didn't seem able to suck in enough of the enervating air. The skin burned, and if metal touched by the sun was contacted by bare skin, some of the skin was left adhering to the metal.

The heat waves shimmering from the baking earth actually hurt the eyes and disturbed the brain as they writhed and twisted in an unholy dance of their own. Yellowish dust arose from the churning wheels of the truck and hung about it because of its slow speed, coating everything in film. It gritted between the teeth and worked its way down inside one's clothing to mingle with the running sweat, and an intolerable itching started where it rested.

There was no wind, and had there been one, it would have done nothing but sluggishly stir the vast mass of heavy heated air that filled the great bowl of the desert set amid the dull and distant mountain walls, like masses of lead poured out upon the sands and allowed to cool into shapeless forms naked of everything but the hardiest of plant life.

Here, a person was as close to the primitive as he might ever get. It was not a world in which man could ever hope to be at home, although it had a deadly fascination of its own.

Perhaps the planet Mars was something like this. The thought was Gary Cole's as he pressed his strong fingers against the base of his skull to try to alleviate the dull aching he felt there. It was temporary relief at best, for as long as that pitiless sun poured its heat upon the great reflecting surface of the Spanish Desert, the aching would remain.

The hills seemed a little closer after some hours of travel. It almost seemed as though they were retreating before the truck like the tide retreating from a vast and desolate beach. There seemed to be little distinction between the earth and the sky because of the ever-prevailing heat haze. It would seem as though the misty-looking haze would protect one from the burning rays of the sun that seemed suspended forever in the yellow sky, but the reverse was more the truth, for the sun was perhaps magnified by the haze which it itself had created.

There was no conversation in the heated cab of the truck. Sue sat with her head resting on the back of the seat, her eyes closed and her mouth partly open for her dry breathing. Tuck sat on a bunk in the rear of the truck, hands clenching the edge of the bunk, head hanging down, while sweat dripped from his face and soiled his khaki trousers or struck the objects lying on the floor of the truck. The drops almost seemed to sizzle as they touched.

How Pardy Willis could survive in this inferno was beyond Gary Cole. The old man was part and parcel of this country, but even so, it didn't seem as though he could survive a day like this one because of his age.

"Look," said Sue. She pointed west.

The sun seemed to be poised on the tips of the mountains. The sky was turning color as the sun sank behind the range. Softly came a warm wind, stirring up the cauldron of soggy heat in the desert. The few scattered plants of the desert began to move slowly and sinuously in response to the siren call of the rising wind and its promise of the cool night sure to come.

The sun was gone, leaving behind it on the western sky a vast painting of red and gold, expressive of its death agony, for that day at least. The heat still hung in the desert, but in a matter of a few hours, it would be cool, and life would move on in better fashion.

Before the light had completely vanished, the truck had reached the place where it had been stuck on the last trip. The deep marks of the wheels still showed on the ground. Beyond the southern ridge rose the dark heights of the hills, and behind them, still farther south, rose the ruffled tops of the Lechuguillas.

Gary stopped the truck on a hard, wind-swept patch of ground. "I think we ought to find a place to hide the truck and head on toward the hills before moonrise. The moon will give us light to hunt for Pardy."

"How do we know he's there?" asked Tuck.

"If he isn't, he's likely dead by now. He'd never survive several days out in this suburb of hell. That would be too much even for Pardy Willis."

"And maybe the Lost Mission is in there too?"

Gary turned slowly. "I was thinking of Pardy first," he said.

"I'm sorry, pal."

Gary nodded. "I'll admit I have been thinking of the Lost Mission, but I also have a feeling that the Lost Mission and Pardy Willis are somehow mixed up together. I can't explain it. Tuck."

"Sue nodded wisely. "You're right, Gary," she said. "I feel the same way."

"That settles it," said Tuck drily. "What chance does an ordinary human being, like me, have against those who, by a gift of the gods, have been blessed with the second sight? This, then, my children, is the story of my life. These visions and messages somehow pass by ol' Tucker and are given freely to those of lesser intelligence but perhaps of greater perception." His voice died away as he saw two heads turn and two pairs of eyes study him speculatively.

Sue grinned. "This is definitely a split personality, Gary. Did you note the precise usage of our native language in direct contrast, as it were, to his usual ungrammatical and uncouth verbiage?"

Gary drove down the ridge. "I have a good mind to lock you two keen-minded individuals in the back of the truck and let you battle it out."

"One thing puzzles me," said Sue. "Why do we have to hide the truck?"

Gary shrugged. "Somebody stole my food and

dumped out my water on my first trip here. Somebody was prowling around the truck the night we stayed at Pardy's place. I don't like to take the chance that someone might find the truck and really do it some damage, so much that we'd be trapped here, and I don't have to tell you what our chances would be to get out of the desert if that happened."

"Keno," said Tuck.

Gary drove the truck into a deep-walled arroyo that cut deeply into a transverse ridge, scarcely five hundred yards from where he had penetrated the hills by means of the great wash that flowed its alluvial fan out into the desert.

The floor of the arroyo was of talus rock, firm enough to hold up the truck and give the wheels good traction. There was no chance of seeing the truck from out on the desert or, indeed, from the nearest hills. It could be seen clearly only from one end of the twisted arroyo or if one were to stand on the very lip of either side of the top of the great gash in the sterile earth.

Gary threw a canvas shelter half over the windshield to keep the forthcoming bright moonlight from reflecting off it and thus giving away the presence of the hidden truck. He took out the rotor from the distributor and hid it behind a rock. Tuck filled two haversacks with necessities and handed a large canteen to each of his companions. Without saying a word to each other, they armed themselves. Gary had his Winchester, while Tuck had the pump shotgun, and Sue buckled the pistol belt about her slim waist. She was a better-than-average shot with either pistol or rifle.

Gary led the way out of the arroyo and slogged through the deepening sand and soft earth of the alluvial wash toward the dark mouth that led the way up, by an easy sloping, into those mysterious, luring hills. It would be necessary to advance into the hills while it was still dark, for it would be quite sonic time before the moon would rise to give them light for their explorations. Time, too, was pressing, for Pardy might be in bad shape if he was in those hills.

None of them spoke as they slogged their way up the wash, with stones and sand grating beneath their booted feet and their breathing sounding harsh. Sweat dripped from their faces. The rocks and sand of the wash still held the terrible heat of the day, and the wind had not yet cleared away the sluggish air.

There was no sight or sound of anything out of the ordinary. Gary couldn't help but think of that robed figure he had seen. He was sure he had seen it, but perhaps he had clothed a shaped rock with the robe and cowl of a Franciscan. Still, it would have taken more than imagination to see the thing move and then point toward the north with a fleshless hand.

Beyond that was the hard, cold fact that he had seen it again, more clearly, near where the truck had been stuck, and that his companion had seen it as well. It wasn't indisputable, but it was certainly a strong argument to the effect that both boys had seen *something* out of the ordinary, perhaps *something out of this world.*

There was no robed figure at the head of the wash. Nothing but the dry, rustling sound of the night wind as it felt its way across those dry, waterless hills. Gary climbed atop a great, tip-tilted slab of rock and took off his hat to let the wind dry his sweating brow. It was hard to distinguish anything in the windy darkness. He gave a hand to Sue and pulled her up beside him while Tuck scrambled up the back way.

None of them spoke. The night held their tongues in check. It wasn't quite the place to awaken the sleeping echoes with useless talk. Besides, *who might be listening at that very moment?*

There was nothing outstanding to see in the clinging

darkness, although Gary peered up toward the area where previously he had seen the moonlight shining softly on a rounded, whitish surface of some kind. There was nothing like it to be seen now.

Gary led the way up the wash. It widened to form a sort of playa between low-walled hills, and here and there, along the sides of the playa, were a few rugged and scraggly desert growths. Perhaps in the spring, when the heavy rains fell for a time, the sun would later produce the exquisite and fleshly desert flowers that would form a lovely carpet upon the harsh earth for a few short weeks.

Their feet crunched through something brittle. Gary knelt and felt about on the ground until he picked up several pieces of the material. He knew at once what they were from the feel of them. They were rounded and thin, smooth and brittle. "More potsherds," he said to his companions.

Tuck moved about. "Man," he said, "the ground over here is thick with them."

Sue looked about. "That indicates that the Indians came here to make their pottery or else they lived close by here."

"It isn't likely they'd come into these God-forsaken hills just to make pottery," said Gary. "Besides, they'd need a lot of water, and it isn't likely they'd haul water in here when it was easier to find pottery clay nearer a source of water."

"Which means," added Tuck, "that they must have had water here when this pottery was made, and they probably lived here."

"I hope it was quite different then," said Sue. "I've seen where some Indians live, even today, and could never understand why they liked to live there, but this place beats everything I've ever seen."

"Lots of time has passed since they were here," said Gary thoughtfully. "There are no records in the Bureau of Ethnology Reports indicating that Indians ever lived here, but then the records are pretty well dated. Trouble is, there isn't even a legend about Indians living here."

"Well, they did," said Sue. She shuffled her booted feet among the pitiful debris left by a vanished people. "Always seems sort of tragic, doesn't it, to find things like this?"

A faint touch of pearly light showed in the eastern sky. The moon was revealing its presence.

"You fellas hungry?" said Tuck hopefully.

"You bet," said Sue.

Tuck arched his eyebrows. "Never thought I'd get an answer like that. It's always me that is hungry."

"This is as good a time as any to eat," said Gary. "By the time the moon lights up these hills, we can be finished."

"Let's get out of the open," said Tuck. "Kinda breezy out here. Ha, ha, ha..."

There was no argument from the other two. The three of them walked to the side of the playa and found a bowl-shaped area among tumbled boulders. While Sue doled out some of the food, Gary stood at the edge of the depression with his rifle close at hand, peering out across the wide playa, half expecting to see a furtive, robed figure whisk past his vision and vanish as quickly as it had appeared.

As they ate, the moon crept up into the sky, lighting its slow and cautious way, tinting the eastern mountains, then flooding down into the Spanish Desert, and by using its invisible but masterful brushes, it began to touch up the landscape with deft magic in brighter colors of silver and pearl. With the coming of the moonlight, the wind shifted a little and made soft and whispered music among the eroded hills, rustling the dry brush and cooling the baked earth.

Somewhere north of the hills, a coyote lifted its voice to welcome the coming of the moon, letting the melancholy howling break away into a series of muted barkings.

Tuck looked quickly at Gary. Gary shook his head. That was a sure enough Brother of the Desert, a brown-and-yellow hided coyote and not the tenuous ghost of old Barkus.

The thin wailing rose again and was followed by another crying into the night of a coyote closer to the sleeping hills. The howlings broke into a series of yappings and then died away.

Here and there, against the darkness of the sky not yet lighted by the rising moon, shone the fitful sparking of stars. The moon began to touch the easternmost hills of the Lechuguillas and to feel its way into the uppermost parts of the arroyos and deep gullies. An owl hung its shadow over the wash and then drifted silently out of sight as it sensed the presence of humans. Somewhere in the hills, the sharp barking of a fox broke the stillness and then died away.

Gary had almost forgotten his companions as he watched the changing mural that spread out before him. From his position, he could see part of the desert floor, the lower spurs of the hills, and part of the great wash up which they had trudged. Nothing moved out there but the gently swaying brush as the wind motivated it.

Sue stood up beside Gary. "Beautiful, isn't it?" she said softly.

"Quite different from today," he said.

"Don't talk about that," she said quickly.

"Maybe we can drive back at night like Tuck and I did the last time we were here."

Tuck was packing away the remnants of food. "If we ever leave here," he said gloomily. "Man, these hills give me the shivers. Funny thing, though—I don't want to leave without taking a look-see at them. Crazy, ain't it?"

"I know what you mean," said Sue.

Tuck's head snapped up. "Amazing," he said. "My dear cousin *agreed* with me on something!"

Sue smiled. "You suppose there are Indian ruins in here?" she asked Gary.

"I doubt it. This isn't cliff-dweller country. If the Papagos were here, they'd live in brush huts, not in adobe or stone huts, as some Indians do. They'd live in wicki-ups, or whatever you call them, and they wouldn't last long in this country."

"Sort of busts up that lead," said Tuck.

"We know they were here. That's all that matters," said Gary. "The metate and the potsherds prove it."

"Doesn't prove there was any mission in here, though," said Tuck.

"That could have tumbled down too," said Sue. "It probably was a small one—maybe just a tiny chapel similar to some I've seen down in Mexico."

Gary led the way from the depression out onto the playa again. The moonlight was illuminating the hills to the south, but the wash and the playa were still deep in shadows. Gary headed due south toward the notch he had seen on his first trip into that area. The more he eyed those jumbled hills and piled-up mountains that looked like wrinkled elephant hide from a distance, the more he realized how much they were cut up by canyons and deep arroyos, with great talus slopes resting against their huge bases, and the more he realized how difficult it would be to find anything as small as a man in that natural maze.

The playa narrowed, became wedge-shaped, and then ended where a great, V-shaped gash thrust itself into the belly of the dry hills like a mortal wound. It was still dark within the confines of the gash, although the surrounding terrain was revealed by the moonlight. A cold breath seemed to emanate from the opening, like the deep exhalation of some monstrous and sleeping creature that might just awaken if disturbed, to rend and tear with claw and fang.

The three explorers stopped in concert as though

halted by an unspoken command. Gary glanced at them. "Ha, ha, ha," said Tuck. "You first, *amigo*."

Gary wasn't too keen to probe into that uninviting darkness, but on the other hand, he didn't want to chicken out in front of Sue. He walked forward and, without hesitation, right into the darkness, feeling his way cautiously, trying not to make too much noise, although he really didn't know why. His boots grated on the harsh ground. Now and then, the branches of thorny growths tugged at his clothing as though to hold him back. They crackled and rustled in tiny, dry voices. "Wait a bit! Turn back! Turn back!" they seemed to insist.

He looked back. He could see two indistinct figures, very close together, a good fifty feet behind him. He couldn't help but grin. Scared as he was, he had an inkling that they were noticing the awesome, haunting feeling of the place more than he was. He turned again and, as he did so, caught a faraway glimpse of that tantalizing expanse of soft whiteness, now first touched by the moonlight. He still could not distinguish it enough to tell what it was, although he was almost sure it was a deposit of lighter rock of some kind.

Gary climbed a rough slope and found himself standing on a level area, something like a shelf on the side of the deep arroyo through which he had come. The area was deathly quiet. He could see a patch of the Spanish Desert to the north. To the south, the hills rose higher and higher to meet the rough flanks of the Lechuguillas. Now and then, Gary could hear the grating of boots against the earth as Sue and Tuck gingerly followed his trail.

Gary looked again toward that smooth, rounded area of whitish rock. It was in such contrast to the rest of the area that he was determined to find out what it was. He rested his rifle butt on the ground and shoved back his hat to wipe the sweat from his forehead. His eyes caught something marked on a flat, up-ended slab of rock behind him, half hidden by a scraggly creosote bush.

He walked toward it and pulled the bush aside. His *eyes* widened. Clearly marked on the rock was a deeply incised cross, with the top and bottom of the upright, as well as each end of the cross arm, splayed out in a sort of leaf effect. Beneath it was carved the numerals *17*.

Gary knelt and eyed the numeral. A piece of the rock had scaled off through erosion and quite likely had taken with it the last two numbers of a date starting with the *17* that now remained.

His two companions puffed up the slope and stood behind him. Gary stood up and stepped to one side. "Look," he said quietly. The moonlight fell fully on the cross and the numerals.

"It proves there must be a mission in here somewhere," said Tuck.

"Or was," said Gary. "Sometime in the 1700's."

"Maybe it just marks the road," said Tuck. "This arroyo is about in a line with the traces of road we followed out on the desert."

"Must have been hard going," said Sue.

Gary nodded. He looked south. "That way," he said. He narrowed his eyes. That whitish patch was so smooth and rounded, it was hard to believe that it had been so made by nature.

"What about Pardy?" said Tuck.

Gary instantly felt ashamed. He had quite forgotten about the old man. "Maybe we ought to call out or something," he said. "Maybe fire a few shots."

"In *here?*" said Tuck. "How do we know who's going to hear us?"

"Such as?" said Sue sweetly. "Maybe a Franciscan in a dusty old robe with no flesh on his hand?"

"Joke all you want," said Tuck. "We seen him, didn't we, Gary?"

"*Saw* him," said Sue. She was looking past Gary now.

"That patch of whitish rock," she added. "Doesn't it look sort of out of place in here?"

"I've been thinking the same thing ever since I saw it the last time I was around here," said Gary. "It doesn't show up unless something shines on it like the sun or moon."

"What else is there to shine on it?" said Tuck with a grin.

Gary did not answer. He walked along the shelf, looking toward that whitish patch that was so intriguing. The shelf dipped down to meet the rising floor of the arroyo, and as Gary descended, he lost sight of the whitish area.

It was still dark at the bottom of the arroyo, but as the ground rose at a slight angle, the moon lighted more and more of the arroyo. He worked his way over a savage tangle of shattered rock and thorny brush, feeling the thorns catching at his boots and clothing, and then, at last, emerged on a level area again. He turned to look back for his two companions and heard their slow progress below him. He turned again, and his eyes widened. The whitish area was plainly seen now, perhaps two hundred and fifty yards from him—smooth and rounded, symmetrically shaped, and at the bottom of the rounded area was a rather sharp line of demarcation, while below that was a sheer wall of rock, perhaps twenty-five to thirty feet high.

Gary walked forward and stopped again. Something shadowy had moved atop the rounded area, and as it did so, the moonlight glittered on something. His breath caught in his throat. The bright object was shaped like a cross tilted far to one side, the upright being nearly horizontal, and to one side of it was a ragged upthrust of some kind of growth that had moved in the light wind that was slowly creeping through the hills. The movement of the brush had revealed the bright object. It *was* a cross, there was no doubt about that!

He moved closer to the strange sight, and as he did so, there came to him, borne on the night wind, the faint, so *very* faint sound of a silvery-toned bell.

He heard them behind him. They came up and stood beside him, wordlessly staring at what he had seen. It looked almost as though it was all formed of rock, earth, and brush by the hand of nature, and yet there was nothing really natural about it. The lines were too straight, the rounded area was too perfectly rounded, and now the moonlight glittered from the hanging cross, which certainly could not have been formed by nature.

"Is it real?" breathed Sue.

The moon was full upon the area now. Gary walked forward, heedless of his two friends, and stopped again when he was two hundred yards from the strange sight ahead of him. His eyes began to pick out other features. To one side of the rounded area was something that looked as though it had been a tower, but earth and rocks had flowed from the steep hill to the left side of the tower and had almost buried it. Desert growths had caught hold with the utter tenacity of their kind to make a frowsy covering of the earth and rocks, partially concealing what remained of the tower.

In the center of the lower part of the rock fall was a large dark opening, with one straight side and a straight top, while earth had poured across it to block a good half of the opening. Gary narrowed his eyes. To the right of the opening was another opening, like a deep-set and narrow window, and this too was partially screened by brush.

Gary half closed his eyes, then opened them widely, and it seemed as though the picture formed clearly, for now, he could see faint lines of carved pillars against the right front of the larger opening and even the very faint outlines of some of the hewn rock that formed the thick wall of what was certainly a building made by the hand of man and not nature.

"What is it?" asked Tuck softly.

"I think we've found our Lost Mission," said Gary.

"Are you sure?"

"Listen," said Sue.

The faint, almost indistinguishable sound of a bell drifted to them on the night wind.

CHAPTER ELEVEN

Mission in the Desert

The three adventurers walked slowly forward toward the ruins so cleverly concealed by nature. On either side of the ancient building, there had been landslides of some magnitude that had flowed earth and rocks to completely bury one side of the building, even spreading out onto the roof and almost covering half of the #yeso-covered dome that shone so whitely in the moonlight.

Time had not dealt kindly with the old structure, for great patches of plaster had fallen from the thick rock walls. Earth and rocks had tumbled down about the sagging bell tower, almost completely burying it. Wind had drifted loose, powdery earth and sand over much of the structure and had flowed up it in a smooth fan against the front of the building. The great doorway was so disguised by earth, rocks, and growths that it looked something like the ragged mouth of a shallow cave unless one was close enough to it and knew what he was looking for, and even then, its appearance could play tricks upon one.

"I can see, now, why this has been lost," said Sue. "Planes could fly over it, and unless the pilots were looking specifically for something like this, they'd never see it. It sure isn't the kind of country a person would fool around in very much, dry and hot as it is."

"Likely any Indians who saw it would give it a wide berth," said Tuck. "You know how superstitious they are."

Gary nodded. "Indians won't come near these mountains for some reason of their own. Likely because the place is supposed to be haunted."

"Speaking of being haunted," said Tuck, "I wonder where our friend is?"

There was no need for explanation. The other two knew well enough to whom he was referring. Still, it was hard to think of anything else other than the discovery they had made.

"The cross was set with bright stones or crystals of some kind," said Sue. "See how it glitters in the moonlight?"

"I was also wondering," said Tuck drily, "about who rang that bell. Are you two listening?"

The wonder of the place seemed to dispel all other thoughts. Gary walked closer to the building, wondering who last had walked that way. It had taken a great deal of hard work and perseverance to build such a structure in such an out-of-the-way place without modern tools and equipment. These missions were all hand-built by a slow and laborious process, but a labor of love must have eased the burden.

He stopped fifty feet from the great door. He could see that one of the double doors still sagged on rusted hinges while the other had either been torn away or flattened beneath tons of earth. He could see just the upper part of the bell tower, and within it, seen through the narrow arched openings, hung a bell. The lure of the place crept into his blood. He walked forward until his right foot rested on a low step, one of a series almost completely covered with drifted sand.

"You going in there?" hoarsely whispered Tuck.

The place was much bigger than Gary had thought it was, for the mass of it was buried beneath the rock fall. Perhaps the roof had caved in long ago from the great pressure upon it. He walked to the door and peered into the darkness, surprised to see some sort of light at the far end of the long room into which he was looking, until he realized that the light came from the moon, which was sending its rays into a large and ragged opening in the roof.

A cool draft whispered from the interior. Gary stepped inside and stopped short. The roof had held up the great weight of earth and rocks to form a sort of cavern under the debris from the landslide. He moved a foot, and the grating sound of it was magnified into an echo that died quickly away somewhere within the huge room.

As his eyes grew accustomed to the dimness, he could see that fine sand had drifted within the building, forming miniature ridges and valleys on the paved flooring of the building. To his right was a deep-set doorway cut into an immensely thick wall. It led into the base of the almost completely buried tower. He wondered whether or not the stairs up to the top of the bell tower still existed. It would be dangerous to enter any part of the building because of the great weight of earth and rocks upon the roof and against the walls, but the temptation was too great for Gary. He looked back over his shoulder. "Stay outside," he said.

Tuck smiled wanly. "We weren't thinking of coming in."

"Speak for yourself, Tucker," said Sue.

Gary shook his head. "*Both* of you stay here."

"I won't," said Sue stubbornly, "and you can't make me."

It was then that the hard and cold look of a Cole seemed to strike her across the face. It was an inheritance of Gary's, directly from his great-grandfather who had fought Apaches and bandits to establish Chiricahua Springs Ranch in bitterly hostile country, carried down through his grandfather who had fought rustlers and outlaws to hold that same ranch, and through Gary's father, who, as a Marine, had earned the Navy Cross fighting in the South Pacific in World War II.

When a Cole looked at you like that, it was best to listen. That was a local saying, and Sue Browne now knew exactly what was meant by that saying. Without another word, Gary walked into the room at the side of the entryway.

There was enough moonlight to reveal a shadowy flight of rock steps reaching up into the unknown darkness of the almost completely buried bell tower. Gary took out his powerful flashlight and flicked the beam up the stairway. The steps were thick in powdery dust. One thing he noted: the dust was undisturbed and evidently had been so for many years. He looked up the stairs. Someone, or *something*, had rung that bell.

He walked slowly up the steps, his footfalls deadened by the dust. The dust wreathed up about his face. A feeling of claustrophobia inched its way into his mind. It wasn't the narrow confines of the stairwell that bothered him as much as the thought of those many tons of earth and rock pressing against the aged outer walls.

His head emerged into the top of the bell tower, and he stood at last beside the bell. It was hung on a framework of thick hardwood with hand-forged strappings and bolts. The old padres had hung it there to last and last, and it had done so, even when the old padres were forgotten dust. He reached out and tapped the bell with the butt plate of his rifle. The soft, silvery tone was as sweet and soft as bardic music.

Gary walked to the front of the bell tower and looked down the sloped earth to his two friends. Their faces were turned up toward him, very white in the light of the moon. He looked across the domed roof toward the far slopes of the dreaming hills. It was almost like a land-scape dreamed up by a mystic artist of scenes of fantasy.

Beyond the old mission church, he could see other structures, some of them nothing more than heaps of rubble, for the roofs had fallen in to fill the interiors, and then the upper walls had succumbed to fall in too, and then the ever-constant winds of the hills and the desert had added to the debris, working patiently for the Spanish Desert to erase, through time, the perishable handiwork of man.

Gary was surprised to realize how large the mission area had been. The wickiups of the Indians would, of course, have been destroyed by time first, long before any of the mission buildings had started to decay.

He looked again at the bell. There was hardly enough wind creeping through the arched opening of the bell tower to make the bell ring. Maybe it had been pure imagination, engendered by the mystical quality of the hills and the long-abandoned mission.

He walked slowly down the stairs and stopped again in the entryway. More light had flooded into the interior of the building, and the powerful flashlight beam picked out features of the long hall, or nave, in which he stood. Gary had visited other missions—San Xavier del Bac at Tucson, the *White Dove of the Desert*, and old Tumacacori, now a National Park in the Valley of the Santa Cruz, south of Tucson and north of Nogales—so he was familiar with the construction of such buildings and their functions.

There wasn't a stick of church furniture to be seen. The niches which had been the Stations of the Cross were empty and had been gutted. Holes had been battered into the rock flooring and into the walls, while great patches of the original plaster had been ripped or had fallen from the basic rock structure of the thick walls. At the far end, he could just make out the sanctu-ary. The wind moaned softly through the openings, like a dirge for the tragedy that had befallen this long-lost place of worship.

Gary walked slowly toward the dim sanctuary. The gilded reredos had vanished. The carving about the niches had been destroyed. Holes pocked the floor and the walls. The five altars were completely demolished. Powdery dust arose about Gary as he stopped and looked up at the faint traces of the plaster palm fronds under the faded dome of the sanctuary.

All this destruction was more than the impartial hand of nature; it showed, without dispute, that man, the great destroyer, had been there. Quite likely looking for treasure, if the work had been done by white men; likely done by the Apaches if done by the hand of red men. But that would have been long, long ago. From the looks of the place, there had been no one within those aging walls for many years.

Gary looked back to see two silhouetted figures just beyond the front entry. To Gary's right was the entry into the old sacristy, a dark hole that wasn't at all inviting. His feet grated on shards of brittle plaster as he walked toward it, flicking his flashlight beam into the darkness. Here, the flagstone floor was comparatively free of debris, although thick in the ever-present dust. He inspected the place in the light of his torch. Everywhere within the building was the feeling of unutterable tragedy and unbearable loneliness.

Gary walked back to his two companions. His footsteps echoed hollowly in the nave. It must have been a beautiful place in the days of its use, bright with paintings and colorful statuary, gilded candlesticks, and exquisite altar cloths and hangings, kept immaculately clean by the padres and their Indian converts.

Sue eyed him. "You look different, Gary," she said.

"Dust," he said drily. "The place is thick with it."

"It's more than that," she said.

He looked away from her. His emotions must be

showing on his tanned face. Gary was not a Catholic, but the thought of the faith and arduous labor the old padres had put into making such a place, so isolated, in such a wilderness of heat and hostility, was enough to stir the emotions of even the most unimaginative of persons.

"Sort of gets you," said Sue.

Tuck nodded. "I'm still wondering who rang that bell."

"The wind," said Gary.

Tuck glanced sideways at him. "Yeah," he said quietly. "I guess that's so." There wasn't much conviction in his tone of voice.

"What about Pardy?" said Sue.

"We can search around here," said Gary.

"Pardy wasn't supposed to know about this place," said Tuck.

"He knew about it, all right," said Gary. "The only thing that puzzles me is that he wouldn't admit it, and he avoided the subject whenever we brought it up. That wasn't like Pardy."

"You saw no signs of him in there?"

Gary shook his head. "There hasn't been anyone in there for years," he said.

They walked past the ruins, clambering over the drifted earth to reach the tumbled-down heaps of the other, smaller buildings. There was no trace of Pardy Willis or of anyone else in the area.

"How did they ever survive in this place, Gary?" asked Sue. She shuddered.

Gary shrugged. "They were under vows, I suppose. They were soldiers of the Cross. You have to hand it to them."

"Yeah," said Tuck. "But here? No water? No nothing?"

"There must have been water here in those days," said Gary. "The Indians lived here, so there would have to be a good supply of water. It took a long time to build that old mission church, so they'd have to have water then.

And, furthermore, they'd only build a mission in a place where they expected a good, continuing supply of water."

"Well," said Tuck, "they were 'wrong there."

Sue looked about the moon-lighted area of decay and ruin. "Seems like they were wrong in more than that."

Tuck grounded his shotgun. "What next, Gary?" he asked.

"We've still got Pardy to consider."

"We'll never find him in here."

"He might have to come to us," said Gary. "There's only one way to let him know we're around."

He raised his rifle and fired rapidly three times in succession. The shots blasted the quietness, and the triple echo seemed to tumble through the hills and slam back and forth inside the canyons, to die slowly away in the distance.

Gary had not wanted to do that. It seemed almost a sacrilege to blast the quietness of the place like that, but there was no help for it.

"Man," said Tuck. "I wonder who heard that?"

"Like whom?" said Sue.

Tuck shivered a little. "Who knows, Susie?" he said.

Gary lowered his smoking rifle. The quietness had flowed in on them once again. "All we can do now is wait a spell," he said. "If Pardy heard that, he might come along. If he didn't, we'll have to keep up the hunt for him."

"He may be miles and miles away from here," said Sue.

The wind moaned softly through the canyons and rustled the dry brush. It sighed through the openings in the old mission church and whispered through the top of the bell tower.

Gary shoved back his hat. "We'll take some pictures of the place in the morning," he said, "so we can take back proof that we found the place. Dad can contact the authorities and let them decide what they want to do about the place. I don't suppose it will ever become a

State or National Park because it's so far out of the way, but they'll probably want to send in some men to inspect it and so forth. Maybe we'll have to show them the way. It's amazing how difficult it is to distinguish the ruins from the surrounding area."

"Did you say we'd take some pictures in the *morning?*" said Tuck.

"Can't very well take them now," said Gary.

"You don't intend to sit around here waiting for the daylight, do you?"

Gary looked sideways at him. "You mean you want to go all the way back to the truck and then climb back up here tomorrow in the heat?"

Tuck swallowed. "Well," he said, "it will be dark before too long, pal. I ain't exactly in the mood to sit around here in the dark listening to that bell ringing with no one there to ring it."

"I'll wait," said Sue.

"Oh, sure!" jeered Tuck. "Brave little Susan! It's nice and light right now, my dear cousin, but wait until it gets dark and the ol' boy in the dirty ol' robe comes nosing around! Just you wait!"

"You can go down to the truck by yourself," said Sue. "I'll stick it out with Gary."

Tuck flushed. "There ain't any water here."

"Our canteens are full," said Sue.

Tuck threw up his hands in despair. "Listen to her!"

Gary sat down on a flat rock. "We can go back to the truck, if you like, then start back up here about dawn. It won't be so hot then. We can get good light from the east for pictures. It's O.K. with me, Tuck."

Sue's face fell. "I thought we'd stick it out, Gary, and maybe we'd see that ghost."

"Brave little Susie," grumbled Tuck. "All you want to do is stay up here alone with Gary."

Sue smiled sweetly. "So what's wrong with that, Tuckie boy?"

"Come on," said Gary. "No use in sitting around here arguing. We can get some sleep and be up here before daylight."

Gary really didn't want to leave, for the place held a compelling fascination for him, despite any thought about the mysterious robed figure he and Tuck had seen, but he didn't want to force his will upon Tuck.

———

GARY LED the way back down the tangled slopes, looking back every now and then at the mission church, noting how cleverly nature's way of camouflaging seemed to make the structure melt into its surroundings when one was at a distance from it.

The journey back to the truck was easy, now, for it was downhill, the desert night was cool, and the moon lighted the way. The truck was not visible until they reached the arroyo mouth, and it evidently had not been bothered, although who would want to bother it puzzled Gary. He reached the truck ahead of the others.

He stopped beside the vehicle and tested the locked driver's door, then walked to the rear of the truck and tried that door. That, too, was locked. He could hear Sue and Tuck arguing about something as they walked toward the truck. Gary grinned. He walked along the right-hand side of the truck to test the right-hand front door, and it was then that he noticed a dark patch of something on the sand just below the outside tap for the thirty-gallon water tank Gary's father had installed in the truck.

Gary tested the dark patch with a foot. It sank easily into the sand. He knelt and pressed a hand on the patch. A cold feeling came over him as he stood up and checked the tap. *It was wide open, and every drop of the thirty gallons had been drained onto the thirsty sand.*

"Hey, Gary," said Tuck, "listen to this latest one of Sue's! She claims..." His voice died away as he saw the look on Gary's face. "You look like you seen a ghost, pal," he added slowly.

"Worse," said Gary. He pointed down at the dark patch. "That represents thirty precious gallons of water."

"A leak, maybe?"

Gary shook his head. "The tank is sound. It was full when we left Pardy's place, and besides, the tap was full open, Tuck."

Three pairs of eyes looked up and down the arroyo. There wasn't a sign of footprints on the sand.

"An animal?" said Sue.

"No," said Gary. "Besides, there aren't any animal tracks either."

"I don't like this at all," said Tuck.

"We've still got the G.I. cans full of water," said Sue.

"And the canteens," said Gary. "That should hold us if we're careful. We'd better hope the truck doesn't over-heat." He unlocked the back of the truck and inspected the interior. Nothing had been disturbed. He hauled out the two full G.I. cans and looked at them, and a cold feeling came over him. He quickly unstoppered one of them and thrust his nose close to the opening. The faint odor of gasoline was mingled with the tinny smell of the water. "Tuck!" he called out.

"Yup!" said Tuck from the rear of the truck.

"Did you fill these cans?"

"Only one of 'em, pal. Sue filled the other. The red one."

"Great, oh, great," murmured Gary. "She filled the reserve gas can with water."

"You said fill two cans," said Tuck.

Gary nodded. "Well, we can use it for the truck if not for drinking."

"How long do you figure we'll be out here?"

"Until we find Pardy."

"Or they find *us*, dead of thirst," said Tuck.

"It's not that bad," said Gary. He checked the second

can. The water smelled clean and fresh. "Don't say anything to Sue about filling the gas can."

"Not me, pal!"

Gary eyed his friend. "What do you think?" he said.

"Maybe the tap was loosened by the jolting of the truck."

"No, there's a safety wire that locks it from opening by accident. We should have fixed it so it couldn't be opened by anyone but us."

"Yeah, but how did we know anyone was going to open it, Gary? Man, that's like handing a death sentence to someone out here. You had the same thing happen to you when you were out here the first time. But why, Gary? *Why?*"

Why, indeed? The thought was Gary's. The air of mystery that hung perpetually over the Spanish Desert seemed to be thickening. He looked at Tuck. "We'll take turns staying on guard tonight," he said. "Let Sue sleep."

"Fair enough."

As the moon drifted down to the west, the desert became almost deathly quiet. Not a breath of wind stirred. Not a creature moved, and the gaunt limbs of the sparse desert growths seemed etched against the light, still and lifeless.

Gary sat in the cab, his rifle between his knees, peering out into the gathering darkness, and then, at last, the darkness seemed to close in on the truck and shield everything from the boy's tired eyes. He could hear the quiet breathing of the two Brownes in the rear of the truck. All doors were locked, but he had let down the side windows partway for ventilation...

Worry came drifting silently through the darkness on great velvety wings and settled down in the arroyo to watch the truck with unseen eyes as the Spanish Desert slept.

Gary raised his head with a suddenness that made his neck twinge in sharp pain. He looked about in bewilderment. A movement caught the corner of his right eye. He had slumped over toward the wheel. He turned and saw something white hanging over the glass of the right-hand window. His flesh crawled as he saw fleshless fingers scrabbling at the glass. Beyond the window in the thick darkness was an indistinguishable form, and he had an eerie feeling about who, or *what*, it was.

The bony hand reached out toward Gary, and he jerked back in terrible fright to hit the horn ring of the truck. The horns blasted the quiet and echoed back and forth in the arroyo. The hand was jerked back. Gary grabbed for his rifle and full-cocked it. He lunged for the doorway and felt for the door handle. The rifle caught on the gear shift, and the trigger was pulled back.

The crashing discharge of the rifle within the narrow confines of the cab nearly deafened Gary. Acrid powder-smoke swirled inside the cab. The door swung open, and the dome light of the cab flicked on to reveal Gary to anyone who might be standing outside. He half fell out of the doorway while Sue screamed piercingly. Gary kicked the door shut to turn off the light and swiftly reloaded the rifle.

The echoes had died away. The smell of the rifle discharge hung in the quiet air. Gary peered into the darkness. To the east were faint pewter traces of light against the dark sky, prophesying the coming of the false dawn.

"What was it?" gasped Tuck as he came running toward Gary with the shotgun in his shaking hands. Sue was close behind him.

Gary shook his head. He didn't want to tell Sue what he had seen.

"I saw it," she said shakily. "A brown- or black-robed

figure was outlined in the light from the cab just for an instant. Oh, that hand! I know now what you mean! There was no flesh on it! What did it want?"

Icy sweat worked down Gary's sides. He walked forward, followed by Tuck and Sue. He drew out his flashlight from his jacket pocket and flicked it on, moving the beam up and down the arroyo. There was no fleeing figure of any kind to be seen.

"No tracks except ours," said Tuck quietly.

"We might have walked on his," said Gary.

"Yeah," said Tuck, but there was no sincerity in his voice.

Faintly, the light of the dawn began to creep down the western slopes of the mountains far to the east. A wind began to whisper over the cold sands. Beyond the arroyo, there was nothing to be seen except the low sand ridges and, beyond them, the hills.

"Whatever, or whoever it is, can sure make tracks out of here when he wants to," said Gary.

"If he makes tracks at all," said Tuck.

"Cut it out!" snapped Gary.

They walked slowly back to the truck.

"I'll get breakfast," said Sue. "I'll never be able to sleep after that." She walked to the back of the truck to haul out the gas stove.

"Maybe it was Pardy," said Tuck.

Gary shrugged. "I doubt it."

"Man, I'm glad daylight is coming, heat and all."

"Gary! Tuck!" called out Sue in a shaky voice.

They ran to her. She was looking down at the ground at the rear of the truck. Both water cans lay on their sides, with the tell-tale dark patches of spilled water about them. The truck door was wide open.

"Empty!" said Tuck. His face blanched. He looked wildly about.

Gary looked at the ground. There were no tracks. He looked up at the sides of the arroyo. The place was empty of any other living creatures but himself and his two companions.

"I'm scared," said Sue.

"You wanted to see the ghost," said Tuck drily. "You satisfied now?"

Gary lowered his rifle. It was no use. Whoever was clever enough to backtrack and empty out the last two containers of water was also clever enough to vanish into the desert without being seen.

"Maybe we'd better get out of here," said Tuck.

There was no argument from Gary. They had just enough water in their canteens to get them to Pardy's or to Mesquite Wells through a long, searing day of heat on the merciless Spanish Desert. He walked to the place where he had hidden the rotor of the distributor. It was gone. He searched the ground inch by inch with no success while a feeling of a deep-seated fear came into his soul.

Gary walked back to the track. "The rotor is gone," he said quietly.

"We'll have to walk out, then?" asked Tuck.

"Not enough water," said Gary.

"What do we do, then?" asked Sue in a very small voice.

Gary picked up his rifle. "There was water at the mission once," he said quietly. "With luck, we might be able to find it." He did not dare say more to the others.

The sun was tipping the eastern ranges when they walked toward the hills. It promised to be the worst day of heat they had yet encountered

CHAPTER TWELVE

Trapped Without Water

If the Mission de la Purisima Concepcion had been haunted by tragedy and a nameless sort of dread at night, it was haunted as well by daylight, with an aura of lingering loneliness as well as the fear of death by thirst to those who ventured into that part of the Spanish Desert.

The sun was hardly up long enough to strike with its merciless heat, but it was already giving warning as Gary led the way into the area that had once contained the various outbuildings of the mission. Even before he spoke, he felt deep misgivings. There could certainly be no water in the area.

"Well?" said Tuck quietly.

"You and Sue scout around together. I'll go by myself." Gary shoved back his hat. "It seems hard to believe that the water supply could just vanish."

"Maybe the landslide covered the springs, or wells, or whatever they used," said Sue.

"There has to be water," said Gary stubbornly.

"Would you mind letting us into the reason you're so certain?" asked Tuck.

Gary looked at him. "Whoever that was fooling around the truck last night has to have water."

"Yeah," said Tuck drily. "From the looks of that hand of his, he sure could use some moisture."

Gary did not speak again. He refused to believe that the robed figure with the bony hand was a ghost, and yet there was no proof that it was human, and it certainly wasn't imagination that had conjured the terrifying figure into existence. It was just part of the brooding mystery that overhung the Mission de la Purisima Concepcion.

"There's one thing for sure," said Sue. "Whether that thing is a ghost or not, he plays for keeps, and you can paste *that* fact into your hat."

Gary walked toward the rear of the mission. Sue always had a neat way of cataloging things. As he walked, he eyed the surrounding terrain, trying to discover a clue to the whereabouts of the water supply of the mission. Perhaps a long drought had forced the patient padres to leave the place, and it was quite possible that water might have come again to the place through the medium of rain.

Perhaps Sue was right. The landslide might have covered the springs or the wells. Certainly, the padres would not have depended on rock *tinajas* for their water supply, like those at Tinaja Alias in the mountains to the southwest. There was usually water in those isolated rock hollows, enough for a parched traveler to quench his thirst and perhaps fill his canteens for the journey to the next water supply. No, he was certain that the padres would never have depended on such an unreliable source.

He worked his way up a tangled slope behind the mission and found a place where he could survey the surrounding terrain. The rising heat and the effort he had made had brought thirst quickly to him, in warning of what he and his two companions could well expect later on, when the very core of the day's heat would hover about the old mission.

He uncased the field glasses and studied the naked hills, hoping to see an outgrowth of dusty gray-green foliage that might indicate a water supply, but there was no such welcome sign. Now and then, he could hear the distant voices of his two companions. If they could find Pardy Willis, the old man would know the way to water, but there had been no indication that the old man was about the place.

Gary cased the glasses, and as he did so, a cold feeling crept over him despite the steadily rising heat. A thought had come to him as he thought of Pardy. Suppose the old man was at the root of all these troubles and mysterious appearances of the ghostly robed figure?

The old man's mind was hardly stable, according to quite a few people who knew him, or of him. He was eccentric and close-mouthed—a man of mystery who knew this country better than any other man—and maybe he had a reason for scaring other people from it, particularly three nosey teenagers. The chilling thought came again to him. It was one matter to scare people away, but to deprive them of water in the depths of the Spanish Desert was the next thing to murder.

Gary walked slowly down the rock-littered slope. The old man did act peculiarly most of the time, and the last time Gary and Tuck had seen him, he had been downright mystifying. He had lied as well about knowing about the cross-inscribed rocks, claiming that he had never seen any while all the time his old dog was buried under a pile of them. He had been downright insistent, too, that Tuck and Gary stay away from the area where they had later found the mission. Pardy would have known about the mission. Gary was sure of it.

It could have been Pardy who had Indianed up on Gary's lonely camp the time his canteens had been emptied and his bay's picket pin had been pulled from the ground in an attempt to let the bay drift off. It could have been Pardy who had fooled around the truck the first time Tuck and Gary had come to the old man's place. He would have had time to cross the desert to get ahead of the slowly moving truck and even more time when it had bogged down to put on an act to scare the boys back out of that area. An act involving a dusty brown robe and a phony skeleton hand.

There had been no sign of him at his place at Lookout Rock when Sue, Tuck, and Gary had arrived there. Then there had been that mysterious cache of fresh new bills hidden in the preserve jars down in Pardy's spring cellar. If Pardy wasn't around Lookout Rock, it was quite possible he was in the mission area, keeping out of sight, showing up only to frighten the trio of teenagers and empty out their water containers.

Gary nodded. Suddenly, he felt better. If Pardy *is* around the mission, he'd have to have water to live. Therefore, there must be water in the area. "Yeah," said Gary drily. "If Pardy *is* around here." He shook his canteen. It was about a third full.

He reached the level area beyond the place where loose earth had flowed about the rear of the large mission buildings and then looked about. If they could find no water within a day's time, one of them would have to make an attempt to go for help, using what little water they had in their canteens and perhaps the water from the radiator of the truck, unpalatable as it would be. Gary would have to go.

The sun was beating down with more power. In a little while, it would hardly be possible to stay out in the sunlight. Gary would make his attempt when the sun was gone, crossing the desert during the cool of the night. There wasn't any chance that anyone would think of looking for them, at least for several days, nor would anyone know where they had gone after they had left Lookout Rock. Bit by bit, the Fates had woven their net about the trio, and all the odds were with the Fates.

Gary remembered with a cold shudder what Pardy Willis had said about that plane that had landed out in the Spanish Desert, the one he had found while on one of his solitary walking expeditions. *"They walked away from it to look for water. Heat and thirst got at 'em. Likely then they crawled into any shade they could find. Maybe under a sand bank. They died there. The wind blew and the sand drifted. The plane was found. The bodies weren't.*

"The old Spanish Desert likes its privacy. Maybe it allows a lone man to travel across it, if he's careful and don't let the desert trick him into thinking he's real safe. Maybe it even lets men build things out there while biding its time, lulling them into a false sense of security. Then it strikes, one way or another, and either kills them off or drives them out. Then, the old desert settles down to get rid of the buildings, like trying to get rid of an abscess or a scabbed wound.

Takes time. Bit by bit the sand drifts. Bit by bit the wind works. Together, the two of them work, and in time, they take back what is really theirs. The naked desert, like God made it during the Creation. You can't ever lick the Spanish Desert. It don't make any difference if you wore moccasins and came to it before Columbus discovered America, or wore a Spanish pot helmet and rode a horse, or walked afoot in a black robe carrying a cross. Maybe you wore a slouch hat and chewed tobacco, talking with a Yankee twang or with a soft Southern drawl, velvet in your voice and steel in your eyes, but the desert licked you just the same. Horses, mules, cars, and then planes. The desert licks them all!"

Gary saw Tuck's head bob up out of a roofless outbuilding and then vanish as quickly as it had appeared. Before too long, they would all have to take shelter from the gathering heat. The mission church would be the best place, for the walls were thick, and the mounded earth and rocks against them would afford more insulation.

Gary walked slowly alongside the peeling patches of wall that showed here and there above the drifted sand and earth until he reached the front of the mission. A cool draft came from within the big building. He stopped at the open doorway and peered within, suddenly alert and tense, although he had neither seen nor heard anything. Whether the place was haunted or not was open to argument, but it certainly gave one the strong impression that it was. He shook his head and stepped back, waiting for Sue and Tuck to join him. This time, he did not want to go in there alone.

————

THE GATHERING HEAT drove Sue and Tuck to join Gary. With their company, Gary was less concerned about entering the mission church, but even so, in the light of day, it was still rather an eerie business. Anything that could close Tuck's mouth from eating or talking had to be eerie, indeed, and the lean one was as close-mouthed as a clam at low tide.

They stood close together in the dusty dimness of the entry, peering into the long nave. At the far end, a shaft of dusty sunlight probed down into the interior of the sanctuary, revealing the despoliation of the holy place, the ragged holes in walls and floor, the battered carvings and plaster ornamentation, the almost utter feeling of tragedy and desolation that hung about the place like a stained and tattered shroud.

"It's horrible," said Sue in a soft voice.

"Don't be afraid," said Tuck staunchly. "We'll take care of you, Susie."

"It isn't that," she said. "It's the air of tragedy that clings here. The remains of the wonderful work those old padres and their converts did so many years ago, first partially destroyed by time, and later by the unfeeling vandals that came and did *their* work, and then left."

"You can get the same feeling at Tumacacori," said Gary quietly. "Even when the place is full of tourists, you can feel it."

"I wish we could feel some water," said Tuck, the practical one.

Gary nodded. He walked forward toward the far end of the long, shadowy nave.

"Wait!" snapped Tuck. "Footprints!" He raised his shotgun.

Gary was startled for a moment as he saw the line of footprints in the thick dust, trending toward the far end of the building, and then he realized who had made them. "Stop acting like Robinson Crusoe, you dope," he said. "Those are *my* footprints!"

"What's ahead of us?" asked Tuck nervously.

"The sanctuary," said Gary. "To the right is the sacristy. I didn't go into it yesterday."

"You going in there now?"

Gary looked back at his friend. "There might be a source of water in there." His voice didn't sound very convincing.

_____

THE STRONG BEAM of the flashlight picked out the details of the sacristy, a deep room, low-ceiled, that was to the right of the sanctuary as one faced it. He walked into the room and glanced toward the narrow doorway to the right that was filled with a flight of steps just wide enough for passage up to the pulpit, located just beyond the door to the sacristy out in the nave. He felt his way up the steps and into the pulpit, glancing back toward his two companions. "Stay there," he said. "There's only room for one up here."

He turned to look out into the nave, and as he did so, his left eye caught a vague, indistinct movement in the entryway. He snapped out the flashlight and leaned far forward to see if he could see what had moved, hoping to see it against the bright sunlight of the outside. There was nothing to see. For a moment, he wondered if he had been imagining things. He quickly flicked on the flashlight and stabbed the powerful beam toward the entryway. Faint dust swirled in the cool draft, but he wasn't sure whether the draft had caused it or perhaps the dust had been disturbed by his passage and that of his two friends.

"See anything?" asked Tuck in a hoarse voice from the darkness of the sacristy.

"No," said Gary. There was no use in worrying them, but in his own mind, he was almost certain that someone, or something, had been there in the entryway, perhaps following the trio of explorers, thinking they were in the sacristy when Gary's sudden appearance in the pulpit had startled him.

"Blast Pardy Willis!" he added.

"What brought that on?" asked Sue.

Gary joined them in the sacristy. "Nothing," he said. "Just for a minute, I was thinking we'd have never been in this mess if it hadn't been for him."

"And we wouldn't have found the Lost Mission," said Sue.

"And run outa water," said Tuck gloomily.

Sue stamped a foot. "Those padres had the faith to build here," she said quickly. "We had the faith to follow our hunches. Now all we've got to do is have enough faith to think we'll find water. Listening to you two, you'd think we were already licked. Well, I'm not! Let's find that water!"

Tuck shrugged. "There speaks the brave heart," he said. "She's right, Gary. We were losing faith."

"Speak for yourself, Tucker," said Gary.

Tuck rolled his eyes upward. "How come I'm always alone in my considered opinions?"

"We won't answer that, will we, Gary?" said Sue sweetly.

Gary did not speak. He played the flashlight along the rear wall of the sacristy. Plaster and other building materials were piled there, partially from the wall and from a great gap in the ceiling that was wedged tightly with brush and rocks, a stopgap built there by the falling of the landslide from the hill beyond the mission.

It was in his mind that there should be another door in the sacristy whereby the priest could enter to don his robes before services rather than to come through the crowded nave. There was such a door in the sacristy at Tumacacori. He leaned his rifle against the wall and placed his flashlight in Sue's hands, then he began to pull rocks and bricks free from the tumbled mass. Tuck gave him a hand.

In an hour's work, they saw the curved top of a door set very low in the wall and hardly high enough for a tall child to use, until they realized that the door was set above a narrow flight of steps that led down to a level lower than that of the sacristy floor.

Despite the insulation of the mission walls, the heat was beginning to penetrate into the building. It took several more hours' work to free the steps from the debris and partially make way into a narrow, vaulted hallway, more like a tunnel, that led from the sacristy toward the hill that stood to the right of the church building as one faced it.

Tuck wiped the sweat from his lean and dusty face and glanced at the canteens. "If we don't find water down here, pal," he husked, "we'll need all of that water in the canteens to keep us from dehydrating, and we won't be any better off than we were before."

The same thought had come to Gary. He'd have to leg it out of the Spanish Desert that night, between dusk and dawn, with a few mouthfuls of water in his canteen, and he was tiring himself out in a perhaps hopeless struggle to find water in the harsh depths of the ruins.

Tuck broke free into a larger open space. He slid down the pile of loose material. "Tunnel," he said. "Hand me that light, Susie. There's a doorway to the right." He played the beam along the tunnel. "Funny-looking tunnel," he added. "Got windows in it."

Gary wiped the sweat from his face. "It isn't a tunnel," he said. "It's likely a hallway that was covered over by the landslide. Can you see anything farther along?"

"Another doorway."

"Plugged up?"

"Not that I can see. Looks like the wooden door is still intact."

Gary crawled down beside Tuck. "Beyond the rear of the sacristy at Tumacacori, there used to be smaller buildings or rooms connected together with a colonnaded arcade, or whatever you call it, in front of them. There was a well or a spring in the area."

"Seems crazy to be in a tunnel that's really a hallway, looking underground for a spring or a well that used to be atop the ground."

"This whole business is crazy," said Gary drily.

Sue slid down beside them with the guns and canteens in her hands. "Where to?" she asked brightly.

Gary took the Winchester from her hands. He didn't think that he'd have to use it, but the feeling of the weapon gave him a courage he had not felt in the past hours of digging. He walked forward across the littered flooring of the hallway and eyed the old door. It looked remarkably well preserved. He lifted the hand-forged latch and pushed on the door. It swung open on a shrill note of rusting hinges, and a draft, musty and dust-laden, played about his heated face. He took the flashlight from Tuck and walked inside the room beyond the doorway, playing the light about. He opened his mouth to tell Tuck to keep Sue back, but it was too late, for the two Brownes had entered the low-ceiled room behind him.

The light revealed a skull, grinning at them from a pile of rags, while a bony hand rested on a broken olla. The hollow eye sockets seemed to probe into the eyes of the three of them as though to say, "*As I am, so shall you be...*"

"Don't get up for us," said Tuck politely to the skeleton.

"One of the old padres?" said Sue quietly.

Gary walked to the gruesome relic. A pair of cracked Mexican boots protruded from the dusty rags. He pulled at one of them and saw the naked bones of the lower leg. "No," he said. "Some poor fellow who likely wandered into the mission in search of water." The instant he spoke, he regretted it.

"Like us," said Sue.

"He might have found water and starved to death," said Tuck.

Gary nodded. The man might have been weak and dying of thirst or hunger when he had crawled in here to die. He looked beyond the skeleton. There was another door there. He pulled at the ring of it after lifting the rusted latch. The door resisted, then opened partway with a protesting of hinges. A trickle of loose earth flowed about Gary's ankles. He worked his way through the narrow opening and, by the light of the flashlight, saw the bases of several columns showing beneath packed earth and rock, intermingled with brush that held the material from flowing farther.

"I think we've reached a colonnaded arcade," he said over his shoulder. "The earth has filled the open area beyond it."

"Where the well might be?" asked Tuck.

"Stay back," said Gary. "This whole place looks as though it might collapse or fill in if you made too much noise."

"You're in there," said Sue.

Gary did not answer. He walked farther into the tunnel made by nature from the works of man. There were several doors, but he didn't try any of them. They were likely storage or work rooms. He began to feel depressed again. There couldn't be any water in here.

"You notice how the air is musty but still fresh

enough to breathe?" called Tuck. "Means there must be an opening somewhere along there."

Gary nodded. He pulled open a door and entered a large room. Broken plaster and pottery grated beneath his feet. A rude table and several chairs stood in the middle of the room. Several thick candles were in rusted wall sconces. He had the eerie feeling that the room looked as it had when the old occupants had left it for the last time so many, many years ago.

The next room was smaller and fitted with an ancient desk and chair but little else. Gary turned to leave, and as he did so, his left boot toe hooked into something, pitching him against the door, which slammed shut with the weight of his body while he dropped the flashlight to the paved flooring. It went out.

For a moment, green panic flooded through Gary as he stood there, the cold sweat breaking out on his body as the thick darkness seemed to rush in at him in gibbering eagerness to unseat his sanity.

He struggled to gain control over himself, then knelt to find the flashlight. He flicked it on. Though the lens had cracked, the lamp was otherwise undamaged. He turned to see what he had stumbled over. It was a thick iron ring, set almost flush into the flags of the paved flooring, in the center of a hardwood trap door. He tried it with no success. He opened the door and called for Tuck. The two Brownes appeared almost instantly.

Gary and Tuck tried to lift the trap door with no success. With the aid of a short length of thick hardwood, they moved the door a trifle. Sue sniffed at the air that flowed from beneath the door. "Smells damp!" she cried. She gave the boys a hand, and the combined strength of the three of them was just enough to lift the stubborn door. Cool, damp air flowed up about their heated faces. Gary dropped flat and held the light down into the opening. There was no stairway, but a rough wooden ladder lay on the paved flagging of the tunnel floor.

"By golly!" said Tuck. "I can smell water!"

"There better be water down there," said Gary. He handed Sue the flashlight and dropped his legs into the hole.

"You going down *there*?" asked Tuck.

"I ain't staying up here when there might be water down there," said Gary inelegantly. He gripped the edge of the hole and let himself down, hanging at full arms' length, breathed a silent prayer, and let himself drop. He landed lightly and then looked up. "Flashlight," he said. He caught it and turned it to examine the tunnel. It was walled with heavy masonry and well-built. Perhaps it had been designed and built as a hideout in the days when the Apaches held most of that country in mortal subjugation.

"How does it look?" asked Tuck.

"Alright. You have any matches?"

"Yes."

"Then go into the next room. There are some old candles in there."

"What do we need them for?"

Gary looked up. "I'll need the flashlight to explore down here. You want to stay up there in the dark, Tuckie, old boy?" Gary grinned cruelly as he flicked out the flashlight.

"I'll go get 'em!" said Tuck breathlessly. His boots grated on the floor, the door squeaked, the next door squeaked, and in a matter of about a minute and a half, Tuck was back in the dark room, trying to light one of the ancient candles. The wick flared up, and then the mellow light filled the little room. "Beats the heck out of me how they can last this long," he said.

Sue lowered Gary's Winchester to him, and he leaned it against the wall while he inspected the old ladder. He tested the rungs and then placed it so that the others could descend if they wished to do so. "You'd better stay up there," he said. "I'll see what I can find down here."

"Be careful," said Sue. Her face was drawn and worried-looking in the flickering light of the candle.

"I will," said Gary confidently. He did not look at her —his feelings might show on his face. He had no choice but to penetrate into the unknown beneath the old mission. No matter what dangers there were down there, none of them could be worse than the peril of dying of thirst.

The tunnel was narrow, hardly wide enough for a person to pass through, and here and there, some of the masonry protruded, with great gouts of heavy mortar hanging from it. The air was cool, and perhaps a little damp, although Gary thought that perhaps his imagination was working overtime, wanting him to think that it *did* smell damp, thus indicating the presence of water.

He worked his way slowly through the narrow passage, wincing now and then as one of his shoulders struck a ragged fang of the masonry, and once he struck his head, a glancing blow against a low-hanging part of the tunnel roof. As he passed, bent low, a piece of the masonry fell heavily from the roof and smashed just behind his heels.

He had no idea of where he was, although he judged that he might be beneath the mission church by now. It was possible, from the looks of the tunnel, that it might have been laid out prior to building the mission above it, perhaps as a trench, walled and roofed with masonry, and then covered by the flagged paving of the mission.

Suddenly, he rounded a corner and found himself in a roughly shaped room, low-ceiled but surprisingly large. His eyes widened as he saw a familiar-looking object sitting on crude trestles in the middle of the room. It was a coffin, shaped of wood, thick with dust, and cracked by time. Gary closed his eyes for a minute, struggling to keep back his fear. It was only a box, he thought, but at the back of his mind surged nameless fear and approaching panic.

He forced himself to approach the box. The lid was slightly ajar. It took all his courage to push the lid to one side. The coffin was empty save for dust. He wiped the cold sweat from his face. Then, as he raised his eyes, he saw something that gave him a greater sense of fear. A robe hung on a peg driven into a crack in the masonry. A heavy brown robe. The robe of a Franciscan monk!

Wild fears rushed through his mind. He remembered all too well that silent, menacing figure he had seen several times, and the sight of that bony hand reaching inside the window of the truck. "Get hold of yourself," he whispered hoarsely. "It's only a robe. Nothing else." His words echoed softly in the room.

It was then that he noticed something on the flagged paving of the room. Something narrow and dark, like a ribbon of blood trickling from the darkness beyond his flashlight beam. He knelt and sniffed at the fluid. It certainly wasn't blood. He touched it with a finger and tasted it. "Water," he said quietly. His eyes followed the dark line, hardly enough to wet the dry stone of the paving. The line ended abruptly at the far wall of heavy, thickly mortared masonry.

Gary walked to the wall and studied it for a possible opening. There was none. He booted the wall several times, but it did not sound hollow. He knelt and felt along the bottom of it, hoping to feel a faint draft, but there wasn't any. Just that mysterious, thin trickle of water from some unknown source, and hardly enough of it to fill a cup.

He could go no farther. The water source was beyond the massive wall. There was nothing to do but return to his friends. He walked slowly back toward the trap door, confused and frightened.

CHAPTER THIRTEEN

Tuck Plays the Count of Monte Cristo

Tuck Browne steadily picked away at the thick mortar in the wall, using an iron bar he had found in one of the rooms, while Gary scraped away with his thick-bladed hunting knife. Sue was examining the coffin and the robe in the guttering candlelight.

Tuck looked sideways at Gary. "This will take hours. Maybe the water comes through the earth from a long distance."

"If you've got any better ideas, pal, you'd better sound off," said Gary brutally. "I'll have to be heading out of here soon if we don't find water down here."

"Funny," said Sue.

Gary turned. "I don't think so," he said.

"I don't mean what you said, Gary. I mean, how did they get this coffin in here?"

"What do you mean?"

She looked at the narrow tunnel entrance. "You couldn't fit it through that," she said.

"Maybe they brought it in here and assembled it."

She shook her head. "It's over six feet long. I don't think you could work a six-foot board through that tunnel, no matter how you tried. Besides, the bottom is one solid board over two feet wide. They'd never have been able to work it through, Gary."

"Might have put it in here before they roofed it over," said Gary.

"*If* they built the tunnel that way," she said.

"I haven't got time to play Sam Spade right now," he said.

Tuck turned. "Maybe we'd better," he said. "Gary, this wall was built at a different time than the rest of the walls. This mortar is much fresher, and the rocks are not the same color."

"So?"

Tuck struck a hard blow against the wall and then picked up a shard of the mortar. "I'd be willing to swear this mortar isn't anywhere near as old as the rest of the stuff."

"How old would you say it was?" asked Sue.

Tuck shrugged. There was an odd look on his face. "Maybe not more than a year or so old, give or take a little time."

"That's *loco*," said Sue.

Gary picked up more of the mortar, felt it, and sniffed at it. He looked at Tuck. "You're right," he said.

"Who could have done it?" asked Sue in a shaky voice.

An icy finger seemed to trace a course down Gary's sweating back. He had suddenly remembered the painstaking labor Pardy Willis had shown in constructing his odd dwelling place at Lookout Rock, and the secret room so well concealed below the old man's living quarters.

"I just wonder where Pardy Willis has been all this time," said Tuck.

Gary looked quickly at him. It was as though Tuck had read his mind.

"It's no use kidding ourselves," said Tuck. "Who else could be behind all this monkey-business? Who else knows about this place but Pardy Willis? What about that money he had stashed away in that hideout of his? Him always acting poor as a church mouse and having all that money in those jars? I tell you, there's something strange about that old coot."

Gary nodded. "What bothers me is his dumping our water. I don't mind the ghost bit, with the robe and all, but when a man dumps out other people's water in this desert, that's the next thing to premeditated murder, and I *don't like it*!"

Tuck nodded. He struck a savage blow at the wall and drove the battered iron bar clear through. A piece of masonry fell heavily on the far side, and a draft of cool air flowed about their heated faces, causing the guttering candles to leap and posture, throwing grotesque shadows on the walls.

Tuck peered through into the stygian darkness. "I feel like the ol' Count of Monte Cristo," he murmured.

Gary picked up the bar and began to pry and work it through the hole. Mortar and masonry fell from the widening gap until he could thrust an arm and a shoulder through and use the flashlight to explore beyond the opening.

Sue shrieked piercingly. Tuck yelled. Gary jerked his arm and shoulder from the hole and whirled. The flashlight struck the wall and fell from his hand to clatter on the paving, going out as it did so. One of the candles had gone out, but in the flickering, daring light of the other candle, a startling figure stood framed in the narrow doorway of the room.

A robed figure, with the cowl drawn low over the hidden face and a bony hand extended toward the three staring adventurers. Sue sagged sideways in a dead faint and struck the side of the coffin upon which stood the candle. The candle fell to the floor and went out. An eerie laughing sound filled the room.

Gary felt along the wall, icy sweat streaming down his face, until he found the flashlight. For an instant, he hesitated with putting on the torch, for he had no desire to see that awful specter standing there, but at least the known was better than the chilling unknown. He snapped on the light. The doorway was empty. For an instant, he thought he heard a muffled voice in the tunnel, and then it was gone, but he wasn't sure about it at all.

Tuck's eyes were wide, and his mouth worked, but not a sound came from him. Finally, he made it. "Let's get outa here!" he gasped.

"Light the candles," said Gary. He knelt beside Sue.

Sue opened her eyes. "Is he gone?" she whispered.

Tuck's shaking hand managed to light a match and then the two candles. The feeble light filled the room.

Gary picked up his rifle and walked toward the doorway. He flicked the flashlight beam up the narrow tunnel as far as he could. There was nothing to be seen. Foot by foot, he worked his way slowly back toward the ladder. The tunnel was empty except for himself. There was no sound from the upper room.

Gary rubbed his jaw. Scared as he was, it was hard to believe he had seen a ghost. He turned to go back, and as he did so, he saw something hanging on a projecting piece of masonry. It was a scrap of thick brown cloth, and it had not been there before.

He picked it from the rock. One corner was darker than the rest and a little damp. He looked at the rock and saw a faint smudge upon it. He touched it and tasted his fingertip, sensing the faint salt taste of blood. He remembered then that he had heard a muffled outcry in the tunnel after the specter had vanished. Whoever it was, it was a man, not a ghost—of that, Gary was quite sure. *But who was it?*

Gary walked back into the room. Sue was leaning against the wall, white-faced and shaken. There was no sign of Tuck, but a faint flickering light showed beyond the opening in the masonry wall, and a weird chuckling sound came from there. Gary looked at Sue. She shrugged and pointed toward the opening. Gary could never have fitted his broad shoulders through the hole, but Tuck was built like a trout, and it would have been difficult, but possible, for him to have wormed his way through.

Gary poked an arm through the hole and swung the flashlight to pinpoint Tuck. The lean one was seated on a box, fondling something in his dirty hands, chuckling to himself like a madman. Something fell from his hands. Gary stared. It was a piece of paper money. He suddenly realized that Tuck had a lap full of the stuff.

Tuck turned. "We're filthy rich!" he cried wildly. "Look!" He threw up his hands, and bill after bill fluttered to the damp floor of the room. He chuckled eerily.

The flashlight beam picked out a pile of small metal boxes neatly stacked against the wall. One of the boxes had been opened, and some bills showed above the edge of it.

"Put down that loot," said Gary, "and help me make this opening big enough for a *man*."

In a matter of minutes, Gary got into the room. He lifted box after box, finding them locked, but each was filled with something, and if the first box was any indication, there was a fortune in bills stored in the room. "I don't get it," he said.

Tuck turned. "Simple enough," he said. "This is where Pardy keeps his ill-gotten gains. That stuff we saw at his place is nothing compared to this."

Gary rubbed his jaw. "If this belongs to Pardy," he said thoughtfully, "the old shyster sure had people buffaloed into thinking he was always dead broke."

"Sure," said Tuck. "What better place to store his money than here? Who'd come here, anyway? No one but nuts like us. No wonder he was trying to scare us away."

"You think that was him in the robe?"

"Sure."

Gary picked up his rifle. "Listen, Count of Monte Cristo. If that old boy owns this money and is so anxious to scare people away from it that he dumps their water out, even the water belonging to supposedly good friends of his, he's hard enough to kill anyone he finds fooling around with his money."

"We still need water," said a small feminine voice from the other room. "All that ill-gotten wealth can't buy a thimbleful in here."

———

GARY WALKED around a protruding rock shoulder and found a thick wooden door set closely into the wall. The ground beneath the mission must be literally honey-combed with rooms and tunnels. He turned the flashlight to the floor and saw that the trickle of water came from beneath the door. He tried the door, but it would not move. With the help of Tuck, the door could be moved a fraction of an inch or so, and that was all.

Gary whittled away at the tough wood with his sheath knife until he could slip the end of the iron bar into it. He put his full weight against the bar, and the door moved a little. Once again, he heaved at the bar. It began to bend a little, but something snapped, and the door moved several inches. Tuck eagerly began to pull at the door.

"Wait," warned Gary. He picked up his rifle. He nodded at Tuck. Tuck opened the door, and the flashlight beam stabbed into the gloom beyond the doorway and reflected from something bright, as though polished metal was beyond the doorway.

"Gold, maybe!" said Tuck. "Or silver!"

Gary shook his head. "Better," he said quietly. "It's water."

"Amen," said Sue softly.

Gary walked slowly into the room. A portion of the

room had been fitted with a rock wall several feet high, and the pool was behind it, a foot deep in clear water, from which a slow trickle escaped over the edge to flow along the floor toward the doorway by which Gary had entered, indicating that the pool was likely fed by a spring. Beyond the pool were two doors. Sagging wooden shelves held various odds and ends. Perhaps the old padres had used the room for storing food that must be kept cool.

Gary tasted the water. It was as fresh and tasty as the water that had given its name to Gary's home, Chiricahua Springs Ranch. At least this was one problem that had been solved.

"I can understand now why our water was dumped out," said Tuck from behind Gary. "With a water supply like this, they could afford to be careless with *our* water."

"But who could it be?" asked Sue.

"Pardy Willis," said Tuck.

"I wonder," said Sue.

Gary looked at her. "Why do you say that? It must be him."

"We never saw the face of that thing, or whatever it is," agreed Tuck, following Gary's line of thought.

"I haven't seen Pardy for a long time," she said, "but I can remember that lovely beard of his. It must have been more than a foot long."

"He still has it," said Tuck, "but it's closer to a foot and a half long and as thick as a mattress."

"Then where was it when we saw that ghost, or whatever it is:" she asked.

"Could have been hidden beneath the robe," said Gary.

"I don't think so," she said.

Gary looked at Tuck. Tuck shrugged.

"Besides," she said, "Pardy isn't a tall man, is he?"

"Maybe five feet seven or eight," said Tuck.

"That figure we just saw was closer to six feet tall."

"How would you know?" jeered Tuck. "You fell into a dead faint, Susie."

She flushed a little and looked questioningly at Gary.

Gary began to fill the canteens with the fresh water. Maybe Sue was wrong, but she was a keen observer. It would have been difficult for Pardy to have stuffed that luxurious beard beneath the robe. The figure had been taller than Pardy, although that might have been an illusion, for the figure had hardly been in sight long enough for one to evaluate its height. "I think the best thing for us to do is to get out of here and report what we've found."

"Yeah," said Tuck. "A lost mission haunted by old padres in dusty old robes and thousands of dollars hidden in the cellars. They'll think we're plumb *loco!*"

"If you've got any better ideas," said Gary, "you'd better air them, Mac, because I can't think of any."

"What about the truck?" said the lean one. "No rotor, no motor, man."

"Then I'll walk out," said Gary. "I've got enough water now."

"We'd better *all* walk out," said Sue.

Tuck looked at Gary over the top of Sue's head and shook his own head. Gary knew well enough what he meant. The two boys might conceivably make the walk out with fairly even odds, but Sue would never make it, and they'd have no way of carrying her if she fell victim to the heat and exertion.

Tuck sipped some of the water. "Sue," he said quietly, "we'll stay here until Gary comes back with help. It's the best way. I'd rather go with Gary to double our chances, but I won't leave you alone here."

"I'll be all right," she said.

"No argument," said Gary. "Tuck is right."

"What about all that money?" said Tuck.

"It isn't ours," said Gary.

"I didn't mean it that way. There's something almighty queer about this place."

Sue nodded. "Like someone's been trying to keep us away from here, and it started when you first came into the area where the mission is, Gary."

"And, it's got something to do with Pardy," said Tuck, "whether or not he's been the one trying to scare us away."

Gary picked up his rifle. He tried one of the doors and found that it led into a small room. He shrugged and left it—it was as empty as a sea shell. The other door opened into a large room, shored up with masonry piers and heavy balks of timber. There was a huge table set to one side. Beyond one of the piers was an open doorway.

"Funny," said Tuck from behind Gary. "I could swear I can smell gas."

"Gas?" said Gary.

"I mean gasoline fumes," said Tuck.

Gary sniffed the air. The lean one was right. There was a faint, almost indefinable odor of gasoline in the room. He walked toward the table, noting that it was comparatively free of dust. The odor of gasoline was stronger there, mingled with something else that seemed vaguely familiar to him. Then it came to him. "Printer's ink," he said.

"Yeah," said Tuck softly.

Gary saw an opening in the ceiling behind the table. He worked his way behind the table and peered up the opening, noting that it was actually a pipe of some sort, driven up into the masonry, and a faint circle of light showed at the upper end, as though it protruded into the open air. Maybe it was a stovepipe. Perhaps someone, at some time, had lived in the place long after the old padres had left. The odor of gasoline was now very strong.

"Someone had a small gas engine in here," said Tuck.

"Look here." He indicated a pair of balks placed on the floor, soaked with oil and smelling of gasoline.

"And they ran the exhaust up through the pipe," said Gary.

"But why?" asked Tuck. "They wouldn't use a gas engine for heating." He eyed the balks and then the hole. "I got it!" he added. "The gas engine was probably used to run a generator for electrical power to run something else."

"Such as?"

Tuck shrugged. "*Quién sabe?*"

Gary rubbed his jaw. Gasoline fumes. An exhaust opening. The odor of printer's ink. An odd thought came to him. "All that money," he said quietly. "Fresh as new-baked bread. What's it doing here?"

Sue looked at him. "Counterfeiters," she said softly.

"Holy Moly!" said Tuck. His eyes widened. "You mean all that money back there is phony?"

"Isn't likely a Federal Mint would be operating out here in the middle of nowhere," said Sue.

Gary shoved back his hat. It was too bewildering to fully comprehend, but the facts surely were pointing to something quite out of the ordinary.

Tuck checked his shotgun. "If this *is* a counterfeiter hideout," he said soberly, "that means we're in deep trouble. They'll never let us get out of here with the information we have. Maybe that's why they swiped the rotor of the distributor. If they know we found this layout down here, they'll sure get a lot more serious about stopping us than running around hiding in a brown robe making like a long-dead padre with the phony skeleton hand and all."

Gary nodded. "What bothers me," he said, "is how they let us get this far. "Maybe they just let us go ahead," said Sue, "figuring that they can always trap us down here."

In the silence that followed Sue's remark, the two

boys looked at each other. The room suddenly seemed a lot colder.

Gary walked toward the open doorway. A flight of steps led upward into thick darkness. His flashlight beam picked out fresh scars on the old masonry steps, as though something heavy had been dragged up or down the stairs. Something heavy like a gasoline engine, and perhaps a small but efficient printing press.

"You going up there?" asked Tuck.

Gary nodded. "We can't stay down here," he said.

"Maybe they've got someone up there waiting for you," said Sue. "Someone with a gun, maybe!"

Gary smiled, but there was no mirth in the smile. "I've got a gun too," he said. "I'll go up first. If anything happens, you go back the way we came. Try to get out of the mission and head out into the desert. You've got water now. You'll have to chance getting to safety."

"What about you, Gary?" asked Tuck.

"I got you into this," said Gary quietly. "You're responsible for Sue, Tuck." He walked quickly up the steps before they could say anything else.

He flicked out the light at the top of the steps, feeling with his hands, identifying a heavy wooden door. He tested the latch. It worked freely. Slowly, he eased open the heavy door. Surprisingly enough, it hardly made a sound, as though someone had oiled the great hand-forged hinges. He narrowed his eyes. There was faint light beyond the doorway. He stepped through into a dusty corridor, partly open to the sky, and realized that the light was coming in from the moon. He had not realized how many hours he and his companions had spent in and about the ruins.

———

IT WAS hard to figure out just where he was until he peered through a great fissure in the wall and realized

that he had come out into a corridor that was partially
—indeed, almost completely—buried by the great fall of
earth from the high-sided hill to the west of the
mission church. His eyes studied the flagged flooring of
the corridor. Faint footprints showed here and there in
the thick dust, heading toward the darkness of the far
end of the corridor, and there were other marks, as
though something had been dragged through the dust
as well.

Gary padded like a cat along the corridor, seeing his
way by the light of the moon, his rifle at hip level. The
corridor ended with a doorway that led into stygian
blackness. Gary paused there for long minutes, testing
the darkness with his senses, and then he could make out
the faintest odor of gasoline. He felt his way into a room,
thick in dust and darkness, and his questing hands
touched metal of some kind.

He could not see a thing, but his hands outlined the
known shapes of a small gasoline engine and a generator.
He felt his way cautiously about the room until his hands
touched something else he could identify. It was a small,
compact printing press. He risked turning on the flashlight. Part of the press had been disassembled, and the
parts placed in strong wooden boxes. The generator was
mounted on wooden skids, upon which it could be
dragged. The light picked out a wide wooden door, made
of rough new planking. A wooden bar lay across rests,
closing the door.

Slowly and cautiously, he lifted the bar, then turned
out his light and eased open the door, letting in cold,
silvery moonlight. The way beyond the door lay between
rough earthen walls studded with shattered rock, and
Gary realized that the door behind him was new, cut into
the old masonry walls of the mission. He eyed the outer
surface of the door and saw that it had cleverly been
painted to resemble the surrounding earth and rocks and,
in addition, had been partially covered with pieces of

brush. The way beyond the door was well concealed with brush.

Gary softly closed the door behind him and worked his way to the mouth of the artificial draw. He sharply drew in his breath. He could see down a rough slope to a wide level area stippled with scrub brush. Miles and miles to the south, he could see the faint, humped back of mountains, and to the right, he could see for miles across open desert, almost as flat as a billiard table. He had not realized that beyond the hills surrounding the lost mission was such open country. There wasn't a sign of a road, a dwelling, or anything else made by man to be seen in those hundreds of square miles—not even the friendly yellow eye of a light.

Gary squatted amid the brush. He knew enough about counterfeiters to know that what they valued most highly were the plates from which the phony bills were printed. From the looks of the money he had seen, the plates were excellent indeed. The press and the generator did not matter, nor did the printed bills, as compared to the value of those plates. They, of course, would either have been taken away or well hidden somewhere— perhaps not even in the mission area.

Gary stood up and peered around the side of the hill. There was no sign of life. If he skirted the base of the hill, he would end up somewhere toward the rear of the mission church. The thing he had to do now was to get back to his friends—after he was sure that the coast was clear—and get them out of the mission area where they could either hide or strike out across the Spanish Desert on foot before the murderous heat of the day came.

He worked his way as quietly as possible through the brush. It gave him an uncanny feeling, thinking about the robed figure that had plagued them and might plague them again. Whoever it was knew that the trio was probably still beneath the mission and might even now be watching for them to appear.

He reached the rear of the mission and looked about. The moonlight bathed the empty ground. It was almost as bright as daylight. Gary started for the front of the mission.

The gunshot blasted the quiet and aroused the sleeping echoes. The echoes slammed back and forth between the moonlighted hills and died away. Another shot aroused the echoes again.

Gary Cole cast caution aside and raced as silently as possible toward the front of the mission

CHAPTER FOURTEEN

Strangers from the Sky

Rifted gun smoke drifted about the front of the mission church. A slim figure was running toward Gary. It was Susan. "He's got Tuck!" she screamed at Gary.

"Who has?" he cried.

"The padre!'

For a moment, her words sent a chill through him until he realized that she meant a man, a creature of flesh and blood, armed with a gun. Gary gripped her by the arm and pulled her toward a place where two ungainly buttresses held up the church wall. He peered around one of the buttresses, rifle at the ready. "Tell me about it," he said over his shoulder.

She gulped. "We wondered what had happened to you. Tuck got worried. We started back the way we came, and when we were on the ground level, we thought someone was following us. Just before we reached the sacristy, Tuck went back a little way to look. I heard him yell. I started to run. He was just behind me, or so I thought. When I reached the front of the nave, I heard the first shot. I looked back and saw Tuck struggling with that robed figure. He hit Tuck with his gun and knocked him down, then called out to me to stay where I was. I ran. He fired again. That's all I know."

"You don't know who it was?"

"No."

"Pardy Willis, maybe?"

"I don't know."

"There was only one of them?"

She looked at him curiously. "*Them?* Do you think there are more than one of them?"

"There is, or was, a counterfeiting operation going on here. I have a feeling that they were getting ready to pull out when we blundered along."

"What will he do with Tuck?"

Gary turned. "This is big-time stuff, Sue. They can't afford to have us get away and inform the authorities."

"What will they do with Tuck?" she repeated.

He did not dare to look at her, for the message would be written on his face. There was likely but one answer. These would be desperate men. "Stay here," he said quietly.

He padded toward the front of the mission church, then stopped and eyed the open doorway. The gunsmoke was gone, but the faint, acrid odor of it still hung in the quiet air. Not a sound came from within the building.

Gary moved softly, but his rifle butt struck the front of the building, sounding loudly in the stillness. He jumped back and raised the weapon.

"I've got your pal here," called out a hard voice from within the building. "You better get rid of your guns and surrender to me. You hear?"

Gary wet his dry lips. As far as he knew, there was only one man in there, but there was no telling where the others might be, and he was quite sure that there must be more than one of them.

"You won't get hurt, kid," called out the man.

Gary thought, *Oh, yeah? Let us get into his hands and they'll never see the three of us again. Lost in the Spanish Desert.*

No trace ever found. That would be the obituary for the three of us.

"I only meant to scare you kids away," continued the unseen man. He laughed. "You know, the old padre bit. The hand was made outa wood and painted white. Pretty realistic, eh?"

You have no idea, thought Gary.

"Make you a deal," said the man. "Drop your gun and surrender. We'll keep you locked up until we get outa here, then set you free, and no harm done. Fair enough, eh?"

Gary eased his way toward the doorway. "All right," he said. He dropped the gun on the hard ground.

"Get out in front of the doorway!"

Gary moved slowly to the doorway, hoping he wasn't exposing himself to a bullet. Feet grated on the dusty floor within the building. "Where's the girl?" asked the counterfeiter.

"Scared. She'll be along."

"Go get her."

Gary risked a glance. The robed figure was just within the entryway, the dullness of blued gun metal showing in the right hand. There was no sign of Tuck.

"Get the girl," repeated the man.

Gary hesitated. He had hoped that the man would approach him, Gary, closely enough for Gary to risk a poke at him. He was big and fast, and handy with the gloves, but the man would have to be close enough for the youth to risk throwing a punch at him. There were a few other tricks Gary knew, judo taught to him by Jerry Black Eagle.

The gun hammer clicked back. "*Get the girl!*" said the man in a low, harsh voice.

Gary dropped low and charged, arms outspread, driving in hard, booted feet hammering on the flags. The gun exploded just over his head as his shoulder smashed into the midriff of the counterfeiter, and the two of them crashed back into the nave in a flurry of blinding dust. Gary rolled free, and a boot cruelly struck his shoulder. "Tuck!" he screamed.

The man was tangled in the robe he wore. Gary kicked up at him, and the man gripped Gary's ankle and aimed at Gary's head with the barrel of the heavy pistol. A gun went off behind them. "Let Gary alone, you big ape!" screamed Sue.

She had given Gary just enough time to break free and dart out of the doorway. He shoved Sue to one side as the man fired, and the slug seemed to whisper evilly within an inch of Gary's head.

Gary rounded the corner of the church a good two yards behind Sue as another bullet whipped through the air. She darted behind the church and turned to hand him his rifle. He gripped it and jumped back between two buttresses. His shoulder struck one of them, and the stinging pain forced him to drop the rifle. It fell beyond the buttresses. He started toward it and then jumped back as the counterfeiter's pistol cracked flatly, spurting dust between Gary and the rifle.

The rifle lay temptingly within six feet of Gary. Six shots had been fired from the counterfeiter's revolver. He'd have to reload. Gary had to make up his mind in a matter of seconds. He stepped out again, and the gun was fired. This time, the slug smashed into the rifle, snapping off the outside hammer. It tinkled musically on the hard ground.

The man laughed. "You have no idea, kid, how fast I can reload when I have to."

Gary wiped the sweat from his face. The rifle was useless now. Tuck had had the shotgun with him. He suddenly remembered that Sue had been carrying the .22 caliber pistol. That was poor consolation. He was trapped between the buttresses, and from the shooting the counterfeiter had just done, smashing the hammer from the rifle, Gary had no doubt that the man was an expert.

"Sue?" called Gary.

"Yes," came her faint reply.

"Do you have the pistol?"

There was a long pause.

"Sue?" snapped Gary.

"I must have left it down under the mission, Gary. I'm sorry."

The moon was shining down fully upon the old mission and the naked hills surrounding it. It glittered from the worn metal of the useless rifle. An ant could hardly cross that illumined ground without being seen. There would be no offer to surrender now. The counterfeiter would take no chances. Tuck was likely doomed—perhaps already done away with. Gary could not risk trying to find him now. His responsibility was to Sue.

Gary thrust out a hand. The pistol cracked. A pitted spot showed on the aged plaster of the buttress, and the mutilated slug sang thinly off into space. The man could shoot like Billy the Kid and was just as deadly.

Gary flattened himself against the forward buttress. There was nothing to prevent the man from coming to get him, and Sue as well. What was holding him back?

Gary raised his head. A faint humming sound came to him. He looked about the area. It was empty of life, clear and sharp in the bright moonlight. The humming sound grew louder, and he recognized it as the sound of a plane flying over the empty Spanish Desert.

He looked up at the clear sky and a moment later saw the reflection of moonlight on the wings of a bi-motored plane flying at low altitude, headed almost directly for the mission. His heart leaped within him. Maybe he could attract their attention. Almost instantly, he cast out the thought. They'd never see him. If he broke into the open, he'd be dead in an instant.

"It's a plane, Gary!" called Sue.

"I hear it," he answered.

A moment later, she spoke again. "It's coming lower, Gary!"

The droning of the engines grew louder. A shadow flitted across the silvered ground as the plane circled over the mission. Gary risked peering up at it. The pistol spat flame and smoke, and the slug splattered against the buttress. Gary winced as tiny shards of plaster stung his face.

"Get away from here," said Gary in a low voice, hoping that Sue, and not the counterfeiter, would hear him. She was safe enough from his fire, but if anything happened to Gary, she'd have little chance to escape.

"I won't leave you," she said.

"You listen to me! I'm going to make a break for it when he runs out of cartridges in his pistol. He's only got three left."

"The plane is very low now, Gary! I think it's trying to land! Yes! Yes! It is!"

He could not see it, but he could hear it well enough. The engines had been throttled back.

"I'll run to it, Gary!" she cried. "It's help!"

He heard her boots grating on the gravel. The pistol cracked again. Four rounds gone, two left, thought Gary. The plane must be very low now. He could hear the rushing of air about it as it neared the ground. They must be going to land in the level area he had seen beyond the hidden entrance to the other side of the mission. The ground was clear enough and hard enough for a plane landing.

Another sound came to Gary. The sound of laughing. He turned to listen. It was coming from the front of the mission. It was the man dressed in the robe. Why was he laughing? A cold chill went through Gary. The realization struck him like the blow of a rifle butt. That was no friendly plane coming in for a landing! Gary had been sure all along that there must be more than one counterfeiter. It would have taken a number of strong men to have brought the printing press and the generator to the mission and manhandled them down into the cellars beneath the mission.

He heard the sound of the plane landing as the wheels struck and the shock absorbers took up the strain. A moment later, the engines were cut, and silence flowed across the dreamy-looking landscape. "Sue!" he yelled. "Stay away from that plane!"

He was too late, for he could hear Sue calling out to the people in the plane.

Gary dashed from his hiding place. The gun spoke. A slug whispered over Gary's head. He bent low and zigzagged from side to side, streaking for cover beyond the open area. The last slug whipped through the slack of his shirt as he dived into a hollow, holding back an agonized scream as catclaw ripped through his clothing into his flesh.

There was no time to waste. He plowed through the clutching catclaw, darted behind a boulder, and then ran like a deer for a deep draw, casting a look over his shoulder as he ran. The plane had settled not far from the hidden entrance to the mission. Two men stood there with a slight figure just in front of them, and there was no doubt in Gary's mind but that it was Sue. She had walked right into a trap. Gary vanished from sight in the draw. He knew he was safe enough. They'd never be able to catch him with the start he had. They were safe enough from him as well, for he was unarmed, and by the time he got help, they'd be long gone in their plane.

He circled back, ending up on a flat-topped hill beyond the area where the plane had landed and where he could see the area to the east of the mission. Small figures moved about beside the mission. Three of them were men; the fourth figure was that of Sue. Gary rested his head on his crossed forearms. He was literally help-less. Maybe Tuck was already dead, and Sue's fate a certainty. What could Gary do against three well-armed and desperate men?

———

As the moon rose higher, he saw two of the men working around the hidden entrance to the mission. He was startled when a violent puff of smoke and flame shot from the hidden entrance, followed by the dull booming of an explosion. Smoke drifted lazily out of the draw and hung in the windless air.

The two men walked unhurriedly toward the rear of the mission, and it was so quiet that Gary could hear their voices, although he could not distinguish what they were saying. He knew that they had blasted the hidden entrance to the mission, thus destroying it and burying beneath tons of earth and masonry the incriminating printing press and the generator.

Gary stood up, screened by brush from view, and studied the mission. Maybe they had already accounted for Sue and Tuck. A cold hatred swept over Gary. It would be easy for him to escape, but that was not the way of a Cole, and he knew that Sue and Tuck would never have deserted him, for that was not the way of the Brownes.

His mind was working swiftly. Certainly, the counterfeiters would no longer require the press and the generator. They were likely going down for the metal boxes stored beneath the mission—the boxes packed with phony money.

There was something far more important than the press and the generator, and even the thousands of dollars of counterfeit money, and that was the engraved plates required to print the money. They were excellent plates. The printed money indicated that. Those plates were worth a fortune, to counterfeiters at least. If Gary could get his hands on those plates, he'd have something with which to dicker for the lives of his two friends.

Gary moved as silently and as unseen as a hunting cat through the silence of the night toward the crumbling ruins of the outer buildings of the mission. He reached a point where he could see the front door. There would be only one way to enter the lower level of the mission now, and that would be through the sacristy, for the way he had emerged from the mission was now blocked by the explosion that had buried the incriminating press and the generator.

There was no sign of the counterfeiters or his friends about the front of the mission. He crossed the open ground swiftly and dropped behind a ledge of rocks close to the edge of the loose earth that flowed about the base of the bell tower.

He could see nothing of the others or hear any sound from them. He climbed up the earth slide and entered a window of the tower halfway to the top of it. He worked his way cautiously down the stairs until he could peer into the dusty entryway. Not a sound disturbed the quiet.

Gary flitted like a shadow through the faintly echoing nave until he reached the sacristy door. He was halfway across the sacristy when he heard sounds coming from the doorway that Tuck and he had unearthed in their search for water. He sped up the narrow stairway into the cramped pulpit just as footsteps sounded within the sacristy and the flickering light of a flashlight cast dancing shadows upon the ancient walls.

The footsteps sounded in the sanctuary and then in the nave. Gary risked a look over the crumbling edge of the pulpit. Two men were walking toward the front of the nave, carrying a board between them upon which rested a number of the money-filled metal boxes he had seen cached beneath the mission. The two of them disappeared outside.

Gary went down to the sacristy. The two counterfeiters were obviously heading for the plane. It would take some time for them to reach the plane, load it, and make the return trip. That meant that one of the counterfeiters was with Sue and Tuck, if Tuck was still alive. Gary would have to take his chances. He still had his sheath knife, and if forced to, he would use it to attack or for defense. His father had taught him a bit about Marine knife fighting.

He entered the buried hallway and padded along it to the room where the grinning skull kept gruesome watch with its hollow eyes. He passed from there into the almost totally buried arcade area. He was forced to turn on his flashlight to see his way into the trapdoor room. The trapdoor was open, and the ladder in place.

Gary gathered all his courage and descended into the narrow, twisting tunnel. If he was caught in there, it would be all over for him. He turned off the flashlight and felt his way along the tunnel until he reached the low-ceiled room where the grim coffin still sat on its trestles. The room was dark. He felt his way across it to the wall he and Tuck had broken through. His questing hands revealed that the wall had been almost completely torn down.

Gary stepped into the room where the counterfeit money had been stored. A quick stab of light from the flashlight revealed that a good half of the boxes were still piled there. Softly, he walked to the next door, that which was behind the protruding rock shoulder. The door was open, but no light showed from beyond it. He crossed that room, listening to the metallic, silvery sound of the water trickling from the rock basin.

He paused at the partly open door of the small room beyond the water room. Not a sound came from it. He crossed it and placed his ear against the next door that opened into the room where the press and the generator had been kept and used. Now, the faint sound of voices came to him. He began to recognize the voice of the man who had been left alone at the mission while his confederates had been elsewhere.

Softly, he eased back on the door until it was open a crack. The voice droned on. Gary wet his dry lips, feeling the icy sweat trickling down his body. If those others came in silently behind him!

The voice was clearer now. "Like I said, it was a real break for the boys and me when we found this place. Imagine the Feds looking for our place of operation out here in the cellars of an old mission."

"It was your plane then that Pardy Willis found?" asked Sue.

The man laughed. "Sure! It was a chartered plane. Max is a first-class pilot. We were flying the press and the generator down to a place in Mexico when we had some engine trouble and landed near here. It was me that had the idea of hiding the press and the generator in here. Took quite a bit of doing to get 'em into the mission then cover our tracks.

"Max drained off the gas in the plane to make it look as though we had run outa gas and then wandered off into the desert to die. There was no way of tracking us down. Max had picked me and Cliff up out in the desert near Yuma. He gave a phony name and credentials to the plane charter service. We had hauled the equipment out into the desert in a hired truck. Gave phony names to the truck-renting outfit. Just left the truck sitting out there with a flat tire to make it look like we abandoned it."

"Very neat," said the dry voice of Tuck Browne.

Gary's heart leaped. Tuck *was* alive, then!

"It was that *loco* old man, the one you call Pardy Willis, who nearly gave the game away," continued the man. "It was him that found the plane. By the time they came in to fly the plane out, we were well located in the mission, and no one was the wiser. The old man began to bother us. Kept prowling around out in the desert. We'd see him now and then. Couldn't keep him away. It was me who had the idea of making with the old robe and the skeleton hand. Sure scared the devil outa the old man. Even so, he nearly gave the game away."

"How so?" asked Tuck.

"Crazy old coot came out here one time and found some of the phony money we had stashed away in here. We weren't wise until we found it missing. We had gone down to Mexico for a while. We figured he was the one who had taken it. Trailed him to his place one night but couldn't get near him on account of that dog of his. We took care of the dog, but we couldn't get at the old man. He'd be watching out over the desert by day and on the moonlit nights. Other times, he was barricaded in that rock of his."

"How'd you get around so fast out in the desert?" asked Tuck.

"Motor scooter. Neat, hey? Quite a sight to see me riding around out in the desert with that robe on. Haw!"

"Noisy little things," said Sue.

"I'd drive close enough before they'd hear the motor, then walk the rest of the way. Wasn't anyone fooling around out here but that old man and you boys. I tried to scare you boys off. Well, you wouldn't learn. Too bad."

"Meaning?" asked Tuck quietly.

There was a long pause. "Well, we can't very well let you nosy kids go tell the Feds about us, can we?" said the man coldly.

Gary wet his dry lips. He couldn't wait much longer. The others would soon return. They would clean out the last of the bogus money on the next trip. Gary stepped back. Something slid against the wall, and he wildly grabbed it before it fell. It was the battered iron bar that he and Tuck had used to break through into the room where the water was.

As he hefted the bar, he heard the faint sound of voices behind him. The others had returned! There was no time to lose. He kicked open the door and charged in.

The counterfeiter turned, pistol at hip level. Gary slammed down the bar, catching the man across the forearm. He yelled hoarsely in extreme pain. The pistol clattered to the flags.

"Run!" yelled Gary to Sue and Tuck.

The counterfeiter struck at Gary with his left fist, staggering him. Gary reached for the pistol, but the man kicked it away. Gary struck him down with the bar and ran after the others. He had reached the steps leading to the upper level when the pistol cracked behind him, thunderingly loud in the confines of the low-ceiled room. The slug smashed into the masonry, mere inches from Gary.

"After them!" yelled the man Gary had felled.

Gary heard the shouts of the others as he sped up the steps. He slammed the door at the top of the steps shut just as the gun cracked again. He heard the impact of the heavy bullet against the other side of the door. Feet thudded on the steps. Metal struck against the wood of the door. The heavy door was shaken. The hinges were old and rusted halfway through. It would only be a matter of minutes before they broke through.

"We're trapped!" said Tuck. He placed his shoulder against the door to help Gary.

Gary shoved him to one side. Tuck fell clumsily, and Gary dropped atop him just as a bullet smashed through a thin part of the door and struck the wall behind the boys. The door shook violently.

Gary gripped Tuck by the collar and dragged him to his feet. "Follow me," he said.

Gary clambered up a loose fall of earth to a narrow opening in the ceiling hardly wide enough to shove a beanpole through. He tore at the ragged edges of the hole with his bare hands, heedless of the pain. Blood trickled down his wrists. He turned and looked at Tuck. "Come on!" he snapped.

The lean one clambered up beside Gary. Gary gave

him a leg up through the hole, Tuck grunting and protesting as the ragged edges tore at his clothing and flesh. He seemed to pop through like a cork from a bottle. He reached his hands down for Sue. Gary lifted her and felt her move upward even as he slid helplessly down the pile of loose earth. She disappeared through the hole.

The door fell with a crash into the corridor. Gary sprinted up the pile of earth, losing two steps for every one he gained. He reached up through the hole, felt hands grip his wrists, and the two Brownes yanked him through, heedless of his ripped clothing and flesh, just as a gun went off in the corridor and neatly clipped the heel from his left boot.

———

THE MOONLIGHT SHOWED full and fair upon the harsh ground. Gary rolled a rock over the hole. Sue and Tuck piled others atop it. Gary tapped Sue on the shoulder. "Pile rocks on there as though to build the Tower of Babel," he said. "Come on. Tuck!" He sprinted down the slope and ran at full speed around the back of the mission, followed by the lean one leaping like a kangaroo.

It was as bright as day. The moonlight gleamed on the shiny surfaces of the plane. Gary turned and yelled over his shoulder. "You're the mechanic!" he yelled. "You go fix that plane so that Jimmy Doolittle couldn't fly it outa here!"

"Keno!" cried Tuck. He bounded with awkward eagerness toward the plane.

Gary skidded around the front of the mission and darted into the echoing entryway, raising clouds of dust as his feet struck the flagging. He reached the sacristy and leaped into it, half running and half sliding down the loose earth beyond the low doorway until he struck the corridor beyond.

He ran through the room where the grinning skeleton lay, with the beam of his flashlight stabbing ahead, then through the next doorway into the half-buried arcade. He yanked open the doorway that led into the room that had the trap door in the floor. The trap door was open, and the ladder protruded into the room. He gripped the ladder and yanked it upward, hearing a muffled cursing from below. He threw the ladder to one side and kicked the trap door just as a gun exploded.

The trap door dropped neatly into place, and the bullet thudded into the underside of it. Gary dumped the ancient and quite heavy desk atop the trap door and piled the heavy chair atop it. He lay across the top of it, his breath harsh in his throat, sweat streaming from his body, and every nerve as taut as a piano string. He had made it with a fraction of a minute.

CHAPTER FIFTEEN

The Spanish Desert Always Wins

The moon was almost gone by the time Gary, Tuck, and Sue had made sure that the three counterfeiters were well trapped beneath the mission ruins. The pile of rocks atop the hole would effectively stop egress at that point.

The trap door had been loaded down with masonry hauled with infinite labor from outside the mission. There was no chance that the three men would die beneath the mission before the authorities would be guided back by Gary. There was plenty of water down there and enough air to keep them alive for days. They'd have to do without food for a day or so, but that could hardly be helped. Their piles of phony money wouldn't buy them a dog biscuit, according to the wise words of Tucker C. Browne.

The three adventurers walked away from the plane. They had found what they had been hunting for—the excellent plates from which the counterfeit money had been printed. There was something else they had found: the small but excellent motor scooter the counterfeiters had used to get about the Spanish Desert in their nocturnal prowlings. The gas tank was full. Gary could reach a highway before dawn on the little vehicle.

"Keep an eye on the boys," said Gary with a grin.

Tuck nodded. "We'll go back to the truck with you. Gotta pick up some chow. Man, I never been so starved in my whole life!"

"Once I contact the authorities," said Gary, "and they see these plates, they'll likely fly in here with a whirlybird to pick up the boys. Maybe I can con them into letting me come along. I'll pick up a rotor for the truck, and we can drive out of here in the style to which we are accustomed."

IN THE FAINT light of the dying moon, they reached the truck. Tuck opened the rear of it. There was a long pause. "Urk!" said Tuck at last. "Man, I thought we were all through with the shenanigans that's been going on!"

Gary ran around to the back of the truck. The steady, insistent sound of snoring came to him. He flicked on the flashlight. A human figure lay on one of the bunks, full beard spreading over the chest, rising and falling as Pardy Willis, in all his glory, slept the sleep of the just.

Tuck shook the old man awake. Pardy sat up and yawned.

"'Bout time you kids got here," he said sourly. "Been takin' a nap while waitin' for yuh. Where you been foolin' around?"

"Listen to *him,*" said Tuck. "Foolin' around..."

Pardy yawned and scratched in his beard. He tilted his head to one side and eyed the battered, dusty trio with birdlike eyes. "Been up to the Lost Mission, hey?" he asked.

"Yeah," said Gary.

Pardy shook his head. "Never get *me* up there," he said. "Place is haunted, I tell you." He planted big feet on the floor of the truck. He held out a blue-veined hand, cupping something in the palm. "Found this, Gary. Part of the truck?"

"The rotor!" said Tuck.

Gary shrugged. "Well, I can drive out now, Tuck. I'll take Sue along. You game to stay alone up there?"

Tuck patted the scooter. "With this at hand, they'd never get near ol' Tucker if they did break loose."

"Who?" said Pardy curiously.

"The ghosts," said Tuck. He grinned.

———

TUCK WAS FIDDLING with the scooter while Gary replaced the rotor of the truck distributor. Gary started the truck motor. "Sings like a bird," he said in deep satisfaction. He shut off the motor.

Tuck mounted the scooter. "Well, anyway, we laid them haunts," he said. "A fella could get nervous sitting up there thinking about such things if he didn't *know*, of course, there ain't no such things as ghosts."

Softly on the windless air came the muted ringing of the mission bell. From somewhere within the dark scope of the empty hills came the howling of a coyote, lifting, rising higher and higher, until it broke off into a sharp, barking sound that rose and fell, rose and fell, then died away into the silence of the desert night.

Pardy Willis shifted his feet. "Ol' Barkus," he said. "I hear him now and then. Ol' Barkus is restless. Sometimes, his ghost keeps that up all night."

The mission bell rang softly in the quiet air.

Tuck cleared his throat. "Well, fellas," he said cheerfully, "we might as well get going. Them three boys are safe enough up there by themselves. I think my Mama will be worried about ol Tucker C. Browne. Let's get a-goin', Gary, ol' pal!"

He heaved the scooter into the back of the truck and clambered in after it, settling himself across from Pardy

Willis. Sue climbed in beside Gary. The motor kicked over, and the headlights stabbed out into the thick darkness. Gary drove from the deep-walled arroyo and turned to drive north across the hard-packed surface of the Spanish Desert.

The Spanish Desert was quiet and dark, except for the humming of the truck motor and the singing of the tires as the headlights bore into the darkness. In a little while, the truck would be gone, and the night hunters would come out.

The silent bobcat would hunt the dainty kit fox while the kit fox was pursuing the timid pocket mouse, and overhead, the velvety winged owl would drift its swift shadow between the earth and the ice-chip stars, searching with its uncanny vision for game. So it had always been, and so it would be as long as the earth existed, for the Spanish Desert was a world unto itself, and no place for man except on a temporary basis.

Bit by bit the sand would drift, and bit by bit the wind would work. Together, the two of them would work, and in time, they would take back what was really theirs. The naked desert, like God made it during the Creation...

TAKE A LOOK AT JUDAS GUN AND HANGIN' PARDS:

Two Full Length Western Novels

BLOODTHIRSTY GUNSLINGERS GET THEIR REVENGE IN THIS CLASSIC WESTERN DOUBLE.

In *Judas Gun*, the prison at Yuma couldn't hold him... The blistering desert couldn't kill him... And the county's toughest guns couldn't stop him. Ken Sturgis was on the hunt for his brother Roy's killers – and not even prison could stop him.

In *Hangin' Pards*, it sure seemed that Holt Deaver had just about the worst luck of anyone in the West. At the age of twenty-five he was dead broke and on the run. He had shot one man in Chloride and had killed two others in less than a week. So when an old, whiskery, murdering no-good offered Holt ten thousand bucks to side him, it looked like a good thing. It was at least a chance for the best of everything if the gamble paid off— horses, food, liquor, and women. It also meant a partnership with a wanted outlaw and a self-conviction for Holt. But the thought of that last chance drove Holt on. Little did he reckon that even if the old rascal kept his word, it wouldn't do much good with six other bloodthirsty gunslingers on his trail.

"The joy of reading Shirreffs' work is in his mastery of pacing and his tough, gritty prose." – **James Reasoner, author of Outlaw Ranger.**

AVAILABLE NOW

ABOUT THE AUTHOR

Gordon D. Shirreffs published more than 80 western novels, 20 of them juvenile books, and John Wayne bought his book title, Rio Bravo, during the 1950s for a motion picture, which Shirreffs said constituted "*the most money I ever earned for two words.*" Four of his novels were adapted to motion pictures, and he wrote a Playhouse 90 and the Boots and Saddles TV series pilot in 1957.

A former pulp magazine writer, he survived the transition to western novels without undue trauma, earning the admiration of his peers along the way. The novelist saw life a bit cynically from the edge of his funny bone and described himself as looking like a slightly parboiled owl. Despite his multifarious quips, he was dead serious about the writing profession.

Gordon D. Shirreffs was the 1995 recipient of the Owen Wister Award, given by the Western Writers of America for "a living individual who has made an outstanding contribution to the American West."

He passed in 1996.